# My Life as a Rat

## NOVELS BY JOYCE CAROL OATES

*With Shuddering Fall* (1964)

*A Garden of Earthly Delights* (1967)

*Expensive People* (1968)

*them* (1969)

*Wonderland* (1971)

*Do with Me What You Will* (1973)

*The Assassins* (1975)

*Childwold* (1976)

*Son of the Morning* (1978)

*Unholy Loves* (1979)

*Bellefleur* (1980)

*Angel of Light* (1981)

*A Bloodsmoor Romance* (1982)

*Mysteries of Winterthurn* (1984)

*Solstice* (1985)

*Marya: A Life* (1986)

*You Must Remember This* (1987)

*American Appetites* (1989)

*Because It Is Bitter, and Because It Is My Heart* (1990)

*Black Water* (1992)

*Foxfire: Confessions of a Girl Gang* (1993)

# *My Life* as a Rat

### A Novel

## Joyce Carol Oates

HARPER LUXE

*An Imprint of* HarperCollins*Publishers*

This is a work of fiction. Names, characters, places, and incidents are products of the author's imagination or are used fictitiously and are not to be construed as real. Any resemblance to actual events, locales, organizations, or persons, living or dead, is entirely coincidental.

FIRST HARPERLUXE EDITION

ISBN: 978-0-06-291151-3

HarperLuxe™ is a trademark of HarperCollins Publishers.

Library of Congress Cataloging-in-Publication Data is available upon request.

19 20 21 22 23  ID/LSC  10 9 8 7 6 5 4 3 2 1

To my friend Elaine Showalter,
and to my husband and first reader, Charlie Gross

# Acknowledgments

In its earliest form, *My Life as a Rat* appeared as a short story titled "Curly Red" in *Harper's Magazine* (2003), which was reprinted in the collection *I Am No One You Know* (Ecco, 2004). Other sections have appeared, in slightly different forms, in *Narrative, Boulevard,* and *F(r)iction.*

# My Life as a Rat

I

# The Rat

*Go away. Go to hell—rat!*
*You don't get another chance to rat on anybody.*
It's true, you will not be given another chance.
There is just the one chance, the first.

# The Omen:
# November 2, 1991

This, I would remember: smelly dark water in the river near shore, the color of rotted eggplant, we'd seen on the way to school that morning and stopped to stare at.

On the Lock Street Bridge. Crossing on the pedestrian walkway. And there, directly below, the thunderous river (a deep cobalt-blue on clear days, metallic-gray on cloudy days) seemed to have changed color near shore and was purplish-dark, smelling of something like motor oil, roiling and surging as if it was alive like snakes, giant writhing snakes, you didn't want to look but could not look away.

My sister Katie nudged me crinkling her nose against the smell. "C'mon, Vi'let! Let's get out of here."

I was leaning over the railing, staring down. Trying to see—were those actually *snakes?* Twenty-, thirty-foot-long *snakes?* Their scales were a winking deep-purple sheen. The sight was so terrifying, I'd begun to shiver convulsively. The odor was making me nauseated, and dizzy.

As far as we could see upstream the oily-purple water came in surges near shore while elsewhere the river was the color of stone, choppy and thunderous—the Niagara River rushing to the Falls seven miles to the north.

We ran from the walkway. Didn't look back to see if the giant snakes were pursuing us.

I was twelve years old. This was the morning of the last day of my childhood.

(**Not our** imaginations. The oily purple water like snakes in the river had been real.

Alarmed citizens in South Niagara had noticed the phenomenon and reported it. There'd been many calls to local authorities and to 911.

On the front page of that evening's *South Niagara Union Journal* it was curtly explained that the *exces-*

sive *discharge of sludge* in the river that morning had been the result of *routine maintenance of the Niagara County Water Board's wastewater sedimentation basins and no cause for concern.*

What did this mean? What was sludge?

When our father read the boxed item in the *Journal* he laughed.

"'Routine.' 'Sedimentation'—'no cause for alarm.' Sons of bitches are poisoning us, that's what it means.")

# Disowned

Once I'd been Daddy's favorite of his seven kids. Before something terrible happened between us, I am trying still to make right.

This was in November 1991. I was twelve years, seven months old at the time.

Sent me into exile. Thirteen years! To an adult that is not a long time—probably; but to an adolescent, a lifetime.

*Who's Daddy's favorite little girl?*

*Violet Rue. Little Violet Rue!*

When I was a little girl Daddy would kiss my pug nose, and make me squeal. And Daddy would lift me in his strong arms, and pretend to toss me into the air so I was frightened but did not let on for Daddy did not like *scaredy-cat* little girls.

There was an intensity to this, the lifting-in-the-arms, the impassioned speech. A delicious fiery smell, Daddy's breath, fierce and unmistakable and I had no idea why, that he'd been drinking (whiskey) but knowing this ferocity to be the very breath of the *father*, the breath of the *male*.

*How's my little girl? Not afraid of your daddy are you?*

*Better not, Daddy loves his little Violet Rue like crazy!*

**Once, before** I was born, my oldest sister, Miriam, had been Daddy's favorite little girl. Later, my sister Katie had been Daddy's favorite little girl.

But now, the favorite was Violet Rue. And would remain Violet Rue.

Because the youngest, the baby of the Kerrigan family.

*Last-born. Most precious.*

Daddy had named me himself—*Violet Rue.* A name he claimed to have heard in an Irish song that had haunted him as a boy.

It was said that *Violet Rue* had been an accidental pregnancy—a "late" pregnancy—but to the religious-minded nothing can be truly accidental.

All human beings have a special destiny. All souls are precious to God.

The family is a special destiny. The family into which you are born and from which there can be no escape.

*Your mother was thrilled! A beautiful new girl-baby to take the place of the others who were growing up and growing away from her and especially the boys she hardly dared touch any longer, their downy cheeks, their prickly cheeks, the heat of their skin, fierce flushed faces she did not mean to surprise, opening a door without knocking, unthinking—Oh. Sorry. I didn't think anyone was . . . Your big brothers who'd throw off Mom's hand if even by chance she touched them.*

*A baby to love. A girl-baby to adore. The innocence of being loved totally and without question another time when she'd believed there would never be another time . . .*

*Of course, Lula was thrilled.*

*Of course, Lula was devastated. Oh God, oh Jesus no.*

*Hardly had she recovered from the last pregnancy—she'd determined would be the last. Thirty-seven years old—too old. Thirty pounds overweight. High blood* pressure, swollen ankles. *Kidney infection. Varicose veins like inky spiderwebs in her thighs fleshy-white as raw chicken.*

*And the man, the tall handsome Irish American husband. Turning his eyes from her, the bloated white belly, flaccid thighs, breasts like a cow's udders.*

*His fault! Though he would blame her.*

*In private reproach he'd blamed her for years for she'd been the one who'd wanted kids and it was futile to remind him how he'd wanted kids too, how proud he'd been, the first babies, his first sons, dazed and boasting to his male friends he was catching up with them God damn it and boastful even to his father the old sod he couldn't abide, as the old sod could not abide him.*

*And she'd been a beautiful woman. Beautiful body he'd been mesmerized by. Soft skin, astonishingly soft white breasts, curve of her belly, hips. Oh, he'd been crazy for her! Like a spell upon him. Those first years.*

*Six pregnancies. Not wanting to acknowledge—(except to her sister Irma)—that these were, just maybe, at least two pregnancies too many. And then, the seventh . . .*

*After the first pregnancy her body began to change. After the second, third. And after the fourth* it began to rebel. Cervical polyps were discovered, that (thank God) turned out to be benign and could be easily removed. Another kidney infection. Higher blood pressure, swollen ankles. The doctor advised terminating the pregnancy. But Lula would never have consented. Jerome would never have consented.

It was not something that was discussed. Not openly and not privately. They were Catholics—that was enough. You just did not speak of certain things and of many of these things there were not adequate words in any case.

As boys went unquestioningly to war, in the U.S. military. You did not question, that was not how you saw yourself.

Those weeks, months your mother spent most of each day lying down. Terrified of a miscarriage and terrified that she might die. Praying for the baby to be born healthy and praying for her own life and in this way Lula Kerrigan not only lost her good looks (she'd taken for granted) but also became permanently frightened and anxious, superstitious. Looking for "signs"—that God was trying to tell her something special about herself and the baby growing in her womb.

A "sign" could be something glimpsed out a window—the figure of a gigantic angel in the clouds.

A "sign" could be a dream, a mood. A sudden premonition.

In the later stages of her pregnancy no one could induce Lula to leave the house. So big-bellied, breathless and pop-eyed she'd become. Eating ravenously until she made herself sick. Gaining more weight. Knowing that her body disgusted her husband though (of course) (like any guilty husband) Jerome denied it. Last thing Lula Kerrigan wanted to do was expose herself to the eyes of others who'd be pitiless, mocking.

*My God. Is that—Lula Kerrigan? Looking like an elephant! Making a spectacle of herself parading around like that.*

Scornful expressions you would hear through your childhood, girlhood—*making a spectacle, parading around.* The harshest sort of denunciation a woman might make of another woman.

*Parading around like she owns the place.*

This would be charged of women and girls who exhibited themselves: their bodies. Particularly if their bodies were imperfect in obvious ways— too fat. Appearing in public when they should be ashamed of how they looked or in any case aware of how they looked. Of how unsparing eyes would latch onto them, assessing. Never was such a charge made of men or boys.

There appeared to be no masculine equivalent for *making a spectacle, parading around.*

As, you'd discover, there was no masculine equivalent for *bitch, slut.*

# The Happy Childhood

We were Jerome Jr., and Miriam, and Lionel, and Les, and Katie, and Rick, and Violet Rue—"Vi'let."

"Christ! Looks like a platoon."

Daddy would stare at us with a look of droll astonishment like a character in a comic strip.

But (of course) Daddy was proud of us and loved us even when he had to discipline us. (Which wasn't often. At least not with the girls in the family.)

Yes, sometimes Daddy did *get physical* with us kids. A good hard shake, that made your head whip on your neck and your teeth rattle—that was about the limit with my sisters and me. My brothers, Daddy had been known to hit in a different way. Haul off and *hit*. (But only open-handed, never with a fist. And never with a belt or stick.) What hurt most was Daddy's anger, fury. That look of profound disappointment, disgust. *How the hell could you do such a thing. How could you expect to get away with doing such a thing.* The expression in Daddy's eyes, that made me want to crawl away and die in shame.

*Disciplining children.* Only what a good responsible parent did, showing love.

Of course, our father's father had disciplined *him.* Nine kids in that rowdy Irish Catholic family. Had to let them know who was boss.

One by one the Kerrigan sons grew up, to challenge their father. And one by one the father dealt with them as they deserved.

*Old sod.* Daddy's way of speaking of our grandfather when our grandfather wasn't around.

So much of what Daddy said had to be interpreted. Laughing, shaking his head, or maybe not laughing, exactly. *Old sod bastard. God-damned old sod.*

Still, when our grandfather had nowhere else to live, Daddy brought him to live with us. Fixed up a room at the rear of the house, that had been a storage room. Insulation, new tile floor, private entrance so Granddad could avoid us if he wished. His own bathroom.

Daddy's birth name was Jerome. This name was

never shortened to "Jerry" let alone "Jerr"—even by our mother.

Our mother's name was Lula—also "Lu"—"Lulu"—"Mommy"—"Mom."

When speaking to us our parents referred to each other as "your father"—"your mother." Sometimes in affectionate moments they might say "your daddy"—"your mommy"—but these moments were not often, in later years.

In early years, I would not know. I had not been born into my parents' early, happier years.

Between our parents there was much that remained unspoken. Now that I am older I have come to see that their connection was like the densely knotted roots of trees, underground and invisible.

Frequently our father called our mother "hon"—in a neutral voice. So bland, so flat, you wouldn't think that "hon" was derived from "honey."

If he was irritated about something he called her "Lu-la" in a bitten-off way of reproach.

If he'd been drinking it was "Lu-laaa"—playful verging upon mocking.

At such times our mother was still, stiff, cautious. You did not want to provoke a husband who has been drinking even if, as it might seem, the man is in a mellow mood, teasing and not accusing. No.

Fact is, much of the time we saw our father, later in the day, he'd been drinking. Even when there were no obvious signs, not even the hot fierce smell of his breath.

Mom had a way of communicating to us—*Don't.*

Meaning *Don't provoke your father. Not right now.*

This Mom could communicate wordlessly with a sidelong roll of her eyes, a stiffening of her mouth.

*Your father loves you, as I do—so much! But— don't test that love . . .*

A painful truth of family life: the most tender emotions can change in an instant. You think your parents love you but is it *you* they love, or the child who is *theirs?*

Like leaning too close to the front burner of the stove, as I'd done as a small child, and in an instant my flammable pajama top burst into flame—you can't believe how swiftly.

But swiftly too as if she'd been preparing for such a calamity for all of her life as a mother, Mom grabbed me, pulled me away from the stove, hugging me, snuffing out the fierce little flames with her body, bare hands smothering the flames, before they could take hold. And trembling then, lifting me to the sink and running cold water over my arms, my hands, just to make sure the flames were gone. Almost fainting, she'd been so frightened. *We won't tell Daddy, sweetie, all right?—Daddy loves you so much he would just be upset.*

Comforting to hear Mom speak of *Daddy.* As if in some way he was her *Daddy,* too.

And so when Mom called Daddy "Jerome" it was in a respectful voice. Not a playful voice and not an accusatory or critical voice but (you might say) a voice of wariness.

*Oh Jerome. I think—we have to talk . . .*

The hushed voice I would just barely hear through the furnace vent in my room in the days following Hadrian Johnson's death.

**Even now.** So many years later. That strong wish to *crawl away, die in shame.*

**When I** was a little girl in the early 1980s my father was a tall solid-built man with dark spiky hair, hard-muscled arms and shoulders, a smell of tobacco on his breath, and (sometimes) a smell of beer, whiskey. His jaws were covered in coarse stubble except when he shaved, an effort made grudgingly once a week or so by one not willing to be a *bearded man* but thinking it effeminate to be close-shaven too. By trade he was a plumber and a pipe fitter and something of an amateur carpenter and electrician. In the army he'd been an amateur boxer, a heavyweight, and while we were growing up he had a punching bag and a heavy bag in the garage where he sparred with other men, and with my brothers as they came of age, who could never, not ever, quick on their young legs as they were, avoid their father's lightning-quick right cross. It was the great dream of my oldest brother Jerome—"Jerr"— that he might someday knock Daddy down on his rear, not *out* but *down;* but that never happened.

And Lionel, Les, Rick. He'd made them all "spar" with him, laced big boxing gloves on their hands, gave them instructions, commanded them to *Hit me! Try.*

We watched. We laughed and applauded. Seeing one of our brothers trying not to cry, wiping bloody snot from his reddened nose, seeing our father release a rat-a-tat of short stinging right-hand blows against a bare, skinny, sweating-pale chest—why was that funny? *Was* that funny?

*Try to catch me, li'l dude. C'mon!*

*Hey: you're not giving up until I say so.*

Girls were exempt from such humiliations. My sisters and me. But girls were exempt from instructions too. And Daddy's special glow of approval, when at last one of our brothers managed to land a solid blow or two, or keep himself from falling hard on his ass on the cement floor of the garage.

*Not bad, kid. On your way to the Golden Gloves!*

Daddy's girls had to suppose that Daddy was proud of us in other ways, it wasn't clear how just yet.

He wanted us to be good-looking, which might mean *sexy*—but not too obviously. Staring at Miriam—her mouth, lipstick—not knowing what to think, how to react: Did he approve, or disapprove?

He'd seemed to be impressed by good grades but report cards were not very real to him, school was a female thing, he'd dropped out of high school without graduating, never read a book nor even glanced inside a book so far as I knew, pushed aside our textbooks if they were in the way on a counter, no curiosity except just once that I remember, pushing aside a book I'd brought home from the public library—*The Diary of Anne Frank.*

What was this, he'd heard of this, vaguely—in the newspaper, or somewhere—*Anne Frank.* Nazis?

But Daddy's interest was fleeting. He'd peered at the cover, the wan girl-face of the diarist, saw nothing to particularly intrigue him, dismissed the book as casually as he'd noticed it without asking me about it. For always Daddy was distracted, busy. His mind was a kaleidoscope of tasks, things to be done, each day a ladder to be climbed, nothing random admitted.

And what pride we felt, my sisters and me, seeing our father in some public place, beside other, ordinary men: taller than most men, better-looking, with a way of carrying himself that was both arrogant and dignified. No matter what Daddy wore, work clothes, work boots, leather jacket he looked good—*manly.*

And the expression on our mother's face, when they were together, with others. That particular sort of female, sexual pride. *There. That's him. My husband Jerome. Mine.*

To their children, parents are not identical. The mother I knew as the youngest of seven children was certainly not the mother my older siblings knew, who'd been a young wife. Especially, the father I knew was not the father my brothers knew.

For Daddy treated my brothers differently than he treated my sisters and me. To Daddy the world was harshly divided: male, female.

He loved my brothers in a way different from the way he loved my sisters and me, a fiercer love, a more demanding love, mixed with impatience, at times even derision; a hurtful love. In my brothers he saw himself and so found fault, even shame, a need to punish.

But also a blindness, a refusal to detach himself from them.

His daughters, his *girls*, Daddy adored. You would not have said of any Kerrigan that he *adored* his sons.

We were thrilled to obey him, we basked in his attention, his love. It was a protective love, a wish to cherish but also a wish to control, even coerce. It was not a wish to *know*—to know who we were, or might be.

Yet, Daddy behaved differently with Miriam, and with Katie, than he did with me. It was a subtle difference but we knew.

He'd have claimed that he loved us all equally. In fact, he'd have been angry if anyone had suggested otherwise. That is what parents usually claim.

Until there is a day, an hour, when they cease making that claim.

**Two facts** about Daddy: he'd fought in Vietnam, and he'd come back alive and (mostly) undamaged.

This was about as much as Daddy would say about his years as a soldier in the U.S. Army, when Lyndon B. Johnson was president.

"I enlisted. I was nineteen. I was stupid."

We knew from relatives that Daddy had been "cited for heroism" helping to evacuate wounded soldiers while wounded himself. He'd been awarded medals—kept in a box in the attic.

My brothers tried to get him to talk about being a soldier in the U.S. military and in the war but he never would. In a good mood after a few ales he'd concede he'd been God-damned lucky the shrapnel that got him had been in his ass, not his groin, or none of "you kids" would've been born; in a not-good mood he'd say only that Vietnam had been a mistake but not just his mistake, the whole country had gone bat-shit crazy.

He'd hated Nixon more than Johnson, even. That a president would lie to people who trusted him and not give a damn how many thousands of people died because of him, Daddy shook his head, speechless in indignation.

Most politicians were *those blood-sucking sons of bitches. Cocksuckers. Fuckers.* Even Kerrigan relatives who were involved in local, western New York State politics were untrustworthy, opportunists and crooks.

Daddy would only talk about Vietnam with other veterans. He had a scattering of friends who were veterans of Vietnam, Korea, and World War II he went out drinking with, but never invited to the house; our mother did not know their wives, and our father had no interest in introducing her. Taverns, saloons, pubs, roadhouses—these were the gathering places of men like Daddy, almost exclusively male, relaxed and companionable. In such places they watched championship boxing matches, baseball and football, on TV. They laughed uproariously. They smoked, they drank. No one chided them for drinking too much. No one waved away smoke with prissy expressions. Who'd want women in such places? Women complicated things, spoiled things, at least women who were wives.

Returning home late from an evening with these men Daddy was likely to be heavy-footed on the stairs. Often he woke us, cursing when he missed a step, or collided in the dark with something.

If one of us left something on the stairs, textbook, pair of shoes, Daddy might give it a good kick out of pure indignation.

In our beds, we might hear them. Our mother's murmurous voice that might be startled, pleading. Our father's voice slurred, abrasive, loud.

A sound of a door being slammed, hard. And though we listened with quick-beating hearts, often we heard nothing further.

Katie had hoped to interview our father for a seventh-grade social studies project involving "military veterans" but this did not turn out well. Calm at first telling her *no, not possible* but when Katie naïvely persisted losing his temper, furious and profane, threatening to call the teacher, to *tell that woman to go fuck herself* until—at last—our mother was able to persuade him not to make such a call, not to jeopardize Katie's standing with her teacher or at the school, please just forget it, try to forget, the teacher had only meant well, Katie was in no way to blame and should not be punished.

*Punished* was something our father could understand. *Punished unfairly*, he particularly understood.

Katie would remember that incident for the rest of her life. As I will, too.

You didn't push Daddy, and you didn't take Daddy for granted. It was a mistake to *assume* anything about him. His generosity, his pride. Dignity, reputation. Not being disgraced or disrespected. Not allowing *your name to be dragged through the dirt.*

There were many *Kerrigans* scattered through the counties of western New York State. Most of these had emigrated from the west of Ireland, in and near Galway, in the 1930s, or were their offspring. Some were closely related to our father, some were distant, strangers known only by name. Some were relatives whom we saw frequently and some were estranged whom we never saw.

We would not know why, exactly. Why some Kerrigans were *great guys, you'd trust with your life.* Others were *sons of bitches, not to be trusted.*

We did notice, my sisters and me, that girl-cousins with whom we'd been friendly, and liked, would sometimes become inaccessible to us—their parents were no longer on Daddy's good side, they'd been banished from Daddy's circle of friends.

If we asked our mother what had happened she might say evasively, "Oh—ask your father." She did not want to become involved in our father's feuds because a remark of hers might get back to him and anger him. Personal questions annoyed our father and we did not want to annoy our father whom we adored and feared in about equal measure.

For instance: What happened between our father and Tommy Kerrigan, an older relative who'd been a U.S. congressman and mayor of South Niagara for several terms? Tommy Kerrigan was the most prominent of all the Kerrigans and certainly the most well-to-do. He'd been a Democrat at one time, and he'd been a Republican. He'd had a brief career as an Independent—a "reform" candidate. He'd been a liberal in some issues, and a conservative in others. He'd supported local labor unions but he'd also supported South Niagara law enforcement, which was notorious for its racist bias against African Americans; as a mayor he'd defended police killings of unarmed persons and had blatantly campaigned as a "law and order" candidate. Tommy Kerrigan was a "decorated" World War II veteran who supported American wars and military interventions, unquestioningly. He supported the Vietnam War until the U.S. withdrew troops in 1973 and it was his belief that Richard Nixon had been "hounded" out of office by his enemies. Naturally Tommy Kerrigan was critical of rallies and demonstrations against the war which he considered "traitorous"—"treasonous." He defended the actions of the police in dealing roughly with antiwar protesters as they'd dealt roughly with civil rights marchers in an earlier era. After a scandal in the early 1980s he'd had to abruptly retire from public life, narrowly escaping (it was said) indictment for bribe taking and extortion, but he continued to live in South Niagara, in a showy Victorian mansion in the city's most prestigious residential neighborhood, and he was still exerting political influence in circuitous ways while I was growing up. It was speculated that there'd been bad blood between Tom Kerrigan and our father's father and so out of loyalty our father was permanently estranged from Tom Kerrigan as well. When a softball field was built in South Niagara and given the name

Kerrigan Field no one in our family was invited to the dedication and the opening game; if our brothers played baseball at Kerrigan Field, they knew better than to mention the fact to our father.

Carefully Daddy would say of Tom Kerrigan that there was *no love lost between our families* though at other times he might shake his head and admire Tom Kerrigan as *the most devious son of a bitch since Joe McCarthy.*

And if anyone asked us if we were related to Tom Kerrigan, Daddy laughed and said, tell them politely *No. I am not.*

**We lived** in a two-story wood frame house at 388 Black Rock Street, South Niagara, that Daddy kept in scrupulous repair: roof, gutters, windows (caulked), chimney, shingle board sides painted metallic-gray, shutters navy blue. When the front walk began to crack, Daddy poured his own cement, to replace it; when the asphalt driveway began to crack and shatter, Daddy hired a crew to replace it under his direction. He knew where to buy construction materials, how to buy at a discount, he scorned using *middlemen.* In the long harsh winters of heavy snowfall in South Niagara Daddy made sure our walk and driveway were shoveled properly, not carelessly as many of our neighbors' walks and driveways were shoveled; in warmer months, Daddy made sure that our (small) front yard and our (quarter-acre) backyard were kept properly mowed. My brothers did much of this work, and sometimes my older sisters, and if Daddy wasn't satisfied that the task had been done well, he might finish it himself, in a fury of disgust. By trade he was a plumber and a pipe fitter but he'd taught himself carpentry and he dared to undertake (minor) electrical work for he resented paying other men to do anything he might reasonably do himself. It wasn't just saving money, though Daddy was notoriously frugal; it had to do with pride, integrity. If you were a (male) Kerrigan you were quick to take offense at the very possibility that someone might be taking advantage of you. Being *made a fool of* was the worst of humiliations.

As long as I lived in the house on Black Rock Street, as far back as I could remember, a project of Daddy's was under way: replacing linoleum on the kitchen floor, replacing the sink, or the counter; repainting rooms, or the entire outside of the house; hammering shingles onto the roof, building an addition at the rear of the house where for a few difficult years, Daddy's elderly, ailing father would live, convulsed in coughing fits that sounded like gravel being rapidly, roughly shoveled.

Daddy was a perfectionist and could not walk away from anything he believed to be *half-assed.*

Daddy kept a sharp eye on neighbors' houses, properties. He did not much care that lawns at other houses were scrubby and burnt out in the summer but he did care if grass wasn't mowed at reasonable intervals, if it grew tall enough to look unsightly, and to go to seed; he cared if trees were allowed to become diseased, and to shed their limbs on the street. He cared very much if properties on our block of Black Rock were allowed to grow shabby, derelict. Particularly, Daddy grew upset if a house was allowed to go vacant, for bad things could come of vacant properties, he knew from his own boyhood with his brothers and cousins raising hell in places not properly supervised.

Back of our house was a yard that seemed large, and deep, running into municipal-owned uncultivated acreage on the steep bank of the Niagara River. There were trees of which Daddy was proud—a tall red maple that turned fiery-red and splendid in October, an even taller oak, a row of evergreens. (But Daddy was unsentimental about cutting down the oak after it was damaged by a windstorm, and he feared it might be blown down onto the house; he'd cut it down himself with a rented chain saw.) My mother tried to cultivate beds of flowers, with varying degrees of success: wisteria, peonies, day lilies, roses assailed by Japanese beetles, slugs, black rot and mold, that often defeated her by mid-summer for Mom could not enlist her older children's help with the property as Daddy could.

Our house was at the dead end of Black Rock Street above the river.

I cried a lot when I was sent away. Any river or stream I saw, even on TV or in a photograph, tears would be triggered. *You have to get hold of yourself, Violet. You will make yourself sick. You can't—just— keep—crying . . .* My aunt Irma pleaded with me.

The poor woman, I was not nice to her. She could not bear a broken heart in a child impossible to heal by any effort of her own.

No matter how far away I came to live from the Niagara River, it has gotten into my dreams. For it is not like most other rivers—relatively short (thirty-six miles), and relatively narrow (at its widest, eighty-five hundred feet), and exceptionally fast-moving and turbulent. As you approach the river calls to you— whispers that become ever louder, deafening. The river is turbulent like a living thing shivering inside its skin. Miles from the thunderous falls like a nightmare that calls—*Come! Come here. Strife and suffering are absolved here.*

That morning in December when you wake to see that the river has frozen all the way across, or nearly; corrugated black ice with a fine light dusting of snow over it, the eye registers as beauty.

*But I had a happy childhood in that house. No one can take that from me.*

# Best Kisses!

A game. A happy game. The way Mom would stoop over to kiss me, suddenly.

When I was a little girl. Best kisses come by surprise!

Lacing her (strong) fingers through my (smaller) fingers. Securing my fingers with hers. Preparing to cross a busy street. *Ready. Set. Go!*

A long time ago when Mommy loved me as much as Daddy did. When I knew (without needing to be told) that Mommy would take care of me and keep me from harm even if this harm was Daddy.

**"It's easy** to love them when they're little"—Mom laughed, talking with a friend. "Later, not so easy."

# Obituary

This clipping from the *South Niagara Union Journal* I saved until it became so dry it fell into pieces in my fingers. An obituary beneath a photograph of a shyly smiling black boy with a gap between two prominent front teeth. Seventeen when he'd died but in the photo he looks as if he could be fifteen, even fourteen.

Hadrien Johnson, 17. Resident of 29 Howard Street, South Niagara. Varsity softball and basketball at South Niagara High School. Honor roll 1, 2, 3. Youth Choir, African Methodist Episcopal Church. Died in South Niagara General Hospital, November 11, 1991, of severe head wounds following an attack in the late evening of November 2 by yet-unidentified assailants as he was bicycling to his home. Survived by his mother, Ethel, his sisters, Louise and Ida, and his brothers, Tyrone, Medrick, and Herman. Services Monday at African Methodist Episcopal Church.

People would ask if I'd known Hadrian Johnson. (The name was misspelled in the newspaper obituary but corrected in subsequent articles.) No! I had not known him—he was a junior at the high school, I was in seventh grade. His sister Louise was a year older than me, at the middle school, but I did not know Louise either.

There were no African American classmates I knew well. All of my friends were white like me and all of them lived within a few blocks of our house on Black Rock Street.

It was only after his death that I came to know Hadrian Johnson. It was only after his death that we came to be associated in people's minds. *Hadrian Johnson. Violet Rue Kerrigan.*

Not that it did any good for Hadrian Johnson, who was dead. And it was the worst thing that could have happened to Violet Rue Kerrigan.

# "Boys Will Be Boys"

*W*as *it wonderful to have brothers when you were growing up? Older brothers? Who could look out for you?*

Girls lacking older brothers would ask me. How wistful they were! Having to fend on their own.

I didn't just adore my brothers, I was proud of them. Just the fact—*My big brothers! Mine.*

For girls are keenly sensitive of needing to be *looked after.* In certain circumstances, like school. Not to be alone, exposed, unprotected. Vulnerable.

Not measurable but very real—the power of *older brothers* to forestall teasing, bullying, harassment, threats from other boys made against girls. The protective power of *older brothers* by their mere existence.

The sexual threat of boys is greatly diminished, by the (mere) existence of a girl's brothers.

Unless of course the girl's brothers are themselves the (sexual) threat.

Parents have not a clue. Cannot guess. The (secret) lives of children, adolescents. Thinking that, because we are quiet, or docile (seeming), because we smile on cue and seem happy, because we are *no trouble*, that our inner lives are placid, and not churning and choppy and terrifying as the Niagara River as it gathers momentum rushing to the Falls.

*Did you adore your brothers, Vi'let?*

*Sure, you had to!*

**It's true.** I adored my brothers.

Not so much Rick, the youngest, who resembled me temperamentally, and who was a reasonably good student, as I was, and sweet-natured, but the other, older boys—Jerr, Lionel, Les.

They were quick-tempered and loud and impatient and bossy. Out of the earshot of adults they were profane, even obscene. They were funny—crass and crude. And loud—did I say *loud?* Voices, footsteps. On the stairs. Opening and shutting doors. Colliding with me if I didn't get out of their way.

Ignoring me, usually. Of course, why'd my brothers take note of *me?*

They were not so polite to Mom, sometimes. *Mouthy,* she'd call them. But in our father's presence, they were watchful, wary. They behaved.

If Daddy became annoyed with one of them he had ways of disciplining: sometimes a sharp, level look; sometimes an uplifted hand, the flat of the hand, a fist.

Flick of Devil-Daddy tongue which the boys could not miss. Hot red, sharp-pointed tongue like a blade slicing their hearts. But in the next instant, gone.

Even so, outside the house the older Kerrigan boys sometimes got into trouble.

Almost there was a hushed reverent air to the phrase—*into trouble.*

The first time I was too young to know what had happened. Nor did Katie know. And if Miriam knew, she wouldn't tell us.

On the phone with relatives our mother spoke derisively: "It's nothing. It's a stupid rumor. Those *liars.*"

Though sometimes her voice quavered: "It's her word against theirs! That's what everybody says, and that's a legal fact."

Near-inaudibly Mom would speak into the phone, in the kitchen. Seated, hunched over, pressing the avocado-plastic receiver against her ear as if trying to keep the words inside from spilling out.

If Katie asked what was going on Mom said, scolding: "Never mind! It's no business of you girls."

*You girls.* Often we'd hear from Mom's mouth.

Her gaze avoiding us, skittering away across the linoleum floor.

We were mystified but we knew better than to persist in questions. We knew better than to ask our brothers who were the ones *in trouble.* (And if we asked Rick he'd shrug us off—*Don't ask me, ask them.*) No possibility of asking our father who was the custodian of all secrets and didn't take kindly to being questioned about anything. And eventually we learned what had happened, or some version of what had happened, as we learned most things not meant for us to know, piecing together fragments of stories as our mother sometimes, with a curious sort of self-punishing patience, fitted together broken crockery to mend with glue.

The girl *whose word was against theirs* was a fourteen-year-old special-needs student at the middle school where Lionel was in ninth grade. Jerr was sixteen, a junior at the high school.

*Liza Deaver* was the name. *Liza Lizard* she was called for her face was splotched like a turtle's shell.

At fourteen she had the body of a mature woman, fattish, slow-moving, with thick plastic-rimmed glasses and lenses that magnified her eyes. She wore slacks with elastic waistbands and plaid shirts that billowed loose over her big soft breasts and belly. We'd overheard our brothers imitating her speech which was slow and stammering and whining like the speech of a young child.

Liza's mental age was said to be nine or ten. And it would remain that age through her life.

Liza was physically clumsy, poorly coordinated, and often made her way swaying and lurching with one eye shut, as if seeing with both eyes confused her. Oddly, unpredictably, Liza sometimes burst out in anger and tears and had to be sent home from school by the special-needs teacher.

We'd heard that, in the special-needs classroom at the school, Liza had some talent for drawing. Except her drawings were of people with large round balloon-faces on small stick legs—just faces, legs.

*Retards*, they were called. *Special-needs* was the adult term, *retards* what others kids called them.

*Liza Lizard* was a cruel name. Yet sometimes it seemed, if boys called this name after her, Liza misheard it, and thought it might be something else, and turned to them with a peculiar squinting smile, a childish sort of hope.

I did not—ever—utter aloud the name *Liza Lizard*. But like other girls I may have sniggered when I heard it.

It is shameful now to recall—*Liza Lizard*. You did not—ever—want the attention of the crude coarse cruel boys to turn upon you and so possibly, yes—you did snigger when you heard it.

No news item about the incident in Patriot Park would appear in the *South Niagara Union Journal*. Only minors were involved, and the (alleged) victim so unreliable.

Sometimes in Liza Deaver's confused telling there were just five or six boys involved. Sometimes, many more—ten, twelve.

Sometimes Liza Deaver remembered a few names. Sometimes, just one or two.

What would come to be generally known was that a *loose group of boys between the approximate ages of fourteen and seventeen, not a gang, not even friends* had cajoled Liza into coming with them to Patriot Park after school. One of the older boys, *not* a Kerrigan, had been friendly with Liza, or rather had pretended to be friendly with Liza, so Liza would boast that he was *my boyfriend*.

The Kerrigan brothers Jerome Jr. and Lionel were not the ringleaders in the assault—if there was an "assault." This was much-reiterated by my brothers. All they'd done (they would claim) was follow other boys tramping through muddy playing fields and past skeletal trellises in the municipal rose garden to the swimming pool, to the weatherworn stucco building where refreshments were sold in summer and where there were foul-smelling restrooms and changing rooms. In the off-season the building was deserted, dead leaves blew about the cement walk. But the restrooms were kept unlocked through the year.

The boy who was Liza Deaver's "boyfriend" led Liza into the men's room saying they had "nice surprises" for her.

It was so, Liza Deaver liked "surprises." Usually candy bars, snacks in cellophane wrappers from a corner store, cans of sugary soda pop. Sometimes these were given to her by kindly persons who knew her and her family and sometimes by others who were not so kindly.

Questioned afterward by parents, school authorities, Family Court officers the boys would claim that Liza had "wanted" to come with them. Going to the park had been "her idea." Into the men's restroom, her idea. She'd told them that she had done such

things with her brothers and other boys and sometimes they gave her "surprises," and sometimes they
didn't.

Liza Deaver denied this. Liza's parents denied it,
adamantly.

Liza Deaver had not been injured enough to require hospitalization but she'd been examined in an
emergency room and treated for cuts, bruises, bloodied nose and teeth, "chafings" in the vaginal and anal
areas. Clumps of hair had been pulled from her head
and (it was whispered) the boys had "grabbed and
pulled out" pubic hairs of which (it was whispered)
Liza had many.

Still the boys insisted that it had been Liza's idea.
They'd been "nice" to her, they said. These gifts
they'd given her: a Mars bar with just a small bite
missing, a plastic bead necklace found in the trash, a
small stuffed puppy with button eyes, a perfumy de-
odorant. (Liza Deaver was notorious for her strong,
horsey odor.) It was not clear how long Liza remained
in the restroom with the boys for Liza lacked a firm
grasp of the passage of time but the boys insisted that
it had been for "only a few minutes"—"definitely no
more than a half hour." It was 5:40 P.M. by the time
Liza limped home, a distance of about a mile; it was
estimated that the boys had led Liza away from school

at 3:30 P.M., though accounts differed about who exactly had been with Liza from the first, and who had
joined later. The fact that Liza had brought home
with her the "gifts" the boys had given her seemed
to suggest that she'd been happy to receive them, for
otherwise—wouldn't she have thrown them away, in
disgust?

If she'd been victimized by the boys, and not a
willing companion, wouldn't she have called for help
as soon as they'd released her, and she was able to run
out into the street?

(Though it wasn't clear that the boys had kept Liza
in the restroom against her will. She hadn't been a
*captive*, they said; she'd wanted to stay, and only left
because it was suppertime, and she suddenly remembered that her parents would be angry with her if she
was late.)

Eventually, it was established that there were at
least seven boys involved in the incident. These included Jerome Kerrigan Jr. and his brother Lionel but
not (it seemed) Les. (Certainly not Rick.) No doubt
there were more boys but the seven who were named
refused to provide the names of other boys—they
were not *rats*.

Poor Liza! Questioning left her confused about the
boys' names but she could (more or less) identify them

by other means, descriptive means and by studying pictures.

Yes she'd gone into the park and into the restroom with them willingly but when she'd wanted to leave they had not let her leave. Yes she'd been held captive by them, in the restroom. No she had not wanted to do the "nasty" things they did to her.

Yes she had told them she wanted to go home. Yes she had started to cry but they just laughed at her. No no *no* she had not told them that her brothers had done these nasty things to her, and other boys and men beside. *She had not.*

It was not clear if Liza had intended to tell her parents that "something bad" had happened to her. After they'd released her she'd slipped into her house by a rear door and was discovered by her mother in a flushed and disheveled state, clothes soiled and torn and misbuttoned, and her face smeared with blood. At once, confronted by her frightened mother, Liza burst into tears and began stammering and sobbing.

It was the "worst day" of their lives, Mrs. Deaver said. They would "never, not ever" recover from what had been done to their daughter whose fault was she was "too friendly" to people who were not her friends.

The Deavers lived in a ramshackle house on Carvendale Road, at the edge of the school district. On

one side of the road was the township of South Niagara, on the other side an unincorporated region of
scrubby farmland, overgrown pastures and derelict
dwellings.

The Deavers were a large family but not as the
Kerrigans were a large family. For the Deavers were
a *welfare family* whose father could not provide for his
wife and many children—nine? Ten? And of these,
what a pity, what a shame, unless it was a crime, as
people said, several were *not right in the head*—what
the kids called *retards.*

Mr. Deaver, when he was employed, worked at the
railroad yard. Mrs. Deaver worked part-time at a local
mall. Several of their children were out of school and
only intermittently employed and the youngest had
not yet begun school.

At Family Court, Liza initially sat mute and
frightened as others spoke on her behalf. Her deep-
shadowed eyes were swimmingly magnified behind
the thick lenses of her glasses. After a while she began
to answer questions in a hushed, hoarse voice. Eventually she began to speak louder. And then she began to
cry, to sob, to stammer, to stutter and to choke. Her
splotched-turtle face was flushed and puffy, saliva
glistened at her lips. Family Court officials who tried
to make transcripts of her not-very-coherent and con-

tradictory accounts would insist afterward that they felt sorry for the "poor, mentally disabled girl"—and for the Deavers, who accompanied Liza and never let her out of their sight—(Mrs. Deaver went with Liza several times to the restroom during the course of the session)—were nonetheless unconvinced that Liza was telling the truth or even that with her impaired cognition she had a clear conception what *truth* might be.

It was generally conceded—*Boys will be boys.* And—*These boys' lives might be ruined* . . . How much worse the situation might have turned out for the boys, if the girl had been seriously hurt!

There were extensive interviews with the accused boys by Family Court officers, with the boys' fathers and their attorney present. (The fathers of the accused boys hired a single lawyer to represent their sons, a local lawyer with connections to the Kerrigan family.) In this way a public hearing in juvenile court was avoided. There were no arrests. No formal charges were made against the boys who were suspended from school for one week.

Liza Deaver was placed on suspension for the remainder of the school year for it was believed that her presence would be "distracting" and "hazardous," in the words of the school principal; Liza herself was known to have a raging temper, and to strike out furiously, in frustration, at younger and smaller children when she believed they didn't respect her. (Liza was usually intimidated by individuals older than herself.) As it happened Liza Deaver never returned to school but was allowed to drop out for "medical reasons."

All this my sister Katie and I would learn, much later. At the time, we knew little.

No one in the family talked about Liza Deaver, so far as we knew.

No one talked about *the trouble*. For weeks Jerr and Lionel were subdued around our mother and wary of our father, like kicked dogs. But cunning kicked dogs. They had 9:00 P.M. curfews. Jerr wasn't allowed to drive for six weeks. Both boys had extra chores around the house. On the phone my mother said, incensed, "It was all that girl's fault! She did it deliberately! Those Deavers better get her fixed! Before it's too late."

When my mother hung up I asked what "fixed" meant. I wondered if whatever the boys had done to her, Liza might need fixing like a broken clock.

Disdainfully my mother said, "Like a cat, spayed. So it can't have kittens people have to drown."

# To Die For

Growing up, we Kerrigan kids knew that our daddy would die for us. No one had to tell us, we knew. Of course, the concept "to die for" was not in our vocabularies. Still, we knew.

In our father's big Irish Catholic family in Niagara Falls he'd been raised with the conviction that families stuck together. Irish immigrants had had a hell of a hard time coming to America, hadn't even been considered "white" in some quarters, like Italians, Greeks, and Jews, until even the 1950s. And so, the Irish stuck together, in theory at least.

Not in theory, but in reality, and crucially, a family had to protect its own. You might quarrel with relatives, a brother or a sister, you might quarrel with your parents but essentially you stuck together, you never deserted or betrayed one another. You never went *outside the family*—that was unforgivable.

Inside the family you never *lied* when it really mattered, and you never *cheated.*

Siding with your brother against your cousin, but with brother and cousin against the stranger.

You would die for your family and you would (maybe) die for your (close) friends the way soldiers would die for their (close) buddies.

Something like this, Jerome Kerrigan had truly seemed to feel for his immediate family, if not all of the Kerrigans. And for the guys in his platoon in Vietnam, he dared not recall without his eyes welling with tears and his mouth working to keep still.

If Daddy was suspicious of strangers he was almost naively trusting of relatives and friends. Often he did household repairs for no payment, wouldn't hear of being paid except in drinks, hospitality, reciprocal favors. That was friendship—loyalty, paying back what you owed. Being generous.

He lent money to people who, he had reason to know, probably wouldn't be able to repay him; he lent money without interest, knowing that this was a disadvantage, for those to whom he'd lent money would repay the lenders who'd demanded interest, and not him. Yet, Daddy could not bring himself to lend money *with interest*—that was not how he saw himself.

And so, Daddy lent money to his heavy-drinking brothers. He provided bail bond for Kerrigans who found themselves on the wrong side of the law—business fraud, bad checks, failure to pay alimony, embezzlement. He did favors for guys in the plumbers' union, for guys he'd gone to school with who'd had bad luck. He respected *bad luck*—it could happen to anyone.

The more kids you have, the more possibilities for *bad luck*. That was a grim fact.

The most extravagant thing Daddy did, that I remember from my childhood, was helping one of his younger sisters buy a house in Buffalo, so that she and her husband could live near her husband's family, who would help her nurse her husband afflicted with some terrible wasting disease like multiple sclerosis. Our mother had not liked this arrangement, she'd sighed and fretted and all but wept over the phone, for a large amount of money was involved, but in Daddy's presence she did not dare complain for, as Daddy would've pointed out to her, *he* was the one with a salary.

At the same time, you did not wish to cross Jerome Kerrigan.

You did not wish to find yourself on his *shit list.* For there were many on this list who were, in Daddy's eyes, *fucked.*

Forgiving was rare. Forgetting, rarer.

And the closest you were to Daddy, the harder for Daddy to forgive.

He liked to quote an Italian adage—*Revenge is a dish best served cold.*

Another remark he favored from the boxing world was *What goes around comes around.* Which was more hopeful for it seemed to mean not just bad but good, too. The good you do will be returned to you. Eventually.

# "Accident"

In November 1991 when Hadrian Johnson was beaten unconscious and left to die on the shoulder of Delahunt Road, and the lawyer who'd defended Jerome Jr. and Lionel Kerrigan at the time of Liza Deaver pleaded their case to prosecutors, the defense of *boys will be boys* didn't work so well for them, or for my cousin Walt Lemire and a neighborhood friend named Don Brinkhaus who was also involved in the beating.

At this time Jerome Jr. was nineteen and no longer living at home. He'd managed to graduate from South Niagara High with a vocational arts major and, through Daddy's intervention, was an apprentice plumber with the contractor for whom Daddy also worked, the largest and best-known plumbing contractor in the city; he had not yet been accepted into the plumbers' union but there was no doubt that he would be as soon as he completed his probationary period. (No African Americans belonged to the local plumbers' union. This would be emphasized, unfairly some thought, in the media coverage of the case; unfairly because there were no African Americans in the local police officers' union, the firefighters' union, the electricians' and the carpenters' unions, among others. The only local union in which black men were welcomed was the sanitation workers' union which was predominantly black and Latino.) Lionel was sixteen, a sophomore at the high school, big for his age, coarse-skinned, easily bored. Even in vocational arts Lionel's grades were poor, he cut classes often, our mother didn't dare report him to our father for fear of a terrible scene. But Lionel was in awe of his independent older brother who lived by himself now in a place near the railroad yard and owned a car, Daddy's old 1984 Chevrolet he'd passed on to Jerr since it was all but worthless as a trade-in. Weekends the two hung out together drinking beer with Jerr's friends, cruising in Jerr's car. Jerr had hated school but now he was hating full-time employment even more, being overseen, assessed and judged. Worse, he hated being a plumber's assistant, actually having to clear toilets of shit, every kind of crap, came close to puking every time he went out.

What their father called *fucking real-life*. Didn't know how the hell long he could take this *fucking real-life*.

At the house Jerr had grown sick of Mom snooping into his life. Overhearing him on the phone. Giving him unwanted advice. Stripping his bed of soiled sheets, picking up his filth-stiffened socks and underwear from the floor to be laundered. Preparing food he was bored with, he'd grown out of eating years ago, had come to hate. Fast-food restaurants were good enough for him, greasy cheeseburgers, heavily salted french fries. Anything that came in a cellophane wrapper strung up in colorful displays at the 7-Eleven, he'd tear open with his teeth in a pretense of rapacity.

When he'd broken up with his girlfriend boasting how he'd left her stranded at a tavern, exactly what the bitch deserved for disrespecting him, there was Mom shocked and demanding to know why he'd do such a thing, she had met Abbie and Abbie seemed like a nice girl, and Jerr came back at her, "Fuck 'Abbie is a nice girl.' You don't know shit about 'Abbie,' Mom. So mind your own fucking business. There's no 'nice girls' just different kinds of pigs."

Mom was so shocked by Jerr speaking to her in such a way, not just the disrespect, the insolence, but also the meaning of his words, the loathing for her, she could not reply but stumbled away to another room.

*No nice girls just different kinds of pigs.*

**Again and** again, *Why.*

But it was like *nice girls, pigs*—there was no *why.*

You would say, the Kerrigan boys had not been brought up that way, and that would be true. And yet.

Going back to a time when our father had attended South Niagara High there'd been incidents involving white boys and darker-skinned boys, especially following Friday night sports events, but these were usually squabbles or altercations between sports teams, rival schools. Rivalry with Niagara Falls High, Tonawanda High, South Buffalo. Some of these teams were predominantly white, and others were predominantly black. South Niagara had integrated teams, our coaches liked to boast. Boys' teams, girls' teams. Football, basketball, softball. Swim team.

Cheerleaders? That was another story.

No incident had involved Hadrian Johnson, who was on both the varsity basketball and softball teams in his junior year.

The previous year, when Jerome Kerrigan Jr. had

been a senior, he'd known Hadrian Johnson slightly, as he'd known a scattering of African American boys at the school, but there'd been no animosity between them—none at all. So Jerome Jr. insisted, and so it seemed to be true.

Lionel would deny "animosity" too. Any "race prejudice"—not *him*.

They would insist, they admired black athletes—Mike Tyson, Magic Johnson, Michael Jordan. Jerry Rice, Barry Sanders. And many others.

They'd been aware of Hadrian Johnson on the high school sports teams for who had not been aware of Hadrian Johnson? Not that Hadrian was a brilliant player, usually he was just very good, very reliable, the kind coaches can depend upon.

Yes it was true, the better black athletes at South Niagara were generally showy, spectacular. They modeled themselves after the great national black athletes whom Americans watched avidly on TV. These were the insolent blacks whom white boys feared, disliked, envied. If these black athletes were not demonstrably superior to the very best white players they were likely not to be chosen for varsity teams for there was much pressure from (white) fathers, that their sons be chosen for teams, and there was (as coaches tried to explain) limited space on the teams; but, granted this fact, in the face of such competition still Hadrian Johnson was chosen for two varsity teams, a favorite of coaches and of teammates.

A black kid, yes. But not, you know—one of *them*.

South Niagara wasn't a large school: fewer than five hundred students distributed among three grades. In some way everyone knew everyone else.

But white students and darker-skinned students didn't mix much. On sports teams and in the school band and chorus, service clubs, but not socially.

Nor was there "mixed" dating. Just about never.

It was ironic, Hadrian Johnson had been an outstanding player on the South Niagara Jaycee boys' softball team, which was comprised of boys from several city schools. Photographs of Hadrian in his Jaycee uniform, to be published in newspapers and on TV, had been taken at Kerrigan Field.

Questioned by South Niagara prosecutors whether they'd had any special reason to stalk and harass Hadrian Johnson, the boys insisted *no*.

They had not "stalked" him—that was wrong. They'd meant just to scare him. And they had not known it was *him*—they hadn't seen his face, not at first.

But had they forced Hadrian Johnson off the road, because he was black?

Vehemently they denied this. Repeatedly, they denied this.

Four white boys driving a vehicle, a solitary black boy on a bicycle, late Saturday night—but no, they were not racists.

It would be bitterly debated, whether the attack had been a *hate crime*, or an assault that had gotten out of control in which race wasn't an issue. If a *hate crime* the assailants were likely to be sentenced to longer prison sentences, if they were found guilty; but there was the possibility, if they insisted upon a jury trial, that they might be acquitted by a sympathetic (i.e., white) jury. If he could devise a way in which such a defense would not backfire and make things worse, in the media for instance, their lawyer was considering the boys might claim *self-defense*.

The boys had been drinking for most of the evening. Two of them were underage which involved the others, for having supplied them with alcohol; the 7-Eleven storekeeper who'd sold them the six-packs was in trouble as well. They'd been driving around, at the mall, returned from the mall, drinking and tossing beer cans. Stopped at Friday's, where there was a crowded bar scene, later at Cristo's (which was taking a chance, our father sometimes dropped by Cristo's on Friday night). Past Kerrigan Field. Past Patriot Park.

Kirkland Avenue, Depot Street, Delahunt. *Saw this guy in a hoodie riding a bicycle on Delahunt looking kind of suspicious to us like he didn't belong in the neighborhood. Something in the bicycle basket looked like could be stolen goods. We did not see his face—we did not know who it was . . .* If they'd shouted after him it was just a way of talking, scaring someone who (maybe) didn't belong in the place he was in. If Jerr aimed the car at the bicyclist it was just to scare him not to run him down at the side of the road.

And the way he tried to escape crawling away, yelling to leave him alone. Like what a guilty person would do.

Like cops, they were. Neighborhood "vigilantes." Keeping strangers from breaking into houses, stealing cars.

Their lawyers were suggesting this possibility. "Vigilantes"?—"fighting crime"? Like the possibility of self-defense.

Problem was, the boys weren't in their own neighborhood. Hadrian Johnson happened to be in his neighborhood.

Yes but they hadn't *known*. Like they hadn't gotten a look at their victim's face until—later.

Delahunt was a darkened road at this time of night.

Strip mall, fast-food taco place, gas station. At Seventh Street there was a small trailer court with a string of unlit lights, from the previous Christmas. Beyond that a potholed street of small wood frame bungalows lacking a sidewalk, called Howard.

Following the bicyclist along Delahunt. For the hell of it.

Well—who rides a bicycle at night? Looked like a tall dude, not a kid. Not a young kid. And what was in the basket?

Reflectors on the back of the bike and the bike looked (they could see, squinting in headlights) like it might be pretty expensive. *Stolen merchandise?*

The bicyclist was acting guilty, they thought. Bumping along on the shoulder of the road. Knew they were there, and coming close to him. Maybe he thought they were cops. So he tried to pedal faster, fast as he could, intending to turn into a dirt lane opening ahead in a field, looking to escape. For whoever was in the car was coming close to him, honking his horn like machine-gun fire. Guys yelling out the windows.

It would turn out that Hadrian Johnson had spent the evening at his grandmother's house on Amsterdam Street a mile away. Sometimes when Hadrian spent time with his grandmother who suffered from diabetes he stayed the night but this night, he did not. Bicycling home to Howard Street along a stretch of Delahunt where if there was traffic it was likely to be fast but there was relatively little traffic at that hour of the night, he'd been ten minutes from his mother's house when a vehicle had come up swiftly behind him swamping him with its bright lights, deafening horn, derisive shouts, curses.

Thud of the front right fender striking the bicycle, a high-pitched scream, the fallen boy amid the twisted bicycle trying to free himself and crawl away . . .

What happened next was confused.

Hard to remember. Like something smashed and broken, you are trying to reassemble.

Still it was an accident. The boys would claim. Had to be, for what happened hadn't been premeditated.

Striking the bicyclist, could see by this time that it was a kid, (maybe) a black kid, but (still, yet) no one they recognized, so Jerr braked the car to a stop, had to check the bicyclist to see if he was all right . . .

True Jerr did stop the car. True they did exit the car.

True they did approach the (injured?) boy who was trying to crawl away from them at the side of the road . . .

(Was it true, all four boys had exited the Chevrolet?

Or had Walt remained inside, as Walt would never cease to claim?)

Here is a fact: nothing of what happened was what Jerome, Lionel, Walt, Don had meant to happen. Which wasn't to say that they remembered clearly *what had happened.*

Just that they'd been drinking. The older guys had gotten the beer for the younger guys. Saturday night. Deserving more from fucking Saturday night. Not ready to go fucking home just yet.

But only seconds, they'd stopped on Delahunt. Not even a minute—they were sure. Vaguely aware of traffic on the road, a vehicle passing. Someone slowing to call out the window *What's going on?* and Jerr yelling back *We called 911, it's OK.*

And then panicked and back in the Chevrolet. Driving away with squealing tires like a TV cop show. And even then they would (afterward) claim they'd scarcely been aware that the badly injured bicyclist was dark-skinned, still less his identity: seventeen-year-old Hadrian Johnson from their own school.

**Shortly after** midnight of November 2, 1991, an anonymous call was placed to 911 reporting a badly beaten young man lying unconscious and unresponsive at the side of Delahunt Road, South Niagara, a bicycle twisted beside him. An emergency medical team from South Niagara General Hospital was immediately dispatched and the stricken young man brought back, by ambulance, still unconscious and unresponsive, to the ER.

The victim would never regain consciousness but would die, of severe brain damage and other traumatic injuries, nine days later.

No other calls to 911 had been reported that night. But the following morning when news of the beating began to spread through South Niagara an anonymous caller reported to police that he'd been driving on Delahunt Road the night before, around 11:40 P.M., when he'd seen a vehicle parked at the side of the road, where someone, it appeared to be a young black man, was lying on the ground bleeding from a head wound as four or five "young white guys" stood around him. It had looked, the caller said, as if there'd been a fight. He'd slowed his pickup then accelerated when the white guys saw him for they were looking "threatening"—"drunk and scared"—and he'd thought he saw one of them with a rifle.

Maybe not a rifle. A tire iron? Baseball bat?

He'd gotten out of there, fast. Hoping to hell they wouldn't get in their car and follow him.

The caller went on to identify the car as a mid-1980s model Chevy, dull bronze, pretty battered, rusted, and dented—"Especially, you could see that the front right fender was bent all in from where they'd hit the kid. You couldn't miss that."

He hadn't gotten a good look at the boys. Just "white kids"—"maybe high school age, or a little older"—but he'd tried to memorize the license plate number: "first three digits—*KR4*—something like that."

# Louisville Slugger

If the fucking bat hadn't been there.

Because none of it had been premeditated. Because it had just happened—the way fire *just happens.*

Because it had been rattling in the back of the car, for months. Why'd he carry the bat loose in the car he'd liked to say *For protection.*

Sort of, he meant it. But it was a kind of joke too.

Because most things, fucking things in his fucking life, were jokes. Which included the bat.

Just his old baseball bat. The label worn off, he'd had for years. Couldn't remember when he'd played baseball last. But the bat was *his*—his brothers had to have their own damn bats if they had a bat at all.

Never thought about it. Not much.

Rattling in the back of the car along with some empty beer cans and other shit, he'd stopped hearing.

Except that night, one of the (drunk) guys in the back snatched it up. And outside, in the confusion, he grabbed it away from whoever it was, maybe Don Brinkhaus, excited and aroused and swinging the bat because the bat was *his* and the bat was fucking wonderful, the solid grip, the weight of it, soiled old black tape he'd wound around the handle how many years ago. He'd never been a great batter, but he was OK. Easily embarrassed and discouraged and fucking disgusted, missing easy pitches, striking the ball not hard enough so it popped up like a little kid might pop it, fell straight down, rolled at the first baseman's feet . . . Wanting to murder any asshole who laughed at him.

But now, no. Fucking bat wasn't missing its target now.

Black kid sprawled on the ground pleading with them to let him go, please let him go, bleeding from his nose and mouth not so hot-shit now. Flat on his back and begging. And the guys jeering, laughing. Swatting at him, kicking.

Like he'd provoked them to run into *him*. Dented the fender of the fucking car, because of *him*.

Natural in Jerr's hands for the bat to rouse itself to life, and get away from him. Furious, fast. Like chopping wood.

The *crack!* of the bat. Or was it the *crack!* of the skull.

But without the bat, maybe not. No.

Wouldn't have *cracked* the skull. And all the blood.

Without the fucking bat would've kicked the black kid a few more times then let him go. Seeing he wasn't fighting back, had gone limp. Probably not able to identify them, his eyes are swollen shut. Blood all over his face. What the fuck. Nobody wanted to kill anybody, that was a fact.

That *was a fact.* They'd swear on the Bible.

Came to him they'd (maybe) mixed this kid up with another black kid, a bigger kid, heavier, older by a year or two. Football player—"tight end." With the bleached-blond white girlfriend. Hanging out across the street from school. *That* motherfucker, they'd have meant to stomp, wipe the smirk off his fat face.

Except for the bat. Fucking bat. None of it would have happened. Or in the way it happened. You could argue it was *mitigating circumstances.* How the bat came to be in Jerr's hands at just that minute.

Because it hadn't been premeditated, bringing the bat. Just in the back of the car where it had been rolling around for months. And so, like an accident. Christ sake it *was an accident.*

And maybe also, could they argue they'd been drinking, and their judgment was off. Buying six-packs and nobody asking them who it was for, how old. None of it would've happened except for that. Which wasn't their fault—there were adults to blame. And the car, his father had given him. Christ! He hadn't even asked for it, he'd known better than to ask his father would've made him crawl, if he had. Surprising the hell out of him, just giving him the car which would have been worth something at least, a few hundred at least, on a trade-in. But he'd given Jerr the car, which put Jerr in his debt big-time. And made Jerr anxious, taking care of it. Every time he came to the house the old man would go out into the driveway and inspect the car and if he didn't say anything that could be worse than if he did for at least, if he did, you'd know what he was thinking. And Jerome Kerrigan was always fucking *thinking.*

Which led to Jerr swerving the damned car off the road. Like wanting to get rid of it. A few beers, you started thinking that way. Hitting the black kid was just collateral damage. You could argue that was an accident, nobody'd known the kid was even there until they saw him. He'd been meaning just to scare the kid, make the guys laugh, impress his brother who thought he was a cool dude but the front wheels hit gravel and swerved, right front fender struck the kid and lifted him, and the God-damned bicycle leaving a dent in the fender him and Lionel would have to try to even out with their bare hands, panting and struggling to unbend it but still the dent is there. Fucking rust on their fingers.

And blood from the bat, they'd have to scrub like hell.

Chain of circumstances, accidents. Could happen to anyone.

None of it *premeditated*. That's the crucial point.

Realizing then, his father had given him the fucking baseball bat. Sure. That's who it was, had to be, making a big deal of it, bringing him to the store downtown to pick it out for his birthday: *Louisville Slugger.* The best.

Now you got to live up to it, kid.

# The Little Sister

Wakened by—something . . .
     Not a flash of headlights on the wall of the darkened room. Not the expansion of headlights on two walls of our room, if a vehicle turned into our driveway.

So that I would think, but only later—*They cut the headlights. Not wanting to wake anyone.*

Still less would I think, at the age of twelve—*This part of it would be premeditated. Leaving nothing to chance.*

And so I saw the time: 12:25 A.M. Someone had entered the kitchen downstairs, from the rear of the house, through the garage. I did not yet know that it was Jerr and Lionel.

Though Jerr had his own place to live now often he

turned up at our house. He'd brought Lionel home, but wasn't leaving immediately. He'd dropped the others, our cousin Walt, and Don Brinkhaus, at their houses.

At this time they had not known, they would claim they'd had no idea, that Hadrian Johnson had been beaten so badly he would never regain consciousness.

Though bleeding badly from head wounds, from the blows of Jerr's baseball bat, they would claim that, when they'd left him, Hadrian Johnson had looked as if he was *all right*.

This I would learn later. In time I would memorize much. Like lifting small stones, pebbles. Lifting, contemplating. Setting down again taking care to put its pebble in its precise and rightful place.

In the small room at the top of the stairs shared with my sister I lay very still hearing voices that seemed to me lowered and urgent. At first I thought one of the voices was my father's—but the other voice was not Mom's.

I went to the door and opened it, just slightly. Eagerly I listened. It was thrilling to me, that Katie remained asleep. That everyone else was asleep—our parents, our older sister, our brothers Les and Rick.

When Daddy was out, or my brothers, I would remain awake waiting for them, if I could keep my eyes from closing. They had no idea how I waited for them. Patiently watching for headlights to flash onto the bedroom wall. That night waiting for Jerr to bring Lionel home and hoping that they'd hang around a while in the kitchen having a beer or two as they often did.

Quietly I left my room and descended the stairs, barefoot. In my pajamas. But no one was in the kitchen.

They'd entered the kitchen, I had thought. There was a draft of cold in the air, a smell of cold, wet leaves. But then they'd gone back out into the garage, leaving the door ajar.

This door was rarely locked. Most doors of our house were rarely locked.

A few inches from the doorway I hesitated, listening. Until now I was not altogether certain that it was Jerr and Lionel who'd come into the house but now I heard their voices which were lowered, urgent. Often I overheard my brothers talking together, their speech was fascinating to me. Yet more, my father's speech was fascinating to me. The language of men and boys— rarely was it directed toward me, I could be only an eavesdropper. While there was never any ambiguity about whether my mother was addressing me.

My brothers were aroused, excited. I could hear only isolated words. *Fuck, shit. Keep it down!*

My brothers never caught me eavesdropping, so little notice did they take of me.

Then, I heard the outdoor faucet being turned on. Were my brothers doing something with the hose?—washing the car?

Through the crack in the doorway I saw them squatting close together just outside the garage where the water from the hose would soak into the soil, not accumulate on the garage floor. There was a light—an overhead light in the garage—a bare bulb, harsh and coated in grime—so that I could see, just barely, that they were washing something: a baseball bat.

Had to be Jerr's bat he carried in his car "for protection." He and Lionel had rolled up their sleeves to wash the bat, and to wash their hands and forearms, vigorously.

They'd brought out soap from the house. Bar of strong-smelling soap on the kitchen sink that mostly just our father used, wiping his hands on wads of paper towels.

My brothers were laughing, nervously. There was something very wrong but I felt an impulse to laugh too. They were only about ten feet away, for I was seeing them at an angle. Thinking *They won't like this. Being spied on. No.*

Still, I remained where I was. Staring. (Maybe) memorizing. Not for a long time would I learn that my brothers were deliberating what to do with the bloodstained bat during these minutes. *The murder weapon* it would be called one day.

They were sober now, they'd have said. Stone-cold sober.

Fucking totally *sober.*

Not really thinking clearly but they knew they had to get rid of the bat, fast. Considered throwing it into the river—but what if it floated? Even weighed down, a wooden bat might somehow work loose and the river would be the first place South Niagara cops would look for a weapon. Nor could they burn it—(would a bat *burn?* The smoke would be detected). Not a great idea to hide it in the trash, even somebody else's trash can on the street and so finally they decided to bury it on the riverbank, in the underbrush. A few hundred yards from the house. There was litter on the riverbank, some of this was compost from Mom's garden. This was a better idea, they thought, than driving somewhere. They'd had enough of the car, for the night.

They'd managed to lessen the dents in the fender. Struggling, with bare hands. Panting, cursing. Next day, in daylight, on the curb by his rented place Jerr would take a hammer and un-bend it more, if he remembered.

In fact, the dents and scratches and (even) blood-smears on the front of the Chevrolet still registered in the name of Jerome Kerrigan would be evident when it was closely examined by police investigators. Like the clothes, socks, shoes my brothers would try to launder that night.

Like the bat, that could not be scrubbed clean by my brothers for its minute cracks and indentations would harbor traces of Hadrian Johnson's blood, unmistakably.

Burying the bat in the underbrush, near Mom's compost—that seemed like a practical idea. I saw my brothers wrap the wetted bat in a piece of burlap and I saw them leave the garage but I could not observe them after this, only to understand that they weren't going far, into our backyard it seemed, or a little farther, on foot.

I was mystified. I had no idea what they were doing. I guessed they might be drunk. Maybe it was some kind of joke.

I went upstairs, back to bed. But I couldn't sleep.

**And then** about a half hour later I heard them re-enter the house. The kitchen. Heard the refrigerator door being (quietly) opened and shut. The sound of beer cans being opened.

Almost, I could hear voices. Soft laughter.

*Jes-sus.*

*Fucking Chri-ist!*

I was sleepless, and I was curious. I was thinking—*Nothing is different tonight.*

Left my room to join them. Their tomboy kid-sister, they favored over Katie and (prissy, bossy) Miriam.

It was so, I adored my big brothers and basked in the glow of even their careless attention. And they loved me, I believed. I'd always believed.

Taking note of me, sometimes. Tousling my hair as you might tousle the hair of a dog. *Hey kid. How're you doing, Vi'let Rue?*

In a family there are allies, and there are adversaries. It seemed to me that my brothers and I were on our daddy's side, and my sisters were on my mother's side.

Wanting to think this. In my naivete.

Because, really I wasn't a *female* just yet. Lean-hipped as a guy, flat-chested, hard little muscles in legs, arms, shoulders—my brothers had to be impressed, I could run as fast as most boys my age, rarely cried or complained, wasn't fussy or squeamish like other girls. If a spider darted across a wall, or a garter snake slithered across pavement, I didn't shriek and run like another girl.

Why was I proud of this? I was.

Walking into the kitchen as if I'd only now been wakened. Daringly said, "Hey guys! Where've you been so late?"

They stared at me in my pajamas as if for a shivery moment they didn't know who the hell I was. As if they didn't know what to do about me.

Both my brothers were drinking beer from cans, thirstily. Breathing through their mouths as if they'd been running. I felt their excitement, I saw the fatigue in their faces and yet something raw, aroused. Unzipped, their jackets were wet in front. They'd been vigorously washing, scrubbing. Their shoes were wet, dark-stained. The cuffs of their trousers. Lionel's big-jawed face looked puffy; a small cut gleamed beneath his right eye. Jerr was rubbing the knuckles of his right hand as if in pain, but a pleasurable pain. He'd taken time to splash water on his flushed face, dampen his long, lank, sand-colored hair and sweep it back from his forehead. Like Lionel's skin Jerr's skin was blemished but he had a brutal handsome face. He had Daddy's young face.

With a tight smile Jerr said, "Over at the Falls. We ran into some sons of bitches. But we're okay, see? Don't tell Mom."

Lionel said, "Yeah, Vi'let. Don't tell Mom, or— him."

*Him.* We knew what *him* meant.

No need to warn me against telling Daddy. None of us would ever have ratted on one another to our father. Even if we were furious at one another, or disgusted, we wouldn't. That would be a betrayal so profound and so cruel as to be unforgivable for Daddy's punishment would be swift and pitiless and for a certain space of time Daddy would withhold his love from the one he'd punished.

I asked who it was they'd been fighting. How badly I wanted to know their secrets. To be like a brother to them, and not just a *sister.*

Though I knew it was futile. They would shrug as they always did when I asked pushy questions. Jerr said, lowering his voice, "You got to promise you won't say anything, Vi'let. Okay?"

I shrugged and laughed. I was feeling wild! Asking, could I have a taste of their beer?

They looked surprised. Had I surprised *them*?

Lionel handed me his can, which was still cold. It turned out not to be beer but Daddy's favorite, Dark Horse Black Ale. The taste was repulsive to me, even the smell, but I was determined to persevere in trying to like it, to see why my brothers and my father liked the dark ale so much, until one day (I was sure) I would like it just fine. I swallowed a mouthful. I was choking, liquid stung in my nose, the guys laughed at me, but not meanly. I managed to say, "I promise."

# The Promise

By Monday news of the "savage beating" of Hadrian Johnson spread through South Niagara. Even in middle school no one was talking about much else. I heard, and I knew.

An African American boy, basketball player and honors student at the high school. Beaten and left unconscious at a roadside. In critical condition in intensive care at South Niagara General Hospital . . .

Our teachers were looking grim, cautious. You could see them speaking together urgently, in the halls. But not to us.

*Better to say nothing. Until all the facts are known.*

I was frightened for my brothers, I was in dread of their being arrested. I would tell no one what I knew.

But already South Niagara police were making inquiries about my brothers, my cousin Walt, and Don Brinkhaus who was, like Jerr, no longer in school. Someone had provided them with the first three digits of the Chevrolet's license plate and a partial description of the car which was traced to our father.

No possible way that Jerome Kerrigan could deny that he'd given the car to his oldest son Jerome Jr., since any number of people knew this; but there was the off chance, Daddy probably told himself, and the police, that the Chevrolet had been stolen and whatever had happened, his sons were not to blame . . . For police officers had allowed Daddy to think initially that the situation was just an accident, a hit-and-run.

*Damn kids lost it and panicked.*

Both my brothers were picked up by police officers and brought to headquarters for questioning. Jerr, just as he was arriving late to work, groggy and distracted, in the Chevrolet with the dented front fender; Lionel at school, disheveled and anxious and determined to behave as if nothing was wrong. We would learn later that Daddy met Jerr and Lionel at the police precinct in the company of the very lawyer who'd so successfully defended the boys against charges of assault against Liza Deaver.

At home our mother was preoccupied, nervous. Several times she hurried to answer the phone, taking it into a room where she could speak privately. By suppertime when Lionel and Daddy weren't back I thought it would be expected of me to ask where they were? Was something wrong?—but my mother turned away as if she hadn't heard.

Where was Daddy, and where was Lionel?—my sisters, my brothers Les and Rick seemed not to know.

In silence we sat with our mother to watch the local 6:00 P.M. news. The lead story was of a *deadly attack on a local teenager by yet-unidentified assailants.*

The victim was *Hadrian Johnson, seventeen. Popular basketball player and honors student, South Niagara High. Beaten, critical injuries, witness driving along Delahunt Road has allegedly reported "four or five white boys . . ."*

A likeness of Hadrian Johnson filled the screen, the photo that would be published with his obituary: young-looking, boyish, sweet smile, gat-teeth.

Our mother was moaning softly to herself. She'd been in an agitated state since we'd come home from school and even now the telephone was ringing, she didn't seem to hear.

My sisters Miriam and Katie, my brothers Les and Rick, remained staring numbly at the TV screen though an advertisement had come on. They were quieter than I had ever seen them. Les said he knew Hadrian Johnson—sort of. Katie said she knew his sister Louise. Miriam, who never dared smoke at home, fumbled for cigarettes in a pocket, lit one with trembling hands and our staring blinking benumbed mother paid not the slightest heed.

How much they all knew, or had guessed, I did not know.

I did not understand how this terrible news could be related to my brothers. There was something I was forgetting—the baseball bat? In my confusion it seemed to me that Hadrian Johnson must have been beaten by the same persons who'd fought with my brothers— *sons of bitches at the Falls.*

Niagara Falls was seven miles away. This beating had been here in South Niagara, on Delahunt Road.

There were long-standing rivalries between the high school sports teams. Sometimes these spilled over into acts of vandalism, threats, fights. Beatings.

That must have been it, I thought. Guys from Niagara Falls, invading South Niagara. Often there were attacks of graffiti on the South Niagara high school walls, obscene words and drawings after a weekend.

From what my brothers had told me it sounded as

if they'd been at the Falls and had been fighting there. Was it possible, I'd heard wrong?

*I won't tell Dad. I won't tell anyone. I promise!*

In the aftermath of the TV news our mother stood slowly, pushing herself up from the couch. With the stiff dignity of one in great pain who is resolved not to show it she made her way out of the room. We saw her lips moving wordlessly as if she were praying or arguing with someone. Her eyes had become glazed, as if she were staring at something pressing too close to her face, she could not get into focus.

She would hide away in the house, in this benumbed state. She would hide like a wounded creature. As after what she called *the trouble* with the Deaver girl for weeks she'd been reluctant to leave the house knowing that she had to encounter friends, acquaintances, neighbors eager to commiserate with her about the terrible injustice to which the Kerrigan boys had been subjected . . .

For it was not always clear, our mother knew: the distinction between commiseration and gloating.

Eventually, the Deaver girl was forgotten. Or people ceased speaking of her to Lula Kerrigan.

From that time onward, we noticed that Mom was becoming more religious. If that's what it was—"religious."

At church she sat stiffly at attention. You would think that her mind was elsewhere, her expression was so vacant. Yet, she would suddenly cover her face with her hands as if overcome with emotion. As the mass was celebrated by slow painstaking degrees, as the priest lifted the small pale wafer in his hands to bless it, to transform it into the body and blood of Jesus Christ, the ringing of the little silver bell seemed to prompt our mother to such behavior, mortifying to those of us who had to crowd into the pew with her— in recent years just the younger children, and Miriam.

It was rare that Daddy came to mass with Mom. Rarer still that Jerr or Lionel came. But Les, sometimes. And Katie, and Rick. And Violet Rue who was usually squeezed between Katie and Mom, a fidgety child, easily bored.

Violet Rue hated church. Oh but she feared church—the sharp-eyed God who dwelt inside the church, and who knew her innermost heart.

Sometimes, when Mom lowered her hands from her face her eyes were brimming with tears.

Tears of hurt, or fear?—triumph? Vindication? You could not say, you dared not look at the shining face.

Making her way to the communion rail then, swaying like a drunken woman, oblivious of her children.

*She* was in the presence of God, she had nothing to do with them at this moment.

A mother's public behavior can be a source of great mortification to her children, especially her daughters. (As our father's never was.) (Maybe because we saw Mom much more frequently in public places than we saw Dad.) The red-lipstick mouth that stood out like a cutout mouth in her pale, fleshy face, the thin-plucked eyebrows that would never grow back, white vein-raddled bare legs in summer and spreading hips, hair beginning to grow gray in swatches—all these were shameful to sharp pitiless eyes. And the exasperating precision with which Mom parked her car, which required numerous attempts. The muffled exclamations, choked-back sobs.

*Oh, God. Help me!*

I adored my mother but also, I guess I hated her. More and more, as I grew older and Mom seemed never to change except to become more exasperatingly *herself.*

After the TV news we went away stunned. It was as if a fire were burning somewhere in the house, no one knew where. I could hear Katie's bewildered voice and Miriam telling her sharply just be still, not to bother Mom.

I wanted to tell them: I knew much more than they did. Our brothers had entrusted me with a secret as they had not entrusted *them.*

For seven hours my father remained with Jerr and Lionel at police headquarters as they were being interviewed. (Not "interrogated," since they had not—yet—been arrested.)

Initially, my brothers denied any involvement with Hadrian Johnson, at any time.

Then, Jerr conceded that just possibly he'd struck something, or someone, driving on Delahunt Road on Saturday night. And he'd been drinking—a few beers. And maybe speeding, a few miles over the forty-five-mile-an-hour limit.

Definitely, he'd heard a *thud.* He and Lionel both. Looked in the rearview mirror but didn't see anything, guessed it might've been a deer, or a bicycle abandoned at the side of the road.

Had anyone else been with them?—my brothers were asked.

At first, reluctant to give the names of the other boys. For they were not the kind of guys to rat on their friends.

At first, shaking their heads *no.*

Though soon, after repeated questions, and Daddy's increasing impatience, they acknowledged *yes*—there were two other guys with them, in the backseat of the car.

And so, my brothers did "rat" on their friends after all. (Would this be held against them?—it did not seem so.)

I would wonder when our father was told by police officers about Hadrian Johnson—what had been done to him, what condition he was in; when this had happened, and what a witness had reported.

When Daddy had no choice but to realize that the trouble his sons were in wasn't just a hit-and-run accident.

After seven hours Daddy was allowed to bring my brothers back to the house. They had not (yet) been arrested. They had been warned, and had agreed, not to leave South Niagara but to be available for further questioning as soon as the next day.

It was after 9:00 P.M. They were exhausted, and they were starving. In the kitchen they ate the supper Mom had prepared for them, kept warm in the oven. No one else was welcome in the room though we were all told—by Daddy, for Mom could not bear to speak—that there'd been a "misunderstanding" by the South Niagara police—a "misidentification"—that would be straightened out in the morning, with the lawyer's help.

Rick asked if it had anything to do with Hadrian Johnson getting beaten and Daddy said angrily *no it did not.*

What we could see of our older brothers, they were looking fatigued, grim. Their jaws were dark with stubble and their eyes were rimmed with shadow. Lionel didn't smirk as he usually did if someone was looking at him more intently than he liked and Jerr ignored us altogether.

Katie and I went to bed, later than our usual hour. And in our beds we lay unable to sleep. Katie said, "I guess Jerr and Lionel are in some kind of trouble from the other night. With Jerr's car? You think—they were drinking?"

Of Hadrian Johnson she did not speak, as if she'd forgotten him.

And I'd forgotten him, too. And the baseball bat.

Strange to be lying beneath a warm comforter, in flannel pajamas, shivering. So hard, my teeth were chattering.

And my head was aching, as it sometimes did when I lay down, my head on a single pillow; too much blood rushed into it. Badly I wanted to just lie there in the dark, not having to see another person, not having to hear another person speak and not having to speak myself. Not having to think about anything that was upsetting, frightening.

*What is it? Why?*

**At first** I thought it was wind scraping branches against the roof of the house then I understood it was Daddy speaking with my brothers in the kitchen below. His voice was low and urgent, their voices were murmurs. At times it sounded as if he was giving them instructions, and at times it sounded as if he was pleading with them. And then his voice was abrupt, as if he was interrupting them. I could not hear words distinctly, for the pounding of my heart.

I was sick with the knowledge of what Jerome and Lionel had done even as I could not quite understand what they had done for still I was thinking of Niagara Falls . . . I had no wish to eavesdrop now. Never would I eavesdrop on anyone again.

It was frightening to me, I did not think that I could lie, if I was questioned about my brothers. If police officers questioned *me*.

I could not lie very convincingly to my brothers and sisters, and I could not lie at all to any adult. I would have to tell the truth. As, in confession, I made an effort to list the "sins" I'd committed, which included sins of omission. If the priest asked me—*What are you not telling me, my dear? What is your secret?* If one of my teachers asked me—*What is it, Violet?—that you should be telling police?*

Through the long day at school I'd been thinking of Hadrian Johnson. Hearing his name spoken, seeing his picture. His face on the front page of the *South Niagara Union Journal.* Your first thought is he's an athlete, he has brought some sort of acclaim to South Niagara, a championship, a scholarship. But then you see the headline.

## LOCAL YOUTH, 17, SAVAGELY BEATEN
### Attack on Delahunt Rd., Police Search for Assailants

Jerr had stayed the night, in his old room he'd shared with Lionel. I wondered if the two were awake as I was awake and if they spoke together or had lapsed into silence, exhausted. I wondered what they were thinking. If they were thinking.

Though I knew better I wondered if somehow it was true—true in some way—that there'd been a "misunderstanding"—a "misidentification."

Already my brothers had a lawyer. So quickly, Daddy had known to, as he'd say sardonically of others, *lawyer up.*

In Daddy's world, to *lawyer up* was to admit guilt. Usually.

But you needed a lawyer, if you were accused of anything. Under the law you were *innocent until proven guilty* and only a lawyer could guide you through the process of such proof.

As the lawyer had protected my brothers and the other boys from serious consequences, at the time of Liza Deaver.

In a paralysis of dread I lay with my hands pressed over my ears as my father continued to question my brothers almost directly below my bed. I wondered if in my parents' bedroom at the end of the hall my mother too was lying awake, unable to sleep, listening for sounds—footsteps on the stairs, a softly closing door—that the ordeal was over, for the night.

Whatever Daddy was asking my brothers, they were giving him answers that were not satisfactory. This, I seemed to know.

Daddy must have been humiliated by the ordeal in the police precinct. He knew South Niagara police officers, and they knew him. He'd gone to school with some of them. Possibly, they were embarrassed for him.

Of the four boys brought in for questioning, Jerr, the oldest, would have seemed the most convincing as he was (seemingly) the most intelligent; Walt, a cousin, the son of one of Daddy's younger brothers, would have seemed the most innocent, and the most easily led. Lionel, uneasy in his body, grown inches within the past year, with the red cut beneath his eye like a lurid wink, would have seemed the least trustworthy. And there was Don Brinkhaus with his Marine-style haircut and broad heifer-face who'd been on the varsity football team at the high school until he'd been expelled from the team for fighting two or three years ago.

Had the guys been driving on Delahunt Road, and had Jerr (unknowingly) struck something or someone on the shoulder of the road?—this was the issue. Lionel wanted to insist that nothing had happened at all. Aggrieving, whining to Daddy—*We* didn't *do it. We* didn't *even see him. They* just *want to arrest somebody white.*

I wondered: Did Daddy believe them?

**And I** wondered: Did Mom believe them?

On the phone we heard her breathless and disbelieving: "It's a trap. They aren't even looking for anyone else. They think it was Jerr's car—the one Jerome gave him. They *think*. But Jerr has said if he'd hit something that night, he thinks it was a deer. He'd washed off the bloodstains, he said. He'd thought it was a *deer*, that was what you would do, if—if it was a deer you'd hit . . . And they are saying, this Johnson boy, this black boy, he'd been involved in drugs. They all are . . . I mean, so many of them are, right in the high school. In the middle school. The dealers are in the Falls, black drug dealers in the Falls and in Buffalo, with ties to New York City. They drive expensive cars—sports cars. They wear fur coats, gold chains, diamond fillings in their *teeth*. They murder one another all the time and nobody cares, the police look the other way because they are *on the take*. It comes up from Colombia in South America, the drug—heroin, I think it is. Opium."

And: "It was a personal connection, this 'Hadrian Johnson' was killed by a boyfriend of his own mother . . . He was beaten to death with a tire iron. They left him to die by the side of the road. The police say, the 'murder weapon' was thrown in the river. And this isn't the first time, there have been other times nobody even knew about, that never got in the papers because white boys were not accused. The media has it out for white boys—you know . . . It's the way it is. But we have a very good lawyer. He says, the murderer is probably Hadrian Johnson's own mother's boyfriend and a major drug dealer, lives in the Falls and the police never touch *him*, he has gotten away with murder a dozen times."

And, later: "We just heard—it was a Hells Angels attack. 'White racists.' A motorcycle gang, in the Falls. They rode to South Niagara the other night, looking for blacks to kill. You see them sometimes in the daytime in military formation—roaring on their Harley-Davidsons. It could have been anyone they killed. That poor boy—'Hadrian Johnson.' Only in high school, and Les says he was a quiet boy, and a good basketball player, everybody liked him. People who have trouble with black kids say they'd never had trouble with *him*."

A swirl of rumors, like rotted leaves in the wind. A plague of rumors and a stink of rumors and yet, nothing came of them. After several days our mother's voice on the phone grew frantic: ". . . no one is supposed to know, our lawyer says it has to be kept confidential, Hadrian Johnson had gotten in a fight with another black basketball player that weekend, over a girl, and 'sliced' him with a knife, and the other boy threatened to kill him, and . . ."

Jerome Jr. and Lionel were summoned back to the police station. Walt Lemire, Don Brinkhaus were summoned. Now there were three lawyers: one for the

Kerrigan brothers, one for Walt Lemire and one for Don Brinkhaus.

Yet, the boys were not arrested. So long as they were not *arrested*, their names would not appear in local media.

Everyone talked of them: the Kerrigans, especially. Somehow it began to be known, or to be suspected, that Jerome Kerrigan Jr. had struck Hadrian Johnson in a hit-and-run accident.

*Not on purpose. Accident.*

*Blaming the kid more than he deserves, because he is WHITE.*

Daddy insisted that Jerr move back into his old room; there'd been "racist" threats against him, and he wasn't safe in his place downtown, Daddy believed. Lionel was informed by the high school principal that he should stay home for a while, feelings were running high between "whites" and "blacks" at South Niagara High and Lionel's presence was "distracting." Mom wanted to keep me home from school too but I was so upset, she relented. I could not bear to miss school—I loved school! And I was sure, I wanted to believe, school loved *me*.

The thought of being kept home with my mother and my brothers day after day panicked me. Trapped in the house where everyone was waiting for—what? What would save them? For someone else to be arrested for the crime?

As Mom said, "Whoever did this terrible thing. The guilty people."

There was the hope, too, that the evidence police were assembling was only circumstantial, not enough to present to a grand jury. Especially, a jury comprised of white people. This was what the boys' lawyers insisted.

Relatives, neighbors, friends of Daddy's dropped by our house to show support. Fellow Vietnam veterans. At least, this was the pretext for their visit.

A call came from Tommy Kerrigan's office, for Daddy. Not clear whether Tommy Kerrigan himself spoke to Daddy or one of his assistants.

Sometimes Mom refused to see visitors but hid away upstairs when the doorbell rang and told us not to answer it. At other times she was excited, insisting that visitors stay for meals. Female relatives helped in the kitchen. Beer, ale was consumed. There was an air of festivity. The subject of all conversation was *the boys*—how badly they were being treated by the police, how unfair, unjust the investigation was.

*Because they are WHITE. No other reason!*

The name "Hadrian Johnson" was never uttered. There was reference to the "black boy." That was all.

Jerr and Lionel didn't speak of Hadrian at all. It was as if the South Niagara police were to blame for their troubles, or rather the chief of police, who'd been an appointment of Tommy Kerrigan's when Tommy Kerrigan had been mayor of South Niagara—*Rat bastard. You'd think he'd be more grateful.*

There may have been friends, relatives, acquaintances who believed that Jerr and Lionel were guilty of what they'd been accused of doing but these people did not visit us. Or if they did, they were circumspect in their emotional support for beleaguered Lula and Jerome.

*Terrible thing. Such a tragedy. Try to hope for the best . . .*

There was much speculation on the identity of the "anonymous witness" who'd provided the first several letters of the Chevrolet license plate. How could police be certain that he was telling the truth? Wasn't it possible he'd deliberately misinformed them? Giving them the first few digits of Jerr's car, to implicate Jerome Kerrigan's son? And daring to specify Hadrian Johnson's assailants as "white boys."

(In the dark, how could a witness be so certain of the color of the boys' skin? He couldn't have had more than a glimpse of the boys at the side of the road. By his own account he'd slowed down for only a few seconds then sped up and drove away.)

(Very possibly, this "anonymous witness" was a black man himself. Involved in the beating himself . . . )

The phone rang repeatedly. Often Mom stood a few feet away squinting at it. She was fearful of answering blindly—not since Liza Deaver did she dare pick up a receiver without knowing exactly who was calling. If I was nearby she asked me to answer for her as she stood transfixed while I lifted the receiver and said *Sorry nobody is here right now to speak with you. Please do not call again thank you!*—quickly hanging up before the voice on the other end could express surprise or scold me.

One day I was alone in the kitchen after school. Staring at the phone as it began to ring. And there was Lionel beside me. Looming over me. "Don't answer that," he said. He spoke tersely, tightly as a knot might speak. Giving me no time to react, to move away from the phone, but rudely knocking me aside though I'd made no move to answer it.

Lionel's mouth was twisted into a slash of a smile. He'd stayed home from school, he'd barely spoken to anyone in the family for days except our father and only then in private. Much of the time he was playing video games in his room. The cut beneath his eye had not healed, he must have been picking at the scab. His jaws were unshaven. The neck of his T-shirt was stretched, and soiled. I smelled something sharp, rank as an animal's smell lifting from him. I laughed nervously, edging away.

Lionel said, in a jeering singsong voice: "Hey there, 'Vi-let Rue'! Where're you going, you!"

I eased away. I fled.

Wanting to assure my angry brother—*I won't tell Dad. Or anyone. I told you—I promised.*

# The Siege

Without regaining consciousness, Hadrian Johnson died in the hospital on November 11.

**Now the** Kerrigan household was truly under siege. Like a boat, buffeted by ferocious winds.

We Kerrigans huddled inside, clutching at one another. Daddy would protect us, we knew.

Jerr returned to work, where his employer and most of his fellow workers were inclined to be sympathetic toward him. Lionel was suspended indefinitely from school.

Fewer people dropped by the house. But Kerrigan relatives were loyal. Staying late into the night in the basement room Daddy had remodeled into a TV room, drinking, talking loudly, vehemently.

Just adults in the basement with Daddy. No kids including Jerr and Lionel.

With so many people in the house it wasn't hard for me to avoid my brothers. At meals they ignored me, as they ignored their younger brothers and sisters, sitting next to Daddy, eating with their heads lowered and addressing one another in terse exchanges. Their lawyer's last name was O'Hagan—you could hear their remarks peppered with these syllables—*O'Hagan*—but not what they were saying.

Since he'd shoved me in the kitchen Lionel rarely looked in my direction. I had come to think that he'd forgotten me, for he had much else to think about. Jerr's pebble-colored eyes drifted over me, restless, brooding. Within a week or so my oldest brother had lost weight, his face was gaunt, his manner edgy, distracted. While Lionel ate hungrily Jerr pushed food about on his plate and preferred to drink beer from a can. Often he lifted the can so carelessly to his mouth, rivulets of liquid ran glistening down his chin. One evening Daddy told him no more, he'd had enough, and Jerr rose indignantly from the table unsteady on his feet murmuring what sounded like *Fuck.*

Or maybe, judging from Daddy's reaction—*Fuck you.*

In an instant Daddy was on his feet too. Gripping Jerr by the scruff of the neck and shaking him as you might shake an annoying dog. Shoving him back against the wall so that the breath was knocked out of him. Glasses, silverware fell from the table onto the floor. There were cries of alarm, screams. Jerr scrambled to his feet ashen-faced but knew better than to protest.

No one dared leave the table except Jerr who retreated like a kicked dog. Daddy was flush-faced, furious. We sat very still waiting for the fury to pass.

In silence we finished the meal. In silence, my sisters and I cleared the table for our mother who was trembling badly. It was frightening and yet thrilling, to witness our father so swiftly *disciplining* one of us who had disrespected him.

That is the sick, melancholy secret of the family—you shrink in terror from a parent's blows and yet, if you are not the object of the blows, you swell with a kind of debased pride.

My brother, and not me. *Him,* therefore not me.

**Our mother** began to say, many times in those weeks—*Those people are killing us.*

On the phone she complained in a faltering, hurt voice. To her children, who had no choice but to listen. She'd been talking to our parish priest Father Greavy who'd confirmed her suspicion, she reported back to us, that *those people* were our enemies

We wondered who *those people* were. Police? African Americans? Newspaper and TV reporters who never failed to mention that an anonymous witness had described "white boys" at the scene of the beating—"as yet unidentified."

*Those people* could be other white people of course. Traitors to their race who defended blacks just for the sake of defending blacks. Hippie-types, social-worker types, politicians making speeches to stir trouble for the sake of votes.

*Taking the side of blacks. Automatically. You can hear it in their voices on TV . . .*

No one in our family had any idea that I knew about what had happened that night. What might have happened.

That I knew about the bat. That there was a bat.

In articles about the beating there seemed to be no mention made of a "murder weapon"—so far as most people might surmise there wasn't one. (Had police actually mentioned a *tire iron?* I had not heard this from anyone except my mother reporting one of many rumors.) A boy had been beaten savagely, his skull (somehow) fractured. That was all.

I wondered if Jerr and Lionel talked about me. Our secret.

They knew only that I knew they'd been fighting that night. They had no reason to suspect that I knew about the bat. Surely they thought that I believed their story of having been in Niagara Falls and not in South Niagara.

*She wouldn't tell. Not Vi'let Rue.*

*You sure? She's just a kid.*

*Anyway, what does she know? None of them know shit.*

# Because . . .

Because *They could not have done that, such a terrible thing* there came to be *They did not do that terrible thing.*

Because *It can't be possible* there came to be *It is not possible. Was not possible.*

Because *They wouldn't lie to us* there came to be *They did not lie to us. Our sons.*

Through the floorboards you heard. Through the furnace vent you heard. Amid the rattling of the ventilator. Through shut doors you heard, and through those walls in the house that for some reason were not so solid as others, stuffed with a cottony sort of insulation that, glimpsed just once, as a wall was being repaired, shocked you looking so like a human lung, upright, vertical.

Like a TV in another room, volume turned low. Daddy's voice dominant. Mom's voice much fainter. A pleading voice, a whining voice, a fearful voice, for Daddy hated whining, whiners. Your brothers knew better than to *piss and whine.* Shouting, cursing one another, shoving one another down the stairs, over- turning a table in the hall, sending crockery shattering onto the kitchen floor—such behavior was preferable to despicable whining which Daddy associated with women, girls. Babies.

And so, your mother did not dare speak at length. Whatever she said, or did not say, your father would talk over, his voice restless and careening like a bull- dozer out of control. Was he rehearsing with her— *You could say they were home early that night. By ten o'clock. You remember because . . .*

They would choose a TV program. Something your brothers might've watched. Better yet: sports. Maybe there'd been a football game broadcast that night . . . On HBO, a boxing match.

*Jerome I don't think that I—don't think that I can . . .*

*Look. They aren't lying to us—I'm sure. But it might look like they are lying, to other people. Sons of bitches in this town they'd like nothing better than to fuck up decent white kids.*

*Don't make me, Jerome . . . I don't think that I, I can . . .*

*You can! God damn it, they might've been home— might've watched the fucking TV. Or you might re- member it that way and even if you were wrong it could help them.*

None of this you heard. None of this you remember.

# The Rescue

By chance you saw.

So much had become *chance* in your life.

Headlights turning into the driveway, in the dark. Your father's car braking in front of the garage.

By chance you were walking in the upstairs hall. Cast your eyes down, through the filmy curtains seeing the car turn in from the street. Already it was late. He'd missed supper. Past 9:00 P.M. No one asked any longer—*Where's Daddy?*

In the hall beside the window you paused. Your heart was not yet beating unpleasantly hard. You were (merely) waiting for the car lights to be switched off below. Waiting for the motor to be switched off. Waiting for the familiar sound of a car door slammed shut which would mean that your father had gotten out of the car and was approaching the house to enter by the rear door to signal *Nothing has changed. We are as we were.*

But this did not seem to be happening. Your father remained in the (darkened) car.

Still the motor was running. Pale smoke lifted from the tailpipe. You were beginning to smell the exhaust, and to feel faintly nauseated.

In the hall by the window you stood. Staring down at the driveway, the idling car. Waiting.

*He is not running carbon monoxide into the car. The car is not inside the garage, there is no danger that he will poison himself.*

Yet, gray smoke continued to lift from the rear of the car. Stink of exhaust borne on the cold wet air like ash.

*He is sitting in the car. He is smoking in the car.*

*Waiting to get sober. Inside the car.*

*That is where he is: in the car.*

*He is safe. No one can harm him. You can see—he is in the car.*

You could not actually see your father from where you stood. But there was no doubt in your mind, he was in the car.

Had Daddy been drinking, was that why he was late returning home, you would not inquire. Each time Daddy entered the house in the evening unsteady on his feet, frowning, his handsome face coarse and flushed, you would want to think it was the first time and it was a surprise and unexpected. You would not want to think—*Please no. Not again.*

You would want to retreat quickly before his gaze was flung out, like a grappling hook, to hook his favorite daughter Vi'let Rue.

It was one of those days in the aftermath of the death of Hadrian Johnson when nothing seemed to have happened. And yet—always there was the expectation that something will happen.

Your brothers had not been summoned, with O'Hagan, to police headquarters that day. So far as anyone knew, the others—Walt, Don—had not been summoned either.

No arrests had (yet) been made but your brothers were captive animals. Everyone in the Kerrigan house was a captive animal.

They'd ceased reading the *South Niagara Union Journal.* Someone, might've been Daddy, tossed the paper quickly away into the recycling bin as soon as it arrived in the early morning,

For articles about the *savage beating, murder* of Hadrian Johnson continued to appear on the front page. The photograph of Hadrian Johnson continued to appear. Gat-toothed black boy smiling and gazing upward as if searching for a friendly face.

You saw the newspaper, in secret. Not each day but some days.

*These people are killing us.* Possibly, your mother meant the newspaper people. The TV people.

You are beginning to feel uneasy, at the window. You are beginning to wonder if indeed your father is actually in the car. And it is wrong of you to spy upon your father as it is wrong to spy upon your mother. Faces sagging like wetted tissue when they believe that no one is watching. Oh, you love them!

In the car Daddy is (probably) smoking. Maybe he brought a can of ale with him from the tavern. Maybe a bottle.

The bottles are more serious than the cans. The bottles—whiskey, bourbon—are more recent than the cans.

In the plastic recycling bin, glass bottles chiming against one another.

Daddy is not supposed to smoke. Daddy has been warned.

A spot on his lung two years before but a *benign spot. High blood pressure.*

More than once Daddy has declared that he has quit smoking—for the final time.

When Daddy smokes he coughs badly. In the early morning you are wakened hearing him. So painful, lacerating as if someone is scraping a knife against the inside of his throat.

Years ago when you were a little girl Daddy would come bounding into the house—*Hey! I'm home.*

Calling for you—*Hey Vi'let Rue! Daddy is home.*

*Where's Daddy's best girl? Vi'let RUE!*

That happy time. You might have thought it would last forever. Like a TV cartoon now, exaggerated and unbelievable.

Now Daddy is showing no inclination to come into the house. (Maybe he has fallen asleep, behind the wheel? A bottle in his hand, that is beginning to tip over and spill its contents . . . ) He has turned off the motor, at least. You are relieved, the poison-pale smoke has ceased to lift from the tailpipe.

*He's coming inside now. Soon.*

There is a meal for Daddy, in the oven. Covered in aluminum foil.

Even when your mother must know that Daddy won't be eating the supper she has prepared for him there is a meal in the oven which, next day, midday when no one is around, Mom will devour alone in the kitchen rarely troubling to heat it in the microwave. (You have seen her with a fork picking, picking, picking at the cold coagulated meat, mashed potatoes. You have seen your mother eating without appetite, swiftly picking at tasteless food.)

It is unnerving to you, the possibility that no one is in the car.

In the driveway, in the dark. Dim reflected light from a streetlight in the wet pavement.

No, there's no one there!

Somehow, your father has slipped past you. You have failed to see him.

Or, your father has slumped over behind the wheel, unconscious. He has found an ingenious way to divert the carbon monoxide into the car while no one noticed . . .

The father of a classmate at school has died, a few weeks ago. Shocking, but mysterious. What do you say?

You say nothing. Nothing to say. Avoid the girl, not a friend of yours anyway.

As, at school, your friends have begun to avoid *you*.

Pretending not to notice. Not to care. Hiding in a toilet stall dabbing wetted tissues against your face. Why are your eyelids so red? So swollen?

But now you have begun to be frightened. You wonder if you should seek out your mother. *Mom? Daddy is still in the car, he has been out there a long time . . .* But the thought of uttering such words, allowing your parents to know that you are spying on them, is not possible.

And then, this happens: you see someone leave the house almost directly below, and cross to the car in the driveway.

Is it—your mother?

She, too, must have been standing at a window, downstairs. She'd seen the headlights turning into the driveway. She'd been waiting, too.

Slipping her arms into the sleeves of someone's jacket, too large for her. Bare-headed in light-falling snow that melts as soon as it touches the pavement, and her hair.

It is brave of Mom to be approaching Daddy, you think. You hold your breath wondering what will happen.

For you, your sisters, and your brothers have seen, numerous times, your father throwing off your mother's hand, if she touches him in a way that is insulting or annoying to him. You have seen your father stare at your mother with such hatred, your instinct is to run away in terror.

In terror that that face of wrath will be turned onto *you.*

You are watching anxiously as, at the car, on the farther side of the car where you can't see her clearly, your mother stoops to open the door. Tugging at the door, unassisted by anyone inside.

And now, what is your mother doing? Helping your father out of the car?

You have never seen your mother *helping* your father in any way, like this. You are certain.

At first, it isn't clear that Daddy is getting out of the car. That Daddy is able to get out of the car.

It has become late, on Black Rock Street. A working-class neighborhood in which houses begin to darken by 10:00 P.M.

In early winter, houses begin to lighten before dawn.

Up and down the street, in winter, when the sun is slow to appear, windows of kitchens are warmly lit in the hour before dawn. You will remember this, in your exile.

Well—Daddy is on his feet, in the driveway. He has climbed out of the car with Mom's assistance, and he does not appear to be angry at her. His shoulders are slumped, his legs move leadenly. The lightness in his body you remember from a time when you were a little girl, the rough joy with which he'd danced about in the garage, teaching your brothers to box, has passed from him. His youth has passed from him. The years of his young fatherhood when his sons and daughters had been beautiful to him, when he'd stared at them with love and felt a fatherly pride in them, have passed.

Transfixed at the window you watch. For the danger is not past yet.

You steel yourself: your father will fling your mother from him with a sweep of his arm, he will curse her . . .

But no, astonishingly that doesn't seem to be happening. Instead, your father has allowed your mother to slip her arm around his waist. He steadies himself against her, leaning heavily on her.

Awkwardly, cautiously they make their way toward the house. Taking care not to slip on the driveway where ice is beginning to form, thin as a membrane.

What words have they exchanged? What has your mother said to your father, that has blunted his rage?

You have drawn away from the window. You have let the curtain fall back into place. You do not want either of your parents to glance up, to see you at the window, watching.

It is a remarkable fact, your father leaning heavily upon your mother, who is several inches shorter than he, and must weigh seventy pounds less than he does. Yet she holds him up without staggering, your mother is stronger than you would have imagined.

Together your parents approach the house, walking cautiously, like much older people, in this way you've never seen. They pass out of your sight, below. You stand very still waiting for them to enter the house, waiting to hear the door open below, and close, so you can think, calmly—*They are both safe now. For now.*

# The Secret I

There is a secret between my mother and me. All these years in exile, I have told no one.

In fact, there are secrets. Which one shall I reveal first?

In sixth grade I'd become friendly with a girl named Geraldine Pyne. Several times she invited me to her house after school, on Highgate Avenue. Her father was a doctor in a specialty that made me shiver—gastroenterology. She lived in a large white brick house with a portico and columns like a temple. When I first saw Geraldine's house I felt a twinge of dread for I understood that my mother would not like me to visit there and would be unhappy if she knew.

I understood too that my father would disapprove, for my father spoke resentfully of "money people."

But my father would not ever know about Geraldine Pyne, and it was possible that my mother would.

On days when Geraldine invited me to her house for dinner Mrs. Pyne usually picked us up after school, and either Mrs. Pyne or her housekeeper drove me home afterward; there was no suggestion that my mother might come to pick me up.

Mrs. Pyne's station wagon was not a very special vehicle, like the long, shiny black Lincoln Dr. Pyne drove. So if my mother happened to glance out the window, and saw me getting out of it, she would not have been unduly alarmed or suspicious.

And Geraldine too, if Mom happened to see her, did not look like a special girl. You would not have guessed from her unassuming appearance (pink plastic glasses, glittering braces, shy smile) that she was the daughter of well-to-do parents, or even that she was a popular girl (with other girls and with our teacher, at least) and an honors student.

Geraldine was an *only child*. This seemed magical to me. As my sisters and brothers, all older than me, seemed magical to her.

"You would never have to be alone," Geraldine said wistfully.

I tried not to laugh. For this was not true, and why would anyone want it to be true? An *only child* could have no idea of the *commotion* of the Kerrigan house-hold.

It was embarrassing to me that Geraldine should confide in me that her parents had hoped for another child, but *God had not sent one.* In the Kerrigan family no one spoke of such intimate matters casually. I could not imagine my mother or father sharing such information with me.

I was grateful not to be an *only child.* My parents would have only me, and I would have only them, to love; it would be like squinting into a blinding light that never went out.

I did not feel comfortable inviting Geraldine to our house for I believed she would be embarrassed for me. Especially, she would see my mother's weedy flower beds, that were always being overwhelmed by thistles and brambles, and coarse wildflowers like goldenrod, so different from the beautiful elegant roses in her mother's gardens, with their particular names Geraldine once proudly enunciated for me, like poetry—*Damask, Sunsprite, Rosa Peace, American Beauty, Ayrshire.* Geraldine would see how *ordinary* our house was, though my father took great pride in it, a foolish pride it seemed to me, compared to the Pynes' house: as if it mattered that a wood frame house on Black Rock Street was neatly painted, and its roof properly shingled, drainpipes and gutters cleared of leaves, front walk and asphalt driveway in decent condition though beginning (you could see, if you looked closely) to crack into a thousand pieces like a crude jigsaw puzzle. Especially Geraldine would wince to hear my older brothers' heavy footsteps on the stairs like hooves and their loud careening voices like nothing in her experience, in the house on Highgate Avenue. And there was the possibility of my elderly grandfather emerging from his hovel of a room at the rear of the house, disheveled, unsteady on his feet and bemused at the sight of a strange young girl in the house —*Hey there! Who'in hell are you?*

But then, my mother discovered that my friend Geraldine's father was a doctor—Dr. Morris Pyne. She was shocked, intrigued. She insisted that I show her where the Pynes lived and drove me to Highgate Avenue to point out the house to her. This was a request so utterly unlike my mother, who rarely left the house except to go shopping and to church, and who rarely evinced any interest in her children's school friends, I'd thought at first that she could not be serious.

"Oh, Mom. Why d'you want to know? It's not that special."

"Isn't it! Highgate Avenue. We'll see."

No one would know about this drive. Just Lula and Violet Rue, seeking out the residence of Dr. Morris Pyne and his family at 11 Highgate Avenue.

It was as I'd dreaded, the sight of the large spotlessly-white brick house with portico and columns, in a large wooded lot, was offensive to my mother. "So big! Why'd anyone need such a big house! Show-offy like the White House." Mom's voice was hurt, embittered, sneering.

Beside her I shrank in the passenger's seat. In horror that, unlikely as it was, Mrs. Pyne might drive up beside us to turn into the blacktop driveway, that looped elegantly in front of the house, and recognize one of her daughter's school friends in the passenger seat of our car.

I tried to explain to my mother that Geraldine Pyne was one of the nicest girls in sixth grade. She was not a spoiled girl, and you would never guess that she was a "rich" girl. A very thoughtful girl, a quiet girl, who seemed for some reason (God knows why) to like me.

"She thinks I'm funny. She laughs at things I say, that other people don't even get. And Mrs. Pyne is—"

Rudely my mother interrupted: "They look down their noses at us. People like that. Don't tell *me*."

I had never seen my mother's face so creased, contorted. At first I thought she must be joking . . .

"Oh, Mom. They're nothing like that. You're wrong."

"And what do you know? 'You're wrong'—like hell I am."

Driving on, furious. I could not think of a thing to say—my mother whose chatter was usually affable and inconsequential, like a kind of background radio noise, was frightening me.

As we drove in a jerky, circuitous route back home my mother recounted for me in a harsh, hard voice how as a girl she'd cleaned "the God-damned" houses in this neighborhood. Rich people's houses. She'd had to quit school at sixteen, her family had needed the income. At first she'd cleaned houses with a cousin, who did the negotiating, then it turned out the cousin was cheating her, so she'd worked on her own. Five years. She'd worked six days a week for five years until she met my father and got married and started having babies and taking care of a house of her own, seven days a week. Her voice rose and fell in an angry singsong—

*quit school, sixteen, got married, started having babies. Seven days a week.*

There was a particular sort of bitterness here directed at me. For I was one of the babies. And I'd betrayed her with my careless, insulting friendship among the enemy.

"In those houses I had to get down on my knees and scrub. Kitchen floors, bathroom floors. I had to clean their filthy tubs and toilets with Dutch cleanser. Toilet brushes, Brillo pads. I had to strip their smelly beds and wash the sheets, towels, underwear and socks. I had to drag their trash containers out to the curb, that were so heavy my arms ached. Sometimes the kids would come home from school before I was finished, and they'd get their bathrooms dirty again, and I would have to clean them again. Sinks I had scrubbed clean, mirrors I had polished, I would have to do again. Piss splattered on the floor. They laughed at me—the boys. God-damned brats. If they even saw me at all."

Distracted by these memories my mother was driving erratically. Her eyes brimmed with tears of hurt. None of us—her children—had ever known of this hurt, I was sure—I was sure she'd never told anyone, for by now I would have known.

"Oh, they thought they were so generous! Sometimes they gave me food to take home, leftovers in the refrigerator they didn't want, spoiled things, rancid things, garbage—'Here, take this home please try to remember to return the Tupperware bowl next week.' I wasn't supposed to spend more than twenty minutes on lunch. I wasn't supposed to *sit down*—they never like to see a cleaning-woman *sitting down,* that's offensive to them. Or using one of their God-damned bathrooms. If you have to wash your hands, use a paper towel. Not one of their God-damned towels. Some of the big houses, I'd work all morning, so hungry my head ached. That house! I worked in that house—I remember . . ."

I tried to protest: the Pynes had not been living in the white brick house so long ago. They had only moved in a few years ago. It had to be other people she was thinking of. Mrs. Pyne was a polite, kind, wonderful woman, not a snob, not cruel—

Bitterly my mother interrupted: "You! Stupid child! What do you know? You know nothing."

I had never heard my mother speak in such a way. It was as if another woman were in her place, savage and inconsolable.

We were slowing now in front of another, even grander house, at 38 Highgate—a Victorian mansion behind a six-foot wrought iron fence with a warning sign at the gate—PRIVATE. DELIVERIES TO THE REAR.

"And this house—I've been in this house, too. And your father has not."

Not sure what this meant I said nothing.

"D'you know who lives here?"

Yes, I did. I thought that I did. But I played dumb, I said *no*. I did not want to incur any more of my mother's wrath.

"Your father never knew. I never told him. That I was a house maid on Highgate Avenue. That my parents forced me to work. Forced me to quit school. And one of the houses I cleaned was 'Tommy' Kerrigan's—this house. Maybe 'Tommy' doesn't live here any longer—maybe he's retired and living in Florida. Maybe he's dead—the bastard! When he was mayor of South Niagara, and married to a woman named Eileen—his second wife, or his third. She was the one who hired me and paid me but 'Tommy' was on the scene sometimes in the morning when I came to work. Just getting out of the bathroom, getting dressed—filthy pig. Once, he dared to ask me if I would clip his toenails! Saw the look in my face and laughed. 'It's all right, Lula, my feet are *clean*. Come look.' Mrs. Kerrigan never knew how her husband behaved with the help—the female help. If she knew, she pretended she didn't. All of those rich men's wives learn how to pretend. Or they're out on their asses like the female help. She paid me below the minimum wage. She paid me in dollar bills. I had to polish the God-damned silver—the

Kerrigans were always having dinner parties. Had to breathe in stinking pink silver polish that made me sick to my stomach. Terrible bleach I had to use, that almost made me faint. And 'Tommy's' side of the bed—shit stains. I'd hoped to God he had not done it on purpose. But I was grateful for work, I was just too young to know better. The black maids would work for less money than we could so after a while, there weren't any white girls working on Highgate. I doubt there's any 'white help' in South Niagara today. Your father never knew any of this. He lived in his own cloud of—whatever it was—wanting to believe what he wanted to believe. Most men are like that. Jerome doesn't know to this day that I ever set eyes on Tommy Kerrigan up close. He doesn't know that I was on my knees in this God-damned house, or in any of these houses. He'd seemed to think that I had no life before I met him—he never asked about it. He'd never have wanted to touch me—if he knew . . ."

We were out of the neighborhood now. My mother was driving less erratically. Her fury was abating, her voice quavered with something like shame. I could think of nothing to say, my brain had gone blank and it would be difficult for me to remember afterward what my mother had said, and why she had said it; what humiliating truths she'd uttered as I sat stiff beside her in the passenger's seat of the car not daring to look at her.

It was the most intense time between my mother and me. Yet, I would remember imperfectly.

By the time we returned to Black Rock Street my mother appeared tired. I hadn't realized that she'd been crying. Her waxy-pale face was damp with tears which she wiped away with a tissue. She'd had a change of heart. She was sorry now, I understood. Cautioning me not to tell anyone what she'd told me— "They wouldn't understand, they would think badly of me. And your father—he would be disgusted with me."

I wanted to protest *No. We love you, Mom.* But the words would not come.

"Promise! Promise you won't tell anyone, Violet. Not even Katie. Just—*no one.*"

Quickly I promised *yes.* My hand on the door handle of the car, desperate to escape.

# The Secret II

And another secret passed between Lula Kerrigan and her daughter Violet Rue.

Watching TV in the wake of the Hadrian Johnson death, which was forbidden—if Mom knew about it.

Watching local TV news and seeing Hadrian Johnson's mother and older brother interviewed. Faces stricken with grief. Dark-skinned faces, and eyes exactly like ours. Hearing words of grief that were our words, we might someday utter. There was Mrs. Johnson clutching a tissue against her eyes, as Mom might have done. A middle-aged woman stooped in pain, shaking her head in bewilderment. Why? Why would anyone want to hurt Hadrian, who was so kind to everyone? Who loved so many people?

I began crying too. I was often crying these days. Tears brimmed close against the surface of my eyes, the slightest provocation made them spill over. *He is really gone. A boy is really dead. They killed him. It is real.* A taste like copper pennies in my mouth, that made me gag.

My mother strode into the room and switched off the TV. She was angry, disbelieving—"I told you, no TV. Didn't I tell you!" She would have slapped me except I shrank away in time.

Continuing fiercely: "Don't you know, for God's sake—they're just doing that for TV. To get attention, to make people feel sorry for them. So that, if they sue . . ."

My mother's voice trailed off as if, for the first time, she heard what she was saying.

I tried to protest: What if one of us had been killed? Beaten to death with a baseball bat? Wouldn't she feel sorry? Wouldn't she cry?

"Baseball bat? What—baseball bat?"

Mom blinked at me, confused. It came to me in a rush—no one knew about Jerr's baseball bat. The *murder weapon* had never been found.

Mom said, stammering, "That—that would never happen to you. Not to one of us. No . . ."

Retreating then to the kitchen. Where I heard a drawer being opened, and shut. A cupboard door opened, and shut. With a pounding heart I followed my mother, scarcely knowing what I was going to say. "It was Jerr and Lionel, Mom. I saw them with the baseball bat. They were trying to wash it in the garage, then they took it away to bury it. They are the ones—the police are looking for." But Mom stood with her back to me, at the sink running water hard. She was furious, trembling. She did not turn to me. She gave no sign of having heard me or of having the faintest idea that I had followed her into the kitchen. On the wall the avocado-colored plastic phone began to ring but my mother had no more intention of answering it than I did.

# Final Confession

The girl who never cried. Never complained.

Not a *little baby* to be scorned by my father and brothers, or petted and fussed over by my mother and sisters.

But now I cried easily. I cried often. I cried so that my eyes leaked tears before I actually began to cry, like a leaky faucet. My skin was sensitive as sunburned skin registering pain when something brushed lightly against it. My eyelids were reddened, inflamed and swollen and itchy as if bitten by mosquitoes.

At home, and at school. At school, and at home.

Saturday morning at St. Matthew's where Mom brought Katie and me so that we would take communion with her the next morning at mass—*Just the three of us.*

Already the older Kerrigan children were drifting away from the Church. Skipping mass impervious to our mother's pleas and threats since Daddy showed no interest in church attendance, only a vague respect for religion—the Church, though not particularly God or Jesus Christ. (Daddy would have laughed in embarrassment if anyone were to ask him point-blank if he believed in either.)

In the church on Saturday morning Father Greavy heard confessions from 9:00 A.M. until noon. Inside the cage-like confessional with its grille like a small window screen the priest sat, you could see just the shadowy profile, you were not supposed to see *him*. He would hear your abashed whispered confession but he was not supposed to see *you*.

In hearing confessions the priest takes the place of Christ. It is the power of Christ to forgive sins, but only if the sinner is genuinely repentant.

I did not know if it was a sin, that I had told no one about my brothers and the baseball bat. I had promised my brothers to keep their secret without knowing what the secret was. They had demanded it of me, and I had said *Yes. I promise.*

From the catechism I knew that there were sins of omission. These were the most difficult sins to contemplate for they did not, in fact, *exist;* not acts but the absence of acts.

In the confessional that smelled of something acrid and melancholy like old clothes I knelt, dry-mouthed. Always my mouth went dry in this confined space. There was nothing in my young life so unnerving to me, so awkward, as confession. Whispering *Bless me Father, for I have sinned. It has been one week since my last confession.*

Each week my mother brought me with her to St. Matthew's and to Father Greavy in the confessional. From time to time there were other, younger priests assisting him but my mother always knew which confessional Father Greavy was using, it was impossible not to know, you could overhear the priests' murmured voices and recognize them even if you could not hear their precise words.

Each week I was obliged to recite a litany of "sins" to Father Greavy. Fortunately, a list of possibilities was provided at the back of my prayer book, which was a prayer book for young Catholics: disobeying parents, mind wandering during mass, telling lies, uttering profanities, taking the name of the Lord in vain. More obscure and more ominous sins were "impure thoughts"—"impure acts"—from which I recoiled in repugnance, even to consider.

These were venial sins, minor sins. Mortal sins were something other, the province of adults.

It was no wonder that my older brothers avoided confession. They had grown too coarse for such examinations of conscience as they had grown too defiant of priestly authority to make themselves small enough to fit into the confessional. Miriam laughed about confession, uneasily; she had not taken communion in months. (For Miriam was engaged. Whatever "impure" behavior was, it seemed unlikely that Miriam could avoid it with her fiancé.)

Preparing ourselves for the ordeal of confession Katie and I laughed nervously together as we'd have laughed preparing for a physical examination in which all our clothes had to be removed and we had to lie naked and shivering, in a flimsy paper gown, on a table. Because "swearing" was forbidden we dared to murmur forbidden words—*hell, damn, God-damn.* Provoking each other to astonishing feats—*shit, shitty, son of a bitch, God-damn bastard. Fu-uck!* We would have been mortified to have been overheard by our brothers or our father whose speech we were echoing, or by our mother who would have been scandalized.

Each week when I finished my anguished whispering of venial sins, my face burning with embarrassment, Father Greavy would reply with forced patience *And is there anything more you have to say, my child?*—and I would murmur *No, Father.*

As if these trivial sins could be of interest to any adult, still less to God! Yet, Father Greavy was obliged to behave as if this were the case.

But today, twelve days after Hadrian Johnson's death, my throat seemed to have closed when Father Greavy asked me the usual question—*Is there anything more you have to say.* I sat hunched and unmoving, unable to speak. Instead, I began crying.

There was a startled pause. I was such a big girl, twelve years old, I had not cried in the presence of others for years, not like this. And I was sure that Father Greavy knew who I was, if not by name, that I was one of Jerome Kerrigan's daughters.

It was clear, Father Greavy did not like this violation of custom. I could hear him breathing audibly. I could imagine his small damp eyes shifting in their sockets, in alarm and exasperation. But the confessor had no alternative to asking me what was wrong, calling me *My dear child.*

And so I told him. Tried to tell him. Sniffling, and choking, and trying to keep my voice lowered so that those who were seated in pews close outside the confessional would not overhear. In a rushed, shaky voice I told him about my brothers coming home late on the night that Hadrian Johnson had been beaten, and what I'd overheard, and seen them doing in the garage, trying to wash a baseball bat—but Father Greavy interrupted me objecting that I had no idea what I was saying. *These are serious accusations.*

At once I was silent. My heart was hammering in my chest.

In a hissing whisper Father Greavy said that my brothers' lives were at stake. No, no! He did not want to hear more.

In an instant the peculiar lethargy of the confessional had vanished. The thick-bodied priest, middle-aged, querulous, with thin rat-colored hair, red-stippled fattish nose, a habit of loudly clearing his throat of phlegm like gravel, had been awakened rudely from his doze and was sitting upright squinting sidelong at me through the small grilled window with a hawk's eyes, alert and sharp.

Father Greavy wanted no more hysteria about a baseball bat. No more about "Hadrian Johnson" who hadn't belonged to St. Matthew's parish. He did not want trouble, if questioned he would claim he'd had no idea who I was. As a confessor he did not wish to know who his penitents were. Nor had he heard the girl's faltering words clearly.

It seemed that confession had ended. The priest muttered words of absolution, sent me away with the instruction to recite six Hail Marys, four Our Fathers. In his agitation he'd forgotten the humble words that ended the rite of confession—*Pray for me, my child.*

Blindly I stumbled to an empty pew. Knelt, and hid my face in my hands. My lips moved numbly reciting the familiar prayers—*Hail Mary full of grace. Our Father Who art in heaven.* My heart beat rapidly yet with a kind of exaltation as if I'd narrowly escaped a terrible danger. I was deeply ashamed but I was also relieved. For I had tried. I had tried, and I had been told to shut up, and could go away now absolved of my sins.

This would be the final confession of my life.

# "Dear Christ
What Did Violet Do *Now*"

Waiting for you. You knew.

Saying *Hey. Where're you goin', kid.*

You were smiling. Grinning. Inane as a Hallowe'en pumpkin.

Yet cautious enough to hold back. Something in your brother's eyes like cracked marbles warned you.

**His favorite** video games had names like Pit-Fighter, Cyberball, Primal Rage. His favorite movie franchise was *Terminator* and second favorite, *Mad Max.*

He'd grown tall, and he'd grown muscled in the shoulders and torso. A thick neck, thick jaws. Shrewd stone-colored eyes beneath heavy brows. In a few years he would be taller and stockier than his older brother he'd long admired. He would be his father's size with his father's way of clenching and unclenching his fists when he was feeling thwarted.

Unyielding as Jerome Sr. Unforgiving.

Many days after the beating of Hadrian Johnson still the cut on Lionel's cheek had not healed. With his broken and dirt-edged nails he picked, picked at it. Unconsciously he picked at it. Each day it bled anew. Each day he wiped his fingers on his shirt, what the hell. What the fuck did he care, he did not care. Not much. Those days, weeks. Waiting. Waiting for the God-damned police to return. Waiting to be cuffed. He'd claimed not to know how the hell the cut had come to be on his face. Who'd hit him, a wild swing of a fist, wild swing of a baseball bat grazing his skin, or walloping him so that he'd almost gone down, who the fuck had it been Lionel did not know but whoever it was he'd like to murder the bastard with his own hands and maybe someday, Christ knew maybe some-day he would.

Bruises on his chest, upper arms as well. Bruises of the color of oil spills. That night they kept asking him about he'd been totally wasted, couldn't remember a fucking thing and that was a fucking fact.

He'd wanted to. You know. Knew at the time. Sure.

Nudging you down the cellar stairs as a prank. Small of the back. You weighed maybe eighty-five pounds. Barely five feet tall. Cracking your head on the concrete floor. Snapping your neck in an instant the way (on TV) a hyena snaps the neck of its prey. Or, he'd have cornered you in the garage one afternoon when you returned home from school and no one else was in the house. He'd have put on Daddy's old cracked leather gloves abandoned on a work bench in the garage. Slipping on the gloves that fitted his hands loosely but comfortably. Staring at you with interest as if tearing wings off a butterfly as he punched, punched, punched your face you had not have guessed was so tender, the first blow would draw blood.

And your head, as you fell. The bone of the skull not so hard and so protective as you'd have wished to believe. Slid down the wall. Cobwebs in the concrete wall, and cobwebs in your hair. Eye sockets broken, hematomas in both your eyes. Lower jaw broken, slack. Broken teeth. Cartilage of your nose smashed. Rapid punch, punch. Rapid punch. Left jab, right cross.

*Keep your fucking mouth shut, now you won't be able to open it.*

Manslaughter was the most they could charge. Not homicide. Chain of circumstances, accidents. None of it premeditated. Christ! Kids so young, they fuck up every day and could not have *premeditated* anything. Like trying to *premeditate* a shit. You could not.

Anyway, they could not. Had not. Just came up behind the kid on the bicycle by chance and never saw his face. They would swear.

**Should've shoved** *her harder down the steps. Should've broke her God-damn head. Fucking mistake, to show mercy.*

You'd imagined that Lionel no longer glanced in your direction. Was no longer aware of you. Distracted, brooding. Gnawing his lower lip, grimacing. Waiting for the phone to ring. He'd never been a boy to think much but now he'd become a creature eaten up by *thinking, plotting.* Like something was inside him, a living thing. And his eyes ringed with fatigue. You'd noticed him frowning in your direction but not at you. Peering behind you and not at your face. Over your shoulder.

*Looking to see if anyone was around. Watching, listening. If Mom was in the next room. If any of them would come to help you.*

When it happened it wasn't the cellar steps, and it wasn't in the garage. No leather gloves. And no warning.

You'd gone outside to check bird feeders depleted of seed, abandoned and frozen at the rear of the house and recalled suddenly when it was (probably) too late, the birds had flown elsewhere. Foolishly you'd ventured outside at the rear of the house where the concrete steps hadn't yet been salted, shoveled of snow.

Indoors your brother Lionel had seemed to ignore you practically yawning in your presence to assure you, fuck he didn't give a shit about you but there Lionel was, suddenly behind you. Close behind you, panting with what must have been (you would surmise afterward) excitement. Shove against your back as if by accident and you are slipping, falling on the icy steps—so fast it happens, you are taken totally by surprise.

"Hey! Watch out!"—Lionel's warning comes late, mocking. And a mock-groan of scolding solicitude— "Ohhh Vi'let—what'd you do?—*hell.*"

The force of the blow against your head has knocked you unconscious. Two, three seconds obliterated—concussed. Waking stunned to find yourself on the icy ground. A pounding at your left temple where something, the sharp ice-edge of a step, has cut the skin thin as paper, releasing a stream of blood. Your left leg is twisted beneath you, the knee is bent impossibly beneath you. So much blood so quickly, you are astonished. Too surprised to worry that you might bleed to death.

You will recall Lionel crouching over you hungrily even as Miriam comes on the run, from somewhere inside the house Miriam has heard you scream though you have not heard yourself scream, and in that instant Lionel is gone—(gone where? gone)—and Miriam stoops over you to lift you carefully, trying to comfort you, trying not to panic at the blood, explaining to you that you slipped on the ice, you hit your head and cut your forehead but you will be all right. And when Miriam manages to settle you onto one of the steps, to make some effort to staunch the flow of blood with tissues in the pocket of her jacket, and finally with the jacket itself, there comes your mother in the doorway unsteady on her feet and staring, scolding, "Oh, dear Christ what did Violet do *now*."

# The Revelation

"Violet? Is something wrong?"—stooping, staring at me with concerned eyes. "Did you hurt yourself?"

For Ms. Micaela could not, dared not ask *Did someone hurt you*.

She knew the rumor about my brothers. Everyone knew the rumor about my brothers. After the others had filed out of homeroom. After the first-period bell had rung clamorous and jeering and I remained in my seat dazed and weak and (seemingly) not sure where I was.

I'd limped into the room well before the bell. Panting and determined not to make a spectacle of myself I'd positioned myself carefully at the desk assigned to me and half-fell into it for I could not (easily, without pain) bend my swollen left knee.

Dry-mouthed, but not dry-eyed. And a dripping nose.

My eyelids had swollen to twice their normal size and were reddened and itchy. If you peered at me you would see my bloodshot gaze peering back at you from out of the swollen eyes and you would (maybe) recognize me but you would (probably) glance quickly away.

Dared not scratch my eyelids with my fingernails yet could not resist.

Such itchiness is painful yet exquisite like touching yourself in the secret forbidden place. Like the itchiness of the mangled skin on my forehead that if it was touched, at once began to hurt. *No, no!*—don't touch.

No one could see the secret wound. Hidden beneath a Band-Aid.

She'd given me aspirin, to help me sleep. Several low-dosage aspirin, for children.

(But was I still a child, at twelve? I did not think so.)

Miriam had wanted to drive me to the hospital last night to have the wound examined, stitched. To x-ray my skull. My knee.

But Mom had been agitated, frightened. So much blood!

Mom had seemed more upset by the blood, the fact of the blood, staining my clothes, my sister's jacket, dripping onto the linoleum floor when Miriam led me staggering into the kitchen, than by the wound itself.

Insisting upon treating the wound herself. Not wanting to *make a fuss.*

Not wanting a hospital, emergency room. The attention of strangers.

And so with shaky fingers treating the wound herself. Applying pressure to it, to staunch the bleeding. Rinsing with cold water. Applying iodine that stung like fire.

Then, neatly covering the cut with a large square white Johnson & Johnson Band-Aid.

Recalling how when the children were young such accidents happened all the time. Cut knees, cut elbows, falls from bicycles, swings, tripping on the sidewalk, banging heads. *Kids!*

It was true, the small wound on my forehead above my left eye turned out not to be very deep. Head wounds bleed like crazy, that is a fact. Getting blood all over everything! *Oh Violet. Isn't it just like you.*

Sorry. Of course I was sorry for having bled onto people's clothing including mine, and onto the floor which Mom kept spotless as best as she could. Sobbing, sniffling, apologizing.

Telling myself I should be grateful that the cut hadn't been deeper, my eye had not been gouged out by the icy edge of the step. And Mom assuring me how lucky I was, damned lucky no serious damage to my face or to my head, clumsy as I'd been, careless.

*Good that your father isn't here, to see this. With all that's going on in our lives . . .*

Relenting then, seeing how pale I was, and apologetic. Kissing my forehead even as she scolded me. As if she couldn't help herself, she was my mom after all.

**In school** I tried to hide. Girls' restroom, farthest stall. Hoping to disguise my limp. (My left knee was swollen like something grotesque—like a tumorous grapefruit. Up and down my leg, nerves felt as if they were buzzing and short-circuiting.) Girls who were friends of mine, or who'd used to be friends of mine, were keeping their distance. Others, who knew the rumors about Jerome Jr. and Lionel, stared at me pityingly. Only Geraldine approached me to ask what was wrong, had I hurt my forehead, and my knee; and I told her it was nothing —"Nothing. Just fell down icy steps." For that was true, in fact. I had fallen down icy steps and struck my head.

Blinking away tears. Trying not to cry. It was so touching to me, that Geraldine cared.

We were not friends now. No longer. Since my mother had scolded me, and said such shocking things to me about the families on Highgate Avenue, and her life before she'd met my father, I had withdrawn from Geraldine.

She no longer invited me to have dinner with her, for I had declined invitations several times. And so abruptly I'd ceased being a guest in the beautiful white brick house on Highgate Street—this was my gift to my mother, who (I hoped) would understand the choice I'd made without needing to speak of it. But at school, in those days after Hadrian Johnson's death, Geraldine approached me as you might approach an invalid, sympathetically but warily.

"Did you see a doctor, Violet? What if your knee is broken?"

"My knee isn't *broken*. No."

I laughed, to suggest what a silly notion. It wasn't the first time in my life that I had banged a knee.

I could not tell Geraldine what I was thinking of, obsessively—my brothers, Hadrian Johnson, the baseball bat. I could not tell her how I'd come to be injured, and how frightened I was of my brother Lionel. Of what he might do to me, when he had the chance.

Nor could I tell Ms. Micaela. I would not.

Seeing how agitated I was, and not in any condition to hobble off to my first class, Ms. Micaela brought me instead to the school infirmary adjacent to the administrative offices. Took my hand, walked with me along the (fortunately) empty hallways as if I were a little kid and not twelve years old. Encouraged me to lean on her, if my knee was hurting. (It was.) Turning me over to the nurse whose name was Ms. Donovan with the explanation that I seemed to have a fever, and had had "some kind of accident at home."

Immediately Ms. Donovan peered at me, and exclaimed at my swollen eyes. A bacterial infection? How long had I had this?

Ms. Donovan made me lie down on a cot in the infirmary, and put cold compresses on my eyelids; took my temperature and noted that my teeth were chattering. "Violet, you're a sick girl. Your temperature is a hundred and one degrees, that's a fever. Your mother oughtn't to have let you out of the house this morning."

The nurse's kindly words, like a curse, made me cry. My pride melted away, I had no strength to protect myself. Whatever I said, the alarmed nurse summoned the principal who asked me what was wrong, why was I crying, had something happened at home, and without knowing what I was doing somehow I was telling him about my brothers Jerome and Lionel and the baseball bat; I was telling him that Lionel had pushed me down icy steps the night before, I was afraid that he would kill me if I told anyone, and I was afraid that my father would be angry with me if he knew, I was afraid to go home . . .

I'd begun crying hysterically. Ms. Micaela, who had lingered in the infirmary, sat beside me on the cot, and hugged me. *Afraid to go home. Afraid to go home.* These words, once uttered, could not be retracted.

Police officers were summoned. One of them was a sympathetic woman my mother's age who gripped my hand and encouraged me to speak, to tell all that I knew—"No one will hurt you. Never again. You will be safe from now on, Violet."

Of course, I believed her. When I recall the police officer's words, and the way she gripped my hand, I feel a surge of relief, hope—*Safe from now on, Violet.*

**That was** how it began. And once it began it could not be stopped.

It would become a matter of public record: the un-solicited, uncoerced, purely voluntary information provided South Niagara police by the twelve-year-old sister of two suspects in the Hadrian Johnson beating death.

In this way the remainder of my life was decided.

# The Bat

The baseball bat subsequently identified as the *murder weapon* in the Hadrian Johnson case was discovered by a South Niagara police search team in underbrush less than three hundred yards from our house, on a high bank of the Niagara River where it had been hurriedly buried beneath a few inches of soil, rotted leaves, and litter.

The team had not needed a warrant to unearth the bat, which my (unthinking) brothers had buried in municipal-owned property.

The bat, its handle wrapped in frayed and faded black tape, had been washed, to a degree, and even scoured with something like a Brillo pad, but minuscule traces of bloodstains and partial fingerprints remained; most incriminating, wood splinters matching those in the bat had been embedded in Hadrian John-son's scalp.

The bat belonged to Jerome Kerrigan Jr. whose partial prints would be discovered on it. And also on the bat, partial prints belonging to Lionel Kerrigan.

The brothers must have agreed not to testify against each other. Not to incriminate each other. Which of them had actually swung the bat when Hadrian Johnson was struck down would not be known with certainty though Walt Lemire and Don Brinkhaus said that they thought that Jerr had kept possession of the bat during the attack—"It was his. He wouldn't have let anybody else have it."

Each was quick to say that he hadn't touched the bat—not for a second. And it had all happened "so fast"—just a few minutes, or seconds, before Jerr yelled at them to get back in his car, and drove them away.

The bat was considered incontrovertible evidence. O'Hagan and the other lawyers advised their clients to cooperate with police, or to give the earnest impression of cooperating with the police; they advised them to plead guilty, not to homicide charges but to manslaughter. Tentative accounts of Hadrian Johnson as a drug dealer, Hadrian Johnson having provoked the attack, Hadrian Johnson having been attacked by other, black assailants which Jerome Kerrigan Jr. and the other boys had only happened to see while driving on Delahunt Road, were immediately dropped, and did not find their way into the local media.

In this way plea bargains were negotiated with county prosecutors, first-degree manslaughter for Jerome Kerrigan Jr. and Lionel Kerrigan, second-degree manslaughter for Walt Lemire and Don Brinkhaus.

Because he was just sixteen Walt was sentenced to five years at a Niagara County youth facility, to be released at the age of twenty-one. Don Brinkhaus was sentenced to seven to ten years at a medium security prison. Jerome, the oldest, received the most severe sentence—nine to fifteen years at Mid-State Correctional Facility at Marcy, New York.

Lionel was sentenced to Mid-State Correctional as well. At seventeen, he'd had to plead guilty as an adult; his sentence was seven to thirteen years.

Of course, all the sentences were immediately qualified—*with the possibility of parole.*

At least there would be no trial. I was spared having to testify against my brothers in court and South Niagara was spared reliving a terrible crime.

Spared having to hear the arguments of the defense that in some way the victim had brought his own death upon himself

The black community in South Niagara protested that these were overly lenient sentences considering the brutality of the attack on Hadrian Johnson and the fact that Hadrian had done nothing to provoke the attack. Some members of the white community (including former South Niagara mayor Tommy Kerrigan interviewed on local TV) denounced the sentences as too harsh, evidence of "black racism" and "black bigotry" in South Niagara.

Within days of the sentencing several black churches in South Niagara were vandalized including the African Methodist Episcopal Church which Hadrian Johnson had attended. Small fires were started along Howard Avenue in a predominantly black neighborhood and young black boys reported being threatened by older white boys on their way home from school.

No one would tell me of these developments—the *white backlash.* I would read of them, piecemeal, over a period of time—weeks, months.

Imagining a *white backlash* like something in the river—discolored, frothing water, thirty-foot-long snakes churning and writhing. Almost I could see this, the terrifying rush of the *white backlash* lapping against the rocky shore of the Niagara River . . .

By which time I was living in Port Oriskany. Eighty miles away. With Mom's youngest sister Irma (who had always liked me, though she'd liked Miriam and Katie a little better) and her husband Oscar Allyn.

They'd always wanted children, it was said. It had been a mystery to me as a child, why.

For a long time waking confused and frightened in this new place, in this new bed. Not knowing where I was, or why. Desperate and hopeful thinking that I would contact the South Niagara police, the school principal, Ms. Micaela—*The bat. I was wrong about the bat. I never saw the bat. The bat is lost, no one has ever found my brother's bat.*

# Safe House

*Safe from now on, Violet.*

Very quickly it happens, an underage child can become a *ward of the county.*

For the protection of the child, the child must be removed from an *unsafe home environment.*

Officers for Children's Protective Services are as empowered as law enforcement officers and can act as swiftly. It is their task to protect the *endangered child.* It is not their task to placate the wishes of any adult nor is it their task to determine if a child is telling the truth, or some degree of the truth. By the time truth is established a child might be severely injured or dead.

And so, without being allowed to return to my home and with just a single telephone call to my mother I was "removed" from my family and placed in a "safe house" for the time being—a foster home for traumatized children and adolescents of whom a number had been beaten and/or sexually abused by relatives predominantly fathers and older brothers.

(Though there were others who'd been beaten, abused, left to starve by their mothers.)

(And others who were retarded, or mentally ill, from households where adults were mentally ill and dangerous to the well-being of children.)

(And others who were *runaways*—a category that overlapped with the traumatized.)

I had not told anyone that either of my parents had ever physically injured me or even threatened to physically injure me and yet it seemed to be taken for granted that indeed I had been injured, traumatized, threatened by one or both of my parents as well as by my brother Lionel. It was explained to me that my family situation did not provide safety for me at the present time; a Family Court judge had approved the order of removal, particularly since my older brothers were prime suspects in the Hadrian Johnson murder, and one of them lived in the house with me.

In the foster home we moved like zombies fearful of being touched. Fearful of being spoken-to, looked-at.

Is mental illness contagious? Mental retardation? I did not want to think so.

Recalling how we'd stared with fascinated dread at Liza Deaver. Liza Lizard. And if poor Liza glanced in our direction we looked quickly away, turned away giggling together.

*No no no. I am nothing like you. Don't look at me!*

In the foster home there came a frequent dream in which the outer layer of my skin was peeled off and oozed blood. In such dreams headaches like corkscrews began and grew worse through the day after I woke up dazed and groggy.

We were allotted aspirin in the facility. Low-dose child aspirin that had no effect upon the hurt in my brain at all.

Here was a surprise—I'd been removed from school as well.

School! But I loved school . . .

It was explained to me that I would be allowed to return to school—soon.

Also, it was revealed to me that my family did not want me back—ever.

My mother and Miriam arrived at the foster home to bring me some of my things. Clothes, books haphazardly tossed into cardboard boxes that were soiled and torn. Winter boots, in a shopping bag with a broken handle. Fleece-lined jacket. Toothbrush, comb. (Both looking battered and shameful to see.) My mother and sister were allowed into the facility only after showing IDs at a security desk and submitting to an interrogation my mother considered "insulting" and for which she seemed to blame me.

When I saw my mother I rushed to her, to be hugged. I was crying, my swollen eyes leaked tears.

But Mom did not hug me, not exactly. Her arms lifted—weakly. It was all she could do not to push me away.

"Violet. What have you *done*."

Her voice was faint yet accusing. A soft fading wail of despair.

It was a shock to me, I was nearly Mom's height. A gangling big girl at twelve and soon to be thirteen, wishing I could shrink to a smaller size to the *Violet Rue* of just a few years ago when my mother and my father too had loved me.

Still I was wanting to think that Mom and Miriam had come to get me. So badly I yearned to be taken home, I did not immediately absorb the meaning of the cardboard boxes.

It was true—I was frightened of Lionel. But Lionel had been arrested by this time . . .

Yes, Lionel been arrested. But no he was not in police custody.

His bail bond, like Jerome Jr.'s, had been posted by

my father and so Lionel was still living in the house and in this way presented a *clear and present danger* for me in the eyes of Children's Protective Services.

*Rat bitch. Rat cunt. We'll take your fucking head off.*

The bail bond for manslaughter was much lower than the bail bond for homicide would have been. Still, Daddy had had to present a cashier's check ($60,000) to the South Niagara district court, to assure that Jerome Jr. and Lionel would not flee before their crimes had been adjudicated; for most of this money he'd had to take out a second mortgage on the house.

It was Miriam who informed me of this news. For my mother could barely bring herself to speak to me at all.

Miriam saying to me, in a whisper, as if a whisper were less accusatory, yes sure there was a chance our parents would "lose" the house. What'd I think? Was I *stupid?*

My mother's hands leapt to her face. As if, not wanting to hear what Miriam had whispered, she'd covered her (bloodshot) eyes instead of her ears.

Miriam exchanged a quick savage glance with me. Meaning—don't upset Mom. Try.

The visit did not last long. Fifteen minutes? Ten?

Slow—at first—as the cranking-up of a roller-coaster ride, as the doomed car ascends the first, sickening hilly loop of track. But then, fast.

Staring at boxes with my things in them on the floor of the cell-like room without recognizing what they were and what they meant.

In a halting voice at last my mother spoke. Through a buzzing in my ears I heard some of what she said.

*Violet how could you! Ruining our lives.*

*Your father can't even talk about it. Can't talk about you.*

*As long as you can stay here you'd better. There's no place for you at home.*

*And don't you dare cry! This is all your doing.*

I had not been away from my mother for more than a few days. In this time she seemed to have aged. Her skin was floury-white. Beside her mouth were deepening lines. Her eyelids, like mine, were reddened and swollen. She was swallowing compulsively as if the interior of her mouth was very dry. (As Katie would tell me later, Mom has been *sedated.* No one knew exactly how many pills she was taking but no one was supposed to speak of it.)

Mom was frowning, distracted. A fly was buzzing at the ceiling.

At a window, another fly. (Or was it the same fly?) (Or were there more than two flies in the room?)

Mom fell silent as if she'd run out of words, and was exhausted. Miriam took up the task explaining to me with twitchy smiles that no matter if Lionel was at home or not I would not be returning home—"Not for a while, Violet."

Instead, "arrangements were being made" for me to live with my aunt Irma and my uncle Oscar Allyn in Port Oriskany, which was eighty miles away.

I heard these words, carefully spoken by Miriam. But I did not really absorb them for I was waiting for Mom to refute them, and to look at me.

*Oh no, Violet. Of course—you are coming home with us. Right now!*

These words I wanted so badly to hear, it would seem to me afterward that my mother had actually spoken them in a trembling voice.

Instead Miriam was saying evasively: "Daddy is very upset, Violet. You know how he can get. Right now, it's pretty extreme. He says he doesn't want you back home—he doesn't want to see your face. He can't get over how you 'went outside the family'—didn't tell him about Jerr and Lionel. And claimed you didn't feel 'safe' at home. Police had a warrant to come into the house. They've been questioning all of us! Even

Mom! We're hoping Daddy will change his mind—in a while. You know, if Jerr and Lionel don't get sent away . . ."

*Sent away.* I might have surmised that my brothers were likely to be incarcerated yet it had not exactly occurred to me that they would be *sent away.*

"Oh, God"—Mom gave a little cry of pain. She couldn't remain here in this terrible place, she said. Couldn't breathe here. She would wait for Miriam out in the car.

This was something that one of us might've said, as children. Rick, or Les, or Katie, or me. *I don't like it here, I'll wait out in the car.*

It was not something an adult would say. It was not something our mother would say. Yet Mom said these words in a hurt, petulant voice, and turned, and walked out of the room, unsteady on her feet but with determination.

I followed limping to the door. Helplessly stared after her. I'd been taken by surprise and had not the strength to call after her—*Mom! Mommy . . .*

"Violet!"—Miriam spoke sharply. "You haven't been listening."

"I—I have been . . . I have been listening . . ."

"Mom isn't feeling well. I had to drive here. Since you—since—falling down the steps, cutting your head—then at your school—saying those things about . . . Well, since all these things, Mom has been very upset, and of course Daddy—Daddy has been *worse*. You're lucky you are here, Violet. Frankly."

Again Miriam explained: —my aunt Irma, Port Oriskany, transfer to a new school. For I could not remain at home, Daddy was adamant about that. And no other relatives in South Niagara would take me in. *Rat* they were calling me. *Never forgive ratting on her own brothers. Saying her parents abused her.*

Miriam spoke rapidly, evasively. In one breath telling me that the situation was hopeless, everyone hated me and would never forgive me, and in the next breath assuring me that Daddy would (maybe) change his mind but not for a while—"You know what Daddy is like . . ."

Trying to recall, had I told police that my parents had *abused* me? I had no memory of this, it had to be a mistake. The woman police officer had misheard me when she'd questioned me at school. But—

Miriam wasn't interested. Whatever I was trying to say, trying to explain, she wasn't interested, her eyes flashed with tears of exasperation, dislike.

My sister I adored but could not trust now. For clearly Miriam was *on their side*.

Roughly hugging me goodbye, kissing me on the forehead. Pressing three ten-dollar bills into my hand—"This is from me, Vi'let. In case you need something. Don't tell anybody I gave it to you, OK? Not even Katie? Promise?"

# Runaway

G ot as far as the Lock Street Bridge before they caught me.

Five miles from the *safe house* to the bridge. On foot, much of the time running / limping.

It was strange, my knee did not hurt so much now. Or if there was hurt, it seemed far away like something occurring in a distant room. For I was desperate to get back home where (I wanted to think) Daddy would forgive me when he saw me. Daddy would let me return to my old room.

At the foster home it was *runaways* who were admired, envied. *Runaways* who were the toughest kids. (One of the girls, a little older than me, sulky and silent, had smudged, angry-looking tattoos up and down her arms.)

Surprising that Violet Rue should be one of them—a *runaway*.

After my mother and my sister left, God damn that I would cry.

Hugging myself tight, arms crossed over my chest, shoulders hunched and face shut up tight as a fist.

*No bullshit. Nobody fuck with me.*

There were black kids in the facility. I felt dread, that they might know whose sister I was. That they might guess.

Except I was just "Vi-yet" to them—if they knew any name for me at all.

And maybe they felt sorry for me. Dazed-looking white girl, with a (soiled) big square Band-Aid on her forehead, something wrong with her left knee that made her wince and limp.

In the facility last names didn't matter. Family names, adults' names did not apply.

Daddy had never liked it, the name *Kerrigan* called up associations with his politician uncle. In South Niagara people tended to either love *Tom Kerrigan* or hate *Tom Kerrigan* so there was the feeling you were being wrongly judged.

But now, with Jerome Jr. and Lionel arrested, their names, faces on the front page of the newspaper, *Kerrigan* would become yet more notorious.

And there was the blunt terrible headline:

## 12-YEAR-OLD SISTER OF SUSPECTS
Provides "Crucial Information" to South Niagara Police
*Hadrian Johnson Investigation Continues*

Fortunately there had been no picture of me in the paper. Not even my name. My brothers were not so lucky for their pictures would appear prominently many times, in many media outlets.

It had not been difficult to escape from the *safe house*. What the staff knew of me was that I was one of those pathetic children who'd had to be removed from her family, for safety; I did not impress them as being daring enough to run away back to that family, and risk further harm.

In the early morning before dawn. Before others were awake.

Skinny enough to push through a narrow space (window opened at the bottom, just a few inches) the way an animal would—one of those desperate creatures who, to be freed from a trap, would gnaw off a paw with their teeth.

Taking nothing with me. Just clothes I was wearing. The fleece-lined jacket with wadded, stiff old tissues in the pockets.

Making my way through underbrush outside the house. Avoiding the long cracked asphalt driveway.

Knowing then to run not on the shoulder of the highway but beside it. Through fields, vacant lots. Behind billboards and along a railroad track.

Some of the soil was marshy, muddy with a thin crust of ice on top. Much of it was littered with the debris of broken trees. Burrs clung to my jeans and thorns tore at my hands.

Thrilling to be outdoors, out of the *safe house.*

I would never return, I thought. They could not make me.

Wildly I thought—*I will hide in our house. In the cellar. No one will know.*

At the city limits the highway joined a major roadway called Denis Boulevard. Now there was traffic. Fields disappeared but there were vacant lots, alleys through which I could make my way. There began to be sidewalks. Swiftly I walked here, I did not dare to run. I did not wish to appear suspicious in the eyes of strangers. I did not wish to call attention to myself in any way and yet it seemed that vehicles slowed, their occupants stared at me.

*A girl! Alone.*

*Why is that girl running, alone . . .*

As I approached Lock Street, and then the Lock

Street Bridge, which would bring me to Black Rock Street and to my house, I began to feel frightened. As if an anesthetic were fading my knee began to hurt. Miriam had warned me—*He doesn't want to see your face.*

At the bridge the pain in my knee intensified. My legs became weak. I could not seem to catch my breath. Wind from the river made my eyes water. Below, the Niagara River rushed dark and glittering in patches like the scales of a great snake but there were no black snakes visible in the water near shore. There was no oily-chemical odor to turn my stomach.

Leaning against the railing of the bridge, feeling suddenly tired. On the pedestrian walkway with my back to traffic. Recalling the morning when Katie and I had seen the snakes in the river.

Not long ago. Yet it seemed long ago.

The morning of the day when Hadrian Johnson had been struck down.

The morning of the day when Hadrian Johnson would begin to die.

There came a sharp male voice behind me— "Hello? Miss?"

A South Niagara police cruiser had glided to a stop beside the walkway. One of the officers had rolled down his window and was staring at me.

He'd recognized me, I thought. Children's Protective Services had sent out an alarm.

Quickly I turned away. Trying not to panic. It would be (falsely) claimed by both police officers that I'd begun climbing over the railing of the Lock Street Bridge, to throw myself in the river, and in that instant the officer nearer me was out of the cruiser and rushing at me fiercely shouting—"No! Stop!" Always I would remember, he was faster than I was. And how fast he was. Gripped my arm, dragged me back from the railing, harder than I could have imagined any adult man might grip me, and when I struggled, sobbing and screaming at him to let me go, he did what law enforcement officers are trained to do, without a moment's hesitation gripping my arm harder, really hard, behind my back, and raising it, even as he tripped me off-balance so that I fell to the plank walkway, now paralyzed with pain, a pain so intense in my upper arm that I could not even scream, I could not even draw breath, losing consciousness as swiftly as a light is switched off.

He hadn't even asked my name. Hadn't taken time. Needing to know only that I was a ward of the court, a *runaway*. And that was the way South Niagara cops treated *runaways*.

**II**

# "Praying for Violet"

"Violet, here. A letter for you . . ."

My aunt Irma could not have been more surprised, turning the letter over in her hand, frowning suspiciously.

"The return address is South Niagara. Do you know anyone named *G. Pyne?* On *Highgate Avenue?*"

Wanting to snatch the letter from my aunt. My letter! But I knew to be cautious.

It was possible, my mother had warned Aunt Irma who was her younger sister not to allow me to receive letters from Geraldine Pyne . . . (But then, Aunt Irma would not have shown me the letter, would she? I was too confused to think clearly.)

This letter was the first that had come for me in Port Oriskany. Weeks I'd been living here, in the beige-brick house on Erie Street that was so much tidier and quieter than my family home, and no one had written to me, and if there had been telephone calls between Aunt Irma and my mother, I did not know about them.

Furiously my mother hissed in my ear—*They look down their noses at us. People like that. Don't tell* me.

Often in my new life I had to shake my head to clear it of my mother's admonishing voice. It was a dread of mine, that others might hear these hissing words as one might hear a radio whose volume has been turned very low.

And often I was slow-witted, sleepy. My eyelids were heavy. I watched the mouths of others (adults) to try to determine the tone of what they were saying for I did not always comprehend what they were saying. By the time a question came to its end, I had forgotten the beginning.

Vaguely I shook my head *yes*.

Or, might've been *no*.

I had forgotten what my aunt had asked me, that was so urgent. My heart beat quickly in anticipation of danger, or of a sudden undeserved surprise.

Reluctantly Aunt Irma surrendered the letter to me. It was clear that she did not trust me—of course, no one in the family could trust me. But Aunt Irma seemed to like me, and to wish (it seemed) that I might like her.

*Childless*, my mother's younger sister was. Whispered in the family. Like a curse.

"Thank you, Aunt Irma."

It was an effort to speak clearly. If you are sleepy your words have an inclination to go soft, slur. Often bizarre dream-figures crowded near to observe me with unnatural interest like piranha fish approaching their prey with caution. So intensely did these creatures listen to what I managed to say, trying to determine the degree of my alertness, and my ability to defend myself against their attack, that I often lost the thread of what I had myself said.

*She expects you to open the letter in front of her. She wants to know what is in it.*

But I would not satisfy my aunt's curiosity by opening this precious letter in her presence nor would I speak of it afterward for I could not share the small allotments of "news" of my life with anyone—there was so little of it. Instead I went away, upstairs into the room designated as *my room,* which had a door without a lock but which door could certainly be closed, firmly; and there I read Geraldine's letter eagerly, tears flooding my eyes so that I could hardly make out the neat schoolgirl handwriting of my closest friend.

*Dear Violet,*
   *I miss you. I am sorry that you are so far away . . .*

It would be a mystery to me how Geraldine had acquired my address in Port Oriskany. Eventually I would ask my sisters but neither Miriam nor Katie claimed to know anything about Geraldine Pyne.

My mother? This did not seem likely.

I might have asked Geraldine herself but I did not. Though I cherished her letters, of which there would be just three, and have kept them all these years moving from one place to another, I did not reply to her—not once.

I began letters to my friend but never finished them. Oh, why? Why not?

Eventually Geraldine ceased writing, and I lost her address.

Of Geraldine's three precious letters it is the last that is the most beautiful and which I have read, reread, memorized. Often I hear Geraldine's words, in Geraldine's voice, in my ears; it is comforting to me as music I have heard many times.

*Dear Violet,*
   *I miss you! I wish that you would answer my letter(s).*

Are you going to school there? Your desk is empty in homeroom and in all your classes and your locker is empty. Ms. Micaela has asked about you but no one knows what to say except you are "gone."

I asked Mom if you could live with us because there is plenty of room in our house. We could share my room or you could have your own room. But Mom said she guessed that might not work out though it was a "very kind" idea. I asked why it would not work out, and Mom said, "Violet has her own family. They will want her back. They will love her again."

I am praying for you, Violet. That this will be so.
Your friend forever,
Geraldine

# Exile

In the first year of being *disowned* I sent homemade birthday cards to my family. (I remembered all their birthdays!) The pleasure was so intense it was almost painful, carefully writing out the address—*388 Black Rock St., South Niagara, New York.*

Even my brothers who were incarcerated at the Mid-State Correctional Facility at Marcy, New York, received cards from me. At least I sent cards. Of course, they did not answer.

Eventually I gave up making cards. There was such childish hope in these cards, I began to feel pitiful even to myself like a dog whose tail is thump-thump-thumping long after everyone has abandoned him.

Instead I sent postcards. Chautauqua Mountains in autumn, Lake Ontario in winter, Niagara Falls shrouded in mist like ectoplasm. Staring down the steep nightmare sides of the Erie Canal at Port Oriskany where I was sent to live with my mother's youngest sister Irma and her husband Oscar who had no children of their own.

Why did I continue for years, more years than I would wish to admit, to send cards that were never answered?—no one would ask this question who'd been *disowned*.

Because you never give up. You never stop hoping.

In my case hoping that Daddy would notice one of my cards sent to someone else in the family, to Katie for instance, and take time to read it as (I had to assume) he wouldn't take time to read one of the cards addressed to him but would rip up the card at once; and, having read it, been moved, or impressed . . .

Never stop hoping because if you do, what remains?

Imagining the first words they will say to you—*We are so sorry! We did not mean it.*

Or—*We did not understand.*

. . . *all a misunderstanding.*

Careful schoolgirl handwriting on the cards. Careful not to say anything that might possibly offend. Each message very brief. Naive, innocent. Unaccusing. Yes, each card was an appeal but (I hoped) not an obvious shameful appeal. Each card was matter-of-fact, casting no shadow. The hope was that, asking for no sympathy, no pity, both sympathy and pity might be extended to me, who asked for so little. (Vain) hope of making my parents feel sorry for me and regret having sent me into exile; to make them consider (I wanted to think) rescinding my exile and inviting me back to the house on Black Rock Street where (I wanted to think) there was still a room for me, the second-floor room I'd shared with my sister Katie from which, in time, Katie herself would move and leave vacant . . .

*How is the weather there in South Niagara? Here it is all snow—6 feet outside my window.*

Or, *Here it is terribly hot. Not even July & many mosquitoes!*

Rarely, I might venture a timid fact. *Starting 10th grade. Have to take the bus, it's too far to walk. (Two miles.)*

*Aunt Irma was in the hospital for four days (gall-bladder). But she is doing well now & says hello.*

(Did my aunt ask to *say hello?* Certainly not. I would never have told her that I was writing to my parents.)

Eventually I would write on the back of a postcard of the Horseshoe Falls in jubilant sunshine *Graduating on June 15, will be giving valedictorian address at Port*

*Oriskany High & have scholarship for St. Lawrence
U. in fall.*

Of all the cards it was this card I'd hoped might
merit a response. For here was something for which
the Kerrigan family might be proud. But my parents
did not write nor did my mother call her sister (my
aunt) to inquire.

It's so, my sisters did send me cards a few times.
The plainest, least expensive *thank-you* cards signed
with just their names—*Miriam, Katie.* As if they were
afraid to write anything more. Afraid to sign *Love.*

All these years I've made sure that my parents have
my current address. Telephone number. Thinking
that one day Daddy will decide it's enough, his little
girl has been punished enough, impulsively he will
call the number he currently has for me, and if I fail to
answer, he will never call again (for that was Daddy's
way, he took offense when you least expected it) but
if he calls, and I answer, Daddy will say in his loud
happy voice—*Hey-yyy—that you, Violet Rue ? Been
missing you like hell.*

# Sleepwalker

In the school library in study period feeling my head grow impossibly heavy, eyelids drooping so that the print of the page blurs and swims. Laying my head on my arms, on the table. And the librarian Ms. Schaeffer wakes me gently, pityingly.

*Kerrigan, Kerrigan. As killers can.*

*But this one is a RAT.*

But no, Ms. Schaeffer's mouth moves differently. She is saying something else, words I can't comprehend.

"Violet! You can't sleep here."

Immediately my head has lifted from the table. My eyes have snapped open. I am sorry, I try to explain to whichever adult this is looming over me and finding me an annoyance. In my voice is the weak appeal *Forgive me!*

Suddenly, I have to go to the restroom. Badly.

Panicked, my need to urinate comes so quickly. A seizure between my legs. Stammering to the startled librarian another apology, and limping away crouched over as if my back is broken.

*Is that her?—Kerrigan.*

*Rat!*

It is true that I am slow-witted in this new school. It is true that I am often lost. Sleepwalking with eyes open. Wandering corridors in the wrong part of the school. Ninth grade? Eighth grade? After weeks still confused where the gym is, and where the cafeteria is. Sleepy-headed. Also, hearing-impaired.

"Violet? Violet! The bell has rung, you should go to your next class now . . ."

(Not asking *Is something wrong?*—they all know that something is *wrong*.)

Though usually I arrive at a classroom just as the final bell rings and so I am rarely marked *tardy*.

Once I am in the correct room, and in the correct desk, and if I can stay awake long enough I am a "good"—"attentive"—"industrious" student. (Noted on my report card by all my teachers.) My grade on quizzes ranges from 97 percent to 44 percent. My homework grades are more reliably high—most of my waking life in my aunt and uncle's tidy beige-brick home on Erie Street is consumed by homework which is much harder here than it had ever been in South Niagara, like shoveling wet sand endlessly on a beach stretching to the horizon.

It's worth it, I am sure. Whatever effort. Perseverance.

For high grades will impress my parents, and shorten the period of my exile.

(I have no doubt that Aunt Irma reports on me to my parents, or at least to my mother. Can't believe that my mother refuses to hear such prideful news of me, that reflects well on the Kerrigan family, or that my father whom I adore will not even hear my name spoken, that the very syllables of my name are a blade in Daddy's heart. Can't believe that no one cares about me *really*. As it is said we can't imagine the world without us.)

In the new school there are black students who regard me impassively, at a distance. If they have heard murmured taunts it is likely that they are utterly perplexed. *Why? Why her?*

Certainly, I have no black friends in Port Oriskany. But then, I have no white friends in Port Oriskany either.

A sly voice murmurs alongside my head. Drifting off to sleep standing upright I am wakened with a start.

"'Ker-ri-gan'—that's your name? Yes? D'you have a relative who's a politician? In Niagara Falls?"

One of the adults waylays me in a corridor. Ninth-grade math teacher with wiry hair and eyebrows like steel wool notorious for his sarcasm.

"Or was it—a trial? Some politician, maybe a mayor, state congressman, on trial? Guilty? Sent to prison?"

Blocking my way. Smiling at me. Something cruel and greedy in his suet-eyes.

"No? You're sure? Well, the name is familiar, for some reason . . . Maybe there are a lot of 'Ker-ri-gans.'"

Pushing past the jeering man, frantic to escape. Suddenly I am wide-awake.

# The Iceberg

Sometimes, a fist in my hair.

*Girl! Wake up.*

And when I awakened whoever had closed his fist in my hair had retreated, whispering and laughing.

More than one of them. I would not want to see their faces.

It was nothing personal, I wanted to think. I had read of chickens rushing at one of their own stricken with illness, scabs. The fury of the healthy for the unhealthy. How weakness cries out to be devoured.

That phrase, with words meant to be ugly and harsh acquired nonetheless a strange tenderness. For what I was being accused of was *love, loving*. I would wonder if I deserved it.

---

**It was** the New Year. And then it was late winter, the first thaw in April and melted ice water rushing frenzied in gutters, spilling across rooftops.

News came to me, my brothers who were incarcerated in the prison facility at Marcy were appealing their convictions.

Or rather, the new lawyer my father had hired to represent them was appealing their convictions

It would be argued that the baseball bat belonging to Jerome Kerrigan Jr. had been illegally seized by South Niagara police. Its whereabouts had been disclosed to police officers by the (juvenile) sister of the accused who'd been led into ratting on them by a police officer without benefit of a parent or a guardian. *If the bat is excluded, DNA evidence acquired from the bat must be excluded. The case against the Kerrigans becomes circumstantial, the convictions must be overturned.*

If this was so there would be new negotiations with the prosecutor. Why would any of the four boys plead guilty even to manslaughter, without DNA evidence linking the Kerrigan brothers to the bat? No *murder weapon* in evidence, anyone might have harassed and beaten Hadrian Johnson that night on Delahunt Road with any weapon.

The single eyewitness might change his account. All he'd need to say was *It was dark, I can't be sure what I saw.*

Through a rushing sound like a distant waterfall these possibilities came to me. Not meaning to eavesdrop I would hear my aunt Irma and my uncle Oscar speaking together in lowered voices.

*Poor Lula!*—Irma murmured. *What a terrible time this has been for her . . .*

And Oscar would say dryly—*Well. It's been a pretty terrible time for the family of the black boy, too.*

There was no doubt in my uncle's mind that my brothers had killed Hadrian Johnson. Or, one of them had killed Hadrian Johnson and the other had assisted. What my aunt thought wasn't so clear.

Within families, it's best not to think at all. Just— *not at all.*

When I'd first come to live with Aunt Irma and Uncle Oscar, Aunt Irma had tried to hug me often in the (mistaken) assumption that because my family had cast me out, and my mother no longer hugged me, or would even speak with me on the phone, a hug from her, my mother's sister, would be welcomed. And if I didn't hug back but stood stiffly, holding my breath, eyes downcast, this did not entirely dissuade

her. *Violet is very shy. Violet is—what's it called?*—
"traumatized."

I cried often. I am ashamed now to recall. As if
tears have ever helped anyone. Even Aunt Irma cautioned me, I would *make myself sick* if I cried so
often, and so hard.

Aunt Irma too was easily moved to tears. She liked
to speak of the many times she'd spent with me when
I'd been a *little, little girl* helping my mother with
child care, staying overnight in the bustling house
on Black Rock Street. Many times she'd bathed me,
sprinkled my tender little bottom with talcum powder
and given me a fresh new diaper. Pushed me in a
stroller along the sidewalk where there were cracks so
the ride wasn't so smooth but *bump bump bump* that
made me giggle. Did I remember?—Irma asked hope-
fully.

Vaguely I would nod, smile. As a doll might nod,
smile. Though I did not remember I would not want
my aunt to know how little she mattered in my life
then or now.

My uncle Oscar was not so sentimental. He'd given
in to his wife's pleas that they take her sister's daughter into their household but often his eyes wandered
over me baffled—who the hell was this awkward girl,
this stranger at mealtimes eating his food, limping up

the stairs, shrinking from him in the hallway and in the vicinity of the (single, second-floor) bathroom, avoiding his eyes. There was no question of Oscar Allyn hugging me to comfort me when I burst into tears. In Oscar's presence I was not inclined to burst into tears. At an accidental touch both of us would have leapt away, affrighted.

*You are not my father. Go away!*

Between us there was established a kind of under-standing. A little distance. But between the woman and me, not sufficient distance.

*You are not my mother. Go away!*

I could not bear to see myself in the mirror. Learned to observe myself sidelong. And then with half-shut eyes. Where the scab at my hairline had fallen away there was a soft, creepy, lurid scar of which I was ashamed and which I tried to hide beneath wispy bangs.

The injured knee was not so swollen now. My aunt took me to a clinic where someone alleged to be a doctor examined it briefly and said it would "heal" if I did not run or strain it.

Yet, I had to run. The yearning to run was very powerful. Sometimes when I was outside and alone a sudden need came to me, like a sudden thirst, that I might run, and run; a fierce joy overtook me, like flames; I ran until my heart thudded in my chest and my knee did begin to ache, my legs grew weak.

*Rat, run! Wait till we catch you.*

It was a matter of fascination to me. Like the lyrics of a song trapped inside my brain. Over, over and over hearing. Over, over and over seeing how Lionel had come up behind me silently, stealthily to push me down the icy steps. So vivid the scene had become, I saw both of us clearly—the girl taken by surprise, the tall boy behind her pushing. It might've been a scene in a movie—I was sure that I had seen it.

There was also the police officer who'd grabbed me. As quickly and as deftly as Lionel had pushed me. At the Lock Street Bridge he'd grabbed me, twisted my arm up behind my back until I collapsed with pain.

Why it was crucial to run. As fast as I could run.

And quickly determine, wherever I was, where hiding places were. Escape routes. A deep sympathy I felt, seeing rats rummaging in Dumpsters that jumped out squeaking and scurried away in crevices to hide.

Aunt Irma tried to comfort me. *You are safe now, dear. Here with us.*

As if I could believe her! As if any of us can guarantee the *safety* of others.

But Irma was anxious, too. In those days before caller ID she answered the phone hesitantly—*Y-Yes? Who is calling?* A knock at the door suffused her with dread.

Recalling once how, when someone knocked at the door, a louder knock than seemed reasonable, Irma had cried to me to go upstairs, to run into the bathroom and lock the door—as if, in the exigency of the moment, she'd given in to the worst of my fears, that one of my brothers might have showed up in Port Oriskany, to murder me.

Later I would think how foolish this fear was. No one intent upon murder would knock so loudly on a door and announce himself.

**Without my** knowing, the years of waiting had begun.

When you are waiting you are neither unhappy nor happy. You are *waiting*.

Half-consciously assumed that I would remain twelve years old stunted and accursed yet time continued bizarrely, indifferently as if the catastrophe of my life weighed no more than a feather, that had already been blown away.

Growing into a tall thin girl with evasive eyes. Chronic puffiness beneath the eyes.

Sullen, sulky mouth. Pale skin, that burnt easily.

Dark hair resembling mad scribbles of crayon. Could not get a comb through my hair and even brushing it was a chore. Yet, I often let my hair go an entire day and a night without brushing and combing, so that snarls proliferated like lice. In this way both indulging myself and punishing myself in a single gesture.

Unlike Mom, Aunt Irma did not dare sweep into my room unbidden, snatch up a hairbrush and a comb to rid my hair of snarls no matter how I protested.

*Look at you! Look at that hair! What a sight.*

*Sit still. Stop squirming. You have beautiful wavy hair—nicer than your sisters'.*

Indeed, I had my mother's hair. So she liked to claim.

How I hated my bossy mother!—scolding, fussing. Slapping me (lightly) to sit still.

But when Mom finished brushing and combing my hair it did look much improved. Had to admit.

Recalling too how Mom would casually wet her forefinger and smooth my eyebrows!—even in the presence of others. A gesture of exasperating intimacy, such as only a mother might inflict upon a child, and that child likely to be a daughter.

But now there was no one to touch me so intimately. No one to so care about me, as if I were herself.

Aunt Irma could not speak assertively to anyone and certainly not to me. It was rare for her to contradict her husband and if she was obliged to disagree with him, she so managed to contort herself, to speak in circumlocutions, the husband had not a clue. To me she spoke timidly even when commenting on the weather. Her requests were uttered not in a firm bossy voice but as pleas. My aunt had no hope of commanding me as my mother would have done for my aunt desperately wanted to be *liked*.

This is the great weakness—wanting to be *liked, loved*. You give up all pride wanting to be *liked, loved*.

It suffused me with contempt, that an adult woman should apologize to me rather than scold me, speak sarcastically to me. For was I not a rat, and worthless? Should I not crawl away somewhere and die?

Instead Irma would flutter her hands—*Oh Violet, excuse me . . .*

*Violet, dear, wait a minute, I'm sorry . . .*

And then I would overhear my aunt on the phone talking to a friend when she didn't think I was within earshot. I would hear my aunt not timid or hesitant but baffled, resentful—*She won't even look at us! It's breaking our hearts! She was never like this before. She has changed. How long has it been now—six, seven months! She should be trusting us by now. But she isn't. She's up in her room all the time . . . Like someone on an iceberg drifting off to sea and you call after them and call after them and finally . . .*

Quickly I edged away. I did not want to hear how these indignant words would end.

# Turnip Face

Each month, first Monday of the last week, Ms. Dolores Herne of the Children's Protective Services came to check up on me in the beige-brick house on Erie Street, Port Oriskany.

Because I'd been removed from my family and released into the custody of relatives, a county social worker was mandated to visit me at regular intervals.

Brightly Ms. Herne spoke with Aunt Irma and me, and then she spoke with me alone, asking in a hushed voice—"Do you feel safe in this household, Violet? Is there anything you would like to share with me, just between the two of us?"

Yes I felt *safe* with my aunt and uncle—of course.

No I had nothing to *share* with a stranger.

Consulting her notes Ms. Herne went on to ask—
"Has anyone from your family in South Niagara
threatened you, since last November? Your brother
Lionel—"

"Lionel is in p-prison."

"Well—has Lionel contacted you? Directly, or indirectly?"

Shook my head *no*.

"He has not? No?"

*No.*

"Not through a family member? Lionel has not
contacted you—definitely?"

A flurry of panic in my chest for the thought
came to me, does Ms. Herne know something I don't
know? Has Lionel been threatening me without my
knowing it?

His prison sentence was seven to thirteen years, I
told Ms. Herne. It had not been even a year yet . . .

A humming sound came to my ears. It seemed that
Ms. Herne was humming under her breath but in
such a way, her mouth clamped shut, I could not be
sure that the low vibratory sound was actually coming
from her throat and not my own.

A strange Turnip Face, confronting me.

"And you have not visited him in prison? I assume."

Shook my head *no*. Trying not to laugh wildly.

Impossible to imagine visiting either Lionel or Jerome. Would my parents have taken me? No.

Could not bear to see the hatred in my brothers' faces. Murderous rage.

*Rat bitch. Rat cunt. We'll take your fucking head off.*

Ms. Herne was peering at her notes, frowning. Obviously she hadn't glanced at these hand-scrawled notes since the last time she'd visited the house; she seemed to have forgotten the crucial details of my case.

"And your older brother Jerome—had he threatened you, too?"

Shook my head *no*.

"At the time your brother Lionel attacked you— according to my report here, pushed you down 'icy steps'—was Jerome also on the premises?"

Coldly I told Ms. Herne *no*. In another minute I would jump up and run from the room, I hated this interrogation so.

"Jerome did not participate in this attack, you believe? To the best of your knowledge?"

Not sure how to respond. Hesitantly nodded my head *yes*.

"You are not in contact with Jerome, either?"

Shook my head *no*.

(But maybe *yes* for I'd sent a birthday card to Jerome, as I'd sent a birthday card to Lionel, and with the card just my signature—*Violet*. Did that count as being *in contact?*)

"And you don't hear from your incarcerated brothers through anyone else, Violet? Anyone in the family?"

When I only shook my head Ms. Herne persisted: "I have to ask, dear. This is crucial to know."

Sitting very still, staring at the floor. A sensation of great weariness came over me, a wish to lie down on the carpet, shut my eyes that were so heavy-lidded, sink into sleep as into black muck . . .

". . . the one who seems to have actually struck the black boy, isn't he? 'Jerome.' And Lionel has refused to testify against him . . ."

Was this true? I guessed it had to be true. Neither of my brothers had testified against the other. The other boys had been vague in their confessions. (Were they afraid of Jerome? That, someday, when they were all free, Jerome might seek them out and hurt them, if they'd ratted on him, as I had?)

Ms. Herne had to know that I'd *ratted on* my brothers. That this was why I'd been exiled from my family and made a ward of Niagara County and was living now with relatives of my mother.

Never dared ask Ms. Herne about my parents—if they had forgiven me yet? if they had asked about me?—for the questions would be so piteous, Ms. Herne would be embarrassed.

Each day I lived in apprehension of hearing sudden, upsetting news from strangers like Ms. Herne, or one of the teachers at school, like the ninth-grade math teacher with the steel-wool eyebrows who seemed to lie in wait for me, daring to ask questions of me in a lowered voice—*You're the girl, are you? Kerrigan? Your brothers are in prison for manslaughter, beating a black boy to death, isn't that you?*

The humming grew steadily louder. I was beginning to hear—*Kerrigan, Kerrigan. Killing can, KERRIGAN.*

"Violet, it says in this report from Family Court that both your brothers' convictions are being appealed. This was back in June. D'you have more recent news?"

Shook my head *no*.

"No?"—Ms. Herne smiled and winced at me as if she was hard of hearing.

*N-No.*

All I'd heard, vague news from Aunt Irma, was that the New York State Court of Appeals was *very slow*. And lawyers for my brothers were *very expensive*.

I wondered if Ms. Herne knew something about

the appeal that I didn't know. That she didn't want to share with me.

"Violet? Are you all right, dear?"

From a long distance the social worker was peering at me. So far away, I could not really recognize her homely turnip-face and her voice was muffled by the roaring of wind.

"—try to open your eyes? Violet?"

Had my eyes closed? I didn't think so—wasn't I looking at the woman? On a ledge she stood, slightly above me. Between us was a ravine into which (I seemed to know) I must not look for there were terrible things in it, broken, mutilated and bleeding.

"Violet! Please wake up . . ."

Ms. Herne was tugging at me, alarmed.

Blindly I pushed hands away. I did not like to be touched.

"—awake, Violet? Try to open your eyes . . ."

My eyes were open! I wanted to curse the staring woman who would not let me alone.

Still Ms. Herne tugged at me, and more forcibly I pushed her hands away.

Except my hands did not seem to move. They were numb, some distance from my body. I seemed to know that they could be operated by a sort of remote control but I had not (yet) mastered this control.

Ms. Herne had vanished, to confer with the woman whose name I had forgotten, who was meant to be a relative of mine reporting to my parents each day of my exile.

Where were they? Around a corner? If I'd been a younger and more childish girl I would have jumped up and poked my head into the hallway to surprise them.

Naive of them to imagine that I could not hear them when they spoke distinctly.

". . . suddenly fell asleep, it seemed . . . I had to catch her from falling onto the floor."

". . . oh, Violet does that . . . sometimes. It doesn't mean a, a thing . . ."

". . . sleep-deprived? There are shadows beneath . . ."

". . . oh no, oh no . . . Her eyelids are just sort of—swollen, and itchy. It doesn't mean a thing."

". . . examined by a doctor?"

". . . oh yes, yes of course. My husband and I—we have . . ."

". . . so sudden, I had to catch her from falling onto the *floor.*"

Then, Ms. Herne had returned and was seated before me smiling insincerely. My eyes were fully opened and nothing seemed to have changed and nothing was out of place.

In the hallway, (possibly) my aunt was eaves-dropping. I could not be certain and could not betray my suspicion by jumping up and looking, for then both women would know that I was aware of their collusion.

"You are absolutely certain, Violet, that you feel 'safe' in this household? That you *are safe?* And that neither of your brothers have contacted you to—to—threaten you . . ."

Oh, why did this not end!

Nodding *yes.* Or was it *no.*

Ms. Herne concluded her visit with the usual questions about school which were, as we all know, trick questions. Gravely taking notes when I assured her that I was "adjusting"—"doing well, mostly."

"You are, you think, 'adjusting'? And 'doing well'—'mostly'?"

*Yes.*

"Well. Goodbye, Violet! I will see you again in—is it September? But please call me at any time if you—if you have reason to call me. Do you promise?"

*No. I do not promise.*

"Yes, Ms. Harm."

"'Herne'—my name is 'Herne.'"

"'Ms. Herme.'"

"'Herne.'"

Smiling at Turnip Face so that she would have no further reason to be suspicious of me. In the other room, if my aunt was listening she too would be deceived.

Another time the woman said, "Goodbye, Violet!"

"Goodbye."

After Ms. Herne was gone a sensation of cold swept through me. For possibly my brothers would be released from prison sooner than anyone had expected? Were already released? And no one would tell me, to alarm me?

To warn me?

# Sisters

*K*atie—*will you tell me? Let me know? If—*
Hidden away in my room with the door shut writing a postcard to my sister. I wasn't sure what to say. Which words to choose. For everyone in the family hoped that my brothers would be released from prison as soon as possible—(except me).

Everyone seemed to think that the convictions were unjust, unfair. So many times it had been reiterated—*It's just because they are white—white boys.* You would think that Hadrian Johnson had assaulted *them*.

*Maybe you could call me? If there is news? Here is Aunt Irma's phone number if you need it.*

Of course, Katie already had the number. I'd made sure that she had the number. Though neither she nor Miriam had called me in the eight months I'd been here.

*If Lionel is released, and if—if he says something about me . . .*

Meaning: if Lionel threatens me with harm.

Katie knew. And Miriam must have known. That I was terrified of Lionel and Jerome being released from prison though having to pretend that I was hoping they'd be released, like everyone else.

*. . . if he threatens me? Will you let me know?*

An appeal into a void. Like leaning over a deep well and calling down inside with your hands cupped to your mouth and waiting, waiting, waiting for the faintest echo.

**Later it** came to me that sending a postcard was not a good idea. If I sent Katie a postcard anyone in the family could read it including my mother.

But if I sent Katie a (sealed) letter Mom would notice that too and be suspicious, and (possibly) open it . . .

I tore up the postcard for Katie. I began a letter to Miriam, who'd moved out of the house on Black Rock Street, I had heard, and was renting an apartment downtown.

Miriam was working as a secretary for a South Niagara accountant. She'd been eager to leave home even before the arrests of my brothers but she'd waited too long, the scandal had been too much for her fiancé who'd broken off their engagement . . .

Hoping that Miriam didn't blame *me*.

Hours were required for me to write a letter to Miriam though it was less than a page. A sensation of dread suffused me. I had not been wanting to think how badly I missed my sisters, as I missed my mother; writing to them was like talking to them, pleading with them, and left me emotionally shaken.

*Miriam! Katie! Have you stopped loving me, too . . .*

*I am so lonely. Please!*

In my letter to Miriam I included Aunt Irma's telephone number and asked Miriam to call me; I was not prepared for Katie calling me one evening a few days later.

"Violet? Hello! Miriam read me your letter to her. She—we—thought I should call you . . . It's good you didn't write to me—Mom would've brought in the mail and seen it. She's out shopping now. I can't talk long . . ."

Katie's voice was sharp, edgy. She seemed both anxious and embarrassed and spoke quickly to guarantee that I would not interrupt.

"What you're asking about, the appeals, whatever the lawyer is doing—I don't know for sure. There's a state 'appeals' court. Tommy Kerrigan is trying to help. He's got 'contacts' in the justice system, he says. He's coming out of retirement—maybe—to run for state assembly if he can get rich people to donate—he's been interviewed a lot on local TV saying his 'nephews' had been hounded into prison because they are *white*. It's kind of—I don't know—kind of *controversial*, people are saying. There's what they call a 'white backlash' here and in Buffalo too . . . Daddy has had to take out more loans. The bail bond was returned but the legal fees are almost as high. It's just terrible what lawyers charge! But Daddy is hopeful—I guess. If the lawyers can get the sentences overturned Jerr and Lionel will be *out*—they won't even have to wait for parole. Jerr has been in some fights in the facility, he's been injured—in the prison hospital. I guess he was stabbed . . . Not sure about Lionel, he's sort of closed off from us. He doesn't want visitors, he says. Only Daddy, once in a while.

"No, they don't talk about you, Violet. Your name is never mentioned at least to me. Mostly they talk about the 'legal case'—they call it. They are upset about Jerr and Lionel and think they were blamed because they're 'white' . . . Miriam and I try to avoid the subject. I don't know how Les and Rick feel—it's hard to be going to school, with people still talking about Hadrian Johnson. I still have my friends, or some of them . . . It's hard, people kind of blame you, but then other people blame *them*— black people. It's like you have to be on one side or the other and people like us, with our name, have to be on the 'white' side. I just try to avoid it! Les isn't doing so well, he cuts classes a lot. Hides up in his room playing those damn creepy video games. Rick is talking about joining the Marines when he gets out of school which drives Daddy crazy. Daddy is out a lot and when he's home he's very tired. He's drinking more than he used to. He had bronchitis pretty bad this winter—still has it. Mom is on some medication—'Xanax.' It's to help her sleep and for her nerves. I hear her crying sometimes—but I don't go running to her. That just gets her angry at *me*." Katie's words were disjointed, aggrieved. She was speaking rapidly as if to get through our conversation, before we were discovered.

It was my turn to speak. My mouth had gone dry.

Wanting to ask Katie—*Don't you miss me? In our room? Don't you feel sorry for me?*

Suddenly Katie was saying, "Oh, God! Mom is coming home. I have to hang up, Vi'let. I'll try to write to you. I'll try to call—if there's news. But don't call here—and don't write, please. Bye!"

"But, Katie—"

Already she'd hung up.

**You'd think** that I would have been devastated by Katie's call but this was not so. I was grateful that my sister had taken so much time with me and had not forgotten me.

Grateful for the emotion in her voice, even if it was an emotion of impatience, repugnance.

Grabbed a jacket from the closet and went outside, to walk by myself, and run. Run, run!

That sensation when you are running and your heart is filled with happiness and you think—*Just a little more! And the heart will burst.*

In October you see thin desiccated vines with withered leaves that still manage to bear flowers—not big bright-colored flowers any longer but small faded flowers. Blue morning glories on my aunt's fence had faded, shrunken. But some vines had attached themselves to a tree and flowers were blooming fifteen feet above the ground, isolated, bravely blue each morning. Before the first frost.

The contact with my sisters was like that. Withered, desiccated. Barely alive. But still, it existed.

# "Mr. Sandman
Bring Me a Dream"

He would protect me. He promised.

Kissing the scar at my hairline. Smoothing the hair back, that he might press his lips lightly against the scar. Making me shiver.

He would *take measurement* of me. *Establish a record.* The size of my skull, the length of my spine, the size of my hands and feet (bare). Height, weight. Color of skin.

Then taking my hand. Pressing it between his legs where he was fattish, swollen like ripe, rotting fruit. Pressed, rubbed. When I tried to pull away he gripped my hand tighter.

*Don't pretend to be innocent,* "Vio-let!" *You dirty girl.*

———

**Sometimes he** called me Sleeping Beauty. (Which had to be one of his jokes, I was no *beauty*.)

Sometimes he called me Snow White.

"I am 'Sandman.' Do I have a *sandpaper* tongue?"

**Seven months.** When I was fourteen.

If it was *abuse* as they charged it did not seem so, usually. It was something that I could recognize as *punishment*.

Each time was the first time. Each time, I would not remember what happened to me, what was done to me. And so there was only a single time, and that time the *first time* as well as the *last*.

Each time was a rescue. Waking to see the face of the one who had rescued me, and his eyes that shone in triumph beneath grizzled eyebrows. Sharp-bracketed mouth and stained teeth in a smile of happiness.

*Vio-let Rue! Time to wake up, dear.*

Mr. Sandman was the teacher who'd sighted me lost in the ninth-grade corridor, when I was in seventh grade. When I'd first come to Port Oriskany as a transfer student. The teacher with the grizzled eyebrows and strange staring eyes who'd seemed to recognize me, who'd interrogated me about my name.

*And now you are in my homeroom. "Vio-let Rue."*

No alternative. Mr. Sandman was the ninth-grade math teacher.

At last, I was *his*. On his homeroom class list and in his fifth-period math class.

For both homeroom and math class Mr. Sandman seated me at his right hand where he could *keep a much-needed eye on you*.

He'd helped me to my feet. Before he'd been my teacher. Discovered me sleeping in a corner of the school library where I'd curled up beneath a vinyl chair as a dog might curl up to sleep, nose to tail, a shabby little terrier, hoping to be invisible and not to be kicked.

No one else seemed to see me. Might've been somebody's sheepskin jacket tossed beneath a chair at the back of the room.

Standing over me breathing hoarsely for so long, I wouldn't know.

*Time to wake up, dear! Take my hand.*

But it was his hand that took my hand. Gripped hard, and hauled me to my feet.

**Why did** you let him touch you, Violet! That terrible man.

*Why, when you would not let others touch you, who'd hoped to love you as a daughter?*

---

"**I am** the captain. You are the crew. If you don't shape up, you go overboard."

Mr. Sandman, ninth-grade math. His skin was flushed with perpetual indignation at our stupidity. His eyes leapt at us like small shiny toads. When he stretched his lips it was like meat grinning, we cringed and shuddered and yet we laughed, for Mr. Sandman was *funny*.

He was one of only three male teachers at Port Oriskany Middle School. He was adviser to the Chess Club and the Math Club. He led his homeroom class each morning in the Pledge of Allegiance.

(In a severe voice Mr. Sandman recited the pledge facing us as we stood obediently with our hands over our hearts, heads bowed. There was no joking now. You would have thought that the Pledge of Allegiance was a prayer. A shiny American flag, said to be a personal flag, a flag that Mr. Sandman had purchased himself, hung unfurled from the top, left-hand corner of the blackboard, and when Mr. Sandman finished the pledge in his loud righteous voice he lifted his right hand with a flourish, in a kind of salute, fingers pointing straight upward and at the flag.)

(Was this the *Nazi salute?*) (We were uncertain.)

Mr. Sandman ruled math classes like a sea captain. He liked to shake what he called his *iron fist*. If one of us, usually a boy, was hopelessly stupid that day he'd have to *walk the plank*—rise from his desk and walk to the rear of the room, stand there with his back to the class and wait for the bell.

On a day of *rough waters* there'd be three, could be four, boys at the rear of the room, resigned to standing until the bell rang, forbidden to turn around, no smirking, no wisecracks, *if you have to pee just pee your pants*—a Sandman pronouncement shocking each time we heard, provoking gales of nervous laughter through the room.

Of course, this was ninth-grade algebra. We were fourteen, fifteen years old. Nobody in this class was likely to *pee his pants*.

(Yet we were not so old that the possibility didn't evoke terror in us. Our faces flushed, we squirmed in our seats hoping not to be singled out for torment by Mr. Sandman.)

It was rare that Mr. Sandman commanded a girl to march to *walk the plank*. Though Mr. Sandman teased girls, and provoked some (of us) to tears, yet he was not cruel to girls, not usually.

Boys were another story. Boys were *Schmutz*.

Bobbie Sandusky was *Boobie Schmutz*. Mike Farrolino was *Muck Schmutz*. Rick Latour was *Ruck Schmutz*. Don Farquhar was *Dumbo Schmutz*.

Was any of this funny? But why did we laugh?

Hiding our faces in our hands. Nothing so hilarious as the misery of someone not-you.

You'd have thought that Mr. Sandman would be detested but in fact Mr. Sandman had many admirers. Graduates of the middle school spoke fondly of him as a *character, mean old sonuvabitch.* Even boys he ridiculed laughed at his jokes. Like a stand-up TV comic scowling and growling and the most shocking things erupting from his mouth, impossible not to laugh. Hilarity was a gas seeping into the room that made you laugh even as it choked you.

Mr. Sandman was a firm believer in *running a tight ship.* "In an asylum you can't let the inmates get control."

A scattering of boys in Mr. Sandman's class seemed to escape his ridicule. Not the smartest boys but likely to be the tallest, best-looking, often athletes, sons of well-to-do families in Port Oriskany. These boys who laughed loudest at jokes of Mr. Sandman's directed at other, less fortunate boys. *My goon squad.*

He'd get them uniforms, he said. Helmets, boots. Revolvers to fit into holsters. Rifles.

They could learn to *goose-step.* March in a parade along Main Street past the school. *Atten-tion! Ready, aim.* He'd lead them.

(Would Mr. Sandman be in uniform, himself? What sort of captain's uniform? A pistol in a holster, not a rifle. Polished boots to the thigh.)

Boys were goons at best but girls didn't matter at all. When Mr. Sandman spoke with a rough sort of tenderness of his *goon squad* it seemed that we (girls) were invisible in his eyes.

"Girls have no 'natural aptitude' for math. There is no reason for girls to know math at all. Especially algebra—of no earthly use for a female. I have made my opinion known to the illustrious school board of our fair city but my (informed, objective) opinions often fall upon deaf ears and into empty heads. Therefore, I do not expect anything from females—but I am hoping for at least mediocre, passable work from *you*. And *you*, and *you*." Winking at the girls nearest him.

Was this funny? Why did girls laugh?

It did not seem like a radical idea to us, any of us, that girls had no *natural aptitude* for math. It seemed like a very reasonable idea. And a relief, to some (of us), that our math teacher did not hold us to standards higher than *mediocrity*—(a word we'd never heard before, but instinctively understood).

In fact Mr. Sandman didn't wink at me at such times. When he made his pronouncements which were meant to make us laugh, and yet instruct us in the ways of the world, he didn't look at me at all. He'd arranged the classroom seating so that "Violet Kerrigan" was seated at a desk in the first row of desks, farthest to the right and near the outer wall of windows, a few inches from the teacher's desk. In this way as Mr. Sandman preened at the front of the classroom addressing the class I was at his right hand, sidelined as if backstage in a theater.

*Keeping my eye on you. "Vio-let Rue."*

Each math class was a drill. Up and down the rows, Mr. Sandman as captain and drillmaster calling upon hapless students. Even if you'd done the homework and knew the answer you were likely to be intimidated, to stammer and misspeak. Even Mr. Sandman's praise might sting—"Well! A correct answer." And he'd clap, with deadpan ironic intent.

As Mr. Sandman paced about the front of the room preaching, scolding, teasing and tormenting us an oily sheen would appear on his forehead. His stiff, thinning, dust-colored hair became dislodged showing slivers of scalp shiny as cellophane.

It made me shiver, to anticipate Mr. Sandman glancing sidelong at me.

*Keeping an eye on you. "Vio-let Rue."*

*Ever since you came to us. You.*

These were quick, intimate glances. No one saw.

---

**Staying after** school, in Mr. Sandman's homeroom.

This was a special privilege: "tutorial." (Only girls were invited.)

Told to bring our homework that had been graded. If we needed "extra" instruction.

Mr. Sandman stooped over our desks, breathing against our necks. He was not sarcastic at such times. His hand on my shoulder—"Here's your error, Violet." With his red ballpoint pen he would tap at the error and sometimes he would take my hand, his hand closed over mine, and redo the problem.

I sat very still. A kind of peace moved through me. If you do not antagonize them, if you behave exactly as they wish you to behave, they will not be cruel to you.

If you are very good, they will speak approvingly of you.

"'Vio-let Rue'—you are a quick study, aren't you?"

With the other girls Mr. Sandman behaved in a similar way but you could tell (I could tell: I was acutely aware) that he did not like them the way he liked me.

Though he called them *dear* he did not enunciate their names in the melodic way in which he enunciated *Vio-let Rue.* This was a crucial sign.

Edgy and excited we bent over our desks. We did not glance up as Mr. Sandman approached for Mr. Sandman did not seem to like any sort of flirtatious or overeager behavior.

Leaning over, his hand resting on a shoulder. His breath at the nape of a neck. A warm hand. A comforting hand. Lightly on a shoulder, or at the small of a back.

"Very good, dear! Now turn the paper over, and see if you can replicate the problem from memory."

Sometimes, Mr. Sandman swore us to secrecy: we were given "rehearsal tutorials" during which we worked out problems that would appear on the next day's quiz or test in Mr. Sandman's class.

Of course, we were eager to swear *not to tell*.

We were privileged, and we were grateful. Maybe, we were afraid of our math teacher.

Eventually, the other girls disappeared from the tutorials. Only Violet Rue remained.

**Each day** came the hope—*Daddy will come get me today.*

Or, more possibly—*Daddy will call. Today.*

Running home expecting to see my aunt awaiting me just inside the door, a wounded expression on her face—"There's been a call for you, Violet. From home."

At once, I would know what this meant.

Even Irma understood that *home,* for me, did not mean the tidy beige-brick house on Erie Street.

And so, each day hurrying home. But even as I approached Erie Street a wave of apprehension swept over me, my mouth went dry with anxiety . . .

For there would be no Daddy waiting for me. There'd been no telephone call.

In the meantime reciting multiplication tables to myself. Multiplying three-digit numbers. Long division in my head. Puzzling over algebra problems that uncurled themselves in my brain like miniature dreams.

Such happiness in the Pythagorean theorem! Always and forever it is a fact, clutched-at like a life jacket in churning water—*the sum of the areas of two small squares equals the area of the large one.*

No need to ask *why.* When something just *is.*

Math had become strange to me. "Pre-algebra"— this was our ninth-grade curriculum. Like a foreign language, fearful and yet fascinating.

"Equations"—numerals, letters—*a, b, c.* Sometimes my hand trembled, gripping a pencil. Hours I would work on algebra problems, in my room with the door shut. It seemed to me that each problem solved brought me a step closer to being summoned back home to

South Niagara and so I worked tirelessly until my eyes misted over and my head swam.

Downstairs Aunt Irma watched TV. Festive voices and laughter lifted through the floorboards. My aunt often invited me to watch with her, when I was finished with my homework for the night. But I was never finished with my homework.

On her way to bed Aunt Irma would pause at my door to call out in her sweet, sad voice, "Good night, Violet!" Then, "Turn off your light now, dear, and go to sleep."

Obediently I turned off my desk light. Beneath my door, the rim of light would vanish. And then a few minutes later when I calculated that my aunt and uncle were safely in bed I turned it on again.

During the day (most days) I was afflicted with sleepiness in waves like ether but at night when I was alone my eyes were wonderfully wide-open and my brain ran on and on like a rattling machine that would have to be smashed to be stopped.

On my homework papers Mr. Sandman wrote, in bright red ink—*Good work!*

My grades on classroom quizzes and tests were high—93 percent, 97 percent, 99 percent. Because I prepared for these so methodically, hours at a stretch. And because of the secret tutorials.

It was true, I had no *natural aptitude* for math. Nothing came easily to me. But much that passed into my memory, being hard-won, did not fade as it seemed to fade from the memories of my classmates like water sifting through outspread fingers.

My secret was, I had no *natural aptitude* for any subject—for life itself.

Keeping myself alive. Keeping myself from drowning. That was the challenge.

**They would** ask *Why.* But lifting my eyes I can see the synthetic-shiny American flag hanging from the corner of Mr. Sandman's blackboard, red and white stripes like snakes quivering with life.

Listening very carefully I can hear the chanting. Each morning pledging allegiance. (But what was "allegiance"? We had no idea.) The entire class standing, palms of hands pressed against our young hearts. Reciting, syllables of sound without meaning, emptied of all meaning, eyes half-shut in reverence, a pretense of reverence, heads bowed. Five days a week.

Our teacher Mr. Sandman was not ironic now but sincere, vehement.

*Pledge allegiance. To my flag. And to the Republic for which it stands. One Nation, indivisible. With Liberty and Justice for all.*

Under his breath Mr. Sandman might mutter as we settled back into our seats—*Amen.*

**Each time** was a rescue. No one would understand.

Boys had been trailing me, calling after me in low, lewd voices.

Not touching me. Not usually.

Well, sometimes—colliding with me in a corridor when classes changed. Brushing an arm, the back of a hand across my chest—"Hey! Sor-ry." At my locker, jostling and grinning.

*Kerri-gan, Kerri-gan.*

*Rat!*

In a restroom where I'd been hiding waiting for them to go away after the final bell had rung I'd asked a girl, Are they gone yet?, she'd laughed at my pleading eyes and told me yeah sure, those assholes had gone away a long time ago. But when I went out they were waiting just outside the door to the faculty parking lot.

Shouts, laughter. Grabbing at the sleeves of my jacket, at my hair as I fled in panic.

Crouching behind a car, panting. Hands and knees on the icy pavement. Desperate for a place to hide trying car doors one after another until I found one that was unlocked. Climbed inside, into the backseat, on the floor making myself small as a wounded animal might. On the rear seat was a man's jacket, I pulled over myself. Meant to hide for only a few minutes until the braying boys were gone but so tired!—fell asleep instead. Wakened by someone tugging at my ankle.

Mr. Sandman's dark face. Steel-wool eyebrows above his creased eyes. "Vi-o-let Rue! Is that you?"

His voice was almost a song. Surprise, delight.

"What are you doing here, Vio-let? Has someone been hounding you?"

Of course, Mr. Sandman knew. All of the teachers knew. Though I had not ever told.

How much worse it would be for me, if I *told.*

I was not sure of the names of my tormenters. It was a matter of shame to me, there were so many.

"Well! You don't have to tell me who the vermin are just yet, dear. You have already been upset enough." A pause. A stained-teeth smile. "I will drive you home."

Invited me to sit in the passenger's seat beside him. Astonishing to me, the math teacher famous for his sarcasm was behaving in a kindly manner. Smiling!

Though glancing about, to see if anyone was watching.

It was late afternoon, early winter. Already the sky was dim, fading.

In my confusion, waking from sleep, I seemed not to know exactly where I was, or why.

Mr. Sandman advised me, I might just "hunch down" in the seat. In case some "nosy individual" happened to be watching.

"One of my teacher-colleagues. Eager for gossip, you bet."

Quickly I hunched down in the seat. Shut my eyes and hugged my knees. I did not want to be seen by anyone in Mr. Sandman's car.

Mr. Sandman's car was a large heavy pewter-colored four-door sedan. Not a compact vehicle like most vehicles in the faculty parking lot. Its interior was very cold and smelled of something slightly rancid like spilled milk.

"You live on the east side, I believe? Is it—Ontario Street?"

This was astonishing to me: How did Mr. Sandman have any idea where I lived?

"Not Ontario? But nearby?"

"Erie . . ."

"You are wondering how I know where you live, Violet? And how I know with whom you live? Well!"

Mr. Sandman chuckled. It was part of his comic style to pose a question but not answer it.

When I was allowed to sit up a few minutes later

and peer out the car window it did not appear that Mr. Sandman was driving in the direction of Erie Street. The thought came to me—*He is taking another route. He knows another, better route.*

And when it became evident that Mr. Sandman was not driving me home at all I sat silently, staring out the window. I did not know what to say for I feared offending Mr. Sandman.

In homeroom and in math class Mr. Sandman was easily "offended"—"deeply offended"—by a foolish answer to a question, or a foolish question. Often he simply glared, wriggling his dense eyebrows in a way comical to behold, unless you were the object of his ire.

However, Mr. Sandman was in a very good mood now. Almost, Mr. Sandman was humming under his breath.

"You know, Violet, it has been a pleasant and unexpected surprise—to discover that you are an impressively good student. Quite a surprise!"

Mr. Sandman mused aloud as he drove. There was no expectation that I should answer him.

"And also, a pleasant and unexpected surprise, to discover such an impressively good student in my automobile, hiding under a garment like Sleeping Beauty."

We were ascending hilly Craigmont Avenue. Still we were moving in a direction opposite to my aunt and uncle's house on Erie Street and still I could not bring myself to protest.

". . . indeed there are some surprises more 'unexpected' than others. And discovering that Violet Rue Kerrigan is one of my better students has been one of these."

*Violet Rue Kerrigan.* The name suggested wonder, in Mr. Sandman's voice. As if referring to someone, or something, apart from me of a significance unknown to me.

Upper Craigmont Avenue was a residential neighborhood of older, large houses. Tall plane trees with bark peeling from them, like flayed skin. Storm debris lay scattered on expanses of cracked sidewalk and broad front lawns. If there had not been (dim) lights in the windows of houses we passed I might have thought that Mr. Sandman was driving me into an abandoned part of the city.

At last Mr. Sandman turned into the driveway of a stone house, bulbous gray stone, cobblestone?—with dark shutters, and a ponderous slate roof overhead.

Crabgrass stubbled the front lawn. A plane tree lay in ruins as if it had been struck by lightning. The long asphalt drive was riddled with cracks. My father would have sneered at such a derelict driveway though he would have been impressed by the size of Mr. Sandman's house. And Craigmont Avenue looked to be a neighborhood of expensive properties, or properties that had once been expensive. "I am the 'last scion' in the Sandman family," Mr. Sandman said, chuckling. "Since my elderly infirm parents passed away years ago my life is idyllic."

*Idyllic* was not a word with which I was familiar. I might have thought that it had something to do with *idle*.

As Mr. Sandman parked the large heavy car at the top of the driveway, some distance from the street, I managed to stammer, "I—I want to go home, Mr. Sandman. Please." But my voice was disappointingly weak, Mr. Sandman seemed scarcely to hear.

(By this time I needed to use a bathroom, badly. But this I could not tell Mr. Sandman out of embarrassment.)

"Well, dear! Why are you cowering there like a kicked puppy? Get out, please. We'll have just a little visit—this time. Just a few minutes, I promise. And then I will drive you home to—did you say Ontario Street?"

"Erie . . ."

"Erie! Of course."

A subtle tone of condescension in Mr. Sandman's voice. For the *east side* of Port Oriskany was not nearly so affluent as the *west side* nearer Lake Ontario.

My legs moved numbly. Slowly I got out of Mr. Sandman's car. It did not occur to me that I could run away—very easily, I could run out to the street.

At the same time thinking—*Mr. Sandman is my teacher. He would not hurt me.*

"We'll have just a little 'tutorial.' In private."

Badly wanting to explain to Mr. Sandman—(now nudging me forward, hand on my back, to a side entrance of the darkened house)—that I was concerned that Aunt Irma would wonder where I was for she often worried about me when I was late returning home from school . . . And this afternoon I'd lost time, might've been a half hour, forty minutes or more, in my stuporous sleep in a car I had not realized was Mr. Sandman's . . . But I could not speak.

Inside, Mr. Sandman switched on a light. We were in a long hallway, my heart was pounding so rapidly I could not see clearly.

And now, in a kitchen—an old-fashioned kitchen with a high ceiling, the largest kitchen I'd ever seen, long counters, rows of cupboards, a large refrigerator, an enormous gas stove, a triple row of burners and none very clean . . .

"I was thinking—hot chocolate, dear? At this time of day when the spirit flags, as the blood-sugar level plummets, I've found that hot chocolate restores the soul."

In the center of the room was an old, enamel-topped table with solid legs. On it were scattered magazines, books. A single page from the *Port Oriskany Herald* containing the daily crossword puzzle, which someone had completed in pencil.

Shyly I agreed to Mr. Sandman's offer of hot chocolate. I could not imagine declining.

Daring to add that I needed to use a bathroom, please . . .

Mr. Sandman chuckled as if the request was endearing to him. "Why, of course, Sleeping Beauty. It has been a while since you have *peed*—eh?"

So embarrassed, I could not even nod *yes*.

"Even Sleeping Beauty is required, sometime, against all expectations, to *pee*. Yes."

Humming under his breath Mr. Sandman escorted me to a bathroom at the end of a dim-lit corridor, fingers on my back. He reached inside the door to switch on the light, and allowed me to close it—just barely.

My heart was pounding rapidly. There was no lock on the door.

It seemed to me, possibly Mr. Sandman was close

outside the door. Leaning against it. The side of his head against it, listening?

Trying to use the toilet as silently as possible. An old, rusted toilet, with a seat made of dark wood. Stained yellowed porcelain at which I did not want to look closely.

Was Mr. Sandman outside the bathroom? Listening? I was stricken with embarrassment.

And then, flushing the toilet. A loud gushing sound that could have been heard through the house.

Washing my hands was a relief. Though the water was only lukewarm I enjoyed scrubbing my hands. Several times a day I washed my hands, took care that my fingernails were reasonably clean.

Noticing now that there were books in the bathroom, on the windowsill. *Crossword Puzzles for Whizzes. Favorite Math Puzzles. Favorite Math Puzzles II. Lewis Carroll's Math Games, Puzzles, Problems.* The books were small paperbacks with cartoon covers, that looked as if they'd been much used.

When I left the bathroom it was a relief to see that Mr. Sandman was not hovering outside the door after all.

In the kitchen he awaited me with his wide, wet smile that made you think of meat. He'd placed two large coffee mugs on a counter and was preparing hot chocolate on the stove, shaking powdered, dark chocolate out of a container and into simmering water.

"You know, Violet—your family is cruel to disown you. Don't look surprised, dear—I know all about it."

Mr. Sandman's expression was grave, kindly. He was not scowling as he did in the classroom. His eyes that usually shone with malice were bracketed now with smile-creases.

I did not know how to reply. It was not surprising to me that Mr. Sandman knew about my family for it seemed to me that everyone must know of my humiliation and shame.

*Her family kicked her out. Rat!*

"It is particularly cruel, dear—labeling you a 'rat.' Yes, yes—I know, I've heard! Always makes me wince."

Mildly and smugly Mr. Sandman smiled. Basking in the power to read my thoughts.

"And what is there about 'rats,' suggesting that an entire species is prone to informing on one another? And that there is something contemptible about this? It seems to me more likely that a dog would inform on other dogs, in its zeal to impress its master, than a rat would inform on other rats. Just my opinion!"

How Mr. Sandman enjoyed this. In a trance I stood staring at him speechless.

"Don't worry, dear. I will protect you. I have nothing against 'rats'—in fact, I am sure that they are maligned in the popular, debased mind. Your white skin has made you an enemy in some quarters. If not a 'double enemy'—a traitor to your race."

Enemy. Traitor. Was this the meaning of their taunts? I had known I'd been a traitor by betraying my brothers . . .

"No, no, dear Violet! Don't look so frightened. Nothing will happen to you that you do not wish to happen."

Was this consoling? I wanted to think so.

In my hands the mug of steaming hot chocolate was consoling. Shyly I lifted it to my lips since Mr. Sandman expected me to drink it; he would observe closely, to see that I did.

The liquid chocolate was thick, slightly bitter. Almost, I'd have thought there was coffee mixed with it. But I was weak with hunger, and with relief that Mr. Sandman had not followed me into the bathroom. And now that I had used the bathroom and washed my hands I could see that Mr. Sandman meant to be kind.

"Would you like to borrow these, Violet? Of course."

Mr. Sandman was leafing through Lewis Carroll's Math Games, Puzzles, Problems. Many of the problems had been solved, in pencil. On some pages there were enthusiastic red asterisks and stars.

"See here, Violet. This section isn't too difficult for you. Shall we do these together?"

Mr. Sandman sat me at the kitchen table. Gave me a pencil. I puzzled over the (comical, far-fetched) cartoon problems as he leaned over my shoulder breathing onto my neck. My head began to swim. "Careful, Violet! Let me take that cup from you."

Could not keep my eyes open. Would've fallen from the chair except Mr. Sandman caught me.

Light was fading. Small spent waves lapped at my feet. Whispers, laughter at a distance. My eyelids were so heavy, I could not force them open . . .

Waking then, sometime later. Groggy. Confused. Not in the kitchen but in another room, and on a sofa. Lying beneath a knitted quilt that smelled of moth-balls, my sneakers removed. (By Mr. Sandman?) Across the room, in a leather easy chair, Mr. Sandman sat briskly grading papers by lamplight.

"Ah! At last Sleeping Beauty is waking up. You've had a delicious little nap, eh?" Mr. Sandman laughed heartily, indulgently.

My neck was aching. One of my legs was partially numb, I'd been lying on my side. Still very sleepy. A dull headache behind my eyes.

"Dear, it's late—after six P.M. Your aunt will be worried about you, I will drive you home immediately."

How long had I been asleep? My brain could not calculate—an hour? Two hours?

Mr. Sandman set aside his papers. He seemed anxious now. His breath smelled pleasantly of something sweet and dark, like wine.

When I stumbled getting up Mr. Sandman gripped me beneath the arms, hard. "Oops! Enough of 'Sleeping Beauty.' You need to *wake up,* immediately."

Walked me into the kitchen, turned on a faucet and splashed cold water onto my face, slapped my cheeks—lightly!—but enough to make them smart. Bundled me into my jacket and walked me outside into the fresh cold air. My knee had begun to ache, I was limping slightly. Quietly Mr. Sandman told me in the car, "This is our secret, dear. That your math teacher has given you—*lent you*—the Lewis Carroll puzzle book. For others would be jealous, you know."

And, "Including adults. Especially adults. *They* would assuredly not understand and so you may tell them 'Math Club.' It's quite an honor to be selected."

Cautiously Mr. Sandman drove along Erie Street. When I pointed out my aunt and uncle's house he drove past it and parked at the curb several houses away.

"Good night, my dear! Remember our secret."

Lights were on at the house. An outside porch light. I feared that Aunt Irma would be looking out the window. That she'd seen the headlights of Mr. Sandman's car pass slowly by.

But when I went inside Aunt Irma was in the kitchen preparing dinner. She asked where on earth I'd been and I told her without a stammer—"Math Club."

"Math Club! Is there such a thing?"

"I'm the only girl who has been elected to it."

If Aunt Irma had been about to scold me this declaration intimidated her. "They'd never have let me in any math club, when I was in school."

And, "Oh, Violet! Did you go out this morning with your shirt buttoned crooked? Look at you . . ."

I did. Cast my gaze down on myself, seeing that indeed my shirt was buttoned crookedly. Shame.

*But why* *would you go back with him again, Violet? Why—willingly?*

**Soon then,** announcing to Aunt Irma that I'd been not only selected for Math Club but also elected secretary.

Which was why I was often late returning home after school. In winter months, after dark.

(And it was true. True in some way. From his several classes Mr. Sandman had "elected" eight students to comprise Math Club. Six boys, two girls. Boys were president and vice president and I was secretary.)

Uncle Oscar seemed impressed, too. When I showed him *Lewis Carroll's Math Games, Puzzles, Problems* he leafed through the little paperback with a wistful expression.

". . . once, I could probably figure these out. I kind of liked math. Now, I don't know . . ."

Later I would find the little book on the kitchen counter where he'd left it.

Living with adults you live with the husks of their old, lost lives. Like snakes' husks, or the husks of locusts underfoot. The fiction between you that you must not allow them to know.

How many times did Mr. Sandman drive me after school to the stone house on Craigmont Avenue? Over a period of seven months it must have been many times and yet when I was asked by shocked and disapproving individuals intent upon establishing criminal charges against Mr. Sandman I would say truly I did not know, could not remember for always it was the first time and not ever did I seem to know beforehand what would happen nor even, in retrospect, what had happened.

How many times do you dream, in a single night? In a week? A year?

Snowy nights. The heater in Mr. Sandman's car. Windshield wipers slapping. Sheepskin jacket, boots. Mr. Sandman taking my hands in his and blowing on them with his hot, humid breath—"Brrrr! You need to be warmed up, Snow White."

Hot chocolate, with whipped cream. Spicy pumpkin pie, with whipped cream. Jelly doughnuts, cinnamon doughnuts, whipped cream doughnuts. Sweet apple cider, *piping-hot.* (Mr. Sandman's word which he uttered with a sensual twist of his lips: *piping-hot.*)

One evening he had a favor to ask of me, Mr. Sandman said.

For his archive he was taking the measurements of outstanding students. All he required from me was a few minutes' cooperation—allowing him to measure the circumference of my head, the length of my spine, etc.

"An archive, dear, is a collection of facts, documents, records. In this case, a very private collection. No one will ever know."

I could not say *no.* Already Mr. Sandman was wrapping a yellow tape measure about my head— "Nineteen point six inches, dear. Petite."

The length of my spine—"Twenty-nine point four inches, dear. Well within the range of normal for your age."

Height—"Five feet three point five inches. A good height."

Weight—"Ninety-four pounds, eleven ounces. A good weight."

Waist—"Twenty-one inches. Good!"

Hips—"Twenty-eight inches. Very good!"

As Mr. Sandman looped the tape measure about my chest, brushing against my breasts, I flinched from him, involuntarily.

He laughed, annoyed. But did not persist.

"Another time, perhaps, dear Violet, you will not be so skittish."

**So many** books! I stared in wonderment. I had never seen so many books outside a library.

Proudly Mr. Sandman switched on lights. Bookcases of dark expensive-looking wood lifting from the floor to the ceiling.

(There were no bookcases in our house on Black Rock Street. Old textbooks gravitated to the basement where no one touched them, they grew moldy and smelly with time.)

Many of the books were old, matched sets. On the

lowermost shelf were *Encyclopedia Britannica, Collected Works of Shakespeare, Collected Works of Dickens, Great British Romantic Poets.* There was an entire bookcase filled with books on military history with such titles as *A History of Humankind at War, Great Military Campaigns of Europe, The Great Armies of History, Soldat: Reflections of a German Soldier 1936–1945, Is War Obsolete?* In an adjacent bookcase, *The Coming Struggle, Free Will and Destiny, The Passing of the Great Race, Racial Hygiene, A History of Biometry, The Aryan Bible, Adolf Hitler's* Mein Kampf: *A New Reading, The Dark Charisma of Adolf Hitler, Origins of the Caucasian Race, Is the White Race Doomed?, Eugenics: A Primer.*

On a special shelf were oversized books of photographs. More military history: U.S., Germany. Tanks, bomber planes. Fiery cities. Marching men in Nazi uniforms, swastika armbands. Saluting stiff-armed as Mr. Sandman saluted the flag in our classroom.

Daddy had hated the army. Daddy had hated being a soldier. I wondered if Mr. Sandman had been a soldier, ever.

There were yearbooks from Mr. Sandman's old schools, when he'd been young. Group photographs of Mr. Sandman's Boy Scout troop (1954, 1955). ("Can you recognize me, Violet? No? First row, third from the left. More Scout medals than any other eleven-year-old.")

On a table were unframed photographs of local landscapes, skies of sculpted clouds, the mist-shrouded Niagara Falls, which Mr. Sandman had taken himself. And one, apart from the others, depicting a girl of about my age lying on a four-poster bed, partly clothed, hands clasped over her thin chest. Long straight pale hair had been spread about her head like a fan. Her eyes were open and yet unseeing.

A girl I'd never seen before, I was sure. I felt a pang of alarm. Jealousy.

Mr. Sandman saw me staring at the photograph and quickly pushed it aside.

"No one you know, dear. An inferior Snow White."

I would not recall the part-unclothed girl afterward. I don't think so. Though I am recalling her now, this *now* is an indeterminate time.

Against the windows of Mr. Sandman's cobblestone house, a faint *ping* of icy rain, hail. An endless winter.

"It is a fact kept generally secret in the United States that Adolf Hitler acquired his 'controversial' ideas on race and on the problems posed by race from us—the United States. Our history of slavery, and post-slavery, as well as our 'population management' of Indians—on reservations in remote parts of the country. How to establish a proper scientific census. How to determine who is 'white' and who is 'colored'—and how to proceed from there."

Mr. Sandman spoke casually yet you could hear an undercurrent of excitement in his voice.

*Adolf Hitler* was a name out of a comic book. A name to provoke smirks. And yet, in Mr. Sandman's reverent voice *Adolf Hitler* had another sound altogether.

I'd left my mug of apple cider in the kitchen, half-empty. I had not wanted to drink more of the hot sweet liquid that was making me feel queasy. But Mr. Sandman brought both our mugs into the library, and was handing mine to me.

"Finish your apple cider, Violet! It has become lukewarm."

Helplessly I took the mug from him. Shut my eyes, lifted the mug to my lips, to drink.

Sweet, sugary apple-juice. A taste of something fermented, rotted.

They would ask—*But why would you drink anything that man gave you? Why, after what happened the first time?*

There'd been no first time. All times were identical. There was not a *most recent time*, and there was not a *present time*.

"Some of us understand that we must archive crucial documents and publications before it's too late. One day, the welfare state may appropriate all of our records. The *liberal welfare state*." Mr. Sandman spoke with withering contempt.

Entire populations were falling behind others, Mr. Sandman said. The birthrates of those who should reproduce are declining while the birthrates of those who should not be allowed to reproduce are increasing—"Mongrel races breed like animals."

When I stared blankly at him Mr. Sandman said, "Violet, you're a smart girl. By Port Oriskany standards, a very smart girl. You understand that the Caucasian race must preserve itself against mongrelization before it's too late?"

I had heard that a *mongrel dog* is healthier and likely to live longer than a *pedigree dog*. But I did not often reply to Mr. Sandman's questions for I understood that he preferred silence.

"'Mongrelization' is the natural consequence of the slack, liberal illogic—'all men are created equal.' For the obvious fact is, in human nature as in nature itself, all men *are created unequal*."

This seemed reasonable to me. I did not feel *equal* to anyone and certainly not to any adult.

My legs were growing weak. Mr. Sandman took the

mug from me, and seated me on a sofa. In his kindly lecturing voice, which was very different from his classroom lecturing voice, he told me that there are hierarchies of *Homo sapiens*, the product of many thousands of years of evolution.

At the top were Aryans, the purest Caucasians—the "white race." Northern Europe, U.K., Germany, Austria. White Russians. The *crème of the crème*. Beneath these were Middle Europeans, and Eastern Europeans, and beneath these Southern Europeans. By the time you got to Sicily you were in another, lower level of evolution—"Though some of the Sicilians are very physically attractive, paradoxically."

There were the Eastern civilizations—Asian, Indian. Here too the lighter-skinned had reigned supreme for many thousands of years though in continuous danger of being infected, polluted by the darker-skinned who resided in the south.

In Africa, Egypt was the exception. A great ancient civilization, and (relatively) white-skinned. The remainder of the continent was dark-skinned—"Indeed, a 'heart of darkness.'"

Earnestly and gravely Mr. Sandman spoke, facing me. His words were incantatory, numbing.

"Black Africans were brought to America as slaves, which would prove a disaster to our civilization. For the enslaved Africans would not remain enslaved through the meddlesome efforts of Abolitionists and radicals like Abraham Lincoln, and so it was inevitable that black Africans were granted freedom, and seized freedom, and wreaked havoc upon the white civilization that had hitherto given them shelter and employment and nurtured them . . . First, the military was 'integrated.' Then, public schools. Then, the Boys Scouts of America!" Mr. Sandman shook his head, disgusted.

"With *integration* comes *disintegration.* Some Negroes wish to dilute the white race by interbreeding while others wish to eradicate the white race of 'demons' entirely. Revenge is only natural in humankind. As species have to compete for food to survive, so races must compete for the dominion of the earth. The Führer understood this and launched a brilliant preemptive strike but his fellow Caucasians idiotically opposed him—who can forgive them! One day there will be a race war. To the death." Mr. Sandman's voice rose, vehemently as it sometimes did in class.

*Führer.* This too was a word out of a comic book. Yet, there was nothing funny about *Führer* now.

"Your brothers, you know . . ."

Anxiously I waited. Mr. Sandman searched for the proper words.

". . . were following their instinct, in the war. Sacrificing themselves."

*Sacrifice* was not a word I would have associated with Jerome and Lionel. Two years had passed since they'd begun their prison sentences at Mid-State Correctional, in Marcy, New York. Their lawyer's appeal had come to nothing, so far as I knew.

From time to time, I heard of them. Only indirectly through my aunt Irma. My older brother's prison sentence had been extended for he'd been involved in a beating in which another (black?) prisoner had nearly died. But Lionel was taking high school equivalency courses. Lionel hoped to be paroled within a year or two.

Each night I dreamt of them. It would become confused in my mind, when I was very tired, that Mr. Sandman was their ally, and that they had been his students, too.

Mr. Sandman said, curiously, "Do you regret it, Violet? 'Informing' on your brothers as you did?"

A paralysis gripped me. I could not move my head—*no*.

I could not murmur—*yes*.

Mr. Sandman was about to ask more, then seeing the stricken expression in my face seemed to take pity on me.

"Violet, have you heard of the fearful science of eugenics?"

To this, I could shake my head *no*.

"Why is it 'fearful,' you're wondering? Because it tells truths many do not wish to hear."

According to eugenics, Mr. Sandman explained, interbreeding—"miscegenation"—was a tragic error that would result in the destruction of Master Races, and free-breeding—"promiscuity"—would result in inferior races having as many babies as they could and overwhelming Master Races with their sheer numbers.

"We have seen how the black race is being contaminated by its own 'thugs'—cities like Chicago have become overrun with gangs and drug addicts. They breed like rabbits—like rats! Slavery is the excuse their apologists give—its shadow has fallen upon all blacks, and renders them helpless as invalids. They have no morals. They are greedy and lustful. Their average IQs have been measured many degrees lower than those of whites and Asians. How many great mathematicians have been Negro? That's right—none."

Relenting then, "Well. Almost none. And they were light-skinned blacks, Arabs. In medieval times."

And, "In all fairness, some dark-skinned persons have realized the danger of promiscuity. Certain black intellectuals and leaders like W. E. B. Du Bois believed that only 'fit blacks' should reproduce—not thugs! The 'Talented Tenth' of all races should mix." But Mr. Sandman shuddered at the prospect.

In my fifth-period algebra class there were just three black students—two girls and a boy. Not often but occasionally Mr. Sandman would call upon Tyrell Jones, a stolid, solemn dark-skinned boy with thick glasses: "Ty-rell, come to the blackboard, please. Solve this problem for us." Because Tyrell was one of the better students in the class, and black, Mr. Sandman seemed bemused by him. Tyrell was not a *thug* certainly. Yet Tyrell was not what Mr. Sandman called *light-skinned*.

"Here, Ty-rell. We are waiting to be impressed."

Mr. Sandman handed Tyrell the chalk, which Tyrell near-fumbled in his nervousness.

Tyrell Jones was in two other classes with me. Teachers were protective of Tyrell for he was cripplingly shy, with few friends even among the black students. He wore heavy tweed jackets that might've belonged to his grandfather. He had allergies and asthma and was often blowing his nose, spraying medication into his mouth out of a small red plastic device he kept in a pocket, to clear his sinuses. His eyes watered. His lips quivered. He did not seem *young*.

Standing at the board in Mr. Sandman's class, chalk in his fingers, he appeared to be paralyzed with fear, staring at the problem Mr. Sandman had scrawled on the blackboard as if he had never seen it before though (probably) he'd successfully solved it in our homework assignment. His eyes magnified by the thick lenses skittered over the class of (mostly) white faces as if, desperate, he was looking for a friend.

I would have smiled at Tyrell Jones if he'd looked at me. Just a quick, small smile. For if I smiled at anyone, I did not (really) want them to see; I did not want to be responsible for a smile.

But I was seated too far to the right, out of Tyrell's range of vision.

Mr. Sandman had been peering at me, frowning. Could he read my thoughts? In my fear of the man was a numbness of intellect: I had ceased thinking rationally.

". . . race war, inevitable. If they can't mongrelize our civilization they will attack us directly. Even Tyrell Jones of whom you seem fond . . . he is no friend of ours."

It made me very uneasy that Mr. Sandman read my thoughts. Often I felt as if my head must be transparent, Mr. Sandman could peer inside.

"They would slash our throats in our beds, if they

could. You will see! And they all know your name—
'Kerrigan.' They know whose sister you are. And your
flamboyant relative—'Tom' Kerrigan. They certainly
know his name."

Vaguely I was aware that my father's uncle was
running again for political office in South Niagara.
In the local newspaper there'd been articles about
Tom Kerrigan's "controversial"—"inflammatory"—
interviews, speeches, accusations. In the recent Republican primary for state assembly Tom Kerrigan had
received more votes than a younger, more moderate
rival. His campaign emphasized "law and order"—
"welfare reform"—"an end to affirmative action." It
was Tom Kerrigan's belief that affirmative action was
the "new racism—against whites."

Of course, Tom Kerrigan defended his young
nephews who'd been "wrongfully convicted" of manslaughter . . .

"Kerrigan is crude, but sometimes crudeness is the
best weapon. A mallet, not a surgical instrument. A
shotgun, not a pearl-handled revolver. Did you know
your uncle well, Violet?"

"N-No . . ."

"You didn't visit his house? He didn't visit yours?"

It seemed that I was disappointing Mr. Sandman. His
wiry grizzled eyebrows knitted over his fierce eyes.

I had not ever met Tom Kerrigan though I'd been hearing about him for as long as I could remember. I'd seen photographs of him—an older man, broad-chested, white-haired, not handsome like Daddy but with a recognizable Kerrigan face. A mean pike mouth disguised by a wide smile.

"Most politicians shrink from associating them-selves with the 'race issue' at the present time. But Tom Kerrigan—he plunges right in." Mr. Sandman laughed, enviously. "As a public school teacher, I am in a very different position. At least, in this northern state. And so, I've had to be the very soul of discre-tion. I never 'discriminate' against Negro students, when they are in my classes. Nothing could be proved against me if the NAACP tried to sue. I never go out of my way to help, or to hinder. But I rarely acknowl-edge them, either. For the most part they are invisible to me."

This seemed sad, and wrong. I dared to ask Mr. Sandman why he didn't like Ethel, Lorraine, and Tyrell, in our class? They were all nice, and Tyrell was smart.

"It isn't a matter of 'liking' them as individuals. As individuals they might be inoffensive. They do behave themselves in our class. It's the race that is a threat.

Suppose the Negroes were carrying plague virus? You'd avoid them then, even if they are 'nice.'"

"But—they don't have the plague . . ."

"Silly girl! They have something worse than the plague. They have the virus that will destroy the white race, from within. Look, I am one of the most fair-minded teachers in the Port Oriskany school district. I give everyone the benefit of the doubt. But the Ne-groes, I do not. I draw the line. I don't 'see' them and I don't want to teach them. I am obliged to teach them, but I am not obliged to 'see' them."

"Did a black person hurt you, Mr. Sandman?"

"Don't be ridiculous! No one has hurt *me*. I've tried to explain to you! This isn't personal, it's principle. Even if I 'liked' one of them, I would not want our race to be contaminated by their genes . . . Some of them are attractive, yes, and even intelligent, to a degree. I grant you, there are astonishing black musicians, singers, dancers. Athletes—of course. But their cousins, brothers, fathers—those are the problems. The weakness of white women, in succumbing to them . . . The race issue in the U.S. isn't black people we know, our students, our servants and the people who work for us, for instance in the school cafeteria, or collecting trash, it's the ones making trouble politically, and the ones who are their relatives. *Thugs* just getting out of prison, or on their way in." Mr. Sandman spoke meanly. Words bubbled up like bile.

He went on, "Your brothers have been martyred because they are white, Violet. I've followed the case closely. It was a mistake for them to plead guilty—their legal counsel was incompetent. I'm convinced they're innocent. They were defending themselves. Or, they were provoked. As I've predicted, there is a race war brewing. We have no choice about whose side to be on."

My eyelids were becoming heavy. Mr. Sandman's vehement words were like blows of a mallet that has been wrapped in a material like burlap. Hard, harsh yet numbing.

It was not an unpleasant sensation, sinking into sleep. For now my heart was beating less rapidly and nervously and my thoughts were not flashing and darting like heat lightning.

**Gently the** voice nudged: "Vio-let? Time to wake, dear."

Gently the hand nudged my shoulder. With an effort I opened my eyes. Seeing a man stooping over me, feeling his humid meat-breath.

Seeing with alarm that the sun had disappeared

entirely from the sky and night pressed against the windows.

In a silk robe I was lying on a bed. A four-poster bed that creaked as the man's weight settled heavily upon it.

The silk robe was royal blue on the outside, ivory on the inside. It required some time for me to realize that something was wrong.

Was I naked, inside the robe? My skin tingled, as if I'd been bathed. Lotion rubbed into my skin. Talcum powder on my breasts, belly.

A shock to comprehend. I could not allow myself to comprehend.

The ends of my hair were damp. At the back of my mouth was something dry and gritty like sand.

"Sleeping Beauty! Time to open those beautiful myopic eyes."

My eyes were open. But I was not seeing clearly.

*Did he—bathe me? Removed my clothes, carried me into the bathroom?*

In the bathroom was a marble tub with claw-feet. An antique tub, deep as an Egyptian coffin. Vividly I remembered.

A worn tile floor, slick with wet. A camera-flash, blinding.

"Ah, good! You're waking up, are you? Yes."

Mr. Sandman spoke distractedly. Perhaps I had slept too long.

He had freshly shaved, his skin exuded an air of heat. His thinning gray hair too was damp, brushed back from his creased forehead. Had Mr. Sandman changed into a fresh-laundered white shirt?

A panicked thought came to me—*He is naked, below.*

But no: Mr. Sandman was fully clothed. White shirt, dark trousers. At school he wore a white shirt, dark trousers, tweed coat. No necktie.

I was very confused. Sitting up, foolishly clutching the silk robe around me. It was shocking to me, to see my bare feet.

*You can't run away. Can't run far. He would catch you.*

*He could kill you if he wished. Strangle you.*

The man was waiting for me to realize. To scream. To become hysterical.

His fingers were poised. It was up to me.

Lying very still trying to summon my strength. Like water, that falls through outstretched fingers. Despair filled me, yet the calm of reason—silly bare feet, I could not run far.

"Your clothes are here, Violet. I had to launder them—they were soiled . . ."

Mr. Sandman spoke briskly, disapprovingly. In-dicating, at the foot of the bed, clothes neatly folded. Strange to see, how neatly folded.

So grateful to see my clothes! I'd been clutching the silk robe around me, in terror that Mr. Sandman would snatch it away.

But he was a gentleman, you could see. The cobble-stone house on Craigmont Avenue. So many books.

Could have wept, suffused with gratitude. For he would allow me to live, and he would forgive me the fear and repugnance in my face.

"Our secret, Violet. Do you understand, my dear?"

Yes. I understood. Understood something.

Understood that I'd been allowed to live. To continue.

Discreetly now Mr. Sandman retreated. Allowed me some privacy.

(A bedroom, dimly lighted. At the windows, dark-ness. The floor was covered in a thin carpet, against a farther wall a tall vertical mirror reflecting pale-shimmering light.)

Hurriedly I dressed. Underwear, jeans. Shirt and sweater. (It did seem as if my panties had been laun-dered, and had not quite dried in the dryer, the syn-thetic white fabric somewhat damp, at the same time somewhat warm.)

In his car driving me to my aunt and uncle's house

on Erie Street Mr. Sandman explained that, after school that day, there'd been an emergency meeting of the Math Club. As the Math Club secretary, I had had an obligation to attend.

"You understand, dear, that if you tell anyone about our friendship it will hurt you most. Your family in South Niagara, who have disowned you, will never wish to 'own' you again. Your relatives here in Port Oriskany will expel you from their home. And I, too, might be shuttled to—an inferior—school . . ."

At this Mr. Sandman chuckled. As if it were so unlikely, the last of these possibilities might occur.

*Bathed me. Held me down. Licked me with his sandpaper tongue. Until I squealed, shrieked.*

*Took my hand in his and guided it between his legs where he was swollen, fattish.*

*Don't pretend, Vio-let Rue. Dirty girl!*

*The face was contorted. Of the hue of a cooked tomato, about to burst. Eyes about to burst out of their sockets. Breath in gasps. Like a bicycle pump, my brothers' bicycle pump, pumping air into a tire, that wheezing sound it makes if you are not doing it correctly, and air is escaping.*

*The hand gripping my hand, so that it hurts. Pushing, pressing, urgently, faster and faster, jamming my hand against his swollen flesh, my numbed hand, as he groans, rocks from side to side, eyes roll in their sockets, he is about to faint . . .*

But no. None of this happened. For none of this was witnessed.

**One day** in secret I wrote on a scrap of paper—*Dear Tyrell, I love you.*

It was not true that I loved Tyrell Jones. I did not love anyone except my parents. And possibly Katie, and Miriam. (Though my sisters were not very nice to me any longer.) (But I would forgive them and immediately love them again, if they were nice to me.) But if I were to write a note to Tyrell Jones I had to say something and I could think of nothing else to say that would justify a note.

This piece of paper I folded over several times. Forced it into Tyrell Jones's locker when no one was in the corridor to see.

Afterward I never looked in the direction of the locker (which was across the hall from my own, near Mr. Sandman's classroom) if I could avoid it. In this way I had no idea if Tyrell ever found the note.

I did not want to know. I did not want to know *indisputably.*

If he'd found the note, and read it, he would have

been shocked. Would've crumpled the note in his fist, and shoved it into his pocket.

*But it isn't a joke, Tyrell. Not a cruel joke.*

*I am not like Mr. Sandman. I am not making fun of you.*

I was too shy to speak with Tyrell Jones. I could not even bring myself to smile at him encouragingly, when Mr. Sandman called him to the front of the room to solve a problem on the blackboard.

Fortunately, Mr. Sandman never made Tyrell Jones *walk the plank.* But I hated it when Mr. Sandman tormented him at the blackboard.

Mr. Sandman's *goon squad* was entertained. Husky boys, with loud laughs. They were not so skilled at algebra as Tyrell Jones but they could laugh at the nervous black boy, for they had the teacher's permission.

Tyrell was one of a half-dozen students in the class who did the math homework correctly. But Tyrell was so intimidated by Mr. Sandman's interrogation, he could not think clearly. His glasses slid down his sweaty nose. So nervous, he fumbled the chalk. Once at the blackboard he began to gasp for breath, seemed to be choking before our eyes, and Mr. Sandman quickly took mercy on him— "Hand over that chalk to Violet, Ty-rell. Let's see if a slip of a girl can solve the problem that eludes you."

Almost you could hear *a slip of a white girl.* But Mr. Sandman had not said that.

The previous day after school Mr. Sandman had given me this very problem to solve. He'd checked my calculations, and helped me with them. So, I knew how to solve the problem and rapidly the chalk moved against the blackboard. Fascinating to observe how an algebra problem is solved. At first it seems hopelessly snarled, like hair. Then, if you are patient, and know the way, it is "solved"—"unsnarled."

I felt how the class stared at me, resentful. Girls in particular hated me. White boys hated me. Tyrell Jones could not even raise his eyes to observe me, in ignominy seated back at his desk, surreptitiously spraying a medicinal liquid into his mouth out of the red plastic device he carried in his pocket.

For it seemed that I must be very smart. Also, I was spared the worst of Mr. Sandman's teasing.

"Very good, Violet. You are a credit to your sex."

*Sex.* The very word aroused a kind of spasmodic titter in the classroom. Though by uttering "sex" Mr. Sandman did not mean (it seemed) "sex" but something clinically neutral, like "gender."

Mr. Sandman clapped, smiling at me. With a bully's gesture he inveigled others to clap too, if but briefly, resentfully.

After the bell rang I tried to follow Tyrell Jones in the crowded hall but he eluded me. And later in the day, when I saw him again, and hurried to catch up with him, I did not know what to say.

Tyrell Jones was my height, though heavier. His eyes glared at me through the thick lenses of his glasses. Before I could draw breath to speak he turned away abruptly.

Our classmates were watching us, curious. Soon, some would burst into wide grins of wonderment, derision. Not with the usual mockery but with indignation. That phrase muttered in my wake.

**"This endearing** little blemish, Violet?—not a birthmark, I think, but a scar?"

Mr. Sandman drew his fat thumb over the star-shaped scar at my forehead. Involuntarily, I shivered.

"Futile to try to hide it, you know. And what caused it?"

"I—fell from a bicycle . . . When I was a little girl."

"Ah! Tragic, in a female so young."

*Tragic.* Mr. Sandman was joking, I supposed.

"Well, dear, if it's any consolation—you were not

destined to be a 'beauty' anyway. The scar gives you character. Other, merely pretty girls tend to be *bland*."

Steeled myself to feel the fat lips against my forehead, to smell the hot meaty breath. Shut my eyes, shivering, waiting.

**One day,** discovering Mr. Sandman's (secret) archive.

A door just beyond the bathroom. A closet, with shelves containing what appeared to be photography albums, dates neatly labeled on their spines. Daring to pull down one of the albums, *1986–87*, stunned to see photographs of a dark-haired girl of thirteen or fourteen posed on Mr. Sandman's sofa, and on the four-poster bed. In some photos the girl was fully clothed, in others partly clothed. In others, naked inside the royal blue silk robe that was so familiar to me.

In the marble tub deep as an Egyptian coffin, head flung back against the rim of the tub and eyes half-shut, vacant. Beneath the surface of blue-tinged water, the pale thin body shimmering naked.

Many photographs of this girl—*M.H.*

Abruptly then, a sequence of photographs of another girl, of about the same age and physical type—*B.W.*

Wanly pretty (white) girls. Thin-armed, with small breasts, narrow torsos and hips. Captured in the throes of deep sleep. Positioned as if dead with eyes shut, hair spread out around their heads. Lips slightly parted and hands clasped on their chests.

Turning the stiff pages, and more photos . . . More (white) girls.

Also, locks of hair. Folded-in notes fastidiously recording measurements—height, weight, circumference of skull, waist, hips, bust.

Clumsily I shut the album, returned it to the shelf. Took down the most recent album which was *1991–92*. But before I could open it there came Mr. Sandman's voice from the kitchen: "Vio-let!"

Mr. Sandman was assuming that I was in the bathroom. In another minute he would come seek me. Quickly I shut the album, returned it to its place on the crammed shelf, shut the door.

Heart thudding in my chest. Such violence, like a fist punching my ribs.

None of the girls I'd recognized. My predecessors.

"Vio-let, dear. Come here at once."

*Already forgetting how in some of the photographs, the camera was close, intimate. Bruised mouth, open. The silk robe had been pulled open, or tossed away. Small pale breasts with soft nipples. The curve of a belly, a downy patch between legs.*

*In one, a girl with opened, dilated eyes. A look of fear. A smear of blood on her face. Hands not clasped on her chest in that attitude of exquisite peace but uplifted as if pushing away the camera.*

*But already forgetting. Forgotten. The ugliest sights.*

*Unless it was myself I'd seen, confused with another.*

*What had he done to this girl? Stared and stared.*

*She'd failed to fall asleep properly. She'd been stubborn, resistant.*

*Or, he had not drugged this girl because he had not wanted her to sleep. He had wanted her awake, conscious.*

*But why was this? Why was one girl treated differently from the others?*

*You are that girl, you wish to think. Always, you are different from the others.*

**Not true** that all times were the same time. For there was the *last time* in Mr. Sandman's house that would not be repeated.

Inadvertently he'd given me an overdose. A fraction of a teaspoon of fine-ground barbiturate dissolved into sweet blueberry juice but he'd miscalculated, or he'd become complacent over the months. For so obediently the stupor came upon me, each time a mimicry of the time before, his vigilance had diminished.

And then, Mr. Sandman couldn't wake me.

*Vio-let! Vio-let! Wake up, dear . . .*

No memory of falling asleep. Only vaguely, something in my hand that had to be taken from my fingers to prevent its spilling.

A terrible heaviness. Sinking downward. Surface of the water far overhead, no agitation of my numbed limbs could bring me to it. Comfort in the dark cloudy water like many tongues licking together.

*Violet! Open your eyes, try to sit up*—the voice came from a distance, alarmed.

Shaking me, and shaking me. Bruising my shoulders with his hard fingers, naked inside the silk robe. My skin still warm from the bath, not yet beginning to cool into the chill of death. Slick creamy lotion caressed into my skin, smelling of lilac. Talcum powder on all the parts of my body that would be covered by my clothes, when I was clothed again.

Except: he could not wake me.

Did not dare call 911 (Mr. Sandman would confess) for then he'd be discovered, arrested. His secret life exposed.

Yet, he did not want the girl to die.

Well, yes—(Mr. Sandman would confess)—the desperate thought came to him, he might let the girl die, he would never succeed in waking the girl and so there was no alternative, he would let her die, and in that way he would be spared exposure and arrest, the outrage and loathing of the community of decent persons, he would be spared prison, how many years in prison, of which he could not bear even a few days. Yet, he did not want Violet Rue to die for (he would insist) he loved her . . .

Or this he would claim, afterward.

His solution was to dress me hurriedly, haphazardly, in the clothes he'd removed from me, and had partly laundered, and partly dried, and to wrap me in a blanket snatched from a cedar closet, and carry me out to his car, stumbling and sobbing; in the car, he drove me to the Port Oriskany hospital, to the ER which was at the side entrance of the building; half-carried, half-dragged me inside the plate-glass doors that parted automatically, and left me there, slumped on a chair; hurried back outside even as a hospital security guard was calling after him—"Mister! Hey mister!" He'd left the car running. Key in the ignition. He would make a quick getaway, was the reasoning. But he was so agitated, within seconds Mr. Sandman collided with a van turning into the hospital drive as he tried to escape.

In the telling it would become a story to provoke outrage, and yet mirth.

For, outside the tyranny of the math teacher's classroom and house, the math teacher was revealed as bumbling, foolish. Bringing an unconscious fourteen-year-old to the brightly lit emergency room of a hospital, a hastily clothed and (seemingly) dying girl, believing that he might abandon the girl there, might simply run back out to his car idling just outside the entrance and drive away undetected, and then, so agitated, such a fool, colliding head-on with the first vehicle that approached him as if in his desperation he'd failed to see . . .

But mostly, the story provoked outrage. Of course!

A mathematics teacher entrusted with middle school students, revealed to have been sexually abusing one of his ninth-grade pupils over a period of seven months, routinely drugging the girl to make her sexually compliant, at last overdosing the girl with barbiturates, bringing her blood pressure lethally low . . .

In the ER the girl whose heart was barely beating was revived. In the hospital driveway the ninth-grade algebra teacher was arrested by Port Oriskany police officers.

Taken into police custody in handcuffs, brought

downtown to police headquarters. Overnight in the county jail and in the morning denied bail by a repelled judge. Suicide watch for the distraught man had raved and sobbed and uttered many wild things, pleas and threats.

It would be revealed that Arnold Sandman, fifty-one, longtime resident of Port Oriskany, faculty member since 1975 of Port Oriskany Middle School, had been accused of "unacceptable" behavior at previous schools, including a Catholic school in Watertown; but he'd been allowed to resign from the positions, and school administrators at two schools had agreed to provide him with "strong" recommendations, to get him out of their districts without a scandal. For there was the uncertainty of several girls' accounts—there was the uncertainty that the girls' parents would even allow them to make statements to the police, which would be revealed to the public. And Mr. Sandman denied all—everything. And Mr. Sandman did speak persuasively. And Mr. Sandman was, all conceded, a capable, if eccentric teacher whose students tended to do well on state examinations; in fact, better on the average than students taught by other math teachers. Jocosely it was said that Mr. Sandman "terrorized" students into learning math, where other, more gentle methods failed.

This time, however, Arnold Sandman would plead "no contest" to charges of protracted child endangerment, sexual molestation of a minor child, drug statute violations, abduction and false imprisonment.

The cobblestone house on Craigmont Avenue would be searched top to bottom. The incriminating archive would be discovered. Of thirty-one girls photographed by Mr. Sandman over a period of eighteen years all but six were identified; of these all but two were living in upstate New York and vicinity; the two no longer living had died "suspiciously" (suicide?) but in no ways (evidently) connected with Arnold Sandman.

Contacted by investigators, none of the identified women could remember being photographed by their ninth-grade math teacher in his home, or anywhere. None could remember having been driven in Mr. Sandman's car—anywhere. None could remember having been sexually abused, coerced, threatened by Mr. Sandman but most could remember after-school tutorials and Mr. Sandman being "very kind" and "patient" with them; a few would recall that their math grades were unexpectedly high—"Which was really wonderful 'cause I wasn't so great in math, with other teachers."

---

"**Violet. Please** try to remember. Tell us . . ."

*No. Can't remember. Don't make me.*

I could not. My throat was shut up tight, there were no words to loosen it.

Too weak to sit up in bed. Fluids dripped into my veins, too weak to eat or drink except clear sweet liquids through a straw.

"Violet? It will help if you look up, dear. Try to keep your eyes open, and in focus . . ."

*No. No. Can't.*

Amnesia was a balm. Amnesia is the great balm of life. Wept with gratitude for all that I did not remember which was confused (in observers' eyes) with what I might be remembering.

The shock of it is, what was intimate and secret becomes public. What occurred without words becomes a matter of (others') words.

*Sexual abuse of a minor. Abduction. False imprisonment.*

In that deep sleep, in which my heart had barely continued to beat, at the very bottom of the marble coffin, I had been protected, safe. Almost I would think that Mr. Sandman's arms had embraced me.

*Vio-let Rue! Vio-let Rue!*

*You know, I love you.*

He had never uttered these words to me, I was sure. Yet often I heard them, confused with voices at a distance. Muffled laughter.

". . . what that terrible man did to you. Try to . . ."

But I did not remember. And Mr. Sandman was my friend. No one else was my friend.

Aunt Irma staring at me, disbelieving. Uncle Oscar, with repugnance.

For I would not testify against the abuser. My eyes were heavy-lidded, my voice was slow, slurred, insolent.

*No. You can't make me. I've said—I don't remember.*

There was a female police officer, questioning me. But I knew better than to make that mistake again.

A (female) gynecologist who would report *no evidence of vaginal or anal penetration, no (physical) evidence of sexual abuse.* A (female) therapist who would report *probable extreme trauma, dissociation.* Ms. Herne from the Children's Protective Services.

It would be held against me that I was uncooperative with authorities who were trying to establish a case of repeated and sustained sexual abuse against Mr. Sandman unless it might be argued that I was a victim, mentally ill, unable to testify against the teacher who'd drugged and abused me for a period of approximately seven months.

Mr. Sandman had been careful, fastidious. My clothes had been laundered—no DNA. (Except an incriminating trace would be discovered on one of my sneakers. Just that trace would be enough to convict.)

If you don't help to convict this terrible man he will hurt other girls, they told me.

I thought—*Other girls will be hurt whether Mr. Sandman is in prison or not. That is our punishment.*

**"Violet. No** one is putting pressure on you . . ."

*You are all putting pressure on me.*

". . . but you must tell us, you must take your time and tell us, all that you can remember. When did that man first . . ."

Ms. Herne was visibly upset. For (she believed) there'd been a special understanding between us, I'd (should have) known that I could trust her. And yet, I must not have trusted Ms. Herne for the abuse had been going on for months when she'd met with me several times and there'd been *no hint.*

Of course, there'd been a *hint.* Plenty of *hint.* Ms. Herne had failed to detect, that was all.

And now with the (ugly, relentless) publicity in the local media it hardly looked as if Dolores Herne of the Port Oriskany Children's Protective Services had been very good at her job, one of her at-risk juvenile clients having been sexually abused, terrorized by a teacher, over a period of seven months and she had *not noticed.*

I'd thought—*Not abuse but punishment. And not the worst punishment either.*

**"Violet! These** beautiful flowers are from Lula."

A half-dozen pale pink roses in a vase, on the table beside my bed.

Irma blushed, adding—"Your mother."

As if I might not know who Lula was! A wave of emotion for my aunt swept through me, a mixture of anger and love.

Wanting to believe but no. Irma had bought the roses herself. For there was no card from my mother, Irma couldn't go so far in deception, forging a card from her older sister who happened to be my mother.

"Aren't they pretty? Lula was very worried about you . . ."

Irma's voice trailed off, uncertainly. Badly I wanted to say *Was she! Really!* But I remained silent.

In fact I was touched to have received two cards while I'd been in the hospital, from Miriam and from Katie.

*Get well soon! Love.*

As if I'd been stricken with flu. As if *wellness* could be expected to come *soon.*

After five days in the Port Oriskany hospital I'd been brought home to the tidy beige-brick house on Erie Street. Weakly ascending the stairs. Out of breath at the top of the stairs. Thinking—*But maybe I have died. This is one of their tricks.*

The slightest exertion left me breathless. Had my heart been damaged?

If my heart had ceased beating in the ER, it had been shocked into beating again.

And of this too I would remember nothing, or almost nothing.

The reluctance to *wake*. A conviction that *wakefulness* is an unnatural state.

*My heart is broken.* Silly, sentimental.

Not living with my family but with *relatives*. Far better than a foster home or a detention facility for runaways.

It wasn't clear that anyone from my family had actually called while I'd been in the hospital. Since Irma had not told me about specific calls I had to assume there'd been none but truly, I did not know, for my parents might have wished the calls to be secret. I was sure that my parents knew about Mr. Sandman, for Irma had to have told them. And they had to have read about him. (Though my name, as a juvenile victim, was kept out of the papers.) It seemed to me likely that Irma and Lula spoke on the phone frequently, even daily while I'd been hospitalized.

It seemed to me possible, that the sisters spoke on the phone frequently. And their subject had to be me.

*Me.* Most piteous syllable in the language.

Anyway, something I'd have liked to believe.

And what had happened to Arnold Sandman? He'd been in custody in the county jail. Wisely, he would not risk a trial. (The prosecutor was calling for a sentence of ninety-nine years.) Instead, Mr. Sandman would follow his attorney's advice and plead no contest, and express contrition, and repentance, and shame for his crimes; and the presiding judge would sentence him to twenty-five to thirty years in the maximum security prison at Attica.

A death sentence. Arnold Sandman would never survive Attica.

None of this was known to me, at the time. Though if I shut my eyes and began to drift in the rapid current that was always there, inside my eyelids, far below the Lock Street Bridge, amid the churning writhing snakes of the hue of eggplant, there came Mr. Sandman to stoop over me, his face no longer jocular and mocking but contorted with grief.

*Violet! You know, of all the girls I loved only you.*

Upstairs in the small neatly furnished room allotted to me lying on the bed that felt as if it were floating over a river. So grateful to be alone, my tears wetted the pillow.

Hours passed. Might've been days. Or no time at all.

There came a timid knocking at a door. A woman begging please, could she speak with me?

Pulled the covers over my head. So that I could see Mr. Sandman more clearly. So that I could hear him more clearly.

At last the timid knocking ceased. Whoever was outside the door had gone away and left me alone with Mr. Sandman.

# "Dirty Girl"

Uncle Oscar who'd never been my uncle. And now, never would be.

The almost-tenderness between us when we'd leafed through the little book of math puzzles together had vanished utterly in the wake of revelations about Mr. Sandman and the (drugged) girl student (who happened to be me) (who happened to be living under Oscar Allyn's roof as a pseudo-adopted-daughter).

Staring at me when Irma wasn't in the room. Tongue poking between wormy moist lips. *You dirty girl.*

# The Stalker: 1997

At the 7-Eleven, a display of brightly packaged video games. Their titles were *Stalker, SWAT Team, Murder 1, Grand Theft Auto, No Mercy, Nuke!*

On the cover of *Stalker* was a digitally produced likeness of a young hawk-faced man with a shaved head, glaring eyes and flaring nostrils, an angry mouth that resembled my brother Lionel's mouth. Or was it the look of steely hatred in the eyes that made me think of my brother.

In the young man's bloody hands, a large machete dripping blood.

*Coming to get you, rat. Rat-cunt.*

*Nowhere you can hide.*

———————

**Quickly I** retreated, feeling faint. Whatever I'd intended to purchase at the 7-Eleven, I left without purchasing it.

My heart was beating rapidly, cold sweat oozed down my sides. The last news I'd had of my brother had been from Katie, the previous week—*Lionel is up for parole on Monday. We didn't even know about it until now! Mom has been praying. Thought I'd better warn you, Vi'let.*

## "You Are Not Wanted"

And then, when I returned home Aunt Irma was on the phone.

I could not bear to overhear. Terrified of learning that my brother had been paroled.

He'd been in the facility at Marcy for five years by this time. Not quite as long as Hadrian Johnson had been dead.

Both of us: *incarceration.*

Yet Lionel was still young: twenty-two.

And I was still young: seventeen.

Upstairs in my room. Threw my textbooks onto my bed. Pressed my hands against my ears. For it seemed to me that Aunt Irma would call to me up the stairs *Good news, Violet! Lionel has been paroled.*

Katie had told me how hopeful the family was. Thousands of dollars had been spent on appeals without results but Daddy refused to give up—if there wasn't the likelihood of a new trial or a commutation of sentence for Lionel there was the possibility of parole for "good behavior." Lionel had been taking courses in the prison, he'd earned his high school equivalency diploma. He'd "kept out of trouble"—unlike his older brother Jerome Jr. who, it was said, was covered in lurid tattoos, a member of the Aryan Brotherhood whose prison sentence had been extended by another six years for participating in the near-fatal beating of another inmate.

In the facility at Marcy the Kerrigan brothers did not see each other. They'd been purposefully separated, in different parts of the prison. Jerome was considered the more dangerous, as Jerome was the older, the one believed to have committed the murder, and now a member of a white racist gang; Lionel had been (only) an accomplice.

Trying to think in hopeful terms: Lionel was not a murderer, Lionel was (possibly) reforming in prison. (*Reformed? Re-formed?* Was that the idea of a penitentiary? Was *re-formation* actually possible?)

Trying to reason that, if Lionel were released on

parole, he would do anything in his power to avoid being sent back to prison.

He would not threaten his sister. He would not hurt his sister . . .

On the phone Katie had said, meaning to be encouraging—*If Lionel gets out, he's paroled back here. Back home. It would violate parole if he left South Niagara, I think. I mean, I think so. The lawyer was telling us. If, like, he tried to—well, you know—find you, in Port Oriskany.*

*Even if he tried to contact you, I think. Any kind of—threat. Or—whatever.*

*One of the terms of the parole would be he kept a distance from you. Didn't try to contact you. Didn't leave town.*

*Did you know, they can do that? It's what parole is—parole for "good behavior."*

Trying to convince myself that my brother, having served time for manslaughter, had an investment in *good behavior.*

It was not often that Katie called me. Helplessly I'd listened to her voice. At such times my loneliness was greatest for when we hung up the silence would be overwhelming.

Whatever I wished my sister to say to me, it was not said.

And Miriam whom I adored, Miriam who'd once been so loving to me—she rarely had time to call. Married now, with a young child, living in Albany, New York, where her husband worked as a chemical engineer.

Miriam was ashamed of the Kerrigans, it was said. She'd urged her husband to get a job in a city far enough away from South Niagara that no one would associate her with the Kerrigan brothers who'd beaten a black boy to death with a baseball bat or the "controversial" politician Tom Kerrigan who stirred racial anxieties and animosities in his (successful) campaign for a state assembly seat.

Miriam felt sorry for me, I'd been told. Maybe a little guilty. Intended to invite me to spend time with her in her new life in Albany, soon.

Neither Katie nor Miriam had said anything to me about Arnold Sandman. No communication except the *get well* cards.

Anything to do with sex, we were shy to speak of. Sometimes when there are no words, that is best.

I wondered what the relatives thought of me now. That girl, Violet! Who'd ratted on her own brothers, got them sent to prison. Sent away by her parents to live with relatives in Port Oriskany where she was abused by a teacher in some unspeakable way.

*For shame! Lucky the pervert didn't kill her.*

"Violet? Come here"—at last, there came Aunt Irma's wavering voice from the foot of the stairs.

By this time I was badly trembling. I had tried not to listen to the one-sided conversation below. Whoever had called Irma had done most of the talking; Irma had murmured in agreement, little exclamations of surprise, sympathy. As I descended the stairs slowly I saw that my aunt was looking grave and I dared to think that the news could not be good—that is, Lionel could not have been paroled. "Such sad news, Violet. Your grandfather Kerrigan has died."

My grandfather! For a moment my mind was blank.

". . . would have been eighty-eight years old in just a week. Of course, he'd been ill for a long time, poor man . . ."

Irma spoke solemnly. Probably she hadn't glimpsed my father's querulous father in many years, and (probably) she'd been my mother's confidante, in Mom's bitter complaints about the old man who'd come to live with us when I was a little girl, in an addition to the house at the rear that Daddy had built for him.

Grandpa Kerrigan—"Joseph Kerrigan"—had never remembered my name. "Mir'um?"—he'd stare at me, frowning. And Mom would say, careful not to seem to be correcting him, "That's 'Violet,' Dad." Grandpa would continue to stare rudely at me as if assessing the name, or me; but next time, he'd have forgotten.

He'd been a handsome man many years before. In old photos, he'd resembled Daddy with stiff dark hair lifting from his forehead, heavy eyebrows, an "Irish look"—it was said of all the Kerrigan men. But now Grandpa's face had slid downward. Folds of flesh hung beneath his chin. He rarely shaved, whiskers sprouted from his jaws at crazed angles like wires. And he'd become smelly: menthol, tobacco, whiskey, soiled clothing, unwashed feet. That particular dark, sour smell that made me gag, the odor of dentures not kept clean.

Miriam was his favorite granddaughter—*the pretty one.* As a young girl she'd known to squirm away from Grandpa as he ran his hands over her body, disguising her revulsion by giggling. Grandpa hadn't liked it when he teased me by tugging at my hair and I'd shrieked and flinched away like a cat.

And Mom, he'd ordered around like a servant, barely remembering her name—"Hey: Loo-loo."

Sometimes he'd winked lewdly at her—"Hey: Missus."

I'd wondered what it might be, to be so old that you

neither knew nor cared who people were. Like a container filling up, and beginning to spill over. Unlike other, older persons in the family Grandpa Kerrigan made no effort to be "nice"—he didn't give a damn if you liked him or not.

Daddy had never gotten along well with his father he referred to as the *old sod*. Both father and son were short-tempered and thin-skinned, too much alike.

Yet, Daddy had insisted upon bringing his father home to live with us when Grandpa became too arthritic and forgetful to live by himself in the falling-down house in Niagara Falls where Daddy had grown up. His wife, our grandmother, had died before I'd been born. In the family it was said that Grandpa had worn her out, he'd bullied and beaten her, yet after her death he grieved for her and drank heavily. Quarreled with his children, became belligerent, paranoid. He'd had an old feud with his cousin Tommy Kerrigan, couldn't say enough crude obscene things about the politician of which the mildest was "God-damn cocksucking crook."

My sisters and I had had to help Mom clean Grandpa's room. And Grandpa's bathroom. Trying not to get sick to our stomachs. If we complained too much Mom lost patience and screamed at us—*What about me? You will help me God damn you.*

But no one could complain to Daddy about Grandpa.

Fortunately for us Grandpa spent most of his time in his room listening to ranting talk radio or watching TV; he didn't care to eat with us though Mom prepared all his meals. Nights he fell asleep in front of the blaring TV, plates and cutlery encrusted with food, emptied ale cans, whiskey bottles on the floor at his feet in filthy carpet slippers. He hadn't set foot in a church in decades—yet, officially, Grandpa was still Roman Catholic and would require a solemn high mass and burial in the St. Matthew's cemetery which was *hallowed ground.*

I smiled, remembering. The clatter of Grandpa's whiskey bottles in the big green trash container one of us (usually one of my brothers, but sometimes me) would have to roll out to the curb for Friday trash pickup . . .

"Violet, what? Is something funny?"

Aunt Irma who was easily shocked, was shocked.

Often it happened, I smiled when a smile wasn't appropriate. Or, I didn't smile when a smile would've been appropriate.

At seventeen, I wasn't a young girl. Not in my soul. No one messed around with me at school, I'd acquired something of the swagger of my older brothers serving time at Marcy. The taunts had long vanished. Ugly rumors of what the "pervert" math teacher had done to me back in ninth grade may have circulated but I knew nothing about them.

With adults I was careful not to offend. I was polite, "mature." Unfailingly I gave the impression of being cooperative. I had absorbed from Mr. Sandman the fact—(I didn't doubt it was a fact)—that persons in positions of power want you to agree with them no matter what they say and that is all they want—agreement, acquiescence. The adults of the world controlled so much of my life, I could not make enemies of them.

It was sheer relief I felt, that Lionel hadn't been paroled. No emotion at all about my grandfather's death except a small stab of hope—*Now Daddy will have one less person he cares about.*

Family meant so much to Daddy, even the *old sod.* One less person in his family would increase the value of the exiled daughter.

". . . sad, that Grandpa has died. When exactly . . ."

As if I gave a damn, *when!* I'd hardly given a thought to my grandfather since I'd been sent away from home.

*Not paroled! Not paroled yet.*

That was all I cared about: my brother, still incarcerated.

Then it occurred to me: there would be a funeral for Grandpa Kerrigan.

A funeral mass—a "solemn high mass"—for all the relatives, and I would go to it—in St. Matthew's Church. Aunt Irma and I would go together, and would sit with my family in a pew at the front of the church.

Like something swelling, opening in my brain: an American beauty rose, a sunburst. *I will go to Grandpa's funeral.*

But when I asked Irma about the funeral she shook her head evasively. "I don't think they want us, Violet. Lula was sounding so tired, she didn't even think to mention a funeral."

*Lula.* So my mother had called. Another time, she hadn't asked to speak to me.

"Did Mom ask how I was?"—breathlessly.

"Y-Yes, Violet. She always does . . ."

*Always.* Fucking damn lie, but I loved to hear it.

"What did you tell her?"

Aunt Irma was staring blankly at me, she'd lost the thread of the conversation.

As if, in an exchange with me, there was ever getting away from *me*.

"What did I tell her?—I told her you were doing well. Very good grades at school. We were talking about your grandfather, mostly . . ." Irma spoke apologetically. "He'd had a stroke, at the end. Last week. He'd been hanging on so long with his emphysema, at the nursing home they said it was like a miracle . . ."

*Miracle!* Bullshit. Almost, I laughed in Irma's face.

Katie had told me, you had to admire the *old sod.* Emphysema, angina, tremors in both hands, deaf, macular degeneration—our grandfather had come close to dying a dozen times but had always recovered, to a degree. In the Catholic nursing home he'd remained as mean as ever like an old snake, very still, cunning, you approached him at your own peril.

"Is the funeral tomorrow? The next day? We could go—we could drive . . ."

"I don't think so." Irma was sounding embarrassed. "Lula didn't ask me to come. She just thought that I should know about Jerome's father dying but—I wasn't close to your grandfather—I hardly knew him."

Irma paused. She may have been recollecting something unpleasant about my grandfather who'd often, for no reason except meanness, made crude comments about women's faces and bodies to evoke laughter in others. And Irma was not the sort of attractive, sexually alluring or vivacious woman whom the old man admired.

I said, "I should be there. Everyone will be there."

"No, Violet. I don't think so . . ."

"Won't they expect you? *Me*?"

My voice rose in distress. Irma caught at my hands, that were flailing about like wounded birds. Even as I thought calmly—*Of course you are not invited, you are not wanted there. Not ever.*

**That night,** in a state of high excitement I called home. Sheerly by chance Katie picked up the phone.

"Oh. God, Violet. I can't talk now . . ."

In my sister's voice was distress, dismay. I did not want to think, dislike.

Katie had asked me not to call her at my parents' number. But I had no other number for her, just yet.

"Christ! Let me take this into another room . . . ."

In the background were voices not distinct enough to be identified. I could imagine Katie slipping away from the others with the cordless phone clutched behind her back, hoping no one would notice.

Not a good time to call. I knew this. The very day of a death in the family. The household would be in an upheaval. Relatives of the deceased man would be dropping by—there were many in South Niagara alone. As usual Mom would be in charge. Mom would be preparing food for visitors. And Daddy would be in an excitable and unpredictable mood.

Soon, Katie would be moving out of the house on Black Rock Street. She was taking courses at the community college and working part-time.

Wanting badly (she'd said) to leave South Niagara where everyone knew about Jerome Jr. and Lionel in prison but she couldn't abandon Mom, as Miriam had.

Yes, everyone still talked about it. *Hadrian Johnson.*

Seemed like South Niagara was divided almost in two: those who believed that four white boys had killed a black boy by beating him to death with a baseball bat, and those who believed, or professed to believe, that the white boys had been unfairly blamed, "railroaded" into pleading guilty and unjustly sent to prison.

The subject was so painful, I did not ask Katie about it any longer. Everything there was to be said had been said many times. *White racists, black racists* were accusations freely flung about.

Especially, I didn't want to know how Katie herself felt.

Problem was, Katie was telling me frankly: Daddy would be really pissed with her if he knew that she and I spoke often on the phone.

As if we spoke *often!*

I was hurt, and I was resentful. But I knew not to betray sarcasm for Katie would soon hang up.

At first Katie was as evasive as Aunt Irma had been about the time of Grandpa's funeral, then she relented: Thursday morning, 10:00 A.M. at St. Matthew's.

This was good news! Two days from now.

Quickly I told her that Aunt Irma wanted to come to the funeral. A plausible lie: Mom had asked Katie to come help her in the emergency.

". . . could drive there, if we left early Thursday morning. We could stay with . . . Well, that would be up to Mom. I guess lots of Grandpa's relatives are coming, from Niagara Falls?"

At the other end of the line Katie was startled, silent. What was Violet saying!

Blithely I repeated that Irma intended to come to South Niagara, to help Mom. And I could drive Irma's car some of the way, I had a driver's permit now.

Still, Katie was silent. I could envision my sister biting her lower lip, staring into a corner of the room.

"Katie? Are you there? Is something wrong?"—my voice cracked with anxiety.

"I—I'm here, Violet. I am—here." There was a blankness in my sister's speech like the blankness in

Aunt Irma's face when I'd asked her a question she had not seemed to hear.

"It's all right if I come, Katie? Isn't it? I mean— Grandpa is my grandfather, people would wonder if I didn't come to his funeral . . . Wouldn't they?"

"Oh, Violet. I—don't know. It's kind of a stressful time for us. Maybe not good to try to 'visit' right now—you know how Daddy feels about you."

"But Daddy would see that I *cared*. About Grandpa."

Katie seemed to be contemplating this. To me, it seemed so plausible that a death in the family would draw us together.

". . . thing is, Violet, it's not a great time for any more surprises. Grandpa had not wanted to be moved to the nursing home. He went kind of crazy, so angry. Breaking things. Shouting. Threatening he'd set the house on fire. We were all afraid of him especially Mom who was stuck in the house with him so much. Daddy was hoping they could make it up before he died, but that didn't happen. Grandpa wouldn't even see Daddy at the end, or anyone. In the nursing home they had to restrain him even after he'd had strokes and didn't weigh more than one hundred pounds. So Daddy is feeling terrible, how things turned out. And he might have to sell the house, to pay lawyers. *That* makes him really depressed, him and Mom both. You know how Daddy loves this house."

Terrible news! The house I'd been forbidden to enter, of which I dreamt every night . . . If my father sold it, there would be no home for me to return to, ever.

". . . and Lionel was up for his first parole hearing this week—I told you. But it was postponed until next month, we don't know why."

Postponed to next month. That was why Aunt Irma hadn't mentioned it, there was no news only a deferment.

A reprieve, it was. I would not have to think about my vengeful brother released to punish me for another four weeks at least.

"Violet? You know how Daddy is . . . How he's been . . . I don't think he would be much different now, if you showed up at the funeral. I mean—he hasn't changed his way of thinking about you. Mom maybe, a little—Mom does say she *misses* you. But . . ."

*Misses me.* But won't do anything about it, will she.

Hearing this I thought—*I hate her more than I hate him.*

For an awkward moment there was silence on the line. I could not think of anything to say, I'd been struck between the eyes by—something . . . Not even sure what we'd been talking about, I'd been so thrown off-balance.

That was the danger in calling either of my sisters. They would try to discourage me. Try to protect me from being told what I did not want to hear which was (as I knew) what I'd already been told and should have known and (indeed) did know. And yet.

"Violet? Are you still there?"

"Where else would I be?"—adolescent sarcasm now.

Katie seemed about to say something further but then as if weary of the subject, or exasperated by me, she murmured only, in a conclusive way: "So."

*So* was a mere expulsion of air, a sigh. I did not want to interpret it *So, Violet, you can see that this is not a good time for you to return home* but rather as a neutral signifier, friendly, informative.

"Katie, thanks! I guess—I will see you on Thursday—at St. Matthew's."

Quickly hanging up then, before Katie could protest.

**Left a** note for my aunt Irma to spare her trying to dissuade me.

*Dear Aunt Irma, I am going to South Niagara for the funeral. I will take a bus. I will be all right. Will try to call when I can.*

How to sign? I hated hypocrisy, damned if I would say *Love, Violet.*

Finally just signed *V.* Reasoning, Irma would know who *V.* was.


**Fistful of** small-denomination bills. Forty-six dollars.

*Chump change* painstakingly saved from babysitting for my aunt's friends and neighbors. Tempted to take (small) bills from Uncle Oscar's wallet left on a bureau in his bedroom but decided against this thinking shrewdly—*One day, might want to take all the bills in that wallet. Not yet.*

With these bills, and not much left over, I was able to purchase a round-trip ticket to South Niagara on a Greyhound bus leaving Port Oriskany at 7:10 A.M. on Thursday and arriving in South Niagara at 9:25 A.M. If the bus was not delayed, and if I could get to St. Matthew's (which had to be at least two miles from the South Niagara bus station) within a half hour, I would not be late for the funeral mass; and if I was late, I would sit quietly at the rear of the church in a pew by myself and my parents would discover me, the end of the service when everyone rose to leave, and understand that I'd hoped to arrive on time but had had to come a distance, from Port Oriskany . . .

Obsessively I rehearsed: Greyhound bus, bus station in South Niagara, Front Street, Huron Avenue, Comstock Street, Bryant, St. Matthew's Church where a priest (Father Greavy) would be saying a solemn high mass for my grandfather's soul.

And again: Greyhound bus, bus station in South Niagara, Front Street, Huron Avenue, Comstock Street, Bryant, St. Matthew's Church . . . I'd begun to tremble with anticipation and excitement.

"Traveling far?"—a stout woman in a pea-colored woolen coat was seated beside me, on the aisle.

"Not far."

"Alone?"

Couldn't she see that I was alone!—I wanted to protest. Of course, I only just murmured *yes*.

The friendly woman was traveling to Buffalo, she said. Where she had family. Was that where I was headed, too? Her voice was warm, confiding.

(Could I pretend not to hear?) (But no, I could not. Could not bring myself to be rude to this friendly stranger.)

". . . South Niagara." My answer was vague as if I wasn't altogether sure and in any case did not want to elaborate.

"Visiting family?"

A pause. How grudging I felt, having to explain myself. And how self-pitying it sounded, in a voice unexpectedly weak.

"My grandfather's funeral . . ."

"Funeral! Oh. I am sorry." The friendly woman ceased smiling like a light switched off.

Holding myself very still. Staring out the window. In dread of having to speak with another person for the next hour and a half when I wanted only to be alone with my thoughts.

But the woman would not relent. Turning to me, like a heat vent suddenly opened, inescapable—"You are traveling alone to the funeral? Will you be all right?"

What a question to ask! Would I be *all right.*

Blood pounded hotly in my cheeks. No one in my life any longer, not Aunt Irma, certainly not my mother, spoke to me so intimately, or seemed to care so much about me as this inquisitive stranger.

"I—I'm old enough to take the bus to South Niagara alone. It isn't far."

"Isn't *far,* but it's a funeral . . . You sure you all right? How old are you?"

Something suspicious and tender in the woman's voice was wounding to me. I could not bring myself to face her. My eyes welled with tears, turned to the passing landscape outside the window.

None of this stranger's business how old I was but I heard myself tell her, barely audible—"Eighteen."

"Eighteen! No."

Because I did not look eighteen? My heart beat in resentment. Why the hell didn't this woman leave me alone!

It was true, I wasn't (yet) eighteen. But I felt much older. I carried myself (I was sure) with the assurance of a young woman in her twenties.

"Where's your family, you got to travel alone to a funeral?"

Intonations of a mother's voice. A mildly scandalized mother. I had a dread of this stranger clutching at my hands suddenly, to comfort me.

"My family is—where I am going. That's where I am going."

So inanely I spoke, my lips felt parched. The frantic thought came to me that I had to escape—push out over the woman, stumble along the aisle to the rear of the bus, find an empty seat . . .

But the bus was moving, the driver would shout at me. The friendly woman would be surprised, and hurt.

"How old was your grandpa?"

"I—I don't know . . ."

"Real old, or just—kind of old? Seventy-five? Eighty? Or—younger? Ohhh, I hope not." Laughing, as if the prospect of a young grandpa dying was especially alarming. "Did you love him a lot?"

*Love him a lot.* How absurd was this!

"Y-Yes . . ."

"Oh, I loved my grandpa a lot, too! Just the one grandpa I knew, the other I didn't know, I guess my momma didn't, either. But the one—I did know, he was a blessed person."

*Blessed.* The word was a blank to me, beyond comprehension.

Oblivious of my discomfort the woman persisted: "Is this grandpa your momma's father, or your daddy's? Were they close?"

Determined not to answer any more inane questions. I would take out a textbook and begin to read.

But heard myself say stammering that Grandpa was my father's father. No, they were not close. But maybe—yes. They didn't get along but they were close. I thought so. Maybe they were. Maybe it was a bad shock to my father, that Grandpa had died. "My father doesn't like things to change. He feels sad, he can't make things better than they are for his family."

Why I was speaking in this way to a stranger on a Greyhound bus, I had no idea. Though I felt sulky, hostile, prickly as a wild creature trapped in a corner my voice was the voice of a child in need of consolation.

"Oh, your daddy will take it hard! They all do. It's like a woman losing her mother—real hard. Like, if they ain't been getting along, it's worse, 'cause they can't make it up, and that's the worst—you can't change how the other person feels, 'cause it's too late. And what you feel—it's too late."

Like warm water the woman's sympathy spilled onto me. A miserable sensation, yet I could not break away.

Heard myself say suddenly it had been a terrible shock to me, news of my grandfather's death. "I guess—I will miss him a lot . . ."

Astonishing, the words that spilled from me. Maudlin tears in my eyes for a grandfather I might have loved if he'd loved me—if, in fact, Grandpa had been a different person. Grieving for a person who'd never existed—like reaching into your pocket and encountering a hole in the fabric. Whatever might've been in the pocket has vanished.

Now she'd pried me open, like a mollusk. Now, the woman whose name was Sarabeth had me in her grip and would not release me. Extracted from me the information that my name was Violet—and that I lived with an aunt in Port Oriskany. That I was a senior in Port Oriskany High School where all of Sarabeth's children had gone—"But they're too old for you,

Vi'let—you wouldn't know them." In turn Sarabeth embarked upon a complicated story of her mother's mother who was born in Macon, Georgia, and married at fifteen, lost her first husband ("something bad done to him by bad people"), and remarried, and traveled north with the second husband in the 1930s—first to Cleveland, then to Erie, Pennsylvania, then to Buffalo, and Tonawanda where Sarabeth's grandfather worked on the New York Central Railroad, and they had eleven children—"And those eleven children, they had children—lots of 'em!" Two of Sarabeth's daughters were teachers and her youngest son was "some kind of expert in computers" in Rochester. "You got to be impressed, my grandma was the great-great-granddaughter of *slaves*. Makes me real happy to think how far we all come!"

Sarabeth spoke without rancor though with an air of incredulity. I could not help but share this incredulity. *Slaves?*

In my distracted state I hadn't registered that Sarabeth was dark-skinned. Girls at school with whom I was friendly were mostly black and I had ceased to notice the color of their skin. The woman's physical presence, her persistent friendliness had been overwhelming to me.

*Worried about my parents not loving me! And this woman is descended from slaves . . .*

Creasing her forehead Sarabeth said carefully: "Vi'let, why are you living with your aunt? Why aren't you living with your family in South Niagara?"

This was the question I'd dreaded. But I had a reply prepared: "Because there wasn't room for me there—in that house."

"Not room for you? How many brothers and sisters do you have?"

"Six brothers and sisters. And my grandfather lived with us. But they don't all live at home now . . . " My voice trailed off, Sarabeth was looking at me with such frank puzzlement.

"How is your momma, Vi'let? You still have your momma?"

"Yes."

"You close to your momma?"

"Y-yes."

"You got sisters, you said?"

"Two sisters."

"Older or younger or—?"

"Both older."

"You get along OK with them, do you?"

"Yes I do! When I see them."

A sinking cadence in *when I see them* that alerted Sarabeth to the possibility of a wrongness.

Discreetly then, Sarabeth ceased her interrogation. Released me from the intensity of her sympathy. Relief flooded through me but also disappointment, regret.

Soon, Sarabeth fell asleep. Her breathing was audible, comforting. Beside her I stared out the window at the countryside beyond the Thruway. Now that there was no one to witness, tears welled in my eyes and spilled onto my cheeks. No idea why.

Delayed by an accident on the Thruway the Greyhound bus arrived in South Niagara thirty-five minutes late.

In a state of anxiety I ran most of the two miles from the bus station to St. Matthew's church at the intersection of Bryant Avenue and Lock Street my backpack thudding between my shoulder blades. And when I arrived breathless and sweating the tall front doors were shut and inside a solemn high mass had begun for the repose of the soul of *Joseph Gabriel Kerrigan (1908–1997).*

Wasn't sure that I'd even known my grandfather's middle name: *Gabriel.*

Printed on the Sacred Heart of Jesus prayer cards, for mourners at the mass to take home with them *in memorium.*

A beautiful name, I thought. And this too was strange: any sort of beauty accruing to my sneering grandfather.

At the altar, a casket banked with white lilies. Grandpa would've laughed in derision, kicked the flowers.

*God damn you all to hell.*

The interior of St. Matthew's was more dimly lighted than I recalled. And more sparsely occupied than I'd ever seen it. Mourners were in only three pews at the very front and none of these was filled.

From the rear of the church I couldn't see the priest clearly—he didn't resemble Father Greavy. He was older, stooped. His voice was rapid and singsong and nasal and the altar boys' mumbled responses were near-inaudible. How annoyed my grandfather would have been, a solemn high mass being said for *him*. Like many—male—Irish Catholics of his generation he'd come to despise the Church. He'd known about "pervert priests" long before the media exposed them. He'd refused to attend mass for decades since my grandmother died and he'd had no way of avoiding a church funeral.

I strained to see: my parents seated in the first pew. Just the backs of their heads I saw yet I recognized them, with a sick, sinking sensation, at once.

They were seated with my grandfather's family—most of them older, white-haired. But there was Miriam, and Katie . . . Rick? Les?

Chilling to me, to see how I wasn't among them. As if I'd never existed.

Six years since my parents had seen me or spoken with me. That encounter at the children's custody *safe house* when my mother walked out to wait for Miriam in the car had been the last time I'd seen Mom and I could not even recall clearly the last time I'd seen Daddy . . .

Strange to continue to call them *Mom, Daddy*.

In those years I'd grown taller and thinner but I had no idea if I looked very different. I had little sense of my appearance at all. My body felt disengaged and numb, transparent as our bodies in dreams. It was my instinct to shun mirrors to avoid an unpleasant jolt— *Rat! Rat-face.*

Mr. Sandman had said that I was beautiful. Yet, when I dared to study my face in a mirror, to see what he'd seen, I could not find it—the math teacher's interest in me was like a mirror reflecting light but it was a distorting and blinding light. After Mr. Sandman's arrest I'd been shown photographs he'd (allegedly) taken of me but the girl in the photographs (sleeping, slack-mouthed, partly clothed or naked) did not look like me.

*Do you recognize this girl, Violet?*

*You don't see that this is yourself, Violet?*

Possibly it had been a trick. I did not trust the therapist, as I did not trust the police. Whatever I told them became their property, to be used as they wished. It was one of the great shocks of my life, how words uttered may be irretrievable, irrevocable.

All this I would explain to my parents. Try to explain. I had never been allowed. But now, today—maybe . . .

Seated alone in a pew at the rear of the church. Badly shivering for the church was damp and chilly. Yet, droplets of sweat like tiny ants ran down my sides inside my clothes for I'd been overheated by running. It was difficult for me to concentrate on the mass, which should have been familiar to me, the priest's chanting of simple monosyllabic words, repeated pleas—*Christ have mercy! Lord have mercy! Christ have mercy!*

The chalice was raised, incense was released. Like a bird's sudden cry a bell rang brightly. There came a shuffling of communicants to the communion rail. I'd forgotten—of course, the funeral mass would involve communion, and I would be excluded for I was not in a state of grace, it had been more than six years since my last confession.

No I did not *believe.* Not in any of it. I was seventeen!

Telling myself that I'd never believed, really. Even as a little girl . . .

Asking my mother what is *sin* and she'd said *bad things you do that you should not.*

It seemed to me now that the Catholic mass was a ceremony of begging, essentially. Humankind on its knees begging God for—what, exactly?

There came a shuffling of communicants to the communion rail. Among the stooped and elderly was my mother, clasped hands before her. Was I the only observer in the church to recognize the rage in my mother's body? In the very set of her shoulders, the bow of her head? Passing by the shiny casket she'd have liked to pound on it with both hands, shout at the old man within.

*Hate hate hate you! Hate how my life was sucked into yours, had to wait on you like a servant.*

*Hate how you commanded me. How you looked at me. Undressing me with your eyes. Filthy old man.*

As child I hadn't known. Now I was no longer a child I understood. Daddy had forced Mom to surrender her life to the old man as she'd surrendered her life to her family when we'd been children.

As she'd surrender her life to him.

In the car driving to Highgate Avenue that day she'd revealed her bitterness to me—*married, babies, seven days a week*. But before that, she'd cleaned other people's houses.

Never had I heard my mother's voice so bitter, yet so exalted in bitterness.

Communicants were kneeling at the rail. Others shuffled forward on canes, walkers. My grandfather's generation was elderly, unsteady on their feet. Even their children were becoming gray-haired, slow-moving. My father would have been tall, dark-haired and vigorous among them but Daddy remained sitting, would not rise to take communion. Probably, Daddy hadn't taken communion since he and my mother were married.

Since I'd come to live with my aunt Irma I had stopped going to church. Each Sunday Irma went faithfully to ten o'clock mass but I had accompanied her only a few times and each time I'd fallen asleep—a stupor of boredom and anxiety. Irma had had to arouse me at the end of the ceremony—*Violet! Wake up!* Unlike Mom my aunt hadn't the power to coerce me into attending church with her nor could she have frightened me into believing in God and sin and the Holy Roman Catholic Church.

*You know what touching yourself is—you know . . .*

*That's a sin, a very bad sin, disgusting. That's the sort of sin you must confess if you want to take communion. And remember, the priest knows when you are lying.*

Father Greavy hadn't wanted to know when I'd told the truth. I remembered that.

At last the solemn high mass was ending: *Go in the peace of Christ.*

The stoop-shouldered priest departed flanked by altar boys in white muslin surplices. (And now I saw that yes, he was Father Greavy after all, grown older and stouter.) Mourners were moving into the aisles. Gravely they spoke together. All were Kerrigans or Kerrigan in-laws like my mother. All had known Joseph Gabriel Kerrigan though probably few had glimpsed him in recent years since he'd left Niagara Falls to live with my father. Their sorrowful faces had to be for themselves—their mortality. Not his.

Daringly, I stood in the aisle. I could not bring myself to approach my parents but I would remain where I stood, they would have to pass by me on their way out of the church.

And now I saw, or thought I saw, my father glancing in my direction. In gatherings like this Daddy was likely to be restless. Impatient to get away from people who yammered at him. Old age and illness had always discomforted him. Weakness in others and in himself.

His sympathy for you if you were sick would quickly burn out.

He hadn't seen me, I thought. Not yet.

Others came between us. Grandpa's surviving sisters, a younger brother. Moving with care as if their bodies hurt them. Canes, walkers. Katie had said that Daddy had arranged for them to be brought to South Niagara for the funeral. Probably they were staying at the house. Distracted and anxious, Mom would have made up beds for them.

Waiting in the aisle dry-mouthed. People were passing me, exiting the church. Did I look familiar to them? Did they recognize me? No one did more than glance at me. I saw familiar faces—friends of my father's from work. Neighbors, relatives. My heart was beating rapidly as I anticipated my parents seeing me—confronting me—and then it would be too late to turn away . . . But there suddenly was my brother Rick, staring. Seeing me. His face registered shock. Rick was older than I recalled, his features coarser. His hair combed in a different style. And then Katie turned, and Katie saw me too. And Katie too registered shock, and a kind of chagrin. Eagerly I waited for her to smile at me, to wave at me, but Katie did not smile, and Katie did not wave at me except to make a frantic, unmistakable gesture—*Not now! Not now!*

For a moment I stood stunned, unmoving. But Katie continued to gesture at me, shaking her head, frowning in alarm and exasperation—*Go away! Go away! This is not the right time, you are not wanted here.*

Blindly I turned away. Blindly stumbling from the church.

Such a coward! Fled.

# Dirty Girl

Gradually it has happened. At first you thought it had to be an accident.

Brushing against you on the stairs, grunting what sounds like *Sorry!*

Pushing open the door, surprising you in the bathroom. When he has just seen you step inside . . .

In the house in your aunt's presence resolutely not looking at you. At mealtimes scarcely acknowledging you where once he'd been at least civil, friendly. Now stiffly polite, grimacing. Lowering his head as he eats noisily masticating his food.

And then, when your aunt isn't close by, openly staring at you. Tongue protruding on his lower lip. Glistening smile.

*Dirty girl. Think I don't know you!*

Coarse flushed face. Swollen nose riddled with broken capillaries.

Gradually, since Sandman. Since the arrest, headlines in local papers.

Gradually over the past year your uncle (in-law) Oscar Allyn has begun to stay away from the house weekday evenings. Returning late from work. Missing meals without calling your aunt beforehand.

Aunt Irma is acutely aware of this change. Baffled, hurt. They've been married for so long!—twenty-six years. Difficult for her to believe that the mild-mannered reliable/responsible husband she'd believed she knew so well is becoming a different person.

On the stairs, in the upstairs hall as he passes, breathing audibly, not minding if you hear, trailing a hand across your back—just a touch! Small of your back—phantom touch. That look in his (heated) face. Quickness in suet-colored eyes like flies alighting on something rotted and delicious.

In your room, on your bed, when you return after school, to your surprise/shock a magazine with a naked, big-breasted blond woman on its cover—*Hot Eye Kandy.*

(Quickly you dispose of the magazine. *Do not* page

through it to see what Oscar has marked for your particular attention.)

Your textbooks, library books, Oscar seems to have leafed through, underlining isolated and seemingly random words in red pencil, in an indecipherable code. Even your math text.

You have begun to be afraid of him. Your uncle (in-law) who'd been so taciturn, courteous, not very engaged with you but friendly enough, for years.

That look of sick yearning. And resentment, anger beneath.

The slack lips. Wet smile. Meat-smile.

Letting his shirt fall open—exposing the rounded, fatty stomach covered in hairs. Matted hair on his chest, rosy nipples.

Male nipples! You'd wanted to laugh wildly.

Pushes open the bathroom door you think you have locked—(has Oscar tinkered with the lock?)—desperately you try to cover yourself with a towel—"Go away! Leave me alone! I hate you."

Red-faced the uncle-in-law mutters his lame apology—*Sorry.* Quickly backed away guessing this time he has gone too far.

As you have gone too far, past a point of no return. Instead of shrinking away in silence loudly crying *I hate you.*

—————

**And now,** no turning back.

Thinking it has to be your fault. It is you, not Oscar Allyn.

Your fault, your aunt's husband has so altered. This past year. Now that you are seventeen and "older"— not a child. Those months since Arnold Sandman was exposed in the papers and people had spoken of little else reacting with shock, disgust.

*That girl! How could she . . .*

*Not testifying against him, what can that mean . . .*

They would not forgive you, for refusing to testify. For refusing to remember. *But I did not want to remember.*

The sickness had entered you like a parasite seeking warm moist cavities in which to take hold, thrive. As Mr. Sandman seeped into you without your knowing and this not-knowing allowed his spirit to invade you utterly.

And then one day. Irma approaches you shyly. Tight-lipped and anxious asking if Oscar has "touched" you—ever?

Very painful for your aunt to ask such a question. Mortifying.

Irma's voice quavers, she has taken your (cold, unresponsive) hand in hers as you shake your head mutely *No.*

No? He hasn't touched you? Or—threatened to touch you?

You too are embarrassed. Resentful of being questioned. It is like Ms. Herne questioning you, and the therapist, and the (female) police officers insisting they have only your *best interests at heart* but will use any and all evidence they can gather from you against you.

But no. You will not tell your tremulous aunt that her husband Oscar has fallen into the habit of touching, not you, but himself, in your presence. At first this too seemed accidental, unintentional, a kind of rough scratching in the region of the groin, nothing extensive or (apparently) deliberate. As if casually but then, gradually, with unmistakable crudeness when you have no choice but to pass closely by the man. And the simpering sounds emitted from his mouth— *Dirty girl! Vio-let.*

As if Sandman has passed you to him. And yet, your uncle expressed great shock and great disgust over the issue of Arnold Sandman, in his reticent way he'd been outraged. Aunt Irma wrung her hands, Aunt Irma murmured *poor child, poor girl* while Uncle Oscar muttered *pervert! Should be locked up and the key thrown away.*

You will not tell Irma how a few days ago Oscar

was standing outside your room, early in the morning, before you left for school, before he left for work. Belt undone, trousers open. So taken by surprise your eyes shifted downward shocked, dismayed, unable to look away. For you'd never glimpsed Mr. Sandman in any state of undress not even his shirt partly unbuttoned. Not even with hair lank and limp and damp falling onto his forehead. Not once.

And then—shocked to hear yourself laugh. Wild snort of laughter.

"Oh what's *that?* You've got to be kidding."

Instantly your uncle ceased the obscene motions he'd been making with his hand, touching himself. Flinched away from your jeering eyes, mortified.

So quickly it happened. You would never have expected this: a thrill of power. That the man could be assaulted in a way particular to him, his maleness.

You realize: the man's power over you is to intimidate you, to make you ashamed. But your power over him is the power of laughter.

For it is very funny. The man's penis, the flabby thighs of the middle-aged man, the stubby flesh between the thighs intended as a kind of weapon, but limp now, slack and defeated. Laughable.

It will happen another time. One more time. Your (drunken?) uncle standing naked and spread-legged in the bathroom doorway, where you can't avoid seeing him, pulling at his penis, face red-flushed as a mask, lips drawn back—your instinct is to recoil, back away, instead you sneer at him as before, daring to take a step forward as if preparing to kick him in the groin.

Again, Oscar retreats. Your laughter rises, the cry of a fierce bird. Your ridicule of the man is merciless, joyous as you call after him—*Asshole! Fat prick! Hate you! Hate hate hate you!*

It is stunning, the sudden animosity between you and the adult man with whom you've shared a household for years. The thrill of it. Like a curtain yanked down, that has been hiding something astonishing. Once, you and your uncle-in-law had liked each other—almost. Shy with each other. Awkward. Nothing sexual in his regard for you—not at all. Almost, at times, a kind of clumsy tenderness—nothing more. In your adolescent indifference you'd scarcely noticed the man, it was your aunt Irma against whom you had to defend yourself for it was aunt Irma who'd wanted so badly for you to love her, that her love for you might not be the vain yearning of a foolish childless woman.

*Oh Lula—I am trying. So hard . . .*

*Was Violet like this with you? Sometimes she won't even look at me . . . And Oscar, he is trying too.*

Disconcerting to recall, when you'd first come to live with the Allyns you and your uncle had often helped your aunt in the kitchen, clearing the table after the evening meal, stacking the dishwasher. Deferring to Oscar, the male, to set the dials and start the machine properly.

Oscar hadn't been staring crudely at you then. You had not been afraid of him then. You'd have been astonished to be told that, one day, the (well-intentioned) (deeply boring) man your aunt had married would be worthy of your hatred.

Not wanting to think—*But I am the one. I caused this.*

When your aunt returns Oscar has left the house. In astonishment Irma asks where on earth has he gone, just before supper?

You tell her you don't know. *No idea.*

But had he said when he'd be back?

*No. Had not.*

As jubilance fades, as your blood beats less fiercely, you begin to feel guilty. *Dirty girl.*

Following this, Oscar avoids you. Conspicuously. But Oscar avoids his anxious wife, too.

He has ceased going to church with Irma. Sunday mornings, Irma drives to church by herself.

This is the dangerous time: alone in the house with your uncle. As soon as you realize, you leave the house also. You walk swiftly, you can walk for miles. You break into a run, exhilarated. Recalling how desperately you'd run to your grandfather's funeral. And how futile the effort.

*You are not wanted. Go away!*

You wonder if it is time for you to go away again. You wonder if Aunt Irma will ask you to leave. Or if you must remain with her, since she loves you.

In all the world, it is Irma who loves you. Yet, you understand that Irma has no idea who you are and if she knew, she would draw back in disgust.

Oscar has fallen into a pattern of returning home late after work. Even on Saturdays he disappears for hours. Irma is helpless to confront him. Irma is stunned, baffled. You think of a cow that has been struck by a mallet, led to slaughter. The brain is annihilated, the legs collapse. Irma holds herself upright by an act of will.

You hear Irma on the phone speaking with relatives, friends. You have the idea that she doesn't speak with your mother, however. A faltering hurt-female voice. A voice that invites sympathy, pity. But also impatience.

It is your fault, you are thinking. *Dirty girl.*

And your aunt had tried so hard to love you. *You!*

Away for hours and when Oscar finally comes home after 11:00 P.M. his unsteady, heavy footsteps on the stairs remind you of your father's footsteps you'd heard as a little girl, lying in bed wide-eyed.

The stricken look in your aunt's face reminds you of the stricken look in your mother's face, you have not recalled in a long time.

Fleetingly it occurs to you, the man could hurt you if he wished. Very badly.

If he has been drinking and is fortified by drink. Not often that you are alone together in the house but sometimes it happens, despite your vigilance.

In your room with the door locked you would be protected (you think) but the door has no lock. Dragging a chair in front of the door is just too pathetic, you are thinking. (Or is it?)

The bathroom door has a lock but it is a loose lock, not reliable.

His footsteps, his presence outside the door. Can't concentrate on calculus. Is anything so absurd as *calculus*—figures on a sheet of paper, that might be crumpled in the man's hand.

You are beginning to sweat with the possibility that he will repay you for laughing at him. It is the unforgivable insult—laughing at the man, the maleness of the man, unbearable to him.

If he wishes he will push open the door. If there is a chair dragged in front of it, Oscar could (probably) send the chair flying. His body has gone soft and slack and yet Oscar Allyn is strong, you have seen him lifting heavy objects for Irma, a stone bench in the backyard she'd asked him to relocate, bags of fertilizer, salt for the winter driveway.

Easily, Oscar outweighs you by one hundred pounds. He has been drinking, he is summoning his strength. His desperation, chagrin. How you have unmanned him with your shrieking laughter. If Oscar wishes he will burst upon you and cause you to scream another way. Your jeering laughter the man has not been sensitive enough to understand is the laughter of hysteria will be permanently silenced. He will hurt you between the legs however he can, plucking at you, his fingers crude, fingernails sharp. Or possibly something he will grab, your hairbrush. The handle of your plastic hairbrush, shoved up inside you.

*Dirty girl. This is what you like.*

Or, if indeed the man has an erection. If the man can sustain an erection. *That* will be his triumph, annihilating you utterly.

Whatever it is, this revenge. You will not register

it fully, you will not live to recall it. In his jubilance he will snuff out your young life, a pillow snatched from your bed as you thrash in desperation, screaming mouth mashed against the pillow, pleading and begging, mute.

All this is the male prerogative. You'd known, watching from a doorway your brothers at their video games. *Kill! Kill! Kill the enemy!* Certainly you'd known, when Lionel shoved you down the icy steps with a prayer you'd crack your skull.

Outside your door the man listens for the sound of your quickened, frightened breathing. Eagerly the man listens to the silence of your fear which is a kind of reverence, an acknowledgment of his power.

Will he smother you, or will he strangle you. Will he force himself between your legs, will he rape you, or will he merely pluck and pinch at you with his fingers, in a fury of impotence, and toss you back down onto the creaking bed, leave you your debased life as if it isn't worth taking from you . . .

In a trance of terror you have not breathed for some time. One of your comforting fantasies since you have come to live in exile has been that you are a soft boneless sea-creature protected inside a shell and (perhaps) it is a beautifully striated shell that camouflages itself amid seaweed surroundings so that it is not visible to the eyes of predators nor could the creature inside the shell hear anything of the outer world, concentrating on its own heartbeat and the coursing of its blood . . . This fantasy you have only to shut your eyes in school, in a classroom. And when you are alone.

But it is inescapable, you are not alone now.

Trapped in your (second-floor) room. In the house with the person who wants badly to defeat you, to defile you, and if defiled you will have to be murdered for he cannot risk your telling on him; it is the fatal move of the victim, the *telling*.

Though perhaps he is thinking—*She didn't tell on the other. The pervert.*

You remain very still. You do not pray but you instruct yourself to remain very still, scarcely dare breathe, perhaps the man will come to his senses, as it's said; will relent, will think twice, step away from the door without grabbing the handle and shoving the door open.

Instead after several minutes of silence tense as a wire strung tight to bursting he will decide to pass by with just a thump on the door, flat of his hand, a gesture that might be interpreted as jocular, mock-fatherly—*Hey there, Vi'let! Just me.*

---

**But eventually** Irma learns. Despite the husband's stratagems, and the niece's determination not to *tell*, she learns. Of course she is deeply shaken, stunned.

Her marriage! Her precious marriage!

Her husband Oscar Allyn of whom she'd been so proud, that he was *her husband*. That she'd acquired, at almost-thirty, a *husband*. For Irma had passed her girlhood in a trance of dread at being left behind—never engaged, never married. The plainest of sisters, yet not the smartest. The *good girl*—born to be a virgin through her (long) life. Her fate would be that of those daughters common in large Irish families, *aunties*, *spinsters* whom others take for granted, condescend to, pity.

She cannot bear it at her age, beyond fifty. Losing the husband. The man.

And yet, the shame of the man's behavior with her sister's daughter, under her very roof—the girl she has hoped to protect and cherish! She prays to the Virgin Mary for solace, advice: What should she do?

Possibly, Irma speaks to the priest at confession. You don't know who this might be, for you'd never gone to confession at Irma's church.

It isn't clear what precipitates the crisis. Possibly Aunt Irma, meek-mannered, fearful of raising her voice, stricken with embarrassment at a ribald joke on TV, nonetheless dares to confront the (drunken) husband on one of the evenings he returns home late.

And possibly, the husband refuses to answer her, or in an outburst of fury has loudly denied "touching"— "threatening"—her niece in such a way that she understands that—of course— he is guilty.

Of course Irma has known. Slow to realize but it's inevitable. The strain between her husband and the girl, tense silences at mealtimes, hostile glances. The husband's flushed face and glaring eyes, the girl's sullen manner. Why, the husband and the girl are not speaking to each other!—she finally understands.

And there is Oscar's clumsy humor. Attempt at humor. Looking at Irma, keeping his gaze fixed on Irma even as (almost, she can sense this) he is keenly aware of the other at the table, the girl. Fumble of a smile. Not acknowledging the girl, at the very table with them. Sick, sagging look in his face, jowls.

He'd become obsessed not with the girl, his "niece" by an accident of marriage, but with the possibilities exacted upon her by another: the notorious pervert Sandman.

The beauty of rot, phosphorescence. An unspeakable filth, beyond comprehension. Certain poisons that impress the tongue initially as sweet—irresistible.

No one knew what Sandman had done to the girl, precisely. Much was speculated but nothing known. Nor did the girl know, herself. Was this not the most delicious part of the equation, that the girl did not know, herself?

Yet it was a fact in the community, like a baptism.

And so one day Irma confronts the girl: "Violet! I have something to tell you, please don't run away upstairs."

# "Violet, Goodbye!"

Never had a chance to say *goodbye* to my family.
Never had a chance to say *goodbye* to Geraldine Pyne, I'd loved like a sister.

Never to my seventh-grade teachers. Especially Ms. Micaela who'd been so kind to me.

Nor did any of these say the words I wish I'd heard and could cherish waking in the night suddenly uncertain of my surroundings—*Violet, goodbye!*

My mother hurrying out of the *safe house* to wait for Miriam in the car. Not a glance back at me, not a murmur of regret, remorse.

My father refusing to visit me in the *safe house* for fear (Miriam would tell me) that he would be so furious with me, in the hearing of others, he'd have been arrested on the spot.

And so, I was grateful that Aunt Irma would say *Violet, goodbye!*

That Aunt Irma would hug me, and weep over me—*Violet, I love you.*

*Goodbye!*

**My aunt** had made her difficult decision: she would tell her husband Oscar to move out of the house.

Surprising me by saying that she'd spoken with a lawyer. Not to explain to the lawyer why she was asking her husband to leave, why specifically, only just that she needed to know the law on "separating"—establishing separate legal residences.

Separation? From Oscar? *Divorce?*

Not divorce. Irma didn't think so. But the Church does allow *legal separation.*

That night, whenever he returned, she would tell him. He must move out of the house.

Why?—he'd know.

Certainly. He would know.

Though Oscar was co-owner of the house. Though Oscar supported the household. Though financially Irma and Violet, wife and (unofficially) adopted daughter, were supported by Oscar.

Better this way, Irma said bravely.

Thrumming with excitement, apprehension. If I'd touched my aunt, might've recoiled from a quick shock.

Though even then she was averting her eyes. For she would not tell me her suspicions. For she'd asked me, weeks ago, more than once she'd tried to draw out of me what was happening in the suddenly strained household, what had Oscar said, or done, or hinted at doing, or threatened to do—she'd tried to question me, in her discreet way, and I had insisted that nothing was wrong.

Going to pack a suitcase for him, this very hour. Two suitcases.

She'd called a downtown hotel, booked a room—*Oscar Allyn.*

For he *must leave tonight.* Couldn't abide the thought of sleeping under the same roof with her husband one more night.

She was excited, her hands flailed and fluttered. So resolute, I wouldn't have believed her capable. Thinking, with awe—*Lula would not be this strong.*

But having to tell her, no. I didn't think so.

Told her that I would be the one to leave, not my uncle. For this was his house. He should stay in his house.

My response astonished Irma. Whatever she'd expected from me, it had not been this.

Yes, I would leave. Better me, than Uncle Oscar.

Calmly I told her. As if it were a decision I'd come to independently of hers.

The remainder of the afternoon, Irma and I talked. So frankly, so freely we'd never spoken before.

The following week, I would be eighteen. An entire lifetime had preceded this birthday. I was not *young*, and could certainly live alone. I would live in Port Oriskany for a while, I would visit Irma often.

At first Irma did not wish to be dissuaded. She'd rehearsed the words she would say to Oscar. No more and no less. Only what he needed to know. (Not that anyone had accused him of anything. Like any guilty man Oscar wasn't likely to ask.) So long she'd contemplated the grave decision, simply to call a lawyer had required enormous courage on her part. To make up her mind as she might *make up a bed*—methodically, perfectly, all wrinkles smoothed out.

Once made, she did not wish to *unmake it*.

But then by degrees, Irma weakened. It was time for me to leave home—her home. There was nothing wrong between Uncle Oscar and me—truly.

Soon I would be leaving for college. A scholarship at St. Lawrence University, three hundred miles away.

I'd planned to work over the summer. I wanted to support myself. She and Uncle Oscar had supported me for years. Now it was time that I moved away.

Tears shone in Irma's eyes. I understood that she'd capitulated.

"Oh, Violet! You're still so young . . ."

"Mom supported herself cleaning houses when she was my age, and younger. But I guess you know that."

Irma peered quizzically at me. "Supported herself *cleaning houses?* Lula?"

"Didn't she?"

"When was this?"

"When she was sixteen . . ."

"Sixteen! I don't think so, Violet."

"But—Mom told me . . ."

"That's ridiculous! None of us were—cleaning-women, maids . . . We were not that poor."

"But—"

Irma was shaking her head, frowning as if she found the subject distasteful.

In any case the decision seemed to be made: I would leave, and Oscar would remain.

This was only right, and just: the Allyns would remain together.

Only as I was preparing to leave I felt a sudden flood of emotion for the tidy beige-brick house on Erie

Street, Port Oriskany. A longing for what I was giving up. And for my aunt Irma who hugged me tightly, wetting me with her tears.

"Violet, goodbye! I love you, honey. I will miss you so. But you are right, it is time for you to move away."

**III**

# The Scar

You've been staring at the scar on my forehead. I see you.

Not clear if it is actually a scar, or a birthmark, or some sort of exotic tattoo.

Of course, you won't *ask*. Not until we know each other better and even then you might be shy, you might hesitate, guessing that I am a moody individual, that I might *bite*.

You can touch the scar, if you wish. It is soft to the fingertips like something other than human skin. An *unborn skin,* you might think.

Very soft, fascinating. Just slightly repulsive.

Here, let me take your hand!—I know that you are curious.

Your touching the scar makes me shiver, shudder. It is very *erotic*.

Often without being aware of what I am doing, I touch the scar myself. My fingertips find their unerring way to the ultra-soft starburst tissue at my hairline, just to touch, stroke. Confirm.

*Yes. It is real. All that has happened to me is real.*

A sensation like flame rushes through me. Breasts, groin. My breath comes quickly, there is a flush to my face.

*All, all is real.*

How did it happen, you are eager to know.

A visible scar is the way to the secret scar between the female thighs with their terrible muscular power to clamp shut.

There, the secret scar for which you are yearning, I see in your eyes.

The most secret place. Fiery-moist, the deep throbbing pulse.

A man sees such a luscious scar, his first thought is—*Let me taste that with my tongue. Let me make that deeper. Let me make that bleed again.*

It is to your advantage to allow him to think—*Only I know how.*

# The Burrow

She'd never begged, I don't think so. That way of saying *Help me, will you? C'mon.*

Pursing her lips for a kiss.

So almost you'd think it was a game, you could play with Mommy just the two of you. The hell with the others, Mommy laughed so you'd know she wasn't hurt.

(Well, sometimes Miriam and Katie helped Mommy with the garden, and sometimes your brothers but mostly what you remember is Mommy and *you.*)

Spreading out sheets of newspaper on the ground so that you could kneel, as Mommy did. Weeding, pruning. Filling up a bushel basket to be dumped at the edge of the property. *Compost.* Where in a few inches of desiccated leaves and soil your brothers would one day bury the baseball bat they'd used to kill Hadrian Johnson, they hadn't taken time to thoroughly clean.

Until your arms ached, your vision blotched in bright sunshine and miniature suns and moons danced wherever you looked.

So busy with the house and kids, Lula couldn't get to the garden often enough. Hopeful in the early summer, planting seeds in methodical rows, putting in plants from the nursery, then in a few weeks weeds were choking everything, couldn't keep the soil tilled, watered. Weeds, slugs. Japanese beetles. Every God-damned summer of her life, same thing.

She wept. She cursed. Seven kids!—and the husband.

Later, the grandfather would come to live with them. Complaining, leering at her legs in shorts that should've been slacks, the *old sod* had a foul mouth and such a bastard, almost you had to laugh.

She'd laughed, mostly. Until she hadn't.

Early-morning Mom might sight a groundhog in the garden, a fat furry creature, surprisingly fast on its feet, scrambling to escape as she ran at him flailing her hands and screaming—*Get away! God damn you!*

Cries of hurt, rage, incredulity as she discovered what the groundhog had devoured that morning.

The little girl was distressed to see her mother so upset. Mommy in her garden appalled at the damage, tears streaming down her cheeks. Ravaged stalks of zinnias in bright happy colors—now just a few fallen petals on the ground. Ravaged tomato plants, just beginning to form green tomatoes round and hard as marbles. Some plants so ravaged and broken, you could not identify them.

Mommy uttering words she could not (could she?) have meant—

*Can't have anything! Not anything! Every God-damned thing I want is taken from me.*

The little girl knew to stand aside, at such times. To avoid Mommy's swerving glaring eye seizing upon her.

*And you! All of you! God damn you . . .*

Truly, the little girl would not remember such outbursts. Angry shining tears on Mommy's face, she would not remember. Years in exile seeing her own angry shining face in unexpected mirrors, sometimes in the very presence of strangers who did not and would never know her, even her name.

Staring in a kind of exaltation. *And you. All of you. God damn.*

**OK, Mom.** *Let me handle it.*

He'd laughed, it was something of a joke. Killing the groundhog appealed to Jerr, you could see.

By this time we'd tried screaming at the animal. The little girl and the mother. And sometimes Katie. And sometimes Miriam. Clapping our hands, chasing it. With clumsy vehemence Mom had run at the panicked animal with a rake, bringing the rake down, hard. Grunting, as the rake leapt from her hands even as the groundhog escaped, easily.

Running fatly, but fast. Disappearing into a burrow at the edge of the property.

Jerr had this great plan, he'd heard from somewhere: drown the garden predator in its burrow. Sure he'd rather shoot the motherfucker to smithereens with a shotgun but he didn't have a shotgun, not even a rifle, though Daddy had a rifle somewhere in the house unloaded and off-limits for his kids. Instead Jerr hooked up the longest lawn hose to a spigot at the back of the house, dragged the nuzzle to the burrow (which the little girl had pointed out to him), and turned on the water full blast as Mom watched from a little distance.

As uneasily we watched. Katie and me. We did not want to see the animal drowned but we wanted Mommy not to cry and to be happy.

At the mouth of the burrow Jerr squatted, peering into it as water rushed in. He wore a grimy baseball cap, reversed on his head. He wore a soiled black T-shirt, shorts. He was no more than thirteen or fourteen but already he resembled our father. In the boy's sharp-boned face the hard, brutal male beauty of the father. Indifference, obliviousness to the pain of others.

Water continued to gush from the hose and into the burrow, noisily. Either the water would drown the groundhog or "flush" it out so that Jerr could kill it by hitting it with a shovel—that was the plan. But after some suspenseful minutes water began to spill out of the top of the burrow, like vomit. No groundhog.

*Oh damn. God damn. It's in there—I saw it . . .*

Mom dissolved in tears. Indignant, defeated.

But one more time, another morning Jerr tried again with the hose, burrow, gushing water. And again no groundhog.

(**Neither her** brother or her mother knew: little Violet had—daringly—led Jerr to the wrong burrow.

Several burrows in the backyard which were easy to confuse. Jerr never knew the difference between them and neither, it seemed, did Mom.)

*How'd my* brother die? *A prison guard shot him.*

*It was claimed that inmates at Marcy had "rioted" and tried to take guards captive. But they were out-manned. Gunned down.*

*Thirty at the time. Well—almost thirty-one.*

*Strange to think he'd got that old—he'd been just a kid when I last saw him.*

*What was he in for?—manslaughter.*

In bars entertaining men with tales of my family. My lost life. Easy to enthrall men if they are slightly older than you are. Never do I tell them that two of my brothers were incarcerated for the murder of a black high school boy. Never do I tell them my last name. If I tell them a last name it is not Kerrigan but Allyn. But usually, I tell no one a last name and usually, no one asks.

# Valentine

Each February I send a valentine to the family of Hadrian Johnson who continue to live at 29 Howard Street, South Niagara. It is a ceremonial gesture, I suppose. The money included is never much.

*I am not a worthless person, am I? This is proof.*

No one knows. There is no one in my life to know. Nor do the Johnsons know who sends the valentine since it is signed only *Your Friend.*

However many small-denomination bills I have been able to put away in a drawer for the past twelve months, I include neatly folded inside the card for the Johnsons.

Might be thirty dollars. Might be sixty-five dollars. This year ninety-two dollars. I am looking ahead to a time when it might be a thousand dollars. Five thousand!

But that will not be for a while, I think.

It is Hadrian Johnson's mother Ethel who is listed in the South Niagara phone directory as the resident at 29 Howard Street. Probably other family members live with Mrs. Johnson, possibly the sisters who were named in the obituary, possibly one or more of the brothers. Could be a grandparent. Grandparents. Of course, I have no way of knowing. The obituary did not speak of a father.

It is Ethel Johnson I envision, as I prepare the valentine. Hadrian's mother I had seen on TV. *Why would anyone want to hurt Hadrian who was so kind to everyone? Hadrian, who loved so many people . . .*

Shut my eyes and I see Ethel Johnson's face stricken with grief. I see Hadrian Johnson's young face.

It is more of an effort to summon the faces of my brothers Jerome Jr. and Lionel than to summon these faces, of persons I'd never known. More of an effort to summon my own face that has grown hazy in memory.

Is it a futile gesture, to send money to the Johnson family? Is it foolish, vain, self-deluding? Desperate?

All these years since leaving home I've brought the obituary from the *South Niagara Union Journal* with me. I have no need to reread it for I've memorized it entirely. (Including the misspelling of Hadrian's name.) I have memorized the face of the boy Hadrian Johnson, seventeen in the photograph.

The clipping has become yellowed, torn. Though I keep it neatly folded and in an envelope.

No other newspaper clippings. Nothing to remind me of that time!

The (unmarked, plain) envelope containing the obituary, like the small-denomination bills I accumulate over twelve months, to send to Ethel Johnson, is kept in a secret place in anyplace I live for I do not want anyone to discover it.

Like all my secrets, it is not likely to be revealed.

The valentines I've sent to the Johnsons are homemade: construction paper, satiny crimson cutout hearts. Silver Magic Marker pen hand-printing *HAPPY VALENTINE'S DAY! Your Friend.* You might think that a young person, possibly even a child, has made the (oversized) valentine which is so obviously the work of an amateur. You might think *But why? Who is this? And why money?*

Mystified by the postmark which is not South Niagara.

Probably the Johnsons assume (if they assume anything at all) that the valentine has been sent by someone they know. Someone who'd lived in the neighborhood but has since moved away.

A girl who'd gone to school with Hadrian. Might've been in love with Hadrian but kept it to herself.

Black girl, surely. Not white.

The first time I sent a valentine to the Johnsons I tried to compose a note of explanation. I did not want to seem rude or mysterious sending strangers a valentine signed just *Your Friend*.

*I knew Hadrian in school. I think of him and still miss him. I am so very sorry what happened to him and I hope . . .*

Threw this away. Tried again.

*I was not in Hadrian's class at school but I saw him play basketball and . . .*

No. I had not gone to school with Hadrian Johnson, I had never seen him play basketball. I had never knowingly seen him at all.

*I did not know Hadrian but everyone who knew him admired him so much. I have prayed for your family. I hope that you and your family believed that there has been some "justice" . . .*

No. No prayer. No justice.

Giving up, then. For there are no words.

And what consolation could it be to the Johnsons, that some sort of "justice" had been done. Four (white) boys convicted of manslaughter, sent to prison. If Jerome Jr. and Lionel had been sentenced to life in prison, or executed, that would not have brought back Hadrian Johnson . . .

Guessing that the Johnsons took no pleasure in knowing that their son's murderers were sent to prison. No pleasure in learning that the elder Kerrigan boy, the one who'd (allegedly) wielded the baseball bat, was killed in prison; or that the parents of the murderers are deeply unhappy, their lives irrevocably altered.

The Johnsons are Christians, I'm sure. Unless Hadrian's death undermined their faith in God.

*Yes I did pray for Hadrian Johnson and his family and for my family too. For my brothers. At the age of twelve no longer really believing in prayer or in God listening to prayer or even in God (most of the time) guessing that God was just another adult trick to make you behave as others want you to behave.*

*If you are wondering who I am, and why I am writing—I am the sister of the Kerrigan brothers Jerome Jr. and Lionel. I am the one who told police about the baseball bat. I am the "informer"—the "rat."*

But I can never write these words. I have no way to speak in my own voice.

Since there is no return address on the envelope containing the valentine, Ethel Johnson will never write to me, to thank me. If she had an inclination to thank me.

In this way I can never feel slighted or hurt.

Or maybe Ethel Johnson would return the money if she had my address. Perceiving that it has been sent by a (white) person with a guilty conscience. *Thank you but we are not in need. Please do not write to us again.*

**As soon** as I mail the valentine to the Johnson family the air around me becomes brighter.

It is February eleventh. Bitter cold here in Watertown, on the Saint Lawrence River near the Canadian border, with a wind that brings temperatures to below zero.

No more than two days should be required for the valentine to be delivered to Howard Street, South Niagara. In time for Valentine's Day.

As usual I have been careful to affix not one, not two, but three first-class stamps to the envelope which is oversized and noticeably thick stuffed with bills.

How airy I feel! A panel seems to be opening in the bleak sky.

I am made to feel light, effervescent. The leaden sensation drains from my limbs.

I am most alive at such times. I am hopeful. My vision is almost too sharp.

I notice things that would otherwise pass in a blur of distraction—gorgeous neon-orange graffiti scrawled against a building like a hieroglyphic, black-capped birds on a wire with feathers puffed-up to twice their natural size. Above the river frothy horizontal clouds of the kind called *cirrocumulus*. The sound of wind in the trees—*soughing*.

Faces of strangers startling and beautiful.

Eyes of strangers startling and beautiful.

Other days are muffled and blurred and pass as if underwater. Must drag myself through them. Force myself to breathe.

*Keeping myself alive* is the goal. Today, I feel this is possible.

# Keeping Myself Alive

Taking money from a man. There's never exactly a first time.

For at the start, it might be (merely) a *tip*. Then, he's paying for drinks. He's paying for a meal. He's paying for tickets. He's paying for gas, or to park his vehicle. He's pressing bills into your (not unwilling) hand.

Later, he's giving you a present. This is formal. An escalation, a declaration. Watching your face as you unwrap the crinkling gilt paper a salesclerk has wrapped for him and imagining the pleasure he is providing you which becomes pleasure flowing in his veins like liquid fire.

*Oh thank you . . .*

Not just gratitude the man wants but evidence that you are surprised, startled, shaken as if he has reached inside you with his fingers.

*. . . thank you I didn't expect—this.*

Like lovemaking when he raises himself on his elbows to observe your face. Alert and jealous needing to know what you are feeling, what is happening to you, what he is causing to happen to you that is exciting to him, thrilling to him because it is he who is causing it, the male penetrating the female, the female impaled upon the male, helpless in subordination to the impassioned and driven energy of the male, extinguished, annihilated.

*. . . love love love you.*

**But also,** the client paid me for my labor. Through the Agency, I was *in his employ.*

**Here y'are,** *honey. For you.*

And—*Keep the change, honey.*

And—*Smile, honey! That's better.*

I was a university student. I could work only part-time. Usually at the minimum wage, or below.

Favoring those kinds of (unskilled) jobs that involve *tips.* Waitress, counter girl, clerk.

These were natural jobs for young females. Inevitable jobs. Not a servant but yes, servile. Sometimes, you wear a colorful uniform with an insignia embossed on your right breast. Sometimes the uniform is flattering, sometimes not-so.

Sometimes you wear a low-cut jersey top, short skirt of a shimmery fabric that barely covers your buttocks. Legs encased in dark stockings. Or, bare legs kept fastidiously shaved, gleaming-pale in the dim light of the restaurant/cocktail lounge like slow-swimming fish.

The (male) hand coming to rest at the small of the back. Or, a series of light, avuncular pats at the small of the back.

*Tips* depend upon the generosity of customers. To a degree, the sobriety of customers.

However it is true that if the customers are male, and if you can lighten their hearts with a smile, or stir their genitals, they may reward you.

*Here's for you, honey. Thaannk you!*

**What you** lose in dignity you gain in tips.

Or, what you gain in tips you lose in dignity.

**Eventually it** is suggested to you that housecleaning will pay more than waitressing. Much less interaction with the client.

It's a different category of female labor. Harder physically though not what is called unskilled. If you are signed up with a reliable agency and if you can work swiftly and yet efficiently, you won't do badly at all.

You swallow hard, considering. There would seem to be, in housecleaning, a kind of security, *home*. The clients will be known to you beforehand, not like the random customers of a restaurant or cocktail lounge. The clients will be, you want to think, guaranteed to be trustworthy

MAID BRIGADE AGENCY OF CATAMOUNT COUNTY. Their billboards of cartoon house-maids are so charming!

As a part-time university student you attend classes in the evenings. Long after the scholarship (of which you'd been so proud: hoping your parents would take notice) has ceased since you'd transferred to another university.

(And why did you transfer from St. Lawrence University?—surely not to sabotage your own university career?)

(Seeing too many familiar faces at St. Lawrence. Shrinking from their startled smiles, stares. Abruptly one day unable to remain *in the place where you are* but desperate to leave, to move, to begin again, *in the place where you are not-known.*)

In this way swaths of time have been lost to you. Semesters begun, abruptly ceased. Months when you could not bring yourself to re-enroll at any university. Minimum-wage jobs, or no job at all.

But now, another university: Catamount Falls. Another chance.

Hope like a helium-filled balloon drifting.

An urban campus bounded by tall pines to the north, to the south the *thrum* of the Thruway. Where you've (tentatively) felt at home. Knowing the particular melancholy of dusk on such a campus, as day students depart and evening students begin to arrive. As incandescent lights come on.

*Here we are! We belong here, too.*

You have surrendered the possibility of being a full-time student. It is likely that you deserve a lowered status, more in keeping with that of an incarcerated person awaiting parole.

This university schedule leaves weekday mornings and much of the afternoons free for (manual) work. You sign up at the Agency for work when you can get it, hoping for work at least once or twice a week.

Because you are new, and inexperienced at housework, and exude an air of plaintive desperation inadequately masked by a brave stoic smile, the Agency will pay you *off the books, in cash* and not by check, as they pay most of their staff. In this way the Agency is not required to deduct taxes from your wages and aren't required to pay you benefits if you get sick or are injured.

It's true, Maid Brigade does have a reputation for exploiting its workers. But not so badly as other local cleaning services.

You are hopeful, reckless. You are stronger than you appear, a girl who never complains, fit for the rigors of housecleaning that will pay better than your other shitty jobs and will not require smiling until your face aches.

Thinking—*If Mom finds out, what will she think?*

Thinking—*Will Mom understand why I am doing this, or will she be ashamed and hate me more?*

# Off the Books

The client was a "doctor"—that is, his name was prefixed by *Dr.*

The client had money, clearly. Divorced, living alone in a high-rise condominium building overlooking the Saint Lawrence River. A reputation for good tips but a short temper, high expectations, don't "engage" with this client you will regret it.

Most of the Agency's clients were women. Wives of well-to-do husbands, in large homes. You did not "engage" with them either if you could avoid it. If you were wise. Often, these clients did not tip. They paid (by check) through the Agency which would then pass on to the worker a small *gratuity*.

Except, I was a new hire. A part-time hire. Not full-time. No benefits. No weekly checks. *Off the books.*

---

**Goes without** saying, OK. But Ava Schultz at Maid Brigade will say it, frank, blunt, no-bullshit which is what people love about brass-blond Ava with studs in eyebrows, nostril and the husky upper arms of a woman who has put in time as a house-cleaner herself.

*Don't fuck with the client, see? Like stealing some dinky thing you think they won't miss because they will miss it.*

*And don't fuck the client. Period.*

**His name** was Orlando Metti. We were to call him Dr. Metti.

I'd been cleaning houses for just two weeks and I was still learning. Still undecided if I wanted to clean other people's houses. If I was that desperate for money. Willing to stoop, to kneel. Willing to scour away other people's grime, filth, shit. Willing to grovel for *tips.* This afternoon I'd been paired with a middle-aged Guatemalan woman named Felice who'd been cleaning for the client for several years. When we arrived at Metti's apartment on the seventeenth floor of a dazzling high-rise building overlooking the Saint Lawrence River Felice murmured to me, "We take off our shoes now, please. When we go in."

Take off our shoes! I hadn't been forewarned. Fortunately I was wearing gray woolen hiking socks without obvious holes, that would keep my feet reasonably warm through the hours of our labor.

**The man** *is a perfectionist. Do not rush through the cleaning, he will complain to the agency. The master bed especially—be very careful making the master bed. Kitchen, bathroom, sinks, tub and shower—be sure that they are shining. Otherwise he will refuse to pay the full fee. He will request that you never return.*

Yet to us, Orlando Metti was surprisingly polite. That afternoon. For we had worked very hard. For we had spent a good deal of time removing, with varying degrees of success, dog-urine stains, and worse, from carpets scattered about the eight-room apartment, made by the client's daughter's little French bulldog, kept temporarily on the premises while the daughter was at college.

Soap and water, bleach. Doggy-Out! in an aerosol spray.

Indeed, the client was polite, almost apologetic.

Assuring us that the "damned little dog" would not be in the apartment much longer, if he could help it.

Metti had been absent for most of the time we were cleaning but returned in time to inspect the premises, as Felice had told me he would do. I held my breath as he checked the interior of the refrigerator, one of the tedious tasks Felice had assigned me.

Held my breath as the (elegantly groomed) client ran his finger along a stretch of counter behind a microwave oven which one might not have thought of cleaning since it was out of sight, out of mind.

A few minor items needed re-checking, re-cleaning of which only one was within my province, the others Felice's.

But Dr. Metti didn't seem grievously annoyed by these minor mistakes only pointed them out with a grimace somewhere between a smile and a sneer as if saying *Gotcha, girls!*

Then, with the dignified magnanimity of the patriarch, though scarcely glancing at us, Dr. Metti declared *Good work, girls!* and pressed bills into our hands as we left the apartment.

Twenty dollars. Was this a generous tip?—it seemed so, to me. For there would be another, second *gratuity* from the Agency included with our payment for the week.

In the glass elevator soundlessly descending to the

ground floor, a fluid vertical slide that made me feel faint, the very smoothness of it, the silence of the descent, a luxury we somehow didn't deserve but were receiving, a bonus, like another tip—(for Felice and I were a brute sort of proletariat labor, there was less romance in housecleaning than in, even, waitressing)—Felice folded her twenty-dollar bill carefully and put it in her handbag. Her face was tired, drawn, petulant. Her thin-penciled eyebrows frowned. Her lips were pursed tight. She'd been friendly with me previously. She'd been patient giving me instructions, advice. But now when I tried to speak to her Felice frowned and shrugged and turned away.

Felice was a bosomy woman, with an air of careworn glamour, barely five feet tall. Awkwardly I towered over her. Somehow this made her rebuff all the more shocking.

Later I would discover from another girl at the Agency that Felice bitterly resented it, that the client had given me the identical tip he'd given her. Though I was only assisting her, and was much younger than she was, and Felice had been cleaning for this particular client for years.

*There was something between them, maybe. No one knows for sure.*

*Felice would never say. But maybe—that was it.*

---

**The following** Thursday, I was instructed by Ava to arrive at Metti's apartment at 1:00 P.M. sharp. I would be cleaning the apartment alone.

But what about Felice? I asked in a panic.

The client has insisted, he wants just one maid. He will pay the full fee as if there were two. He said—*Just the girl next time. Not the other.*

**Please** was a word this client often uttered. *Please* was so pleasant a sound in Metti's deep-modulated voice, you did not (immediately) register it as a command.

*Have you a few extra minutes, please?*

Or—*Do you have time to do an errand for me? Please.*

Soon it became routine. If Dr. Metti returned before I'd finished cleaning the apartment he would ask me to do something extra on my way home, a "personal errand"—a "favor."

Would I *please?*

Seeing my hesitation (for I had a class at the university that evening) quickly adding that he would pay me extra. Of course.

*Directly to you—is it Vivian?—Violet? Not to the cleaning service. Cash in hand.*

A shivery sensation, the possibility of *cash in hand.*

That's to say, from Metti's (warm) hand to mine.

Exhausted from several hours of housecleaning nonetheless I smiled at the client. Taking care that my shoulders not slouch and hoping that I did not look as disheveled as I felt.

Had to smile—I suppose: no matter that I'd explained to Metti that I had a class in the evening he seemed never to recall from one week to the next. As if the cleaning-girl in his employ existed only when Metti was conscious of her and ceased existing otherwise.

For I understood how easily Metti could fire me. All it would require would be a telephone call to the Agency and I would never see him again, as Felice was never to see him again.

(Poor Felice! When we encountered each other at Maid Brigade she stared at me in contempt. Her indignation was such, the hurt brimming in her eyes so intense, I had to turn away, shamed.)

Few other clients tipped so generously as Dr. Metti, it seemed. Few were as attractive as Dr. Metti.

So I said *OK, yes.* Whatever additional tasks Metti wanted from me did not seem like such a burden.

Agreeing was in fact a kind of pleasure. Smile smile for the attractive (male) (unmarried) client who seemed barely to glance at me but who tipped more generously than anyone in my experience.

I had not surrendered my dignity. I didn't think so. Metti had not laid a hand on me—had not come close.

As an animal—to avoid punishment, to assure nourishment and approval—can learn to behave contrary to its nature, and convincingly, I smiled at Orlando Metti. And I smiled.

**Saving what** I could of the money I'd earned *off the books* to send to the family of Hadrian Johnson that would be, in the end, after months of housecleaning, nearly one thousand dollars.

No one in my life to ask me—*But why? It will not bring him back, will it?*

# Rat, Waiting

It was a time when I'd begun to wait more explicitly.

With more clarity, apprehension: as the term of Lionel's incarceration began to wind down.

For it seemed to me, I was serving Lionel's sentence too.

Seven to thirteen years, and there'd been the expectation at the time of sentencing that of course Lionel would be paroled. *Good behavior. No infractions of rules. Support of prison chaplain. High school equivalency diploma.*

Yet, it did not happen. As the years passed, no parole.

Why, wasn't clear. Decisions of the Mid-State Correctional Facility for Men at Marcy were classified. No explanation.

I'd given up writing to Lionel. No more cards, terse cheery sisterly notes flung into an abyss deep as the Grand Canyon.

Before I'd left Port Oriskany Ms. Herne had advised me to maintain contact with the parole board at Marcy. *Just so that you are warned, Violet. If your family fails to tell you.*

Hadn't wanted to ask Aunt Irma if my parents blamed me for the fact that Lionel hadn't been (yet) paroled.

(Tactlessly, not meaning to be cruel, Irma did reveal to me that my parents blamed me for my oldest brother's death. Of course, this would make sense to them: Jerr wouldn't have been incarcerated, wouldn't have been killed by a guard in the prison, if the *rat-sister* had not sent him there.)

Jerr hadn't even come up for parole. He'd been in trouble at Marcy from the start: targeted by the Aryan Nation as one of their own and grateful to be accepted in a prison facility with so many black prisoners. Lionel was serving his sentence differently, in a different area of the prison in which gangs were not so powerful. Yet each of Lionel's requests for parole were turned down and it was looking as if Lionel would "max out"—serve his full, thirteen-year sentence.

I had nothing to do with the parole hearings. I wondered if relatives believed that I had and were spreading upsetting rumors. The parole board did not call me to speak to them on or against my brother's behalf, and I did not volunteer.

My terror at what Lionel might do to me when he was released had not vanished nor even faded but floated in the shadows at the edge of my vision, I dared not turn my head too quickly and risk seeing it. Still, I would not interfere in his parole hearings.

Would not beg the parole board—*Don't let Lionel Kerrigan out! He will come to murder me.*

Though surely it would be known by the Marcy parole board that my brother had threatened me at the time of his arrest. That he'd "assaulted" me. Had to be in his computer file. Cross-referenced in the Niagara County Children's Protective Services reports, in Ms. Dolores Herne's social worker's reports. Nothing could dislodge or delete those files. Dating back to 1991, they could not be modified or expunged. Certainly it was known that I'd been removed from my parents' house, to protect me from my brother. At the time a murder suspect.

When Lionel is released I will be twenty-six years old. That is much older than twelve, and yet I feel that my life stopped at the age of twelve. I was as *young,* and as *old,* as I would ever be.

Lionel will be just thirty. Jerr's age when he was killed.

Will thirty seem *young,* to Lionel? I have no idea what he looks like now for I can imagine my brother only as he'd been at sixteen.

I am not so sure that the prison will notify me when Lionel is finally released, as the parole board might have notified me. The prison doesn't have my most recent address for I'd moved numerous times since. The telephone number I'd provided them no longer exists.

*Don't want to know. Better not to know.*

*Take your chances . . .*

Ms. Herne has no way of reaching me, if indeed Ms. Herne even remembers me. In fact, I am sure that Ms. Herne does not remember me. I am sure that my folder in her files has been marked CLOSED. I am far from a vulnerable child now.

Possibly, Ms. Herne is retired by now. Turnip Face. I blamed her, for what exactly I don't know. Turning my brothers against me. Never letting me see my family again . . .

Out of contact with so many persons who might

have helped me. If my life as a rat ever ends I will look back upon these years in the way you would look back upon a fever-dream in which the dreamer is in a continuous state of pursuit, desperation.

*Serving my term. No parole!*

# Sorrowful Virgin

*M*  *aybe he will see me, soon. Acknowledge me.*
    *That is all that I want: to be seen by him.*

**Wanting to** please the man who was not readily pleased. Wanting not to disappoint the man who was frequently disappointed.

For more than once when I was cleaning his apartment I'd overheard Orlando Metti on the telephone speaking harshly to someone at the other end who'd been presumably silenced, abashed by the man's speech precise and cruel as rapid face-slaps with the palm of a hand.

Someone female, I had to assume. Ex-wife, or another woman. Fluttering moth-wings, broken.

But to me, Metti was courteous. What pride I took in this!

Gentlemanly, soft-spoken. Expressing (mostly) satisfaction with the work I'd done. Pressing *tips* into my hand.

It was a matter of anxiety to me, standing only a few inches away from my well-groomed employer, that possibly/probably I smelled of my body after hours of dragging a vacuum cleaner through the apartment, stooping to scour tub, shower stalls, toilet bowls, tile floors. Cleaning, polishing, buffing fixtures until they gleamed with manic and pointless intensity as I'd been instructed.

Sweated through the thin white T-shirt, you could see the shadowy outlines of my breasts, nipples. If you wished to look.

My forehead was damp, oily. The little star-shaped scar at my hairline throbbed with heat.

Out of shyness/cageyness I did not exactly look Orlando Metti in the face. My wistful glances at the man were sidelong, covert. It had become my way to register the world in quick sidelong glances hoping that the world would do no more than glance at me in turn.

Metti was amused by me, it seemed. The little star-shaped scar intrigued him but (of course) (as it intrigued many men) he was too polite to inquire about something so personal.

"Would you like a drink, Violet?"

So unexpected a question, I thought at first that it might be a joke. A test? Heard myself stammer *No*.

Standing very still, smiling inanely.

At Maid Brigade we'd been warned of certain of our (male) customers but no one had named Orlando Metti as a threat.

"Are you sure? Wine spritzer, vodka soda?"

The damp T-shirt was sticking to my skin. Damp hair straggling down my neck, hot-tingling scar on my forehead. Determined not to scratch the scar with my fingernails and inflame it.

"I guess—not. But thank you, Dr. Metti."

"Next time then?"

"I—I don't know . . ."

Metti laughed at my stammering reply as if I'd meant to be amusing.

Now staring more frankly at my forehead—the scar that felt so livid, alive. Wondering if indeed it was a scar, or a birthmark. Tattoo?

*Would you like to tongue it? Kiss it? Suck it?*

Feeling dizzy, as Orlando Metti smiled at me.

"Y'know, Violet—you could take a shower here. I mean—if you wished. Before leaving."

Another unexpected remark I could not answer. My face pounded hotly with blood.

Metti laughed again, and relented: "All right, Violet. Don't look so alarmed. We'll plan for some future time. What I'd like you to do now is—"

Drop off clothes at the nearby dry cleaner. Drop off a prescription at the nearby drugstore. Or, take the dog for a quick walk, he hadn't the time or patience for his daughter's damned dog today.

*He meant to insult me. Allowing me to know he could smell my body.*

*He meant to excite me. Allowing me to know he could smell my body.*

**The Game.** Following this Metti would leave money scattered about the apartment for me to discover. And small expensive items—jade cuff links, coins from foreign countries, figurines of crystal or mineral, so small they could easily be slipped into a pocket.

One- and five-dollar bills. Half-dollars, quarters, dimes and nickels in unexpected places like drawers used to store towels, linens.

*Are you tempted, Violet? Go right ahead, dear. Help yourself.*

*Plenty where this comes from!*

And when I'd become accustomed to discovering bills of small denominations, which I always left where I found them, there was a twenty-dollar bill made to look as if it had casually fallen between a bedside table and a bed—and here, on the floor of a closet, amid shoes, a fifty.

A fifty! This was serious money, to me.

Of course, I was not tempted. I would never steal from Dr. Metti even with his tacit permission. But the game excited me.

For the nature of a game is uncertainty. How will it *end?*

And who will be *winner?*

A treasure hunt, it was. Except nothing would be moved far from its place of discovery, so that Metti could have no reason to think that it might be missing.

The bills, I would leave in plain view, on a tabletop. Which is where a cleaning-woman would naturally leave something she'd found on the floor in a room.

Articles of clothing to be put in the laundry, with pockets—frequently there would be coins in these pockets, even folded bills. (Since all clients leave items in pockets, I could not determine if this was part of Dr. Metti's game, or accidental.) Felice had instructed me: check all pockets before putting clothes in the laundry, place items you find in a small basket in the laundry room where the client is sure to see them.

But the bills and other items scattered through the apartment had not been there when Felice and I had cleaned it together.

*This is new. This is for my sake. But—no.*

By this time I had cleaned for other clients at the Agency, uneventfully—all women. No games. No one remotely like Orlando Metti.

**Working alone** in the apartment I became apprehensive, anxious—waiting for the client's key in the lock. Waiting for him to return.

Obsessively shutting off the vacuum cleaner so that I could hear more clearly if he was at the door—but no. Not yet.

I'd learned: Metti had been divorced eighteen months before. In the rooms of the apartment there were no visible reminders of a past: no photographs of a family.

No wedding pictures, family pictures, baby pictures. Not even pictures of Metti at a younger age. Works of art, framed, under glass, prints and lithographs by artists of whom I'd vaguely heard, on the walls, tastefully neutral colors, abstract designs. A row of framed

Modigliani prints, ethereally thin nudes, young girls with beautiful mask-faces, small sculpted breasts. That was all: nothing personal. As if the man had divorced not just a wife but also an entire shared past.

Wistfully I thought—*That is the way.*

*The only way of salvation.*

Digging out weeds. Yanking out weeds. Toss onto the compost, into a bushel basket.

Recalling from my mother's garden how quickly even the sturdiest weeds would go limp, begin to die.

This was heartlessness, and heartlessness meant survival. Extirpate the past like weeds.

Metti wasn't a medical doctor, I'd learned. Instead, an administrator at the Saint Lawrence Biomedical Institute, a research center. His degree was not an M.D. but a Ph.D. How rich was the man? I wondered. Not knowing what *rich* might mean, exactly.

Forty-three years old. At least six feet two or three. Towering over me as I'd towered over Felice. Or so it seemed.

And there was comfort in this, the man's height. As there was comfort in the man's confident manner, the modulation of his voice, the very dark eyes, the air of restraint and reticence where another man, in such close quarters with a lone young female, might have exuded an air of sexual aggression.

Beautiful clothes he wore. Closets of clothes. Shirts of fine cotton or linen, in pale, pastel colors, with thin stripes. Trousers with a precise crease. Sports coats of soft wool flannel, rich tweeds. (There were several suits in Metti's closets. But I would never see Orlando Metti in a suit.) Handsome leather shoes, black. Always kept polished to perfection.

He'd asked me to polish these shoes, once or twice. *See if you can remove the scuff. Thanks!* The elegant shirts that required ironing were done at the dry cleaner's and not entrusted to a cleaning-woman.

Sometimes he asked me, would I pick up these shirts? An errand that wouldn't take more than a half hour. Usually.

And sometimes he asked me, could I run out to the drugstore and pick up a prescription refill and while I was there, in the store, could I buy a few small items for him?—*Thanks so much.*

A terrible sick rage stirred in me, for the individual who lived in this lavish apartment. Who owned such elegant clothing, and who took advantage of his employee's wish to please him. His employee's need to survive.

*Your mother oughtn't to have let you.* This voice, I could not recognize. It was not an accusation, I wanted to think.

---

**Falling in** love with an employer. You have to be very naive, foolish, or stupid. Or desperate.

**Housework is** grim work. Housework is solitary work. You are made to toil in the service of another's house. You are made to inhabit the interior of another's life. You are made to experience an unnatural and one-sided intimacy.

Hairs in drains, stains in toilets and on sheets, indefinable smells that make you gag. Clothes, underwear carelessly flung down for someone else to pick up. Disheveled beds, soiled towels. A spillage of shoes underfoot, no matter if they are expensive leather shoes—too much intimacy.

The scummy condition of his safety razor. Broken, yellowed bristles of old toothbrushes, for what unfathomable reason saved beneath a bathroom sink.

Dishes encrusted with food, soaking in gray water in the kitchen sink. In the dishwasher, more dishes, glasses, silverware encrusted with food which I would have to chip away with a knife, scrub off with steel wool, before they could be properly washed in the machine.

Scattered through the rooms of the apartment were dirtied glasses. In some of these, remnants of alcohol that smelled sharply. Whiskey glasses, wineglasses.

Beer glasses. Occasionally, those delicate glasses I'd learned were for champagne.

Felice had taught me: start the laundry as soon as you can. Strip the beds, gather the towels, haul the soiled-laundry baskets into the laundry room and start the machine. The time you spend housecleaning should approximate the time required to do the client's laundry for you may have to do more than one load and you must make sure that the clothes are sufficiently dry before you leave. Especially, you must not—ever—put away damp things, for the client will discover them and be unhappy.

Wash, dry, sort, fold, put away. Repeat.

Felice had taught me: never leave a room until you've checked it thoroughly, all the corners, ceiling, floor, and beneath furniture especially beds where filth can gather. Then, check it a second time.

Still, Dr. Metti had not valued Felice, much. She'd assumed a good relationship with the (single, male) client who tipped more generously than other clients but he'd dropped her, the more experienced house-cleaner, with a single curt call to the Agency.

*Just the girl. Not the other.*

When Ava informed me I'd felt a sensation of panic. But then, later, satisfaction. For I'd been preferred, unfairly.

Fact is: one day I would be Felice. And another young girl, not beautiful but young, with that expression of naive curiosity, wonder, sexual possibility in her face would supplant me.

*You know I want to fuck you, dear. Is it—Violet?*

I knew this. But, I did not wish to know this.

Thinking of how my mother, as a girl, cleaning houses on Highgate Avenue, had been approached by her employers. Some of her employers.

For all that I knew, my young mother had allowed these strangers to exploit her. She may have clipped the old man's gnarly toenails, she may have massaged the old man's flaccid body. Certainly she'd have said *yes* if he'd asked her to do extra work for him without the cleaning service being any the wiser. *Off the books.*

Thinking these things. Dragging the vacuum cleaner from room to room while in another part of the apartment the lonely little French bulldog was barking. *Here I am! Feed me! Free me! Love me!*

Each Thursday the forlorn sound of the little dog barking tore at my heart. Yet I could not allow Brindle to run free as I worked, he would cause too much commotion. Nor did Metti allow him in most of the rooms for he had a mischievous habit of dribbling urine.

The little bulldog was someone else's responsibility, not mine. I wanted to think so.

When at last I opened the door to the sparely furnished, carpetless small room in which he was kept Brindle blinked at me in astonishment as if for a magical moment he'd convinced himself that I was not a stranger but his beloved mistress, who seemed to have abandoned him; then the frantic barking began again. I was hurt that Brindle didn't seem to recognize me from the previous week. Or wouldn't forgive me for being the wrong person.

Each week, I had to win the little dog's trust another time. Each week, the little dog's tremulous affection, that seemed scarcely distinguishable from terror.

How strange, this breed of dog! A miniature bulldog, scarcely as large as a cat, with a very short, compressed face, bizarrely flattened pug nose, enormous wide-set shining eyes that bulged in their sockets. Deep-chested, short-legged, dwarfish. His coat was stiff-haired, brown mingled with white. Yet there was something elegant about the dog, so unlike the coarse-haired mongrels of my childhood who were free to roam the neighborhood and were never "walked" on leashes.

You had to laugh at Brindle, he took himself so seriously. No idea of his small size though when he tried to run, he sometimes tripped and fell. To me he displayed bared teeth, raised hackles. Panting, and growling deep in his throat. Sharp toenails that clattered against the hardwood floor as he slid and skidded about trying to gain traction and rush at my legs. I wondered—was this miniature animal going to attack me? Bite *me?* Hadn't I been the one to take him on a walk the previous week when the master hadn't had time for him?

"Brindle, no. I am your *friend.*"

He'd overturned his water bowl. He'd devoured all his dry food. A puddle on the tile floor—urine. Quickly I cleaned up the puddle, mopped and cleaned the floor before Metti arrived and was furious.

Bleach, Dutch cleanser. Windex. Doggy-Out! Paper towels. With rubber-gloved hands fending off Brindle feinting and rushing at me.

Felice had been frightened of the little bulldog, taking him at his own self-assessment. She'd complained of having to clean up after a dog though (it seemed to me) this was hardly the dog's fault, that he was so neglected; Brindle had no choice other than to make messes indoors, and wherever he could in the apartment when he was able to run freely barking and knocking things over with the joy of abandon. Felice had told me that Brindle belonged jointly to Metti's ex-wife and their daughter, and that the daughter was away at college in another state and couldn't bring

Brindle with her; the ex-wife was living somewhere not far away but in another city, unable or unwilling to take on the responsibility of the *damned little dog*.

I could not decide if the deep-chested bulldog, with his short legs, and ridiculous mashed-in face, was ugly or in his eccentric way beautiful. It seemed sad to me that he was so lonely for companionship. Ravenous for food and for affection. Dutifully I fed him, and replenished the water bowl, that had become scummy since last Thursday and would have to be scrubbed clean. With a tissue I tried to wipe away mucus that had gathered in his eyes but he shied away from me with a little whimper as if I'd hurt him. Badly the room reeked of dog, I dreaded Dr. Metti reacting in disgust and blaming me.

Last time he'd said, reprovingly—*This place needs airing out. Please.*

A previous time he'd said—*Not all the stains are out of that rug in the foyer. Try again. Please.*

I wondered if anyone had spoken to Brindle with affection since the previous Thursday. Or had spoken to Brindle at all.

After he'd eaten, and sloppily lapped up water, Brindle reconsidered me and decided that I was his friend. His stubby little tail whipped back and forth. His hindquarters quivered. My heart was suffused with an exasperated sort of affection for the *damned little dog.*

But exertion caused Brindle to pant, wheeze. I knew that miniature bulldogs are prone to respiratory ailments. Their joints become arthritic as they age, they are susceptible to many health problems. The compact little creatures are bred for display, not for survival. Not for their own sake but to flatter an owner's vanity.

Brindle had lulled me into petting him, and speaking to him, and not watching the opened door behind me; he managed to dart past me, out into the hallway skidding on his toenails, and into the living room where I dreaded he would leak urine in his excitable state, onto the newly shampooed soft-beautiful-beige-woolen carpet from Ecuador . . .

"Oh, Brindle. Oh *no.*"

I wondered if the little French bulldog was the punishment the former Mrs. Metti and the daughter were inflicting upon Metti for his having expelled them from his life.

By the time I finished re-cleaning the carpet, and putting away most of the laundry, and dragging the vacuum cleaner back into its storage closet, there came a sound of a key in a door—the door opening at last. Metti had returned.

A shock of anticipation ran through me. Like Brindle, in an instant I was alerted to the arrival of the master.

Hesitantly Brindle trotted toward Metti. His hindquarters were quivering. His tail moved hesitantly. He was eager to greet the master yet fearful of the master. I didn't want to think that the master sometimes "disciplined" him—struck him or gave him a kick.

"Ah. You're still here, Violet—is it? Violet."

Metti greeted me courteously. I saw his eyes moving on me more readily than in the past, when he'd scarcely noticed me at all.

With an effort, Metti greeted the little dog. Laughed at the dog's antics. Damned if he'd acknowledge how irritated he was with the dog, in my presence. Like a parent with a disfigured and obstreperous child, wishing to be rid of it but not when others were observing.

I was feeling very warm. Metti's gaze made me uneasy. Through a roaring in my ears I could barely concentrate on what he was saying. The gist of it was, could I *spare a few minutes* to do a favor for him, by taking Brindle for a quick walk?—"I will pay you of course."

It was gratifying to feel that Metti had come to depend upon me in such ways; yet, it made me anxious that I had already spent so much of the afternoon cleaning the apartment, and dealing with the little dog, I hadn't had time to complete the reading assignment for that evening's class. Also, during the housecleaning it had come upon me with a small thrill of horror that I had yet to prepare a one-page, single-spaced critique of the assignment, to be handed in that evening.

But I had to say *yes*. I could not say *no* to the man who smiled at me so warmly, and who had secreted bills and little treasures for me in his apartment, as a game; or as a suggestion of what I might claim, if I wished.

When I returned from walking Brindle in the light-falling snow Metti greeted me at the door and took the dog's leash from me. He thanked me profusely, and asked me another time if I would like a drink before leaving; but now I did tell him *no*, for really I had to leave. My pulse was quickened, snowflakes were melting in my hair. I could not raise my eyes to Metti's face for I wondered if I seemed beautiful to him, in that instant.

"Tell you what, Violet. Stay, have a drink, and I'll drive you home. Or—to the university? D'you have a class tonight? I think you said."

Metti was breathing audibly as if he'd been running. He did not step toward me. Yet, I would recall that he'd stepped toward me.

Quickly I told him *No thank you.* Suddenly eager to escape.

Not even noticing, until I stepped dazedly out of the elevator on the ground floor, that the bill Orlando Metti had pressed into my hand at the door was a fifty-dollar bill.

**I'd considered** informing the Agency that I didn't want to return to Dr. Metti's apartment. *And why? Has the client harassed you?*

No. No!

*If you won't fuck me, you're done. We'll give it another week or two. Understand? Sure you do, you're not stupid.*

**Jerr says,** OK, let me fix it.

Squatting beside my bicycle. Frowning at the jammed chain.

I'd been riding my bike in the street when something happened to make the wheels lock, I'd fallen tangled with the bike, shuddering with pain as my right leg was dragged against the pavement so that my jeans tore at the knee, a bright burst of blood seeped through the fabric.

Blue Schwinn bike with balloon tires, already an old, discontinued model when Daddy brought it home for me, a trade for carpentry work he'd done for a friend. I'd been ten years old, totally thrilled.

Falling from the bike on Black Rock Street within sight of the house but there'd been no one to hear my cries, I'd had to drag myself home limping and bleeding.

And now, Jerr is repairing the bike for me. For in my dreams of my brothers, Jerr is alive. He and Lionel are just boys. When they'd liked Violet Rue, or anyway had tolerated Violet Rue, as the youngest sister who adored them.

The time before I'd learned to fear them. Before they'd learned to despise me.

**Shame. The** ex-wife who calls Metti too often, leaves (drunken?) rambling messages on his answering machine which I am tempted to erase out of shame for a woman so abased, abandoned.

*Never! I would never.*

*Absolutely never beg.*

*Not me!*

———————

*Evidence.* **In** each of the (three) bathrooms, in the sinks, on the tile floors, in shower drains there have been strands of hair conspicuously longer, different in color from Orlando Metti's hair which is dark, gray-streaked.

In a bureau drawer in his bedroom, a silky black nightgown—smelling of faint, fragrant perspiration.

Yes, I'd pressed the nightgown against my face. Yes, my eyes had closed in a swoon of angry rapture.

On a bathroom counter, a half-empty tube of maroon lipstick.

On a shelf in the shower, an unfamiliar brand of hair conditioner.

On a bedside table, a jar of what appeared to be face cream or moisturizer, a French brand—*Yves Rocher.* So rich and buttery, I am tempted to rub some of it on my face.

Quickly removing the rubber gloves from my hands, that stuck to my fingers. Always, the gloves felt moist, even wet inside. I thought there had to be a tiny pinprick in the rubber but I haven't been able to locate it. Hated the feel of the gloves and wished never to have to wear them again.

It was rare that I paused to examine anything in a client's house. The women whose houses I cleaned had little that appealed to me—clothes, jewelry, cosmetics, husbands. *Possessions.*

I wasn't jealous/envious of their lives. In thrall to the husband, or rather to the idea of the husband of years before now fading, vanished.

Recalling my mother's stricken face when Daddy stared at her coldly, insulted her. *Look. You were the one who got pregnant, not me. You were the one who wanted children.*

Sure he'd loved her. This was the voice of love. Sometimes meant to hurt, and sometimes just for laughs. For other men, husbands of other wives, could be counted upon to laugh heartily.

In the bathroom mirror the face was a wan hopeful girl's face. Not a bad-looking face, I thought.

The scar at my hairline might've been a birthmark. Or a clever little rose tattoo. More than once I'd seen Metti glance at it and his glance linger. An exquisite sensation, to imagine the man pressing his mouth against it.

Also, I'd changed the color of my hair since the previous Thursday.

Metti had seen my hair as brown. If he'd noticed at all. Now it was glossy-jet-black, with "russet-red" highlights. Shorter, with bangs that fell to my eyebrows.

Changing the color of my hair at intervals. Though I knew that no one was stalking me still it seemed prudent to take measures to prevent someone from stalking me.

And the maroon lipstick, that smelled like overripe grapes.

I wasn't so shy when I was alone. People who believed they knew me would've been astonished to see how brazenly I rubbed the fragrant French cream onto my face, neck, hands.

Telling myself no one would know. Whoever owned the cream had left it behind. If she did return, she wouldn't ask Metti what had become of it. Or, she'd have forgotten it herself. Or, Metti would never bring her back.

Maybe he tired of them, quickly. That was the male prerogative.

More than one woman. I was sure, examining the evidence.

Thrilling to me, that my employer was cruel to women. Adult women.

In years I was an adult woman—twenty-five years, seven months. But so slender, lean-hipped, with small breasts and a flat belly, at a little distance you might have mistaken me for an adolescent boy, in T-shirt and jeans.

Not unlike the Modigliani nudes on the living room wall. So it had occurred to me.

*Just the girl. Not the other.*

Indeed I was smelling of my body. For I'd been working very hard. Determined to do a good job for Orlando Metti, to earn the generous tips he gave. To please the man, to avoid a look of displeasure, disappointment in his face.

Should I take a shower?—would that please him? I would clean up after myself, if I did.

The idea was thrilling. I could hardly breathe, considering. But had not Dr. Metti invited me to take a shower in his apartment? Smiling at me, enjoying my discomfort. Taking care to call me by my name— *Violet.* To prove he hadn't forgotten my name.

How many girls, women whose names the man had forgotten. Shaken off like something on a gleaming leather shoe.

Quickly then, before I could change my mind, I stripped off my clothes—T-shirt, flannel shirt, jeans, underwear. Gray woolen socks. Rare for me to glance at myself in the mirror for I did not like to be reminded of who I was but I saw now that my small hard breasts had oddly large, soft-looking nipples, a pale brown, like freckles. There was a shadow at my belly, a kind of cleft. A swath of downy pubic hair. The pallor of my skin suggested illness or malnutrition but it was the winter pallor of the Irish, the Kerrigans.

In a bathroom drawer I found a shower cap, saw with interest that there were several blond hairs stuck to it, which I shook out. One of Metti's women.

How many, I could not guess. Perhaps two or three. Or more. I had not once encountered any woman in the apartment, leaving or arriving. Yet there'd been the evidence of soiled sheets. Mucus stains, lipstick stains. Though I stripped the king-sized bed in Metti's bedroom as quickly as I could, not wanting to see anything, half-shutting my eyes that I would be spared seeing anything, yet it was my sense that yes, Metti's bed was often slept-in by more than one person, and for all that I knew, Metti had changed the bedsheets himself during the week, or one of the women had changed the bedsheets replacing soiled sheets with clean sheets out of a sense of delicacy, decorum.

Languorously I stood beneath Metti's elegant nickel-plated showerhead, slowly I soaped my body, and let hot water stream down my torso, belly, legs. Even before I shut off the shower, and rubbed myself dry in an enormous soft towel, I began to feel sleepy.

Removed the shower cap, fluffed out the glossy-black hair. Still there was maroon lipstick on my mouth, smudged. The buttery-rich cream had worn off in the shower and so I applied more to my face, flushed now from the heat of the shower.

Made my way barefoot, wrapped in the towel, to the room where Metti kept his liquor. Had not Metti invited me to join him in a drink, more than once? Of course I'd always declined. But now, brazenly I went to the liquor cabinet and poured an inch or two of whiskey into a glass.

It was an experiment: observing myself. Smiling at Metti as he handed it to me. *Thank you, Dr. Metti!*

In small cautious swallows I consumed the whiskey. When men bought me drinks I did not always drink them but found ways to dispose of them. But when I did drink, I became sleepy. And now, I was very sleepy.

I intended to dress quickly, and to complete the housecleaning. If Metti was to return home before I left, he would return in about forty minutes; he'd already left a tip for me on a table in the foyer, a sign that he might not be returning.

I had not yet taken the tip. That would be my reward, when I completed my housecleaning.

In Metti's bedroom the bright sunshine of an hour before, that had spilled through the tall windows, had become muted, bleak. The king-sized bed was awkward to make, requiring a fitted bottom sheet. As soon as I'd arrived to do the cleaning that afternoon I'd stripped the bed to throw the sheets into the laundry and in the interval I'd begun to make the bed with fresh sheets. You do not want to use the same sheets each week. Nor hang the same towels in the bathroom each week. In the midst of making the bed I'd become diverted by the Yves Rocher face cream on the bedside table.

So very sleepy, I had to lie down on the bed. Shut my eyes for only a moment, I thought.

Should've removed the maroon lipstick but too tired. If Metti saw, he would know . . .

But too sleepy. Sleep like ether lifting into my brain.

Then I was asleep. That delicious voluptuous sleep like floating in dark water. No dreams, for the water is too shallow. Yet the water is deep enough to cover your mouth, nose, eyes. And soon then, it seemed that I was being wakened—not by a light switched on to blind me, nor by an exclamation of surprise, but by a sudden presence close by.

The man had returned, and was standing in the doorway of the room, staring at me.

Utterly astonished. Staring.

Outside the tall windows the wan winter light had shifted. Hours had been lost, it was much later in the day. There were no lights in the bedroom.

A single light in the hall fell slantwise onto me sprawled naked in the oversized towel and my arms outflung as if I'd fallen from a height, helpless.

"Violet! Hello."

At last Metti spoke. His voice caught in his throat, he was deeply stirred. His face was livid with feeling. I thought—*He is furious with me. He will fire me.*

Then I thought—*He will make love with me.*

"Violet. My God."

This was not an Orlando Metti familiar to me. This was an abashed man, totally taken by surprise, smiling, but dazedly smiling, almost at a loss for words.

"You are so beautiful. So sad. Like the *Sorrowful Madonna*—or maybe—*Sorrowful Virgin* . . . Can't remember the artist's name, something like Rossi, or—Bellini? Italian Renaissance . . ."

In the doorway the man stood indecisive, tentative. This was his bedroom, and that was his bed, and yet: What was permitted him? He had not yet removed his overcoat. His dark, graying hair glistened with melting snowflakes. He was waiting for me to give him permission to approach. He did not want to misunderstand. He did not want to make a terrible mistake. He did not want to be accused of a sex crime. He did not want to be sued by Maid Brigade, or blackmailed by the naked girl wrapped in a towel in his bed.

By this time I was sitting up. Groggy, uncertain where I was. An aftertaste of whiskey in my mouth. (Was I drunk? Who'd made me drunk?) Hugging the damp towel close about myself.

Yet strangely calm. Not at all frightened. For whatever happened, had happened. And whatever was yet to happen would happen, beyond my control.

At last unable to resist Metti stammered: "Violet? May I—OK if I—touch you? Is that what you would like?"

*Yes. Yes. If you will pay me extra.*

# Damned Little Dog

Following this, things happened swiftly.

Like that morning in school when Ms. Micaela took me out of class. And then to the school nurse. And then, the principal. And then, the police officers.

*Safe now. Safe now.*

For he adored me, he said. Crazy for me.

How beautiful I was. How *sorrowful*. Never seen such *sorrowful eyes*.

No more cleaning his apartment! In fact, he would pay me *not to clean his apartment*.

No more doing his laundry! Scrubbing his toilets! Vacuuming the floors! Cleaning up after the damned little dog!

The identical fee each week, with a tip. Of course. Cash.

"No more housecleaning for you, Violet. Tell the Agency you are quitting."

Intoxicated with his own generosity. The suddenness of love.

Gay, festive. Exuberant. "Darling, we must celebrate!"

Wine, champagne. Struggling to open a bottle of champagne that kept slipping from his fingers.

Panting with laughter, together. Already I was drunk, before I swallowed the first fizzing mouthful in a sparkling-clean glass that, the previous week, I'd washed myself by hand, and carefully dried.

Kissing me, a flurry of mothlike kisses. He was an eager lover, unexpectedly tender. Unexpectedly careful. Not to press too hard, not to weigh too heavily.

A perpetual quickened breath, heated skin. Astonished eyes. Hands framing my face as if he'd never seen anything like me before.

"First time I saw you, I knew. Crazy for you."

True? Not true.

Mistaking my silence for evasiveness. Mistaking my insecurity for mystery.

"But then, you are so young. So much younger than I am . . ."

Wistful. Not (yet) resentful.

———

**"You must** call me 'Orlando.' C'mon! It isn't hard."

"'Vio-let.' Never known a 'Violet' before."

Then, "That's your actual name, is it? On your birth certificate?"

**If other** women called while I was in his presence he would not pick up the receiver. How gratified I felt, to be preferred by this man.

Orlando wasn't available. No!

Cruel of him to listen to the woman's faltering message played back and then in mid-sentence deleted.

Only one of these women was the ex-wife. The daughter never called.

The excitement over *Violet* seemed to have been the discovery of a beautiful sorrowing virgin/Madonna inside the cleaning-woman's loose-fitting clothes. T-shirt, jeans. Gray woolen socks.

A quite attractive female-body, where no body at all was expected.

Kissing the star-shaped scar at the hairline. A man is attracted without his knowing. Kissing, sucking.

A shudder running through two bodies in an instant.

And now, searching through the apartment for a gift to give the shy-seeming/sullen-seeming girl to make her smile. A memento.

A necklace, turquoise beads, slipping it over my head, beads tangling in my hair—"Beautiful! Perfect."

(Had the necklace belonged to the daughter, left carelessly behind? I would find several dark hairs tangled in the beads and tug them out, bemused.)

Maroon lipstick was his favorite—"Classy. Sexy."

Ivory Translucent makeup, powder. Mascara to emphasize the deep-set mysterious eyes. Glossy jet-black hair parted so that the little star-shaped scar was exposed.

He'd always thought, since he'd been a kid, the natural look was overrated. Nobody's turned on by some face not so different from a young guy's.

"Here, buy some things for yourself. Not drugstore cosmetics. Take it all. Go on! I'd start a credit card account for you, but . . . ."

Voice trailing off as a rueful memory intruded.

**Then again,** he was sober. Hadn't had a drink all day.

Well, maybe at lunch. But only a glass, two glasses, red wine.

Brooding, vexed about something. The jubilance had faded from his voice. Calling me from his office at the research institute, voice lowered.

On the phone he'd purchased for me that he might

call me at any time on it and I must answer immediately: "Hello? Violet? Where are you?"

A phone purchased for me with an (unlisted) number only he might know. *No one else could call me on that phone.*

"It's a deal, Violet? Yes?"

Very exciting, I thought. The sensation of fingers encircling a neck, beginning to tighten.

Driving in his car along the river. That fleeting sense of gratification, the car is a Jaguar.

Beautiful car, soundless engine. The driver's hand falls from the steering wheel onto the girl's thigh, squeezes. Hard enough to leave faint bruises she will discover that night.

"Tell me about yourself, Violet. You have so many secrets!"

It was true, I was very quiet in Orlando Metti's presence. In a daze of unreality, that an adult man should claim to adore *me*.

"What are you studying? Did you tell me?"

Another time I told him. Another time he seemed to be listening, as a father might listen to a child's recitation, hearing the child's voice, smiling in delight at the child's voice, not hearing actual words.

Though Metti seemed impressed that I was taking university courses in the evening school yet he could not seem to comprehend that I had to actually attend classes. Dinner with him? Drive to the Warburton Hotel, twelve miles away?

"But why not? You can miss a class now and then."

Or: "You can miss a class now and then for Christ's sake."

**"I think** that is the most beautiful name—'Violet.' Is it your actual name?"

"None of it is important, Violet. Don't give it a second thought."

"Do you trust me, Violet? I want you to know that you can trust me."

*Yes yes yes.*

*No certainly not. But yes—I will try.*

"Is something wrong, Violet?"—no longer bantering. An edge in his voice.

Came to me, and took my hands in his. The sensation of his touch so warm, so comforting, tears welled in my eyes and threatened to spill over onto my cheeks.

Came to me, and took both my hands in his. Hard.

The recoil was so unexpected, tears welled in my eyes and spilled over onto my cheeks.

He liked to kiss, suck at the little scar. He liked to kiss, suck at the soft-brown nipples, making them hard as little pellets. He liked to kiss, suck at the moist cringing tissue between my legs, that was an opened wound, that would never heal.

*Insinuating himself into me like a parasite. Snug in my warm moist places, that he could fatten himself on me without my knowledge yet with my complicity.*

**Liking her** best when she was "sorrowful."

Gently he would ask, "Is there something eating at your heart, Violet?"—the very sound of her name wondrous in his voice.

**Didn't dare** ask. Recalling how her father disliked personal questions.

"Her? The ex? Nothing to say. 'Been there, done that.' *Fini.*"

**Finished with** Maid Brigade! She has met the kindest most wonderful most generous man who has promised to pay for her college tuition—"Think of it as a loan, dear. No interest. No due date. No strings attached."

*No strings* attached. He has called the phone installed in her rented room in the wood frame house on Cayuga Street seventeen times in succession. Why no answer, where the hell is she?—"You're sure, nobody else knows this number?"

---

**Anyway, you're** paid off the books. Owe them nothing, they don't owe you anything.

Still: you are thinking yes, you will continue to work for Maid Brigade. On non-teaching days. Exclusively female clients.

Not lying to Orlando Metti. Not exactly.

Good to get your hands on all the money you can. While you can.

**Twenty-dollar bills.** Fifty-dollar bills. A one-hundred-dollar bill, pressed into my hand.

Smiling to myself. *Well. You've earned it, Vi'let.*

Some of it is required to keep myself alive. Some of it is hidden in a drawer, to be sent to the Johnson family on Howard Street, South Niagara, in next February's Valentine.

**Opening the** gilt-wrapped little box. Fumbling, my fingers are clumsy.

As Metti stares greedily, grimly.

(OK. I'm drunk: with this man drinks aren't optional but obligatory.)

Lifting the bracelet out of tissue paper. Gold-plated. Heavy, unwieldy. Telling the man *beautiful so beautiful thank you.* Immediately I see that the clasp is impossible, never will I be able to put this beautiful bracelet on my wrist by myself using just one hand. Never will I be able to put it on my wrist unassisted.

Nor is Metti sober enough to assist right now.

"Shit! Fuckin thing is so fuckin small. . . . Should've had you along with me in the fuckin store."

Metti's face darkens with blood. It is the first time I have seen him so furious. Trying to open the miniature clasp, then to close it properly, is too great a challenge for the man's fingers; his coordination is poor when he has been drinking, like now.

"God-damned fuckin . . ."

My solution is to take the bracelet from Metti. Close the clasp using both hands. Then attempt to squeeze the bracelet over my hand and onto my wrist which turns out to be not so easy.

"What're you doing? You're gonna break it . . ."

Still I continue for I understand that the gold-plated bracelet must be put on my wrist. There is no way to endure the next hour if the bracelet is not on the wrist of the gift-recipient to be modeled for the man.

Turning the bracelet, tugging at it, trying not to wince with pain as I squeeze it over my knuckles, or nearly.

"Be careful! You're gonna break it . . ."

Metti is sounding already aggrieved. His face is dangerously flushed.

In his medicine cabinet I have seen prescription pills: hypertension.

". . . if you do, your arm is gonna be the next to break . . ."

Laughing as if it's a joke. Yes probably meant to be a joke.

But at last the bracelet is on my wrist, and looks beautiful indeed, and the gift-giver is gratified.

"Like it, eh? Looks great on you."

*Yes yes yes. Thank you.*

"D'you like it? Huh?"

*Yes yes yes. Thank you.*

"Solid gold-plate. Wasn't cheap. Don't have anything like this, do you, sweetheart?"

*Noooo. That is correct.*

"In fact, you don't have much of anything, do you, Vi'let? I mean—nice things. Like this."

*Noooo. Correct.*

Leaning over to kiss him. In fact feeling grateful. In fact a surge of something like yearning.

But he grabs my head, presses his mouth against my mouth, hard as he'd never done before.

Tongue poking into my mouth, jabbing like an angry man shouting.

"Y'know, Vi'let—you are the skinniest girl I ever fucked since—high school." Laughing so his jowls quiver, drunk-glistening eyes fixed on mine to see how I am taking this frank revelation.

Seeing the faint hurt smile on my face, as if relenting: "Hell, all my girlfriends were skinny, then."

**No longer** do I house clean for Orlando Metti. Now that I've been promoted from servant to girlfriend.

Yet: "The damned little dog has made a mess again. D'you think you could clean it up? Please? Makes me feel like puking just to smell it."

And: "Damned little dog is all excited you're here, listen to it! OK if you take it out for a walk?—please."

And: "Damned little dog needs to see the vet, it's been wheezing and sneezing. Running nose, eyes. D'you have time to take it, Vi'let? Please."

This is a surprise. Well, not much of a surprise. Not possible for me to say *no*.

Metti explains that he has been paying the son of the building superintendent to take Brindle out at least once a day. But the boy isn't dependable—"Not like you, Vi'let."

In a rush the little French bulldog comes yipping, whining, wheezing, sneezing against my legs. Shuddering with love, need. Trying to climb up into my lap though I am not sitting but standing. Lapping his soft moist tongue against my hands. Dribbling urine onto my shoe. (Fortunately glaring Master doesn't notice.)

Poor little Brindle! Desperate to be loved, saved. His toenails click against the hardwood floor, so eager is he to avoid Master.

It is true that the little bulldog has been wheezing, sneezing, snuffling, struggling to breathe recently. Each time I've seen him he has been sounding worse. Both his big dark shiny wide-set eyes are runny and one of them, the left, is obscured with mucus, which I have tried to wipe away.

Still not convinced that Metti is serious about my taking his daughter's dog to the vet's but yes, Metti is serious. It seems that I have been promoted another time to something like close relative, family member. Sharing household responsibilities, for Metti has an "urgent" business call to make and does not have time—tonight—for the damned little dog.

Provides me with address for Dog Haven Veterinary & Kennel—not close by, far side of town. Calls a taxi. Slips several bills into my hand.

"If the treatment will cost more than seventy-five dollars, tell them to put him down."

Not sure that I've heard this correctly. Standing before the man smiling uncertainly.

"OK. One hundred dollars. But get an estimate first, before they start some fancy treatment."

"'Put him *down*?'"

"*Put to sleep.*"

Seeing the stunned expression in my face Metti says quickly that the damned little dog has been a drain on his finances for years. First, his daughter had to have a "Frenchie"—two thousand dollars for a puppy from a breeder. Then, medical bills. Turns out that a normal "Frenchie" has to be taken to the vet two, three times a year. Like dumping money down a rat hole. Plus, Brindle isn't an "obedient" dog—he's "spoiled rotten." A bulldog's life span is only about ten years and this one is almost that old. He'd been supposed to stay with Metti for just a few weeks but five months have passed and now the ex-wife is claiming she has medical problems and the daughter isn't returning his calls—"So fuck them."

Brindle's skinny tail is hidden between his shivering hindquarters. Big runny eyes are uplifted, searching my face.

*I know. I have heard every word.*

By the time we reach the veterinary I have convinced myself that Metti—(difficult to think of him as Orlando)—is only joking about having Brindle *put down*. Maybe it's a test of my integrity, loyalty.

Certainly, no father would have his daughter's dog *put down* without even warning her . . .

Sad to think, poor Brindle is not a young dog. Now I can see that his small size is misleading. The slightly sidelong, slouching walk is probably arthritis and so it is touching when he tries to trot, to keep up with me. He seems oblivious of the fact that his legs are ridiculously short.

In the vet's waiting room we sit, wait. Minutes fraught with terror are stoically endured. A succession of dogs of varying sizes passes by Brindle crouched beneath my chair tugging at his leash not forward to escape but backward against the wall, as if to drag me beneath the chair with him.

Trusting me with his daughter's dog . . . Is this proof of Orlando's faith in me? A wifely sort of duty, here? Wanting to think so.

At last when the waiting room is nearly empty it is Brindle's turn. He balks at walking on the floor like a normal dog and must be carried in the arms of a husky young woman in a blue smock who laughs at him—"What a frowning little face! What's your name?"

I am invited to accompany them into an examination room. I am impressed with the young woman vet's skill at handling the tremulous little animal. Her coercion, her power over him is so subtle, Brindle does not even think of rebelling.

The exam is lengthy and thorough. Eyes, nose, ears, mouth. Lungs, heart. Then, Brindle is taken out of the room for more tests and returns abashed and big-eyed, trembling. *How much, how much is this going to cost!* I am beginning to be anxious myself.

My assumption is that Metti will pay by credit card when he's billed by the vet. He seems not to have given me much money for the taxi and the exam—only about forty dollars, of which I have spent nine dollars on the taxi.

In my wallet are a number of bills, twenties, fifties, which Metti has given me in impulsive moments. I have not counted them up, only allowed them to accumulate. Not knowing how much money there is in my wallet makes me feel as if the money, and the obligation it would seem to entail, are not quite real.

Sometimes Metti seems aware of how much money he gives me as if he is keeping track of every dollar. Other times he's extravagant, negligent as a drunken rich man whose pockets are overflowing with gold coins.

*Here y'are, sweetheart. For you.*

*. . . little smile? Yes!*

The young woman is telling me that Brindle has an infection in his left eye—a tear in the cornea has caused an ulcer possibly caused by a scratch, a poke, or a kick. It will take a while to heal. She gave him an injection today and he will have to have antibiotic drops in the eye three times a day for the next five days.

How will this be possible? I am wondering. Metti would never have time for the treatment, even if he'd been willing to do it. And I could not come to his apartment so frequently. . . . Three times a day!

Also, the young woman tells me that Brindle has a gradually worsening respiratory condition that should be treated sometime soon.

Also, Brindle's toenails were becoming ingrown, so she clipped them.

Also, she took a blood sample. The results should come in from the lab in a few days, she'll have the front desk call me.

Seeing the pained look in my face during this recitation the young woman assures me that over all, Brindle is in good health. His main problem is, it seems that the "sweet little Frenchie" has not been made to exercise. Fatty tissue is beginning to form around his heart. He isn't an old dog but he has some of the health problems of an older dog.

"How old is he?"

"I'd say around five."

*Five!* And Metti is ready to euthanize him.

Awkwardly I tell the young woman that Brindle isn't my dog. He belongs to the daughter of a friend, who's in college and can't take care of him right now. "That's why I don't know how old he is . . . I'm just a friend of the family."

"Well, you are Brindle's friend."

Something almost intimate in this remark, so off-the-cuff, casually uttered.

Briskly now the young woman sets Brindle down on the floor, tugged at his leash and inspired him to walk, waddling on foreshortened legs, out of the examination room and to the front desk. There was a measure of sobriety in the little bulldog's manner, as if he understood the gravity of the situation and was not going to behave willfully.

At the desk, I am given a bill: one hundred forty-six dollars. This includes the price of the antibiotic eyedrops.

Staring at the bill. Shocked.

Not knowing what to do. . . . Except of course I am not going to tell the smiling young woman that she should *put down* Brindle.

Counting the bills in my wallet. Two hundred sixteen dollars. More than anticipated, this is enough to save Brindle.

Seeing my hesitation the young woman tells me that, if I can't pay the full price now, I can pay a deposit this evening and the rest later. But I assure her, I have the money. I can afford it.

Curious probably, that I am paying the bill in cash. Yet, the transaction is completed and we are free to leave.

In the taxi returning to Metti, I hold Brindle in my arms. The stress of the adventure has exhausted us both. Quivering and licking my hands Brindle begins to doze.

When I return to Metti with Brindle in my arms Metti stares at the little bulldog astonished. As if he hadn't expected me to bring Brindle back.

"Well! Thank you, Violet . . . How much was it?"

"Seventy dollars. You'd given me seventy-five."

"Did I! Well—that's good news . . ." As if he'd expected the bill to be higher.

"The vet said his eye has been injured. She gave him an injection. There might be a scratch on the eye, or someone might have kicked him . . ."

Metti is scarcely listening. So surprised that Brindle has been returned alive, he doesn't know what to say.

I tell him that I will have to come over, to give Brindle eyedrops. For five days. But I can do this without bothering him, when he's at work.

Metti says that's fantastic. What a fantastic job Violet has done, taking care of the *damned little dog.*

"My daughter will be relieved if she ever finds out."

Later, in his bedroom Metti kisses me roughly. Handles me roughly. Affectionate yet chiding as one might cuff a pet that has not yet disobeyed but is considering disobeying. His kisses are stinging, punitive. Wayward hands squeeze my bare shoulder, the nape of my neck. He suspects that I am deserving of punishment but could not have said why.

*Well, you* are Brindle's friend.

These kind words, I will cherish in my heart.

**Friend of** a friend, his kid is getting a new car. Twelve-year-old Honda Civic they're getting rid of, for a few hundred dollars Metti will take it off their hands, for me.

*Oh my God thank you, Orlando! Thank you.*

*First car entirely mine, in my life.*

*I love you.*

**First car** of my own. It is so kind of Metti, so generous!—I think of the man with gratitude, a wave of emotion that must mean love.

Each time he says to me, with a wink, how're you

doing for gasoline, darling?—pressing a bill or two into my hand.

Now I can drive to the university instead of taking a bus. I can drive to my housecleaning assignments instead of taking a bus. And when Metti summons me, I can drive to his apartment building instead of taking a taxi. *Hey. Missing you like hell, babe. The key will be downstairs with the doorman, let yourself in. I'll be waiting.*

**By the** time I acquire the Honda Civic, Brindle no longer requires eyedrops. But I can drive to Metti's apartment on weekdays if it isn't out of my way, to check on the lonely little bulldog. Without Metti knowing.

Brindle's left eye has healed but his vision appears to have dimmed. Over the injured cornea, something like a translucent grayish film has grown.

Once, arriving in the late morning at Metti's apartment, on a day when Metti is sure to be away, I encounter the new cleaning-woman the Agency has sent. Tall, big-boned, with ash-blond hair, very pale eyelashes and eyebrows, a young woman of about thirty, somewhat coarse skin and no makeup except red lipstick brightly smeared on her mouth.

Shyly she stammers hello. She speaks with an

accent—Polish? She has no idea who I am. Daughter? Girlfriend? (Not wife: she will know that Orlando Metti doesn't have a wife.) We have never met at the Agency and there is little likelihood that we will.

But I don't explain myself, for it is not the cleaning-woman's business to know who I am.

**"Was that** you I saw? I think it was."

"When? Where?"

". . . walking with a guy, looked like he was 'African American'—or what do they call themselves: 'black.' The other day on Division Street."

Calculating rapidly when this could have been. For Division Street was near the university's sprawling north side, intersecting with Cayuga which was where I lived in an old Victorian house that had been con-verted into rental rooms.

Except for me, the other tenants in the house were graduate students and of these, most were foreign, and male. A neighbor of mine was a young Pakistani studying engineering, sometimes we walked together for a block or two. But I was not even sure of his name.

"Just curious. You say you don't have friends at the university but you looked pretty friendly then, the other day. Who's the guy?"

The instinct is to say quickly *No one!—no one really.* For this is the truth.

Yet, if the truth is ineptly uttered it can fly back to strike you. It can be deadly.

And so you said carefully: "I think it must have been one of the Pakistani students who lives in my building. He's studying electrical engineering."

*Pakistani.* The identification seemed to disappoint Metti, his interest rapidly faded.

**Metti has** told me, his daughter is coming to visit! At last.

Staying just a weekend. And when Leila leaves she will be taking the damned dog with her.

This is surprising news to me. It is not really happy news. For I will miss the little French bulldog. How strange the apartment will be, how quiet, without Brindle barking, skidding on the hardwood floor to greet me when I arrive. To inveigle treats from me, behind Master's back. And when I leave him, whispering *Good night!* wriggling his bottom in a paroxysm of dismay.

Why would I want to come to Orlando Metti's apartment, if Brindle is not here?

If Metti has no more need to say: Could you take the dog for a walk?—please.

---

**But then,** the daughter cancels the weekend. The father's face darkens like something clotted.

Wise to avoid the subject. Wise to just get drunk, avoiding all other subjects.

**Rare that** Metti asks me about my life apart from him. As if it doesn't occur to him that there might be a life apart from him.

Except, in this subdued mood of his. Since the daughter has failed to visit him Metti has been unpredictable.

"OK, Violet. Tell me."

"Tell you—what?"

"Whatever it is, you've never told me."

Uneasily I am laughing, in the man's arms. For in a man's arms you are never *easy.*

"Where do your people live, Violet? You never talk about them."

*My people!* This does not sound like Metti speaking.

But I think—*Shall I tell him? Something.*

Not the sad, sordid tale of my brothers beating a black boy to death. No. Nor the worse tale of my informing on them. *My life as a rat.*

". . . sometimes I find myself thinking about a boy in our neighborhood who died when I was in sev-

enth grade. I don't know why, I think about him—
'Hadrian Johnson.'"

There. The name has been uttered. Scarcely daring
to breathe I wait for Metti to respond but he does not.

"You've never heard the name?—'Hadrian Johnson.'"

Metti thinks. "No. Why should I?"

"He was a basketball player, I think his team won a
state championship . . ."

Is this true? I don't think so. Somehow, the possibility comes to me, as a reasonable remark to make.

". . . you wouldn't have heard of him in Catamount Falls. He lived in South Niagara. Where I—
where 'my people'—are from . . ." My voice trails
off, uncertain. Is Metti even listening? He has a habit
of asking me a question, not listening to the answer,
like a man turning on a radio or a TV, comforting
background noise.

"He went to school with my brothers. High school.
He played basketball and baseball. His picture was
in the paper—in the sports pages. People—some
people—were jealous of him . . . There was a fight,
Hadrian was attacked, killed. . . . He was only seventeen."

My voice is shaking. It is inexplicable to me, why
I am telling Orlando Metti this, and why the words
are so flat, halting, feeble, lame. As if each word is a

pebble sticking in my throat. *Oh but everyone loved Hadrian Johnson, he was beautiful.*

"The boys who hurt him hadn't meant it—really. They'd been drinking. Not Hadrian—I don't think that he'd been drinking. He'd been bicycling home from his grandmother's house. The boys were—white boys . . . Hadrian Johnson was black."

Metti says nothing. I am hoping that he has fallen asleep. I scarcely dare to move, for fear of waking him.

"Did I say that already? That he was black? But it wasn't 'racial.' People in my high school got along—mostly . . ."

Unexpectedly then Metti says, "People think too God-damned much about 'race.' Especially 'African Americans.' Or whatever they call themselves now."

This remark is so irritable, so *annoyed,* as if a fly were buzzing overhead, I am shocked into silence.

Baring my heart to speak of Hadrian Johnson, and this man's response is to be *annoyed.*

"It's some kind of obsession—'race' obsession. Some of us are frankly tired of."

Waiting for me to continue but no. Not just now.

**In a** quasi-public place he kissed her. This was not like him, for he did not want to be seen in public with her (usually). And yet, it was beginning to be like him, for since the disappointment of the daughter, and since she'd lied to him about the dog, though he had no way (of course) of knowing that she'd lied, he was behaving differently, and there had come the realization, belated, abashed, that it was no longer appropriate to say that he was behaving differently because now he was behaving as (almost) she expected him to behave, even in a quasi-public place like the parking lot behind the Warburton Hotel where patrons returning to their cars beneath tall flood lights might glance in the direction of the sleek black Jaguar whose driver seemed to be leaning over, hunching over, a smaller trapped female figure gripped in a headlock.

Kissed her. Except it was not a exactly "kiss"—rather, an assault with his mouth. And his tongue, protruding belligerently into her mouth.

She felt panic, that she would suffocate. Trying not to gag.

But she could not shake herself free—he was gripping her head in his both hands. Crude mimicry of sexual intercourse, the female mouth the receptacle, helpless to resist the male.

Then, when at last he released her, as if it had been mere passion that had overcome him, or some obscure invitation of her own exacerbated by alcohol, she tried to take some initiative, kissing the man in little butter-fly flurries, to indicate affection, playfulness. A sort of sexual giddiness. Not serious.

A girl's kisses, or a child's. She had kissed men like this often, in the past—this one had seemed to like it. He had seemed to like her.

Now, it wasn't clear that this one liked her. Not much.

Leaning away from her, laughing, as if the assault had been merely playful, already forgotten, or soon to be.

"Where were we going?—oh yes: *home*."

**Those nights** he insisted that she remain with him, in the apartment.

In the master bedroom, in the bed. Gripping her tight, tight as death.

So that she thought, marveling—*He loves me! This is love, this need.*

So lonely. In his life so lonely. He had no one but her, now. But he would *have her.*

He slept naked, his body oozed sweat. On his feet he towered over her, in bed his body was like some-thing fallen, inert. Running his hands over her eagerly telling her, he would never hurt *her.* Everyone else had turned against him. Everyone he'd ever trusted.

His wife had turned their daughter against him. His wife had become a bitter crazy person to spite him. She'd been beautiful, she had ruined her beauty to spite him. If she killed herself as she was threatening to do, it would be to spite *him*.

A man in such distress, you must comfort him. Console him.

You *must not* contradict him.

Asking suddenly as if he'd just thought of it, was she sleeping with someone else? While she was sleeping with him?

Was she sleeping with *black men*?

He wouldn't be angry, he said. He promised.

If she would tell him the truth, that was all he wanted. If she felt that she could trust him, if she trusted him with her life, that was all he wanted . . .

Sinking into sleep as a man sinks into a bog. Sinking sinking until nothing remained not even the outline of the sunken body and so she was not required to answer, this time she had been spared.

**Maybe instead** of marrying her he will murder her.

Fuck her, in a way that (seriously) hurts. And another time that way, or two or three, until it's stale to him, and the sight of her and the smell of her and the sound of the female pretending to moan with passion is revolting to him, almost by accident he snuffs out her life.

*Christ! Didn't know what I was doing.*

*A moth the size of a butterfly hitting the glass lampshade, batting its wings, the most beautiful moth I'd ever seen but the sound of it made me grab it in my fist not knowing what I meant to do and then it was— well, crushed, dead . . . And turned out to be the girl in the bed with me, that I hadn't even remembered was there, that was crushed. Dead.*

**Returned from** walking the little bulldog on his comically foreshortened legs. And there was Orlando Metti glaring at me in disgust. A look in his face as if he'd like to give the little dog quivering in fear of him a good kick to confirm the reasonableness of the fear.

"Y'know what, darling?—take him."

Smiling at Metti, for I had no idea what he meant.

"'Take'—where?"

"Take him with you. When you leave here. Just— take the fucking dog out of here."

And now I knew, and wanted to think that Metti was joking.

"But—Brindle is your daughter's dog, Orlando."

Pausing, for the name *Orlando* feels strange on my tongue, like Szechuan pepper, a numbing sensation. "You can't give away your daughter's dog . . ."

"Fuck this 'daughter' shit. She isn't here, and you are."

"But—"

"D'you want him, or not?"

"I—I—I can't—"

"All right, then. Forget it."

Snatching the dog's leash from my hand, yanking the little dog so that he cried out in pain and terror as Metti dragged him away to the back room.

Stunned, for a moment paralyzed. No idea what to do, what to say that would not inflame the man more.

Then, pleading: "Orlando? Please, wait—why don't you call your daughter? Explain the circumstances here—"

Metti shut the door on the little dog he'd shoved inside the room with his foot. So traumatized was Brindle, he wasn't even whimpering.

"I said, fuck the 'daughter.' Fuck the 'circumstances.' I asked you if you wanted the God-damned dog, and you said *no*. You've made your wishes known, darling. So shut up about the subject."

Soon there came a faint whimpering sound from beyond the door. I put my hand on the doorknob, and

Metti shoved me away with a curse. *Damn you. Fuck you.*

He has made a dinner reservation, we must both leave now. But the stricken look in my face annoys him, I want to spend a few minutes with Brindle to calm him, comfort him. But Metti says, we have to leave now. This minute. Now.

Then, in an instant he has changed his mind. No dinner. Or, rather—he will go alone.

"Just get out, Violet. That face of yours, the way you are looking at me, you'd better get out before I break it."

**Later, he** will call, apologize. Your lover is very skilled, practiced at apologizing.

Calmly you listen. Calmly you tell him *No thank you.*

You stay away from him. You have been fore-warned. Next time he may break your face. You are determined—*There will be no next time.*

**Next time** you step into Metti's apartment, there is a noticeable quiet.

No barking, no excited whining, whimpering. You are uneasy missing the sound of toenails clicking on the floor.

Though the doggy-odor lingers. You wonder if Metti realizes.

"My daughter showed up after all. She took the dog with her."

Metti pauses. Gauging your response.

"He's out of my life now. No more dogs."

Another pause. Metti is enjoying this, watching your face.

It is three weeks, two days after he'd told you to leave. After he'd dragged the little bulldog into the back room, slammed the door.

So frequently Metti has called in the interim, begging you to take him back, give him another chance. So frequently apologizing, he's been under strain at the Institute, one of the major investors threatening to pull out, lost his temper about the damned dog but would never hurt *you*.

Assuring you, he has cut back on his drinking. Seriously!

Acknowledges it was a problem. Absolutely. Broke up his marriage, both him and his wife drinking too much except the wife, like most women, couldn't handle it.

But now, he's all but stopped. A glass or two of wine at dinner. Weekdays. When he misses you most.

And so, you've agreed to see him again. A few

times. Hard to say no when the man gives you the most exquisite gifts—silk scarf with label YVES SAINT LAURENT, pair of gold-plated dangling earrings (to match the bracelet), fifty-dollar bills to help out, as he says, with your "education."

"You'll miss Brindle, darling. I know. But he's better off now—he always loved Leila best."

You wondered if any of this could be true. Smiling at Metti not quite meeting his eye. Not wanting to see a wink.

*Of course the damned little fucker is gone, and good riddance.*

But you could not think this. You could not accept this. You were feeling dazed, uncertain of even the guilt you should be feeling if there were cause for guilt.

Weakly you said, "Well. Brindle won't be so lonely now."

Metti laughed. "That's right, darling. Brindle will never be lonely again."

Eyes stinging with tears. You could not allow the man to see, to gloat. Turning from him sick with hatred of him, and self-loathing, now it was too late.

**But I** *could not have taken him! Not then.*

*Could not—he belonged to the daughter . . .*

*In my life, there is no room for a dog.*
*My life as a rat.*

**Not the** *sorrowful virgin/Madonna* now. Instead it came to be *bitch, slut.*

Something had been flung open. Wild winds, quickened pulses.

His fingers probing, poking. Discovering you where you were moist and open. Yearning.

Learn not to flinch. The most sensitive part of a woman's body, raw nerves. Unbearable if wrongly touched. Not tenderly.

Can't help yourself, crying out. *Oh.*

Hey. Sorry. That hurt?

(You know it hurts, God damn you. Stop.)

His excuse is, he gets *carried away.*

So beautiful. You are so (fucking) beautiful.

Lying very still. Eyes shut in a kind of prayer. That he will love you, as he has said. Protect you forever.

*Know what?—I think you need to be my wife, Vi-let.*

*My little wifey-wife I will know where the fuck she is every minute.*

**Have you** had sex with black men?—he asks.

At last. At last he asks. Has wanted to ask this question for a long time (he admits).

Several inches of Johnnie Walker splashed into a glass. Glint of merriment in the rogue male eye.

You are not drinking whiskey. Not tonight. Too much risk.

Yet, a drunken elation courses through your veins. Slyly hesitating just long enough (as if) not seeing how your lover is becoming excited.

Shaking your head ambiguously. Reply could be *no.* Or, reply could be *Not a question I will answer.*

OK, then. Give me an approximate number, please.

So ridiculous! You want to laugh at him. But no, maybe not.

Feeling reckless, brazen.

Hear yourself tell him—Eleven.

Eleven!—he is astonished, awed. Literally, his lower jaw drops a slow inch.

Well. E-lev-en. And this was—beginning when?

Eager to know. Dreading to know. Eyes fixed upon you, whiskey-colored.

Now hearing yourself tell the man that you hadn't been counting high school. Middle school. Too out of it, smoking dope in those years. You'd thought he meant actual men—adults . . .

Whiskey glass lifted, clicking against his teeth. He regards you with something like loathing, fascination. Mild disbelief.

In high school? Fucking *middle school*? So young? Jesus! How many?

How *many?* We didn't count.

Laughing at him now, the look in his face. Who was counting?—you want to know.

And this was—when? How old—? Like, sixteen? Fifteen?

Around then. Or earlier. Eighth grade? Seventh? White girls, I mean. Girls who fucked black boys. Who weren't afraid.

You—weren't afraid?

Why'd we be afraid? Black boys were the best.

I—I think—that must be—amazing . . . How many?

Why'd we count? Nobody counted. That's a crude question.

Possibly now you've gone too far. *Crude* is not a word one would ordinarily apply to Orlando Metti.

But you are laughing. First time ever, maybe. In such circumstances.

You're lying, aren't you? Laughing at me.

Laughing at you? Why would you think that, Orlando.

Frowning to show how God-damned serious you are. But the laughter bubbles up again, like bile.

*Are* you?

*Am I*—what?

Lying. Laughing at me.

Shaking your head, could be *no.* Could be *yes.*

Measuring the distance required for you to flee, to get out of the way of his fist.

As for the *men,* not boys but *black men,* there've been eleven.

Is that including now? The present time?

N-No. . . . Not right now.

But you have hesitated, he has seen. Not so drunk he can't see. Asking you the crucial question. Perceiving how you take it.

When was the last one, then? The last black fuck?

Not meaning to provoke the man. But yes, meaning to provoke the man: making a show of counting on your fingers as if calculating how long you've known Orlando Metti.

Well. I guess—seven months ago. Approximately.

Here in Catamount Falls?

Of course! At the university.

Is he—are you—now?

Told you *no.* Not now.

Were you ever seriously involved with any of them? Like—in love . . .

Licking his lips for this is not easy. *Love* has a clinical sound in the man's mouth. But has to ask, has to know. Burning to know. Excitement, not knowing what the answer will be.

Again that vague inclination of the head, maybe *no*. Or—*yes*.

And did you—do you—compare?—a black lover, white lovers . . . ?

"Compare"—how? You mean the size of the male penis? Black male, white male?

How blunt you are, how unexpected: uttering the word *penis* to confound the man staring at you in disbelief.

For not previously in his knowledge of you have you been so frank. Drawn to the *sorrowful virgin/ Madonna* discovered asleep in his bed Orlando Metti is finding this revelation hard to comprehend.

Matter-of-factly you tell the amazed man that it is true, exactly as white men fear, the black penis is larger.

Even a relatively small black male, you continue, with the air of one imparting a reluctant truth, yet a truth that must be uttered, will have a proportionately larger penis than a white male.

Really! Is that so.

Smiling, a ghastly insincere smile. As if the (white) man's fear has been confirmed. All that he'd dreaded, turning out to be an open secret.

You begin laughing, suddenly. A snort of laughter though this exchange is (possibly) not funny at all but dangerous.

Which is why it is funny—*danger.*

Time now to explain to the astonished (white) man that it has all been a joke. Keep that fist from flying wild. Striking you in the face. But does a joke not-funny qualify as a joke?

Having to go through the motions of the joke as you'd gone through the motions of lovemaking how many times.

You would tell him—*Actually, I have not slept with any black man. I have not slept with eleven men. I have never known eleven men.*

But no, you don't say this. Like hell you will say this, to undo the spell.

Suddenly Metti is livid. Saying, Why don't you shut up, Violet.

Still you are laughing. You are thinking, Kill me, strangle me. Go ahead, you bastard.

Shut up, shut up, *shut up.*

Looming over you. The bully shaking you. Saying crude things to you. If there'd been a leash around your neck he would have dragged you as he'd dragged the little bulldog. Thrown you into a room, locked the door.

Still you can't seem to get serious, your face is melting. So funny!—outrage of the white male.

Should strangle you, Violet. You fucking cunt. That would stop you laughing at me.

No. It wouldn't stop me.

Wild laughter as he lunges for you, but you are no longer where you'd been.

Scrambling to your feet. Grabbing at clothes. Not shoes, you've forgotten shoes. Fuck shoes.

Wanting to flatten you on the bed. Smelly trodden bed. His heavy body weighing yours down, helpless. Shoving himself inside you deep as he can for your words have excited him as nothing has excited him recently. He would tear off what remains of your clothing, raging rogue male. No matter that this rogue male is middle-aged, fattish at the waist, jawline loose-jowled, breath coming fast and shallow as his heart thumps desperately in his chest. No matter he no longer recalls who you are, which one of them you are who has disappointed him, betrayed him, escaped him. You are the fucking cunt, the cunt-to-be-fucked until you scream in pain, to his ears the most delicious pain; until you are bleeding, the male rogue has thrust himself inside you like a samurai sword piercing your guts.

But too quick for him! Not-drunk but all of your senses alert you slip from his clumsy hands, slip beneath his hands, quicksilver as a roused fox. In your fingers a pewter candlestick holder, must've been seeing this on a nearby table for the past several minutes without registering its meaning. Out of nowhere you've grabbed the pewter object to swing at the enraged face, jubilantly you strike the face between the eyes, not a hard blow but stunning to the man who has never been struck in such a way, by one he'd imagined he might easily subdue. This gives you time to swing the weapon a second time, and much harder. Almost, you imagine hearing the eye socket crack, the cartilage of the nose crushed, you see the panting man losing his balance, falling. Hard.

Splattering of blood. Whimpering, moaning. But you have no mercy, without a backward glance you are ecstatic in flight descending seventeen vertiginous floors to the ground and running shoeless out into the harsh cold air—*Running for my life.*

**And each** time you think of Orlando Metti, wicked laughter bubbles up like bile.

And each time you think of Orlando Metti, you feel a rush of something like contrition, a kind of remorse, regret, not for what you'd done but for the fact that you have done it, and Metti will not forgive you, and will not forget.

Only a matter of time, you think. Before Metti seeks you out.

He knows where you live, he'd driven you home numerous times, before he'd given you the Honda Civic. He would know your university schedule except he'd never listened carefully, vaguely he might recall that you are on campus on Thursday evenings.

Of course, he calls. Late-night calls on the specially installed phone. You listen, and you do not answer.

Unlike his ex-wife, Metti doesn't leave lengthy messages. He is too shrewd to threaten you. Too shrewd to leave proof of any intent to do you harm.

All he will say is, in a deceptively jovial voice—
*Hel-lo, Vi'let. We have a little something to discuss.*

**And then,** the Agency calls.

Not Ava Schultz but the manager, a man named Dwyer to whom you'd never spoken before. Dwyer is harsh, disgusted. Informing you that Orlando Metti has accused you of stealing from his apartment. He claims that you took jewelry, articles of clothing, money. Unless you give it back he will call the police and press charges.

You wonder if this is a joke. But no, Dwyer is panting on the phone. No joke.

Weakly you protest: Metti gave you gifts. All those items were gifts.

He'd given you a car, too. A Honda Civic. (But Metti isn't accusing you of stealing the car, at least.)

Disgusted Dwyer commands you to come to the Agency and bring the "gifts" with you.

In the Honda Civic you drive to Maid Brigade Agency. You have brought with you the gifts your lover gave you in the first flush of his desire for the *sorrowful virgin/Madonna*: turquoise bead necklace, gold-plated bracelet with the tricky clasp, earrings that match the bracelet, gorgeous red silk scarf by Yves Saint Laurent.

You are uncertain what to do about the money Metti gave you over several months. You have never added it up but believe it must be nearly a thousand dollars, most of it spent in the effort of keeping yourself alive and the rest set aside to send to Ethel Johnson next February.

Have the bills been gifts, or tips?—impossible to know which might be which by the time of the breakup.

Damned if you will return *tips* to that man. These *tips* you have earned on your feet and on your back.

Deeply embarrassed, you lay the gift-items out on

a counter for Dwyer to contemplate. Each object is clearly expensive, of high quality. You'd been thrilled to receive each, at the time. You'd worn the turquoise necklace most frequently, at the university; the other fancier items you'd worn solely in Metti's company, which pleased him.

In fact, if you didn't wear something Metti had given you, sulkily he'd ask why.

Does Dwyer believe you? Are these the first accusations Orlando Metti has brought against one of his cleaning women? With childlike vehemence you insist—*I did not steal these things! I did not.*

Yet you worry, your vehemence is not convincing. A truly innocent girl would be more crushed, perhaps. Wounded.

Since Dwyer is damned angry with you, he is in no hurry to give you the benefit of the doubt. No good reason for him to take your side in a disagreement with a customer. You will not be asked to work for the Agency again, but Orlando Metti is a valued customer.

Very embarrassing to concede to Dwyer, who questions you closely, that yes, you'd become "involved with" the client.

"Involved with"—what's that? Slept with him?

Mortifying! The skin on your face seems to be contracting with shame.

Yes, you'd been warned. Very clearly you'd been warned. Naively you had not listened.

Impossible to claim—*But I was in love with him. I thought.*

*Wanting the man to love me. To take care of me.*

That had been the wish, beyond even the wish for money. The hope that, when Lionel came for you, Orlando Metti would protect you; your life so altered by him, Lionel would never dare come for you at all.

You realize this now. How transparent! Pathetic. Yet, somehow you had not known.

For forty minutes Dwyer interrogates you. As Metti has enjoyed humiliating you, now the manager of Maid Brigade enjoys humiliating you. And you are willing to be humiliated, you are apologetic, abject. The fear that you may be arrested by police, jailed for theft, unable to convince authorities that you are not a thief, has been rising in you, like a fever.

You tell Dwyer that you don't want any of the gifts. You'd rarely worn them, except in Metti's company. Please, would he return them to Metti! Maybe that will placate him.

Dwyer regards you with some measure of sympathy. Though mostly he is disgusted with you.

Telling you that Metti is very angry. On the phone he was shouting. Sounded as if he'd been drinking.

You're damned lucky he didn't call the police immediately.

Dwyer concedes, Metti's account is suspicious—claiming you stole the items over a period of weeks. If you had, and he'd noticed, why hadn't he reported the thefts at the time? Why would he wait until you'd stolen a half-dozen items, and then report it? And if he gave you the car, and the title has been made over in your name—obviously you hadn't stolen it. And if he'd given the car to you, probably he'd given the other gifts too.

Dwyer thought probably the police would see through Metti's story. Accusing a woman of stealing from him. Former cleaning-woman. As a story, it was suspicious. Also they wouldn't be inclined to take Metti's side, rich guy living by himself, divorced, in the fancy high-rise by the river, bringing women home. They'd know the type.

Before Dwyer you stand meek, humbled. It is flattering to the man, how humbled you are, a girl (at one time) sexually attractive enough to have provoked a man like Orlando Metti to give her expensive gifts, and God knows how much in *tips*.

You are not so attractive now, you understand. Stunned by the accusation that you are a thief. Stammering as you tried to defend yourself. With sluttish haste you'd dressed that morning, thrown on soiled T-shirt, jeans. Not a thought of a shower. Smelling of guilt. Rank underarms. Coldly Dwyer stares at you, face, breasts, belly, hips, legs. Feet. And raising his eyes again, in slow male assessment finding you lacking.

Saying meanly that the police might not like you, either. Figuring you were taking money from the customer for sex which makes you, in some eyes, a hooker.

This opprobrium you accept, it is your due. Taking money from a man, any man, even if earned, is a kind of *hooking*. You will not contest this.

Dwyer says the police aren't stupid, they'll see through Metti's story. But still, they might bring you in for questioning. He pauses, savoring this possibility.

Still you have nothing to say in your own defense. It is all true, terrible. Almost you feel a kind of exhilaration, that this hostile stranger has seen you so exposed, naked.

Time to leave. And leave your hard-earned "gifts" behind to be returned to the giver. Maid Brigade is dismissing you. Not even as a part-time laborer paid contemptuously in cash, off the books, will you be welcome to return though only recently you'd been one of the Agency's most diligent workers, uncomplaining and uncomplained-against.

Dwyer adds, laughing: "You must've done something to really piss this guy off, Vi'let. Count yourself lucky he called us first, not the cops."

*Count myself lucky. Yes!*

**But then,** there was no clear end. For Metti called me a few days later leaving messages of abject apology, insisting he didn't want the gifts back, there'd been a "tragic" misunderstanding—the fault of the Agency.

When I didn't answer, didn't return his calls Metti came by the place in which I was living, a weatherworn Victorian dwelling north of the sprawling university campus. Metti had seen the residence exclusively from the outside, and at night. Somehow he made his way inside and upstairs unerringly to my room on the second floor determined to speak to me but I hid from him behind a locked door. "Violet! Try to forgive me. I've been a little crazy, I think. I never expected that kind of behavior from *you*. Betraying me. Sleeping with—those men. I'd believed I was the only one." He began pounding on the door with a fist. "It's your life, Violet. You have a right to your own life. I can see that. I'm a father, I am not a jailer. A girl—a daughter—can fuck anybody she wants to. Any color. I know that. I am not contesting that. But I'd thought you had promised me. Must've missed something, I was sure you'd promised me. When you took gifts from me. Money. There was an agreement. There is an agreement, if a woman accepts gifts and money. But not you, you lied to me. But no, I am not accusing you, Violet. You're very young. You're not too young to know better. This isn't going to end here, Violet. There's too much left undone. We have much more to say to each other, dear. Women don't walk away from me, not like this. They walk away when I tell them—*walk*. This isn't over yet, Violet. You lying cunt. Not by a long shot."

Then, footsteps descending the stairs. Inside I was cowering. Inside I was calculating how I might escape through a window, breaking the window with a chair, a badly rusted fire escape outside the window, possibly it would hold my weight. And there was a pair of scissors, gripped in my hand. But then suddenly, Metti was retreating. From the window I saw the man make his unsteady way to the Jaguar parked crooked at the curb, where it had attracted some attention from several guys, admiring its sleek dark missile-shape. I wondered if Metti would pause to look back at me, if he would wave. If I would wave at him.

And now, I thought—*No more*.

---

**Yet still,** there would be more. It did not (yet) end. For a few days later when I returned to the house on Cayuga Street it was to discover, on the small front porch, barking and whimpering as I approached— Brindle! The little French bulldog secured by a short leash to a porch railing, a flimsy red scarf about his neck, badly twisted so he'd nearly throttled himself.

"Brindle! My God."

Astonishing—Brindle was alive, and Brindle was *here*.

Afterward I would wonder if Metti had been boarding him at a kennel, after our disagreement. He'd wanted me to think the worst, as a way of punishing me.

I would wonder if Metti had changed his mind about having the bulldog *put down* or whether in fact no veterinarian would consent to do such a thing. Whether Metti's daughter had told him definitively that she didn't care to take the dog back.

Brindle was overcome with joy to see me. His deep-chested dwarfish body quivered, shook from side to side with the agitation of his skinny tail. His left eye was cloudy but luminous. He was panting, slathering spittle on my hands.

"Oh, Brindle. What the hell am I going to do with you . . . ."

Whether in derision, or for some other motive, Metti had tied the red silk scarf around Brindle's neck, over his collar. In his agitation the dog had torn the delicate material with his claws and soiled it.

I wondered if Metti was somewhere close by, observing. I did not want to look for him—the Jaguar parked on the street. No. I carried Brindle up the stairs, to my room. And here too, a surprise—an envelope stuffed with cash, pushed beneath the door.

Ten one-hundred-dollar bills. One thousand dollars!

No note, not a word. Just the dog, the scarf, the envelope filled with cash. Somehow this did not (yet) feel like an end.

**And so** now, I would leave Catamount Falls. I would notify the telephone company, disconnect the phone. (Metti paid the phone bills: he would see that I'd terminated the account.) The previous week was the end of the university spring term, many of us would be departing soon. I felt a sudden stab of regret for that other life, the life of which Orlando Metti had no knowledge, my life as a university student who came onto campus only after dark—diffident, diligent, dutiful—a young woman who sat near the front of classrooms taking notes as if her life depended upon it.

Packed the Honda Civic with the little French bull-dog (in a secondhand carrying cage: I didn't trust him to behave himself in the car) and my (few) possessions. On the way out of Catamount Falls dropping by the Agency to say goodbye to Ava Schultz who'd become my only friend there and to inquire if they'd heard more from Orlando Metti.

Ava said she hadn't heard anything. It was supposed that, since I'd returned the things Metti had claimed I'd stolen, Metti was appeased and would not cause more trouble.

I asked her if Metti was continuing as a customer and she said sure, she thought so. Metti hadn't actually had any complaints about my housecleaning. He'd paid his bills more or less on time. Over the years, other women the Agency had sent to him, most of them had worked out OK. He'd never accused anyone of stealing from him before me.

"You need to be more cautious, Violet. Next time you'll know better." Ava laughed.

Told Ava that I was leaving Catamount Falls and she expressed surprise though maybe not so much surprise, considering. Asked me where I was going and I told her I didn't know yet—"I'm just running for my life."

# Tongue

**t**hrust into your mouth to impale you,
subdue you. The man's tongue thick
like a snake not warm but weirdly cool, clammy.
Predator-male tongue prepared to thrust and penetrate
until you choke to death.

*Bitch. Slut. Lying cunt.*

*This isn't over yet.*

**"Oh, Brindle. *Stop.*"**

Soft flopping tongue on my face. Soul of the dog is
the tongue.

Laughing, pushing the little bulldog away. A dog's
mouth is not exactly clean.

Waking in this new place. Relieved to be alive.

Premature heat of May, white-tinged sun falling directly on my face since I have not (yet) put up blinds, curtains. Outside the window is a balcony, a railing that casts bars of shadow against the windowpanes, onto the bed, on my face as I lie in bed awakened by the funny little dog wanting only to kiss me.

Three hundred forty miles from Catamount Falls and from the high-rise apartment overlooking the steely St. Lawrence River. Though I have yet to precisely calculate the miles, it is probably about the same distance to South Niagara. East and south of the city of my birth, south of the Mohawk River in a hilly and mostly rural region of New York State in which I have never lived and where I know no one.

Here, Orlando Metti will never find me. I am certain.

If I'd remained in Catamount Falls the man might have persevered. Out of bitterness, spite. I'd have had to move from Cayuga Street to another rental. But Metti could not hate me so very much, he'd hardly known me. Soon, another girl/woman would attract his eye. The pale blond cleaning-woman speaking accented English, maybe.

In another few months Metti will have forgotten my name. And he has to be grateful to be rid of the *damned little dog.*

It is a new life in Mohawk, New York. A new interim life.

Not my true life but a provisional life. Improvised, calculated.

Slowly, assiduously since the age of eighteen I have been accumulating credits in the state university system. I have had many interruptions in my education. Entire epochs of my life seem to have disappeared. I have never been able to attend college full-time and now the State University of New York at Mohawk has accepted me as a transfer student in the School of Social Work with just five more courses before graduation.

In Mohawk, a town of less than twenty thousand inhabitants, I will look for a new way of supporting myself. I will change my hair color to its more natural shade of brown. I will walk the lively little French bulldog along the river at least twice a day and see who it is I will encounter in this territory entirely new to me.

*What an adorable little dog! What is his breed? What is his name?*

A dog is a disguise I'd never anticipated.

# Uncanny

*H*im. *But—who?*

He was approaching me on the campus walkway. First morning of the fall term.

Facing me, not exactly seeing me. Making his way deftly through loose surges of students moving more slowly along the walkway oblivious of him, his very presence.

A dark-skinned man, young, yet middle-aged. Dignified, self-absorbed, intent upon his destination. His briefcase was a handsome matte beige leather, a relic of another era, clearly heavy. His manner was severe. Something about the sobriety of his bearing and his clothing, the "sport coat" in a muted color that might have been gray, beige, or blue, the fresh-laundered white shirt and dark, dull necktie, made me think he might be an older, foreign-born graduate student. The black plastic-framed eyeglasses and the boxy-shouldered coat suggested a culture other than American and a style very far from fashionable. And no American student, even an older graduate student, would wear a coat and tie, let alone carry a briefcase.

Briskly he passed me. Ascended a flight of steps, disappeared into a sandstone building.

At the foot of the steps I stood staring after him. A sensation of terrible yearning came over me, to follow him up the steps . . . The uncanny sensation that you know who someone is, unmistakably you recognize the face, that's to say the essence of the face, the (unique) face you'd known in a previous lifetime except now in the confusion of the moment, in the excited leap of your blood, you are unable to recall who this person is, or was.

Yet, I was not sure that I wanted him to see me. I was not sure that I wanted to be forced to recall how this person and I knew each other.

It should not have been surprising to me that I might encounter people here in Mohawk whom I'd known years ago in Port Oriskany and in South Niagara. Often in Catamount Falls I'd encountered former classmates whose company I avoided, for I did not want to recall exactly how they knew me, and what they knew of me and my family—*Kerrigans.*

Seeing in their faces that flicker of recognition—*Is that her? The girl who ratted on her brothers and sent them to prison.*

Not that they would have been cruel to me, but even their kindness and sympathy would be painful. And their pity.

And even if this were not true, it would seem true to me. Like an indelible stain that has in fact been removed, yet its imprint will always remain in the memory, a shadow of a stain.

Half-consciously then I avoided the area of the campus where I'd seen the dark-skinned man with the briefcase. In the sandstone building were the departments of economics, political science, statistics and I was taking none of these courses.

A few days later I saw him again walking on campus, carrying his briefcase. Amid undergraduates wearing the most casual attire—T-shirts, shorts, jeans—he looked almost comically dignified in sport coat, white shirt, tie. I wished that someone would greet him so that his masklike face might break into a smile.

That uncanny sensation of trying to recall a dream! Even as the dream fades.

On the walkway I stood staring after him. Almost, I could remember him—but he'd been younger then. If only he would turn, and see me, and not always be running away as if he wished to avoid me, too.

# First Aid

On his short legs Brindle was struggling to bring me something gripped in his jaws. At first it seemed that he'd managed to kill a creature smaller than himself but no, turned out to be the denim bag I carried instead of a purse, and inside the denim bag a small first aid kit.

No idea where I'd acquired this first aid kit whose contents I examined with mounting excitement: Band-Aids, a roll of gauze, small bottle of disinfectant, small scissors, also nail clippers, (white) adhesive tape. Box of cough drops, lozenges, tube of sunscreen, lip gloss. Asthma inhaler, red plastic. Small bottle of ibuprofen. Toothbrush, very small tube of toothpaste.

How strange this was! Yet my reaction was curiosity rather than alarm. Discovering deeper in the bag a Swiss army knife, an eight-ounce aerosol container of pesticide (to be employed like Mace in the event of an emergency), a wad of blood-stiffened Kleenex and a single seashell earring which I did not recognize as my own.

Had to laugh, this treasure trove was utterly baffling.

Demanding of the little bulldog—*Where'd you get these crazy things?*

Impudently Brindle stood on his hind legs and began licking my face. My hands, my arms were paralyzed at first, I could not push him away . . .

And then I was wakened rudely, abruptly. Of course it was the little dog energetically licking my face with his soft slovenly tongue.

Above me the mashed-in brown face loomed like a moon in shadow. Bug-eyes so wide-set they shone like the eyes of a lunatic. And the damned tongue, the panting slithery tongue, making me shiver, shudder, laugh—"Brindle, stop! *No.*"

I was in bed. In this new, slightly uncomfortable bed in this new place in—was it Mohawk, New York? Where sheer chance had brought me in my panicked flight from Catamount Falls.

Recalling now, as remnants of the dream lapped about me like a shallow stream, that the small red asthma inhaler had belonged to my high school classmate Tyrell Jones.

Of course!—Tyrell Jones.

Had I ever seen another asthma inhaler in the intervening years?—I was sure that I had not.

And now it came to me: Tyrell Jones was the dark-skinned man with the briefcase whom I had seen on campus . . .

It was not surprising that Tyrell Jones was a student here at the State University at Mohawk, as I was. Now I could recognize Tyrell's odd, distinct manner of carrying himself, the self-conscious posture with which a naturally shy boy might carry himself in a school situation. Tyrell's close-cropped hair had not changed much. Possibly Tyrell was stouter, less boyish. The wire-rimmed eyeglasses he'd worn in high school that had given him a prim schoolboy look had been replaced by chunky black plastic glasses that disguised half his face.

It was a shock, to think that Tyrell had to be my age—twenty-six.

*Twenty-six!* Not young. At least in my case, not young at all considering that my true life has yet to begin.

**Painful to** recall how I'd left a note in Tyrell Jones's locker—*I love you.*

What had I been thinking!—I could not imagine.

So young at the time, naive and impulsive. Imagining a sort of kinship between Tyrell Jones and me, each of us tormented by the math teacher whose name I'd made an effort to obliterate in my memory.

Now it seemed to me significant that Tyrell Jones was a student here at Mohawk. That we'd glimpsed each other—(for I had no doubt, Tyrell Jones had noticed me)—could not have been an accident. Though I'd come to Mohawk more or less by chance, as a branch of the state university that would honor my transfer credits without difficulty, I could not believe that it was purely chance that Tyrell Jones was also here.

After the day when Tyrell had almost collapsed in math class, unable to breathe, I'd done some research on asthma in the school library, fascinated and appalled. *A sudden inflammation of the sinuses, the nasal cavity, a sensation of suffocating precipitated by pollen, exacerbated by emotion, particularly anxiety, fear.* In a local drugstore I'd examined asthma inhalers, fascinated and appalled. For perhaps one day Tyrell would collapse and I would be the one, the only one, to know how to "save" him . . .

These memories returned to me now, lying in my bed in Mohawk, New York. Had I actually been *in love* with this boy, with whom I'd never exchanged a sentence? No other boy of those years had meant anything to me emotionally. I had not even any memory of any other boy. Young men with whom I'd been involved, sexually, in recent years, and including now my older lover Orlando Metti, had not meant so much to me as Tyrell Jones had meant, though I was sure that Tyrell would be baffled if he ever learned.

Or maybe, Tyrell wouldn't be baffled. Maybe, seeing me, recalling when he'd seen Violet Kerrigan last, he'd have immediately understood.

**"C'mon, Brindle!** You're a bulldog—a hunter."

Walking with Brindle a mile or so to the university campus though I had no classes that morning. At the sandstone building intending to visit the departments of economics, political science, statistics but encountering, in the first department, a mailbox belonging to JONES, TYRELL M.

As it turned out, Tyrell Jones wasn't a student here. Not even a graduate student. In fact, Tyrell Jones was an assistant professor, a faculty member at Mohawk.

How stunned I was at this revelation. How stricken with embarrassment, shame! While I'd been taking university courses for years, dropping out, transferring, beginning again, wayward and uncertain as a rudderless oarless boat on a fast-moving stream, squandering my youth, Tyrell Jones had kept a steady course. He'd earned a Ph.D., or so I assumed. He'd joined the faculty of a respectable state university branch and was teaching a subject of which I knew virtually nothing—economics.

I was proud of him. I was happy for him. Almost I felt that I might burst into tears.

I had not seen Tyrell Jones since graduation at Port Oriskany High. Like me, he'd been awarded a four-year tuition scholarship to one of the state universities. Like me, he'd received other prizes at commencement among them a math prize.

I recalled that, after Mr. Sandman's abrupt departure, a substitute math teacher was hired to finish the semester. Despite his high grades in math Tyrell had not been selected by Mr. Sandman for membership in the Math Club but the substitute teacher, Ms. Frankl, made up for this injustice by selecting him; in our senior year Tyrell was elected president by the eight or ten members (including me). How wonderful it was, I thought. Tyrell Jones had not (evidently) been harmed by the racist Sandman. Perhaps, unlike me, Tyrell had been able to forget him.

"What a darling little dog," the departmental secretary cried, smiling at Brindle, as everyone did who encountered the feisty little bulldog. And lifting her eyes to me. "What breed is he?"

I told her, as I told everyone who asked. Numerous people each day, strangers who smiled happily at the little dog, as at me, with a warmth they would not have thought to exude to me, otherwise.

In such ways, sudden friends are made. Sudden alliances, linked by a naive and sentimental affection for a miniature bulldog with disconcertingly wide-set bulging eyes, who had come to adore this public role, and to beg me, tugging at his leash, for ever more attention.

The newly befriended departmental secretary struck up a conversation with me. Told me, when I asked after Professor Jones, that he was "new since last year" at Mohawk and "a very nice—quiet—person." She paused as if she had more to say and then thought better of it.

"Is Professor Jones the first black professor in economics?"—innocently I asked.

"Why, I—I think he is, yes." The woman paused, frowning. She might have thought it was a kind of rudeness, to have even noticed that the new assistant professor was black. "He is a 'new appointee'—the department has a special grant for 'minority hires.' Are you one of his students?"

"No. An old friend from high school."

"Really! And where was that?"

"Port Oriskany. We were in the same math class."

"You're the same *age*? Really?"

The woman's eyes moved over me, doubtfully. In my casual clothes, bare legs and bare feet in sandals, I did not look like a contemporary of Professor Jones.

In Tyrell Jones's mailbox I left a note—*Hello, Tyrell! Do you remember Violet Kerrigan from high school? My number here is—*

Walking back across the campus with Brindle tugging at the leash I felt so suddenly happy, I was frightened for myself. I had placed a bet that could not fail to win. For if Tyrell Jones did not call me, that would probably be a good thing: I might seriously fall in love with him, or he with me, and one of us might be badly hurt, or both; or, if Tyrell did call me, and we saw each other, and began to be friends, or perhaps more than friends, this might in fact be the greatest good luck of both our lives, all the more precious for being shared.

# "Maxed-Out"

Think you should know, Violet. Lionel is *out*.

Never granted parole. Served the full sentence. What's called *maxed-out*.

News that should not have been surprising. News I'd been expecting.

News to make me swallow, hard. Groping for a place to sit, my knees have gone weak . . .

News that I am determined to interpret as *good news*.

**Because my** brother has *maxed-out,* he has no obligation to see a parole officer. He has no obligation to report to anyone in authority, even a counselor or therapist. He has no obligation to avoid the company of other ex-convicts or what are called *known felons*. He has no obligation to live within a designated area, he is free to live anywhere he wishes without the surveillance of any state corrections authorities for he is no longer their responsibility.

If my brother is apprehended by police for drugs, carrying firearms, driving above the speed limit, causing a public disturbance—he will not be immediately shipped back to prison as he'd be if he were paroled for it's crucial to understand, Lionel is not *on parole*. Lionel has *maxed-out*.

In an upbeat voice Katie has informed me of these matters. She has informed me that our brother Lionel has moved back to South Niagara. Staying with Mom and Dad in their new house until he can get a job, maybe then he'll move out to a place of his own.

Thirteen years he's been incarcerated! Thirteen years of life he has lost.

Imprisoned May 1992. Released May 2005.

Of course, it isn't easy. Lionel is—well, Lionel is what you'd call *withdrawn*.

Stays in his (attic) room. Up late watching TV (downstairs) or playing video games (upstairs). Sleeps late. Never uses the phone. Hasn't contacted his old friends. Not even sure if they still live in South Niagara. Eats some of his meals in his room especially if Mom has invited guests to dinner—relatives who wants to see Lionel, or Katie herself.

Give the poor kid time, everyone says. Traumatic to be released from a maximum security prison after thirteen years when you were only seventeen when you went in.

Almost half of Lionel's life *inside.*

It is the general belief among family, relatives, friends, no longer examined, still less questioned, that Lionel and Jerome Jr. were "railroaded" into confessions. South Niagara PD, prosecutors. Tried and found guilty in the media, targeted for being *white.* A general belief that the youngest sister Violet had something to do with the convictions. In some quarters, the youngest sister Violet had much to do with Lionel being rejected for parole time after time after time over the thirteen very long years.

You know that isn't true, Katie. (Trying to speak calmly.)

*I* know it isn't true, Katie says. I try to explain if the subject comes up . . .

Is that what Lionel thinks, too? (I have to ask.)

Oh God!—Katie laughs. Who'd know what Lionel thinks about anything? It's not exactly like we *talk.*

Mom keeps marveling that Lionel has become *so polite.* Nothing like the rough loud kid he'd been . . .

Good. How good, Lionel has become *polite.*

Having summoned up the courage to call my sister as I do every few months. Check in with Katie. Just to inquire casually how she is. How Mom and Dad are. And Miriam, and Rick. And Les.

These brothers, remote to me as boys with whom I'd gone to school but barely knew.

Katie is my dear friend. Katie is my precious link, my only link to my lost life. Miriam has become distant, distracted; Miriam does not encourage me to call her, for she is very busy with her domestic life—young children, ambitious husband. Not once in my life have I spoken on the phone with Les or Rick. I've sent them cards as I've sent cards to others in the Kerrigan family but (no surprise) they have not ever responded.

I would fear calling either of them, they've been turned against their *rat-sister* and have come to hate me as Jerr and Lionel had.

Of course, Daddy is helping Lionel look for a job. Daddy has connections everywhere in the city, men who owe him favors. At Marcy, Lionel took courses in business math, accounting, English; he acquired experience in auto repair, welding, masonry, carpentry. Skills that are needed in the workplace. Decent-paying work. (No: not plumbing. Never the slightest interest in plumbing.)

*What does Lionel look like now?*—I don't dare ask.

One thing, Vi'let, Lionel *has not* asked about you. So maybe don't worry, OK?

He hasn't?

*Has not.* Not that he'd ask me anything but Mom has told me, Mom wants me to know so (maybe) I can pass it on to you.

At this revelation, this tiny crumb proffered me, my heart leaps. *Mom wants me to know so (maybe) I can pass it on to you.*

Mom knows that we talk on the phone, then?

Well—hard to say what Mom knows, or doesn't know. Like with Dad, they don't talk about you, ever.

OK. Thanks.

Well, I mean—that isn't news to you, Violet? Is it? After thirteen years?

No. You are right.

Look, I'm sorry to—whatever. But you asked. So I told you. But the thing is, Mom sort of knows that we are in communication, and she definitely told me that Lionel has never asked about you, so why'd she tell me that, unless she thought I'd (maybe) tell you?

To this, I can't think of a reply. Wiping tears from my face, as Brindle rears up on his hind legs, on the sofa beside me, to eagerly lick my face.

Brindle, *no!* Stop that.

Katie asks what's going on there? Who's—what's—"Brindle"?

Brindle is a dog who has come to live with me, I tell Katie.

You have a dog? Really, Violet? How'd that happen?

His owner didn't want him. His life was endangered.

What kind of dog? Katie is sounding surprised, a little envious. Though mostly relieved that the conversation has swerved onto a safer subject.

He's a little guy. Miniature bulldog.

*Bulldog!* Aren't they ugly?

Brindle is nudging and pushing against me, skinny tail flailing. His big bug-eyes shine like black fluorescence. Is the little bulldog ugly, or—beautiful? Close up, Brindle panting in my face, licking my face, it's impossible to judge.

Katie fires more questions at me. Between us is the marvel that Violet has a dog, that Katie had no idea that Violet has a dog, the sisters know so little of each other now.

Katie asks me about Mohawk University, what courses am I taking here. Why did I transfer from Catamount Falls. How do I like living in Mohawk, she'd looked it up online and was impressed, it's in a kind of tourist area, Mohawk River Valley, New York State wineries, Finger Lakes. Of course, Mohawk is pretty small—exclusive of the university enrollment, population six thousand.

Waiting for Katie to ask if I've made friends here. Any special friends here.

But Katie doesn't ask, out of discretion perhaps imagining that I am as lonely as people in South Niagara imagine I must be, and deserve to be, in my involuntary exile.

Katie doesn't ask, and I don't tell her.

*I have a very close friend here. Someone I'd known in high school in Port Oriskany. What there is between us would be hard to explain for much is silence.*

It has been a good conversation, I think after Katie hangs up. I am trembling, but then I am always trembling when I call my sister, and this evening it's worse than usual of course since the news has come at last, unavoidable, unsurprising, yet devastating as a poisonous gas hissing into the house—*Our brother Lionel is free, "maxed-out."*

# The Misunderstanding

He was sure: he was being followed.

Left the Shamrock at about 11:00 P.M., headed for his car. The lot behind the tavern was filled so he'd had to park across the street in the Bank of Niagara lot deserted at this hour.

Aware of them behind him. Murmuring together, about him. Muffled laughter like distant thunder.

Thought he'd seen them earlier, on the street by the movie house. Black kids. Except these looked older, taller.

That tight sensation in his brain. Hearing the faint *beat beat beat* of what sounded like somebody hammering at a distance but (the doctor had said) was the very beat of his blood, in his brain.

Twenty-four hours Jerome had been monitored, wearing a blood-pressure cuff on his upper left arm beneath his clothes, that contracted to the point of pain every half hour during the day and every hour of an interminable night and the discovery was, he had a condition called *hypertension*. Sure, he knew what this was. Every old person they knew had *hypertension*. The old sod had had *hypertension* along with a dozen other ailments but he'd lived to be—eighty-seven? Going strong until the day he died. Stubborn old bastard, never gave up whiskey.

Jerome had cut back on his drinking, some. Also cut back on salt. (Lula now used low-sodium salt, cooking. Why food tasted flat to him now.) He didn't smoke much these days anyway, cigarettes were so damned expensive, and made him cough like hell, mornings. Taking the blood-pressure pills seemed to help. He guessed the pills had helped but the refill had run out. Hadn't been back to the cardiologist in a year. If the *beat beat beat* kept him awake at night sometimes or pausing short of breath at the top of stairs he'd resolve to make an appointment but next day, so many distractions he hadn't time. If he'd mentioned to Lula she'd have made the appointment for him, marked it on the calendar in the kitchen, she'd have nagged him about keeping the appointment but

he never got around to mentioning it to Lula for specifically that reason (the nagging) and now they were
in one of their spells of not-speaking to each other
because he'd (supposedly) hurt her feelings over some
trivial matter and God damn if he was going to make
it up to her when it was so trivial he couldn't remember what the fuck it was, even.

Not that he gave a shit that the woman imagined
she was punishing him, he did not.

Oh fuck, he *did.* Felt like hell when his wife turned
away from him. And he knew, she wasn't feeling so
well lately. All of the kids gone from the house now,
just the two of them but God damn he wasn't going to
grovel.

There'd been other women. He hadn't been faithful
to Lula. Not one of the men, the husbands he knew,
he'd grown up with, guys he'd gone to school with,
not one of them had been faithful to their wives and
(yet) most of the marriages had endured. They were
Catholics, the marriages endured even when love wore
out, frayed like much-laundered cloth in which stains
remain. *Till death do us part*—bullshit like everything else in the Church but still, he and Lula were
together.

What had kept them together was Lula forgiving
him. And what allowed her to forgive was loving him.

A woman's weakness, love without question. Love without doubt. Love like oxygen you'd suck through a filthy broken straw, fall on your knees in mud, anything to survive because you can't live without him.

She wasn't going to let him go, she'd said. After it had come out he'd been seeing someone and wasn't going to apologize. He could try to make her hate him and even so, if she'd hated him, even then she would not let him go. That was *love*.

Crossing the street to avoid the young black men. Had to be five, six of them. Not that he was afraid of them. Walking fast. Not too fast. A car double-parked nearby, door open. Rap music from the car loud, grating. Punk music, you couldn't understand the words. Had to be cursing whitey. Mocking whitey. He had the car key in his fingers that had gone cold as ice. There came a shout—*Hey mister!*

Black gangs had targeted him before. It was deliberate, premeditated. They'd targeted his sons Les and Rick who'd had nothing to do with whatever had happened to Hadrian Johnson but who gave a fuck about that, nobody gave a fuck about actual justice.

Had to be, these punks knew who he was. Not a day of his life in South Niagara after all that publicity, KERRIGAN in headlines for weeks, that half the black population in the city didn't know who he was. Whose father he was.

Soon after Jerome Jr. and Lionel had pleaded guilty to manslaughter and were sentenced to prison the vandalism began. Windows broken in Jerome's car parked in the driveway, tires slashed. Rocks thrown at the front of the house, garbage dumped on the lawn. Vehicles speeding past the house at night, shouts and threats. Jerome had had to guard the property with a (borrowed) rifle. Him, Les and Rick, some of their friends. Armed and ready with guns. Black Rock Street vigilantes, they called themselves. (White) guys from other neighborhoods, some of them total strangers to the Kerrigans, volunteered to help protect the Kerrigans from their enemies. *If one of them sets foot on my property I have the right to kill him*—Jerome Kerrigan had been quoted, actually misquoted in the papers for what he'd said had been different, he was sure—*If anybody sets foot on my property to attack my family or me I have the right to kill him. That's the law.*

There'd been a South Niagara PD cruiser parked out front of the house, two weeks or so. Two cops. Still the kids had to go to school, Les and Rick, poor Katie so anxious she'd started pulling hairs out of her scalp.

Lula had been terrified to sleep in the house. Terrified it would be set on fire, they'd die in their sleep. Took Katie and stayed for a while with relatives in another neighborhood till things quieted down after a few weeks.

If Jerome's uncle Tom Kerrigan had stayed out of it, that might've been better. But there came old fiery Tommy Kerrigan back into the public eye campaigning—again—and winning—again. You'd wanted to think that the wily old bastard had retired from politics but no, he'd been vehement and energized, winning the Republican primary on a campaign of *law and order, fair treatment for all races*—meaning that "whites" were being mistreated in South Niagara as elsewhere in the U.S., his own nephews were "victims" of black racism: persecuted because they were white. Such bitterness Tommy Kerrigan stirred up, virtually all of South Niagara was divided: pro-Kerrigan, anti-Kerrigan. He'd singled out no one by name because that wasn't Tommy Kerrigan's style but it was implicit that certain black leaders, black ministers, liberal white politicians, were responsible for the gross "miscarriage of justice" that had sent his nephews to prison.

Years later now. Things had quieted down in South Niagara. Tom Kerrigan had retired from politics at last, permanently. Had to be over eighty. He lived in Naples, Florida, with his (much younger) wife, said to be incapacitated by a series of strokes. But one of his Republican protégés was a U.S. congressman and another was preparing to run for state senator. Jerome Kerrigan could not escape the ignominy of his name.

God-damned unfair, he'd always had black friends. Veterans like himself. Race issues hadn't entered into any of their exchanges for twenty years or more and then suddenly, they stopped seeing one another.

Why his God-damned blood pressure was high. Just thinking about it like poking a sore tooth. Plus money. *Always* money.

At work that day feeling dazed from the early-morning until late. Head tight. Pounding pulses. Probably not a good idea to stop for a drink but badly needed a drink. Also, the Shamrock was a place where Jerome Kerrigan was known. For himself, not his name or his damned uncle. At the bar, the familiar soothing incantation of complaint. The speech of his friends as it had once been the speech of his elders. A kind of harmony, in complaint. Corrupt politicians, union officials. Whoever happened to be mayor, governor of the state. President of the U.S. Jerome could count on it, he'd know virtually all of the men in the Shamrock beyond a certain age. Young guys he wouldn't know but older guys, he would. He'd gone to school with some of them. He'd gone out with their sisters, their wives—long ago. His kids knew their kids, or had once. He'd had disagreements with all of them but could not have said what the disagreements were, for the most part. A fixed number of people you know, you can't feud with all of them but must relent, forgive. Certainly, forget.

It was a taboo subject among the men, how families disappoint. Maybe you could complain about your old drunk father but not about the wife—not really. Joking, harsh joking, might be OK but nothing too personal, private. Nothing about the wife's health. Mention *chemo* and your best friend's eyes go blank. And talking of children, grown-up kids and how they turn out—pretty much forbidden.

If you love them something terrible happens to them. Though if you stop loving them the pain is worse, like a limb torn off.

Never forgive Violet. His baby Violet Rue.

Jerome Jr. and Lionel he'd forgive, before her. His sons had made stupid choices. It was drinking that had been the stupid, fatal choice—every bad decision that night had followed from that.

Ran in the family. Irish genes. Everybody knew: drinking made you drunk, and drunk made you stupid.

Though they were sober when they'd lied to him. To *him*. Claiming they were scared, didn't know what to do, panicked and drove away and afterward begging him to forgive them and so he'd forgiven them eventually, though he was disgusted with them, and disgusted now when he recalled. His grief at losing Jerome Jr. was contaminated with this disgust and with the fury of disgust that his sons, his oldest children, had so betrayed him.

But the daughter had never said she was sorry. She'd never asked to be forgiven. Wanted to be *loved* as if nothing had gone wrong between them.

His heart had been lacerated, the daughter's betrayal was an open wound even years later. For he'd loved her best.

It wasn't that she'd spoken to the police about her brothers but that she hadn't come to him first, to tell him. Together, they'd have worked out what to do. But she had acted heedlessly, without consulting him. Her *father*.

She had gone outside the family, that was the unforgivable sin. And old enough to know, not a child.

Thinking of this, how his daughter had betrayed him, felt as if his heart were lacerated anew, he could not bear it. His breath came short, a vise seemed to be tightening around his chest. His anger, his fury—collapsed into a pounding fist.

"Hey mister—you OK?"

He was on his knees. The ignition key had slipped from his icy fingers. Pulses beat harder, harder—he pitched forward onto the pavement with a strangled cry as the boys approached cautiously, staring at him.

"Mister? Hey?"

"He's drunk?"

"Somethin wrong with him, see—his face . . ."

Warily they circled him. A white man, looked like an older man, they'd be blamed for knocking him down, taking his wallet. But couldn't just let him lie there struggling to breathe so one of them ran into the Shamrock Tavern yelling there's a man fell down outside, somebody call 911 for an ambulance.

By the time the ambulance arrived not one of the black teenagers remained in the vicinity. Got out of there in their car and on foot, fast as they could.

White cops gonna show up, see black boys and a white man down on the street and suspect the worst. And if they tried to run then, risking a bullet in the back.

# The Return

Hesitantly Katie has said, she thinks it will be *all right.*

I am wondering what *all right* means.

If I return to South Niagara. Stay with her and her family.

For my first real visit in more than thirteen years. A week, two weeks?

If Mom will agree to see me, that is all I want.

For Daddy has died. (It is difficult for me to utter these words—*Daddy has died.*)

*All right now*—for Daddy has died, and the bitterness has died with him. It is hoped.

Or possibly Katie means it is *all right* for me to return to South Niagara though our brother Lionel has been released from prison and is living here. *All right*—Lionel won't murder me.

It is hoped!

**On the** phone we'd cried together. And seeing each other, first time in years, we hugged each other, hard. And we cried.

"Oh, Violet! I am so sorry."

*So sorry I cut you out of my life. So sorry I ceased to love you.*

In that instant I forgave my sister. Of course.

We did not seem to each other like adult women. Grieving for our father we were young girls again as if no time had passed.

Years that had drawn us apart. My sister had been my closest friend and she was married, she'd had a baby (a daughter) without me. Scarcely with my knowing. How was it possible?

Now, Katie would be my sister again. No mistaking the relief in her face, her happiness at seeing me, running to greet me, hug me, as I drove up in the Honda Civic, peering through the windshield at addresses in an unfamiliar part of South Niagara—West Cabot Road.

"Oh my God, Vi'let—it's *you*."

Laughing, in each other's arms. Tears shining on our faces hot as acid.

From my aunt Irma I'd heard the (belated, shocking) news. My father had died of a massive stroke the previous week. He'd been drinking heavily, it was said. Strangers had found him in the street outside the Shamrock Tavern, they'd called an ambulance but he didn't survive the night.

Both Katie and Miriam tried to contact me but had only outdated phone numbers. Irma recalled that I'd transferred to the state university at Mohawk and in this way managed to be connected with me through the university's student affairs office, after some difficulty. *Oh Violet. I have sad news . . . .*

The family was in shock. Jerome had died so suddenly, without warning—so young, at only sixty-four.

But I thought—the stress of Daddy's life! His feuds, his hatreds. He'd worn himself out fighting enemies.

Thirteen years, a son in prison. The other, older son killed in prison. The daughter who'd betrayed him. Never can you outlive the shame, the ignominy, if you are a man of pride. Each day you are reminded anew. Each day is contaminated.

Still, I'd stubbornly believed that Daddy would relent and forgive me, one day. So long as it was a choice of his and not forced upon him by anyone else, that might have been possible.

Deciding on a whim one day to call me. Summon me.

*Hey Violet Rue! Been missing you like hell.*

# In My Mother's Garden

K atie insists yes it will be *all right*.

Of course, she has prepared Mom. And Mom is expecting me.

Not in the house in which we'd grown up at 388 Black Rock Street but in a smaller house in the same neighborhood, a half-mile away.

I am nervous! Wiping my sweaty palms against my jeans.

I am driving to this house, alone. In the trunk of the Honda Civic are several potted plants for my mother's garden which Katie has helped me select at a local nursery.

Katie thinks it is better for me to go alone. Next time I visit Mom, she will come with me. But this first time— "Just the two of you. That will be better, I think."

It is heartening to me, Katie assumes there will be a second visit. That Mom will be happy to see me, and want to see me again.

Katie has cautioned me not to be shocked by our mother's appearance. Five months ago she'd had surgery to remove a small growth beneath her arm, near her left breast. The cancer had been stage 3, metastasized to several lymph nodes. But the surgery went well, radiation and chemotherapy have gone well, just a few weeks remaining of the treatment.

All this is news to me. Another shock. Katie assures me, Mom didn't want most people to know about the cancer. She'd told her, of course. She'd told Miriam. And a few relatives, close friends. But she hadn't told her sister Irma, she hadn't wanted Irma to come visit her, make a fuss. *Making a fuss* was what Lula most dreaded.

Of course, she hadn't told the boys. Les, Rick. Lionel.

If she'd been able to keep the secret from Daddy, she'd have kept it from him. As it was, she'd hidden the worst of the side effects from our father, sleeping much of the day when he was at work so that she was strong enough to prepare a meal in the evening, and managing her appetite so that she was able to eat at least part of the meal with him, to deflect his suspicions. She'd made up her face, she'd looked almost glamorous. Wore loose-fitting clothes so he wouldn't notice how much weight she'd lost. As soon as her hair began to fall out she'd had it buzz-cut so that she could be fitted with a glamorous wig, virtually identical with her own hair when she'd been young and healthy and she'd made sure that Daddy never saw her without that wig.

Amazing! I am filled with admiration for my mother. Thinking how little I knew her.

And did that work?—I have to ask.

Katie laughs. "Well—maybe. You know what men are like."

"Do I? What are men like?"

"They can't face much reality. If they can tell themselves a woman isn't sick, not seriously sick, if that's at all possible it's what they will tell themselves because to think otherwise is terrifying to them."

"And was that the case with Dad?"

"He couldn't face it, that Mom might be seriously ill. If Miriam or I tried to bring up the subject he'd cut us off. He stayed away from the house a lot. At work, and after work. Not so different from the way he'd always been, in fact. They had that kind of marriage—the wife stays home. The man screws around."

"Oh, Katie! That sounds harsh."

"Mom dealt with it, she was OK. Not happy, but OK. Every woman she knew who was married had the same experience. She couldn't have left Dad even if she'd wanted to, she had no income. All she'd ever done was 'keep house'—take care of children. Then this thing that came along, like a stake through the heart of the marriage."

*Thing that came along.* The way our family had learned to speak of the murder of Hadrian Johnson. A thing, an event, an action that had *come along.*

"It wasn't just that Daddy had affairs—had sex—with other women, that they couldn't talk about. He and Mom never actually seemed to acknowledge what Jerr and Lionel *did.* It was like they couldn't—just couldn't comprehend it . . . All Daddy talked about was lawyers and appeals, how to get the convictions 'overturned.' He had his fixed beliefs, no one dared challenge him. The stress made him unbalanced, ill. And then it killed him." Katie pauses, wiping at her eyes.

It has been something of a shock to me, to hear such remarks uttered by my sister. This sudden aerial perspective of our parents' marriage is new to me. And this new sister, so thoughtful, analytical—this hardly seems like the timid girl I remember.

"But Daddy loved Mom, in his way. He loved us all—that was what made him so dangerous. When you love someone like that you can turn on them viciously—the way Daddy turned on you."

Wanting to ask my sister—*But do you think Daddy would have forgiven me? Eventually?* But no, of course I won't ask.

**It is** true, I am frightened of seeing my mother after so many years.

Last glimpse I'd had of Mom she was walking away from me in the "safe house." Drugged and unsteady on her feet but determined to escape me.

Hard to avoid acknowledging the fact that my mother had abandoned me. Made me into an orphan. Why?

*She'd loved your brothers more. No—she'd loved your father more.*

Like a memory of having been poisoned by something you'd eaten. Barely managed to survive. And yet—here is the food again . . . And you are hungry.

But Katie has assured me: Mom wants to see me, this will not be an unpleasant surprise to her.

Our grandfather's funeral had been too soon. They wouldn't have been ready to see me yet, Katie says. But now . . .

And yet: I am shivering with anticipation, that somehow in her medicated state, distraught or depressed from Daddy's death, Mom will not remember that this visit has been planned, that I am in South Niagara staying with Katie.

Or, Mom may remember. But may have changed her mind about seeing me again.

*Rat-girl! You.*

Driving to the new address that is only a few blocks from our old house I am making a conscious decision not to drive by 388 Black Rock on the way. The house in which I'd lived for twelve years. The only house I remember, deep-imprinted in my soul.

Better not. Not now. Another day.

For on Black Rock Street I will see—again—the dead end, the uncultivated land, dirt paths leading to the edge above the rushing Niagara River.

The scrubby-wooded area where my brothers buried the baseball bat. Where they'd buried the murdered black boy, kicked dirt and leaves over him in his shallow grave . . .

In some of my confused dreams, this was so. The murdered boy buried with the baseball bat in a shallow grave.

In another dream, I'd seen my brothers kick other things into the grave—broken bicycle, a baseball cap . . .

Have to shake my head, to dislodge these phantasmal memories. So many years haunted, I am not always sure what is real, and what is not-real; what I have seen with my own eyes, and what I have imagined might have been by my eyes if I'd been in the right place at the right time.

Oh!—here is the "new" house. As the family calls it.

A mild shock, the house at 111 Harrison Street is considerably smaller than my parents' old house, more ordinary, even run-down, though also shingled wood-frame painted gray, on a smaller lot.

Just a stoop at the front. No real second floor except what appears to be an attic room beneath a peaked roof. (Where Lionel is living?) One of numerous post-war houses *cheap-built* as Daddy would say with a sneer, along streets like Harrison.

Probably my father repainted this house, did some repairs. With a mortgage he'd bought it as a temporary measure, deeply in debt from lawyers' bills. Must've pained Jerome Kerrigan to live here, a man who'd taken such pride in maintaining his property.

Badly cracked asphalt driveway is so narrow, you'd hardly imagine that a full-sized car could drive on it. A blighted elm, most of the tree removed, only a trunk remaining in the front yard.

In a working-class neighborhood it had seemed

crucial to mark small distinctions. Black Rock Street with a row of houses overlooking the Niagara River was acknowledged to be a superior place to live set beside lesser streets like Harrison. *See what I have done for my family*—a father's statement of pride.

So nervous, I have been sitting for several minutes in the car parked at the curb trying to summoning my courage. It's as if the outer layer of my skin has been peeled away. I have not told Tyrell Jones much about my life, nor has Tyrell asked me though yes, he does know who I am. Impossible to have grown up in Port Oriskany without being familiar with the name *Kerrigan.* But I'd told him that my father had died suddenly, I had to depart at once for South Niagara and so—would he take Brindle home with him for a while?—and without hesitation he'd said yes. Of course.

Tyrell also said *Whatever happens, Violet—there will be some logic to it.*

*Logic!* I want to believe this.

My wish is to live a life in which emotions come slowly as clouds on a calm day. You see the approach, you contemplate the beauty of the cloud, you observe it passing, you let it go. You do not dwell upon what you have seen, you do not regret it. You are content to understand that the identical cloud will never come again, no matter how beautiful, unique. You do not weep at its loss.

**Ringing the** front doorbell in a state of such anxiety, I am (absurdly) relieved when no one answers. I am carrying a red climber rose for my mother's garden, gripped in my arms against my chest like a shield.

Katie has told me, probably Mom will be in her garden. If no one answers the door just go around to the back.

Mom had chemotherapy yesterday. She will be feeling the effects today. One of our young cousins is staying with her, looking after her until Katie can come over in the late afternoon.

Strange, unnerving, to walk around to the back of the little wood frame house at 111 Harrison Street which I have never seen before. Underfoot the grass is scruffy, gone partly to seed. All of the blinds at the windows have been pulled down. How like trespassing this feels, in a fairy tale in which the clueless young girl blunders into the forbidden and will regret it.

A mild shock, turning a corner of the house, and there is an ordinary backyard, a small plot of tilled soil, a few flowering plants, shrubs, and there, in splotched sunshine, seated in a canvas lawn chair with a straw hat partly covering her face—an older woman in loose-fitting clothes with white skin, delicate features like a smudged watercolor. My mother?

"Mom?—hello . . ."

Here is the true shock: my mother stares at me blinking rapidly, without seeming to recognize me. Then she smiles, stiffly.

"Mom? It's Violet. I—I'm visiting Katie."

Swallowing hard, for this is awkward. (Should I come to my mother, to embrace her? Take her hand? Kiss her? I am carrying the rosebush in my arms, and will set it down at her feet.)

"I—maybe Katie told you?—I'm staying with Katie at her place for—a few nights."

My mother is beautiful!—that is my first impression.

Her skin seems translucent. Her mouth is thinner than I recall, but touched with lipstick, lightly. In the shadow of the straw hat, her eyes are large, luminous.

"Mom? It's Violet."

The thought occurs to me—*She doesn't know who I am.*

"Aunt Lula? You have a visitor."

A strapping big-thighed girl in bib overalls hurries out of the house to facilitate the visit. Evidently she is my cousin Trix whom I scarcely recall as a little girl, and Trix is trained as a nurse's aide, staying with Aunt Lula whenever she's needed.

"Aunt Lula? Look: somebody's brought you a present."

Foolishly I stammer there are more rosebushes in the car . . . for Mom's garden.

Determined not to burst into tears and yet within a few seconds, I am weeping uncontrollably.

"Oh hey, Vi'let—it's OK. Your mom is doing really well, there's nothing to be sad about. Aunt Lula? See who's here? It's 'Violet.'"

My mother has continued to stare at me, with an expression of slow-dawning recognition. Her voice is hoarse and near-inaudible: "'Violet'—?"

My mother is not exactly welcoming me but neither is she turning away from me in repugnance.

Probably, her memory has been affected by the chemotherapy. Though Katie has prepared her for my visit, she seems to have forgotten.

"'Vio-let'?"

Of course, I too am changed. Changed enormously. Can't even remember what I must have looked like, when my mother last saw me.

Twenty-seven years old! Not a girl any longer.

I am stooping to embrace my mother in the chair, awkwardly. I see that her eyes are grotesquely bloodshot. Her skin is unnaturally pale, brittle-looking as if it might disintegrate to the touch. Beneath the wide-brimmed straw hat, that gives her a quasi-glamorous look, the strawberry blond wig is slightly askew.

"Oh, Mom! I am so sorry."

How natural it seems, to apologize. Always, the easiest recourse.

An effort for Mom to lift her arms but she manages to lift her arms. Awkwardly I am crouched above her, trying to hug her without hurting her. Such frail arms! Such a frail body! Lula had once been fleshy, comforting in her ample breasts, hips; now I am concerned that I may bruise her.

"Violet. Hello . . ." Still Mom seems uncertain about me, who I am or why I am here. Her voice is scratchy, barely audible. But she is alert to the fact of the red climber roses, a gift. "These are pretty! Thank you."

"For your garden, Mom. I'll help you put it in."

I am wondering if, with her bloodied eyes, Mom can even see the little roses clearly. She grips my wrist to steady herself.

Mom is wearing a loose-fitting sweater and slacks, bedroom slippers on thin white feet. A chemical odor wafts from her body, pinching my nostrils. Seen close up the strawberry blond wig is obviously synthetic; a human-hair wig would have cost a thousand dollars. But I don't doubt that Daddy was deceived by this wig, or wished to be deceived.

I am wishing that Katie had warned me about the bloodshot eyes. Broken capillaries from the chemo, must be. And the pungent odor! I am close to gagging.

Seeing that I am distracted, shaky, tears running down my cheeks, my nurse's-aide cousin Trix shoves a box of tissues at me. Offers me a glass of grapefruit juice—"Your mom loves this and it's good for her, not too much sugar." Drags another lawn chair over for me to sit in, close by my mother.

Daringly, I take one of Mom's hands. Thin, cool, papery skin, veins visible through the skin, and no rings—this is not a hand I have ever seen before. And so *soft*.

No rings, her fingers are too thin. I wonder if she misses them. If she will ever wear them again.

"Oh, Mom. Gosh . . ."

No words but inane words. At such times, words stumble and fade, fail us.

Mom manages to squeeze my hand in return, weakly. Though (possibly) she isn't altogether certain who I am, why I am here, what is happening, she behaves with a woman's natural instinct for what is expected of her.

Squinting at me: "Are you staying long? Do you live here now?"

Interpreting—*Are you the one who is staying here long? Are you the one who is living here now?*

I am not sure how long I am staying. A week? Two weeks? How long will I be welcome?

I tell my mother that I don't live in South Niagara just now. I am living temporarily in Mohawk, New York. Finishing college at last.

I would tell Mom more—why it has taken me so long to complete college, what I am studying and what I hope to do after college—but she has become agitated suddenly.

"Is Katie here? Where is Katie?"—Mom glances about worriedly.

"Katie is not here right now, Mom. Katie is coming over later."

"Why isn't Katie here? I thought—they said . . ."

*But I am here. I am Violet. I am here with you now.*

". . . they were going to bring Dad. Katie was. He's there now, he has his own floor of the house. You know how your dad takes over," Mom says with a breathless little laugh, tugging at my wrist as if trying to pull herself up, or to pull me down. "Anyplace he is, he just—takes over . . . They gave him his own truck, at work. He never took orders from anybody."

Excitedly Mom is gesturing with her hand in the direction of the street. Does Katie live in that direction?

I am wondering why Katie hadn't warned me that Mom doesn't seem to know that Daddy has died. Or maybe it is painful knowledge that waxes and wanes and she has lost the strength to maintain this knowledge for now.

Tomorrow, I will visit our father's grave in the cemetery at St. Matthew's. Katie has offered to come with me but I think I will go alone.

Katie has said that our brother Rick calls Mom each Sunday evening. He'd had a bad spell with drugs after high school but went into rehab, now he's a counselor at a rehab facility in Boise, Idaho. Our brother Les seems to have disappeared for the time being: he'd been living in Buffalo, working in a small parts factory, married, two young children, then in the process of a divorce he disappeared without notifying anyone and might not even know that Daddy has died, Mom has had cancer.

Of course, Miriam calls all the time. Visits when she can, from Albany.

*And then there's Violet Rue. Where has Violet Rue been!*

Of the seven Kerrigan children only Katie remains in South Niagara. Years ago she'd wanted desperately to leave but had not left, remained in South Niagara because of our mother and now it looks as if she will never leave, she has said.

How like a gigantic tree, a family. No matter if the tree is badly damaged, beginning to die and to rot, roots are entangled underground, inextricably.

As Mom and I struggle to speak together, faltering, lapsing into silence and beginning again, our cousin Trix has been hovering nearby. Watching my face, gauging my emotions like a trained professional.

(Does she expect me to faint? Burst into tears again, like an overgrown child? Strange to see a younger cousin regarding me like a medical worker.) Seeing that Mom and I are doing reasonably well Trix offers to bring the other rosebushes from my car and trots off—breaking into an elated run—eager to exercise her strong, muscled legs.

Husky girl in her early twenties with a big easy smile, a thick ponytail bouncing behind as she runs. Badly I wish to know Trix, to have known Trix as she was growing up. One of many cousins! I have lost all my cousins. I have virtually no family. It is my fault almost entirely—I might have tried harder to keep them even when they'd rejected me.

Feeling a stab of guilt, how I'd taken Aunt Irma for granted. I vow: I will call Irma, visit her soon. I will behave in a way to allow her husband Oscar to know that whatever took place between us, or did not quite take place, I've forgotten, forgiven.

"Aunt Lula, look! Gorgeous roses for *you*."

Trix has returned with the other bushes which she sets down in front of my mother.

"Oh, thank you! Are these from—?" Mom glances about, uncertain. In the fog of her confusion she yet retains a wifely, motherly instinct for not wishing to hurt anyone's feelings.

"From Violet, Aunt Lula. You know—*Violet*."

"From me, Mom. For your garden."

Now, we have something to talk about. Something to look at, to regard together, to admire. And I can identify the roses for my mother. The red climber rose is *Dublin Bay*. The yellow rose is *King's Ransom*. The exquisite pale pink/lavender rose is *Sapphire*.

While Mom looks on blinking and smiling Trix and I plant the rosebushes in her garden. The soil is moist, dark, almost bare of weeds; obviously, someone has been helping my mother with the garden which is flourishing with bright-colored zinnias, dahlias, delicate coneflowers, marigolds, bachelor's buttons as well as several rosebushes in reasonably healthy condition.

"Remember, Mom? Those Japanese beetles that used to eat your roses?"—the memory returns to me, with a flood of childish nostalgia.

But Mom doesn't seem to hear. She is looking tired now, her eyelids flutter and droop. It is all that she can do to keep awake, observing Trix and me digging holes with a shovel and a hoe, setting the rosebushes carefully in place, watering the roots, covering the roots with soil. Exhilarating to work with Trix, my so-capable cousin.

How grateful I am for the beauty of flowers. Thank God for beauty, a balm to the soul.

Trix goes away, returns with more grapefruit juice. Mom makes an effort to drink but her hand shakes, she spills some of the liquid onto the front of her smock, which I dab with a tissue. Mom laughs, and reaches for my hand. Impulsively, she kisses it.

"Well. Here you are—'Violet Rue.' Why did you take so long?"

# Forgiveness

"Violet. Hello."

Lionel's voice is cracked, hoarse. In prison he'd *injured himself,* as prison medical records would state. Mysteriously crushing his larynx in an "accidental fall" in the way that, if you'd suspected that another man had injured your brother, whether another prisoner or a C.O., would seem to indicate that he'd been kicked in the throat, hard.

Of course, if that were so, if Lionel had been violently attacked in the prison, kicked repeatedly in the throat, possibly his assailant had even jumped on his throat as he lay on his back on the floor, intent upon crushing every bone in his throat, Lionel would not have told authorities about the assault. In prison you dare not *snitch.* You dare not *rat.*

"Lionel! Hi."

Shyly you take your brother's big-knuckled hand which is extended not to you exactly but toward you, guardedly. As if, if your hand recoils from his, Lionel is prepared to quickly draw back his hand, too.

Cold fingers, somewhat stiff, unyielding. You can feel the wariness in your brother's body as you'd feel in an animal that is tensing before leaping away. Or leaping at you.

Shy with your brother whom you have not seen in more than thirteen years.

Yet eagerly you stare at each other. Strangers trying to see in the face of the other a trace, a clue, explaining the connection between you.

Lionel seems to be mystified that your hair isn't the color he'd expected—yet, now that he thinks about it, he can't seem to recall the color of your hair when you were a girl.

Like his own, you tell him. More or less.

His own?—Lionel touches his hair, his close-cropped head. As if he can't recall the color of his hair, either. You would describe it as wheat-colored, light brown. Not a remarkable color. Not darkly dramatic like your father's hair before it had become threaded with gray. Not strawberry blond like your mother's hair when she'd been young.

Mild panic in Lionel's eyes. Unless you are imagining it.

No doubt, there is a glisten of mild panic in your eyes.

*Are we really doing this? Are we really—here?*

Like the meeting with your mother yesterday, this meeting with your brother has been arranged by Katie at the "new" house on Harrison Street where Lionel has been living following his release from prison. Elsewhere in the house your mother is lying down trying to nap and your cousin Trix is chatting on the phone with a friend.

About time you guys got together, Katie said brightly.

The casualness of *you guys* is encouraging to you. Maybe it has all been a misunderstanding on your part, the animosity of both your brothers? Maybe it had been mostly an accident, Lionel pushing you down the icy steps?

You wonder if Lionel even remembers it. That time of confusion and unease, dread. When the arrest of your brothers had seemed imminent and yet, the arrest of your brothers had not (yet) occurred.

You wonder if you are remembering the episode correctly: If the steps had been icy, possibly you'd just slipped?

Lionel is having difficulty smiling. Moving his mouth. An effort. Ice pick eyes. Creased forehead of a much older man. Finally he manages, his smile is a shriek of pain.

You think—*He is trying to forgive. It is not easy for him.*

You have been smiling, too. Smilesmile as waitresses learn to do while hoping to be tipped.

Awkwardly you speak together. Lionel is reticent, you will have to do most of the talking. Ask him questions that are easy to answer. No threat. No implied judgment. You have been told that Daddy helped get him a job at Neilson's Lumberyard which is familiar to you from childhood, natural to ask him about that job, also if he has gotten together with friends from high school, though (it seems) that is not a great question since Lionel falls silent, grimacing. *Of course, don't ask him that! Your brother is an ex-convict. He has been shamed in the eyes of his old friends and of everyone who knew him.*

Your voice sounds hoarse too, thin and insincere. You have not been able to decipher all of Lionel's words but haven't wanted to ask him to speak louder for perhaps he can't.

Thinking if you'd glimpsed this man on the street it's likely that you would not have recognized him.

Passing him, you would avoid making eye contact.

There is a plaintive look to Lionel's face, an air of reproach, hurt. His skin has become coarse, putty-colored. He is heavyset and slow-moving where once he'd been lean and muscular, hyperactive and impatient. His eyebrows are thick and well defined. You can imagine that some women might find him attractive—except for the habit of derision into which his mouth naturally shifts.

Lionel is thirty-one years old but could be a decade older. He has never lived alone. He has lived only in your parents' house and in the maximum security prison facility at Marcy. Until recently he has never had to take care of himself as adults do: shopping for clothes and food, preparing food for themselves, driving a car. Katie has told me how when Lionel had first returned to South Niagara he'd seemed terrified of leaving the house. She'd volunteered to drive him to the mall to shop for clothes and other items and he'd virtually panicked, paralyzed at the sight of so many people of whom (he was sure) many were aware of his identity. He'd frozen on an escalator. He'd ducked into a men's lavatory to avoid someone he thought he knew from his high school class. He'd sweated in a state of terror as Katie drove, flinching at intersections.

Tragic, how Daddy died, so soon after Lionel returned home to live.

He'd been stunned by the death, hid away in his room and refused to attend the funeral mass or visit the cemetery.

Since then Lionel has grown more adjusted to the outside world. He has said he likes working at the lumberyard where he has no need to interact with customers, simply follows orders as he'd done in prison. He intends to acquire a driver's license, soon.

Defiantly Katie says, as if this is an argument she has been making, to her husband perhaps: we have to help Lionel. He's my brother. Whatever happened is behind us now. He's served his time.

*Served his time.* There is comfort in such familiar words.

This is true, you are thinking. You will help Lionel, if you can.

Wildly the thought comes to you—*Move back to South Niagara. Live with Mom and Lionel. Get a job here . . .*

You recall how as a boy Lionel admired and emulated his older brother Jerome Jr. but he'd also been intimidated by him, harassed and bullied. Without Jerr goading him Lionel would never have committed any crime still less such a terrible crime.

As Lionel speaks haltingly in his hoarse cracked voice you are thinking these things. Wishing that you dared speak to Lionel openly. But there is this shyness between you, each uncertain what the other exactly remembers, and what emotions the other still harbors.

Groping, blundering at a reconciliation. If that is what this is.

At last Lionel asks you about your life. It is an effort for him, you can see—he dreads to hear that you are doing well, and that you are happy; even as he seems to want to hear that you are doing well, and you are happy. You hesitate to tell him about Tyrell Jones but you are able to show him several snapshots of Brindle.

Lionel peers at Brindle in miniature. What kind of dog is that? Some kind of rat terrier?

*Rat terrier.* This is accidental, you think. This is not meant to mock or wound.

You tell Lionel that Brindle is a miniature bulldog. A very sweet dog.

Why didn't you bring Brindle with you to South Niagara?—Lionel doesn't ask.

Reason is: if something happens to you here. If (as you'd thought, back in Mohawk) there was actual danger here, from Lionel. Better to leave Brindle with Tyrell, the two get along well with each other.

Now, the reason seems silly. The morose man in front of you, your brother Lionel, slack-bodied, prematurely middle-aged, is nothing like the angry vindictive young man you'd been imagining for years. Preposterous to think that he'd ever wanted to kill you . . .

You hear yourself tell Lionel that you are completing a degree in the School of Social Work at the State University at Mohawk. Your plan is to go to graduate school and get a master's degree. You don't tell him *All I have lived through, in exile—I want it to have been for a purpose.*

Hoping that it doesn't sound boastful, that you have been working as a (minimally) paid intern with Mohawk County Family Services. In this underpaid/understaffed office you have been entrusted with responsibility, perhaps you appear to be a trustworthy person. You keep late hours in the office, available if you are needed. You are the one who holds the frightened child's hand, the one to whom the battered wife, daughter might speak in lowered voices. In your backpack are the better eyelid-wipes, not the cheaper eyelid-wipes available in most drugstores. In your backpack is a store of over-the-counter painkillers which you will provide as needed, sparingly. Because you look younger than your age and might (almost) be one of them, teenaged girls feel comfortable with you for you are not likely to judge them. Unlike your superiors you are not very verbal. You are likely to be quiet. As the battered are quiet. The intimacy of silence is natural to you. You know how harsh and abrasive speech can be, to the wounded. Better silence until the right words come.

Guardedly Lionel is listening to you, or gives that impression. He has not exactly looked at you yet but rather has cast sidelong glances at you that seem wistful, yearning. You have been anxiously waiting for the fury to erupt but there seems to be none.

*He is tired. Beaten down. Is it all over?*

You put out your hand, to take Lionel's limp, bigknuckled hand. It is not a decisive gesture—it can be withdrawn in an instant. You are trying to remain calm. Not to cry. You understand that, in prison, an inmate must not cry. A man must not cry. You want to give comfort to this wounded man but you are not fully at ease with him, not yet. You are cautious, fearful.

Wanting to explain to Lionel how it had happened. Not why, you have no idea why. But how it had happened was *too quickly.*

That morning. In the school infirmary. Your skin had been burning, feverish. You had not been thinking clearly. You had not thought of consequences. Strangers had questioned you, meaning to be protective and kind. In the confusion of the moment you had not known how not to answer them.

Uttering certain words to a police officer. Not like uttering identical words to a priest. *Safe now, Violet. You will be safe now.*

It is not possible to explain to Lionel. The words will not come. The child you'd been has been lost, can't be reclaimed. Your brother is confronted only with *you.*

Though you continue to squeeze the big-knuckled hand which neither resists nor yields to your own.

In this pause, the visit seems to be over. In this silence, some understanding has been reached. Each of you is relieved, exhausted. Pent-up breath is expelled, you are feeling almost giddy rising to your feet.

There is a moment when the two of you should embrace. It is up to you, the female, to clasp the male in your arms—though Lionel is taller than you by several inches, heavier by fifty or more pounds.

*He has not forgiven you. No.*

*But you must forgive him.*

**But then,** as you are about to get into your car, Lionel calls after you—"Vi'let?"

And you turn, and see that Lionel has followed you from the house, blinking and smiling in the sunshine, relieved, giddy like one who has been released from a cave.

He has called you "Vi'let"—as your brothers called you, when you were a girl.

So touched by this, you scarcely hear what Lionel says next.

"I was thinking—maybe—we could walk over to the old house? Just to look? OK?" It is the most that Lionel has said to you, in a single outburst.

Your half-formed plan is that on your return to Katie's house you'd drive along Black Rock Street. Over the Lock Street Bridge. And afterward, you might drive across town to Howard Street, to see the house in which Hadrian Johnson once lived.

These intentions, lurking in the periphery of your consciousness while you'd been speaking (awkwardly, haltingly) with Lionel in the house.

So close to Black Rock Street! A five-minute walk.

Each time you think of seeing your childhood house again you feel a leap of excitement. As a child might feel, daring herself to touch a wire that might give her an electric shock.

In Mohawk, in Catamount Falls, in Port Oriskany for years you have consoled yourself, and tormented yourself, with the prospect of returning to your old, lost house. Most of your dreams seem to originate there, in the room you'd shared with Katie. Even dreams of the present are likely to be set in the old house. *Where am I? Where is this? Oh—yes . . .*

Imagining Hadrian Johnson's house is different. In life you've never seen it. Not once.

Vaguely you'd known where the Johnsons lived— Howard Street. And the boy's grandmother on Amsterdam. And there was Delahunt. But you have no actual memories of these places. All you have are feelings—excitement, anxiety. *Forbidden places. Not for you.*

Of course, you're not at all certain that Ethel Johnson still lives at 29 Howard Street. That any of the Johnsons still live there.

But Lionel isn't suggesting a visit to Howard Street. Just walking over to Black Rock a few blocks away.

Katie has confided, once your parents moved out of the house on Black Rock a few years ago, they'd never returned to see it. Avoided Black Rock like the plague—*Would've broken Mom's heart to see it.*

You know from Katie that Lionel has few friends in South Niagara. He works at the lumberyard, comes home. Doesn't drive his own car, rides with a co-worker. Sometimes eats with Mom and whoever is visiting with Mom, most often just eats up in his room, door shut. Plays video games, watches TV. Something of a recluse, if that's what you'd call it. But now, smiling at you, Lionel seems eager, hopeful. His face is animated. His watery eyes shine.

You tell Lionel yes of course—"That's a great idea."

Lionel is dressed warmly for this balmy September day. Long-sleeved dark pullover stiffened with dirt at the cuffs, khaki pants with many pockets, thick-soled hiking boots which he's required to wear at the lumberyard. His skin is even coarser, seen in the light. His uneven teeth are faintly stained, yellowish. The thought comes to you, sympathetic and repelled—*He couldn't brush his teeth very well. In prison.*

Lionel says OK but just one minute—he'll be right back, has to get something—runs inside the house, returns carrying a brown paper bag, and inside three cans of beer cold from the refrigerator.

"Like, if we're thirsty. OK?"

You notice that since he has become more animated Lionel is punctuating his speech with a nervous tic: OK.

And you laugh and tell him: "OK."

At the curb Lionel asks about your car. Impressed

that you own a car, have a driver's license. As if Violet Rue has surprised her big brother, all grown up.

"Did you buy the car new?"—Lionel can't resist asking.

"N-No. Not new."

From Katie you know that Lionel hasn't (yet) acquired a driver's license. If and when he gets a license he will have the use of your father's car which is in the garage, not often used. For all practical purposes it is Lionel's car now but you don't mention this.

Nothing to make Lionel think that people are talking about him. Nothing to provoke suspicion, anxiety.

How surreal it seems to you, walking to Black Rock Street with your brother Lionel. Side by side, companionably, with the brother you'd feared for so many years. Badly you wish that your father could see you—the two of you.

Trying not to despair, that your father has died before you could be reconciled. You have been hoping that your mother will confide in you—*You know, Violet, Dad really had forgiven you. He'd said so many times.*

If Daddy saw you with Lionel, he'd have understood that Lionel has forgiven you. Why not, then, him?

Lionel has put on dark glasses, to protect his eyes from the sun. Like you, he walks with a slight limp, as if with each step he is resisting pain. You would never inquire of course but have to assume that he was injured in prison.

Your injured knee has long since mended. You can walk swiftly, and you can run. But if the knee begins to ache you know better than to persevere. A day, two days without straining it—you are all right again.

You wonder if Lionel has noticed the little star-shaped scar on your forehead? You've found a way to comb hair over it, at a slant so that it is almost invisible.

Though Mr. Sandman had shrewdly observed: it is futile to try to hide your scar.

Tyrell has not seemed to notice the little scar. Tyrell with his tucked-in smile and awkward poise. Have to assume, a black man in a white world sees more than he feels obliged to acknowledge.

Here is a surprise: Black Rock Street. Turn a corner, you are there.

How dismayed your father would be that houses on Black Rock Street have been allowed to deteriorate. A neighbor's driveway is badly cracked, there's a home-made FOR SALE sign at the curb.

Several houses in need of paint. Roof repair. Trees needing pruning. You see with your father's sharp eye, his instinct for imminent ruin. You have come to feel the burden of adulthood of which children and adolescents know nothing: the responsibility of maintaining property.

And there at 388 Black Rock is our house. Stopped in your tracks, you stare and stare.

"Fuck"—Lionel murmurs, shaken. He takes a can of beer out of the paper bag, opens it.

The sight of the house. After so long. It does appear smaller than you recall though it is larger than houses on either side. And it is still painted your father's preferred gunmetal-gray. Shutters, front door a lighter shade of gray. The roof appears to be in good repair.

A new railing on the front stoop? Black wrought iron? You try to remember if the railing had been there, years ago. Not sure.

Blinds in the windows are up, not pulled to the sills like the house on Harrison Street.

Your heart is pounding rapidly, you can barely breathe in dread of seeing something awful—something that would injure your father's pride. But nothing has much changed, you think.

Fact is, 388 Black Rock Street is hardly a distinctive house. But it is well-kept, respectable. And the driveway looks new. Trash cans at the curb look new. New-model station wagon in the driveway, bicycles leaning against the garage.

Lionel is staring at the house as he drinks beer out of a can. So distracted, or disoriented, it takes him a while to even think of offering you one of his beers but you say *no thanks*. Possibly not a great idea to be drinking on the street, and so quickly as Lionel is doing.

"It's so strange, isn't it—that other people live there . . ."

Your voice is tentative, wary. A spell has descended upon you and the tall thickset young man beside you panting as if he has been running.

Lionel murmurs a vague assent. Or maybe just again—*Fuck*.

An acknowledgment of surprise, unless the absence of surprise. Strong emotion, unless the absence of strong emotion. Lionel is drinking beer thirstily though (you guess) Lionel isn't thirsty at all.

Oddly—though it doesn't seem odd at the time—you think it's good your brother's fierce concentration is directed at the house and away from you.

The family house, sold to pay debts. Hundreds of thousands of dollars of legal fees. Punishment suffered by the family for the sons' crimes.

But Lionel isn't thinking this, you are sure. If he feels unease, agitation, it's for different reasons.

". . . it's almost like someone could look out the

window upstairs, and see us—and—wonder who we are . . ." You pause, not altogether certain what you are trying to say: "—I mean one of *us*—like Miriam—looking out the window and seeing us here—grown-up, and changed from who we were . . ."

Though your words are nonsensical Lionel grunts emphatically: "Yeah."

Pausing, to swallow the last of the beer in the can: "Shit, yeah."

Your ally, you think. In this strangeness.

For a few minutes longer you and Lionel stand on the sidewalk before the house, staring and blinking as if you could never get enough of seeing whatever it is you are seeing: a house like many others in the neighborhood, and in South Niagara; what might be called a *family home*, two story, neatly painted, scattered tall trees, evergreen shrubs, what appears to be a flower bed or garden alongside the house where your mother once tried to establish a garden. You find yourself smiling, recalling the groundhog that infuriated your mother, running with astonishing alacrity to its burrow, leaving behind a ravaged garden.

Lionel says: "Remember the God-damned groundhog, Jerr and I killed?" Lionel laughs, crumpling the beer can in his fist.

*Killed?* You don't remember this.

"Slammed the fucker with the shovel. Flattened his fucking head."

Such vehemence, such an air of righteous indignation. "Mom told us to. Chased him all over the Goddamned yard."

You are feeling just slightly faint, off-balance. No memory of a groundhog being chased all over the yard with a shovel, let alone killed . . .

But here is a more disturbing memory: how, beyond the rear of the property, in the no-man's-land above the river, your brothers hastily and carelessly buried the baseball bat that would incriminate them. So unreliable is memory, so surreal, you could swear you'd seen them kicking leaves, compost, debris over the body of Hadrian Johnson dumped into a shallow grave with the bat.

Muttering to himself, laughing, Lionel fumbles for another can of beer and cracks it open. Offers this one to you—(if the gesture is mock-gallant you chose not to notice)— and you see yourself take the can from his fingers out of a wish to seem friendly to your brother, not to seem not-friendly to him, not wishing to offend him, or to suggest (to him) that you imagine yourself superior (to him), lifting the can still cool from the refrigerator to your lips, and taking a (small) swallow.

Then handing it back to Lionel. As if this is something the two of you do frequently, sharing a can of Molson's on the street.

Such rapport between you! Indeed if someone were observing the two of you from the second floor of the house, your father for instance, frowning and staring, shaking his head in (bemused) disbelief, he would identify you not only as *sister and brother* but as *close friends, companions.*

But you are choking, just a little. Swallowed the (bitter) beer the wrong way.

"Weird. 'Family' means so much to people."

This is Lionel's observation. Quite unlike anything you have heard Lionel say.

"Well. There isn't much else, is there?"—a likely reply, a female/sister reply, though you are not convinced that it's so. "I mean, for most people."

Lionel shrugs. Drinks. Something angry, aggrieved about your brother's thirst.

Brightly you say: "It's said that if life has no intrinsic meaning just having a family, keeping together, and alive, and keeping yourself alive, can provide the meaning."

These are words that you have heard, or have read. These are words Tyrell Jones would understand. Perhaps Tyrell is the originator of these exact words.

Ironic that you of all people should be repeating these words as if you knew fully what they might mean.

In that instant thinking—*I will have my own family. I will begin—soon!*

The turning point of your life. This instant on the sidewalk at 388 Black Rock Street. When you leave South Niagara, which will be soon, you will begin the campaign to establish this new life.

Lionel says, skeptically: "There're different kinds of families. You get born into some, but others just come along. Sometimes—it's just one person."

Again, this is not like anything you've ever heard from your reticent brother. Any of your brothers.

You wonder if Lionel is referring to his experience in the prison. You wonder what he endured, so many years in a facility in which for part of that time he'd had to have been one of the youngest inmates.

County prosecutors insisted upon charging Lionel as an adult, and sending him to an adult facility. Jerome Jr. and Lionel had both gone to the maximum security facility at Marcy. The other boys, likely as guilty as Lionel, or no less guilty, were treated more leniently. Your cousin Walt Lemire was sent to a youth facility from which he was released at twenty-one. Don Brinkhaus you'd heard had been long ago paroled from a medium security prison.

You feel the unfairness of the sentence, as Lionel would have felt it. The injustice. How the world has been poisoned for him, the air he has had to breathe.

You wonder if Walt Lemire and Don Brinkhaus know that Lionel has been released from prison and decide yes, of course they know. Their families would have informed them.

You wonder if they live in the area, now. If Lionel has made any attempt to contact them.

Probably not. For why?

Reluctant to leave the old house, yet it's time to leave, walk away. Just—turn, walk away.

The last time you will see the house. You are sure.

Still, you are restless, excited—you and Lionel both. Not ready to return to the house on Harrison Street. No.

Making your way to the dead end several houses away, without needing to exchange a word.

The first wilderness you'd known. Where, as a girl, you'd been warned not to "play"—*You never know who might come along!*

Warned by your mother, many times. But the injunction could hardly be enforced for the dead end was so close, and overlooked the river.

Municipally-owned land, never cleared and developed for building, a sprawling rectangle that encompasses several acres. Behind houses on Black Rock Street above the river, a narrow strip of land between private property and the river; at the dead end a wooded area crisscrossed with dirt paths, overgrown with brambles and wild rose, poison ivy and sumac. In underbrush near the street there are litter, debris, a filigree of rotted newspaper, leaves. Skeletal remains of once-living things like squirrels, birds. You smile to see familiar dirt paths through the underbrush, unchanged since the last time you were here.

Following one of the paths toward the river. Steep dizzy drop to the river below.

It's a clear-sky day, the Niagara River is slate-blue. Dark rushing water churning as if alive.

On the farther shore the cliff is exposed shale. Appearing wet, glistening. Staring from the window of the room you'd shared with your sister thinking there'd been rain, a recent shower, but no, just sunlight on sharp-edged rock.

Bramble bushes catch at your legs, clothes. More litter on the ground than you recall. Partially burnt logs, scorched grass. Discarded beer cans, bottles. Lionel tosses down an emptied can for why not?—already so many.

Fascinating how this path remains, maintained by generations of children, teenagers. Anonymous.

Adults know nothing of such places hidden from (adult) view: vacant lots, tumbled-down trees, storm debris, ancient litter, rot.

Broken plastic, Styrofoam, mangled and rusted remains of a bicycle—some of this trash might have been here when you were a girl. For who would remove it?

If you were to move back to South Niagara, you think. To live with your mother. Take care of your mother who needs you. Take care of your brother who needs you. Early evenings when you'd drift to the dead end on Black Rock Street. Needing to be alone. In love with loneliness, melancholy.

Happiness is not reliable. Melancholy is reliable.

Below, a steep drop to the riverbank. Mostly rubble, sharp-looking rocks, construction debris—chunks of cement, rusted cables. If suddenly you need to escape, you are thinking. This is the only route.

Dangerous, treacherous. You have not climbed down the (partly eroded) path in fifteen years.

High above the river hawks are rising on drafts of invisible air. Gliding downward on fantastically wide-spread wings. Such grace, beauty. Sparrow hawks with scaly clawed feet, stabbing predator beaks.

Is it possible that Lionel has already finished the second can of beer. He is drinking compulsively, with an air of impatience, anger. Cracks open the third without, this time, thinking of offering even a sip to his sister-companion.

Saying suddenly, with an air of wonder as if the sight of the languid hawks has stirred him: "It wasn't Jerr. People wondered. They thought it had to be him but it wasn't. It was me."

"What do you mean?"—you have to ask. Though a chill has passed over you, you know exactly what Lionel means.

"The one with the bat. I mean, the one who took the bat, when Jerr sort of let it drop. Like, he'd gotten scared. Freaked. So I took the bat, his hands were weak. It was like my hands took it from him, like the bat took my hands, and—I guess—I killed the black kid. Guess it was me. It wasn't 'killing' exactly, it was like finishing something that was started. But it wasn't Jerr like you all thought. Dad thought, too. And Mom." Lionel swallows a large mouthful of beer, chokes a little, laughs. "It was me—'Lionel.'"

Your skin is crawling. Your mouth has gone dry. You are trying to remain calm. This is just conversation, you think. Just something your brother is saying in this secluded place where no one will hear him. Except you.

Lionel laughs, with that air of wonder, incredulity.

That he has made this confession to another person? To you? That he once did such a thing? Committed such an act? Laughter like pebbles shaken inside a tin container. Laughter that turns into a fit of coughing.

Lionel has succumbed to coughing several times since you've seen him. Harsh, hurtful-sounding as if his throat is scraped raw.

Saying now, ruefully: "Christ! Like I got lung cancer or something. Had to quit smoking at Marcy after twelve fucking years when they banned it. Let you smoke all you could afford until the last year I was there, then stopped it cold, like they didn't give a shit if we all went crazy. Like, we would've killed for a smoke."

When you don't reply to this vehement outburst, standing very still, staring at the hawks above the river, Lionel adds, laughing in the way he'd laughed as a teenager, joking with a friend: "A fuck or a smoke. You'd kill for the one but you'd really kill for the other."

Quickly turning, to walk away from your brother. A mistake! A mistake to have come here.

Your accelerating heartbeat is a signal: you will have to run.

But Lionel has been awaiting this moment, lunging after you just as you break into a run, seizing your left wrist and turning it, hard.

"Where're you going, you! Rat-bitch. Cunt. You ruined my life. And then you fucked up my parole." The hoarse voice is bitter and aggrieved and yet elated. At last!

Hopeless to plead with Lionel, you know it will be futile. Only make him more furious.

Turning your wrist until you fall to your knees in pain. Agony. Is he going to snap your wrist, continuing to turn it? His face is livid, engorged with blood. The elation of revenge. So many years in preparation, now released, explosive. Lionel kicks you down onto the ground, grunting as he kicks your back, legs, your unprotected belly, with his heavy boot. Horror washes over you, your brother will kick you to death and leave your body here to rot in this wild place only a few hundred feet from Black Rock Street . . .

There comes a rush of adrenaline to your heart like a shot.

Somehow you have crawled away from him, the kicking boot, you have managed to scramble to your feet, though your body throbbing with pain, and the disbelief of pain. Like a wounded animal you are running from the predator, empowered by fear, terror. You have no choice but to take the downward, dangerous path, the path that is partly eroded, a nightmare path of exposed roots like desiccated nerves, no choice but to flee skidding and sliding down this path, toward the riverbank, for your maddened brother is blocking the way to the street, and the underbrush is too thick for you to take any other route back to the street.

Lionel is screaming at you but isn't going to follow you—not down the steep path. He doesn't trust his legs, his coordination. His eyes.

Frustrated, he picks up something to throw at you as a spiteful child might do—a clump of dried mud.

"I'll kill you. Murder you. Cunt! Rat!"

Making your way down the path, sliding partway on your buttocks, afraid to stand upright for fear of losing your balance and falling. It is at least thirty feet to the riverbank below. Trying to think clearly, to recall where there's a fork in the path that will lead uphill through a hillside of brambles and into the strip of land behind the old house. If you can do this—if the path doesn't collapse into the river, or you don't fall—you can escape between houses, you think. There are no fences dividing the properties. Even if Lionel pursues you, you have a chance to escape him.

But it has been years, this stretch of the path is badly overgrown. Thorns tear at your clothes and skin, you are bleeding from a dozen small cuts. Panting through your mouth, sweating. There's a harsh odor here of something chemical, like nitrogen.

You remember—the smell of the river, beneath the Lock Street Bridge. Discolored water like thirty-foot snakes. You are nauseated, gagging. As if the earth is crumbling beneath you, you are in danger of losing your balance, falling onto the rocks below . . .

But now, suddenly—the fork in the path. Overgrown, but you have found it. Struggle uphill, on hands and knees. Grabbing desperately at exposed roots, at grasses—haul yourself forward.

By this time your furious brother has ceased shouting. Or you are out of earshot and can't hear him. You are flooded with adrenaline, in a delirium of terror that is close to exaltation, such certainty—but also anger, rage. That you were so deceived, so blind— your brother had been planning to attack you all along, you'd had no idea.

*Wanting to forgive him. To love him. Take care of him. Wanting to be forgiven. How could you!*

# The Guilty Sister

"Oh, Violet . . . Really?"

You have told Katie that you've just had a call from a friend in Mohawk, you must leave South Niagara today and return.

In fact, within the hour. Though it is already early evening, and you will have hours of night driving ahead on the Thruway.

Katie stares at you uncomprehending. Clearly she is very surprised, and hurt. *Just when we'd started to be sisters again! Violet has always been so—unpredictable. Disappointing.*

Searching your face, hoping not to see whatever she fears to see, that you are withholding from her.

(Though you will tell Katie what happened, in a day or two. When you've recovered and feel that you can speak on the phone calmly, convincingly.)

Managed to wash your dirtied face, quick when you entered the house. Grateful Lionel hadn't bloodied your nose, blackened an eye. Wincing with pain, he'd kicked you hard in the back, lower back, legs, lurid bruises will blossom across your lower body but safely hidden inside your clothing where Katie, for one, will never see.

Palms of your hands scraped, bleeding. How you'd hauled yourself up the steep hill, desperate not to die . . . You shake your head, no. Not something you will want to recall if you can help it.

Your hands, scrubbed with soap, stinging, are still shaking badly. Managing to repack your small suitcase which you'd only just unpacked. Too distracted to help you Katie stands in the doorway staring.

"But what about Mom, Violet? What should I tell her?"

*Tell Mom that I have escaped with my life.*

"Tell Mom that I love her. I will call her, I will keep in touch. I will come to see her again, soon. Sometime."

Not wanting to think—*But Mom won't remember me. Already, Mom has forgotten me.*

"We'd thought you were going to stay a week at least, Violet. There are relatives who want to see you . . ." Katie's voice trails off, she doesn't want to sound reproachful. Though yes, your sister is disappointed with you. Again.

You are thinking—*relatives*. But why did these *relatives* make no effort to contact you, let alone see you, for thirteen years?

"Who is this friend who has called you, Violet?"— Katie sounds skeptical.

"A friend. No one you know."

*Of course. You know no one in my life.*

"I will keep in touch, Katie. I will be back, I promise."

"Will you!" Can't help herself, Katie is an older sister. And you—

*Violet Rue.*

But Katie rouses herself, to help you pack. Though there is little to do, you have brought so few things. Telling you it would be a much better idea to drive in the morning, in daylight, when you are not so upset . . .

To this, you make no reply. Katie scarcely knows how upset you are.

*But what about Lionel?*—Katie has not asked.

And so you will wonder, Does Katie know? How much does Katie know? You assure yourself: Katie could not have guessed how dangerous your brother is, or she would not have arranged for you to spend time with him alone.

*Our brother is a murderer. He is not the person you want to think he is.*

"Oh, Violet. I feel like—like I have failed you. . . . Forgive me."

"Hey. Forgive *me*."

Katie begins to cry. You hug your sister, pressing your hot face against her neck. So much to tell her. But no, not now. Now is not the time.

# Howard Street

Driving along sparsely inhabited Delahunt Road. On your way out of South Niagara, to the Thruway headed east.

Gas station, fast-food restaurant, auto dealership, remnants of a trailer park, open fields. A potholed road, wide rutted shoulder where (you recall) Hadrian Johnson was bicycling when your brother Jerome, Jr. steered his car at him . . .

But where, you aren't so sure. Possibly, you never knew.

Amsterdam Street, where Hadrian's grandmother had lived. Howard Street, where Hadrian's mother, Ethel Johnson, lived. Lives?

North along Delahunt, searching for Howard Street. You'd thought that Howard Street was here, intersecting with Delahunt, but the street signs are unfamiliar, and not all the streets are marked . . . Not sure what to do for you have passed at least two (unpaved) streets without signs, either of which could be Howard. This is a part of South Niagara you don't know, miles from Black Rock Street and the Niagara River—*Where colored people live.*

As your mother might've said, carefully. Or your father.

Any of the Kerrigans. Any of the white people you'd known.

Though not your grandfather Kerrigan, he'd have uttered a harsher term . . .

Might be best to drive a little farther, if you don't see Howard then make a U-turn. Not much traffic on Delahunt at this time of day.

At last, you see a sign for Howard Street—you think. But closer up, you see *Powell.*

Finally at the city limit you make a U-turn in the road, return. But this time you have no better luck. The Honda Civic is an economy car without a tracking system. Your cell phone is a rudimentary model—only just a phone. You feel shy about turning onto one of these streets where small bungalow-type houses are set in surprisingly large lots, at the edge of the city.

In the western sky the sun has spilled out at the horizon, a pale orange-red, slowly, then rapidly fading behind hills. Dusk.

Not an ideal time to be driving any distance. As Katie has warned you.

On Delahunt there appear to be no street lights. On the small side streets you aren't sure.

A convenience store, at a corner. You could go inside, inquire about Howard Street.

But you hesitate, you drive past. And now a gas station—is it open? No? Seeing belatedly that it appears to be open though the interior is dimly lighted . . .

At last you catch sight of a street sign—*Howard.*

No wonder you'd missed it, the sign is turned sideways.

And now, driving slowly along Howard Street. Blocks of small woodframe houses. Howard Street is paved but badly potholed. Vehicles parked on both sides make driving difficult. Without lights house numbers are indistinct. And not all houses seem to have numbers. You are squinting to make out numerals on mailboxes. Beside doors. *Forty-four? Eighty-eight?*

It is late, you should have come earlier. Should have come yesterday. Still shaken from your brother's assault, not thinking clearly. Not seeing clearly.

Beginning to feel panicked. No idea where you are.

But yes, you know where you are. Just no idea where Ethel Johnson's house is.

Approaching a more populated neighborhood. The large scrubby yards have vanished. Brownstone row houses built close to the curb. Trashcans at the curb. Vehicles parked close together in the street.

You are disappointed, you have long imagined Hadrian Johnson's house standing by itself. Ethel Johnson whom you'd seen on TV, for whom you'd felt great sympathy, living in a house of her own. With maybe a garden behind it—hollyhocks, wild climber roses, morning glories. Receiving the Valentines you'd sent, puzzled, but smiling, as she opens the oversized envelope, examines the Valentine so obviously hand-made with care, tenderness . . .

Stopping the car at one of the rowhouses. But the numeral beside the door appears to be *twenty-one*, not *twenty-nine* . . .

You are startled by a knock on the window beside the passenger's seat. You lower the window, a young woman peers inside, asks what sounds like *Can I help you?*

You tell her, you are looking for Ethel Johnson. Who lives, or used to live, at twenty-nine Howard.

The woman doesn't hear you, you must repeat your question. Your voice is faint, hopeful. Apologetic.

In your white skin, confronting this stranger. Of course you are apologetic, it is a tic like your brother ending each remark with *OK*.

Your jaw has begun to ache, speaking in a normal voice is painful. Your eyes are aching too, the vision in both eyes has blurred.

The young woman can't help you, it seems. Doesn't seem to know where *twenty-nine Howard Street* might be, unless she hasn't heard you clearly.

Awkwardly you manage to turn the Honda Civic around in the narrow street, drive back in the direction of Delahunt, slowly, leaning over the steering wheel, peering at house numbers. Oncoming headlights are blinding. It is too late! Too dark! What a bad idea this is. Brake your car, back up to let another driver through the narrow street, with excruciating slowness.

Hoping that he won't scrape the side of your vehicle. For you have no business here, on Howard Street.

Like dirty water the futility of the search washes over you. Never will you share with Tyrell Jones the logic of this naïve quest.

At last! On one of the dour narrow brownstones built only a few feet from curb is the numeral *twenty-nine*. To your disappointment the house is darkened.

"Oh. God *damn.*"

Still, you get out of the car. You knock on the door. As if you might entice whoever is inside, hiding in darkness, to declare herself to you.

Elsewhere on the block is the glow of warm lights within houses, mysterious lives. Drumming music, TV voices uplifted. More headlights threading their slow way along the narrow street.

Another driver, a woman, having parked her car in a nearby driveway, sees you on the front step of the rowhouse and approaches you. For a confused moment you think that she might be the friendly woman from the Greyhound bus, the woman whose concern for you made you cry, then you recall that Sarabeth lived in Port Oriskany. This woman is no one you know and she is much younger than Sarabeth and not smiling as Sarabeth would smile.

"Ma'am? You're looking lost, can I help you?"

"Yes, thank you! I'm looking for Ethel Johnson."

"Who?"

"Mrs. Johnson? Ethel? She used to live here . . . twenty-nine Howard Street."

Smiling so hard, your face aches. The woman stares at you, frowning.

You repeat your awkward query. You consider uttering the name *Hadrian Johnson*—but do not.

Politely the woman asks if you are from the—(you can't decipher the word, perhaps a proper name)— you tell her, "I don't think so. No."

No idea how to identify yourself. No idea really why you are here in this neighborhood you know nothing about and where no one knows you. Your head is wracked in pain, your knees are shaky. You cannot—quite—absorb what it means that this very day you were beaten, kicked. Cursed. And if you were to meet Hadrian Johnson's mother Ethel, what could you possibly say to her?

So many cards you'd written to her, and thrown away. Perhaps that is best, to write, and throw away. Your yearning, your inexpressible longing. Maybe best, to spare the murdered boy's mother a reminder of her loss, after so many years.

The woman repeats her question asking if you are from *the people Mrs. Johnson worked for* and this time you understand: your white skin signals that you are looking for an employee of your family, a cleaning woman perhaps.

Not a friend, an employee. You feel a wave of shame, the woman has judged you by the color of your skin.

Of course it's a reasonable assumption. You understand.

You tell the woman no, you are not from that family. You thank her and tell her that you will come back another time to see Mrs. Johnson. *N Nothing important, just—wanting to say hello.*

Return to your car, you've left the key in the ignition and the motor running. Not thinking clearly. Take care, you can have an accident easily in such a state.

Behind you on the sidewalk the woman remains, watching as you drive away. She has been more curious about you than suspicious. She has not been unfriendly—exactly. In the rear view mirror you see her figure retreating until it has vanished in the darkness of Howard Street and you've returned to Delahunt where there are tall street lights and you can breathe more deeply.

Next time you are in South Niagara you will do better, you promise yourself. You will knock on Ethel Johnson's door in the daylight, and you will introduce yourself.

*Just hello.*

# Home

In the Honda Civic, headed east toward the Thruway. Buoyed by waves of relief so intense it feels like happiness.

At last headed back to Mohawk. *Home.*

Night isn't an ideal time to be starting off on a drive of several hours by yourself but you are eager to escape South Niagara. The air feels oppressive here, difficult to breathe. So close you'd come to being murdered in this place, kicked into insensibility. And maybe, as a parting gesture, your brother would have set his foot upon your exposed throat as you lay helpless on the ground, pressing down, grinding down, exactly as someone had done to him.

The joy of silencing another, forever!—you have

never felt such joy but you have come to understand it, in others.

Is it true, as you've promised your sister, that you will return to South Niagara, soon? To see your mother, and to see Katie? To see where your father is buried in the hilly cemetery behind St. Matthew's Church?

No. You will never return.

But—yes. Maybe.

*Never say never.* A frequent remark of your father's, of the nature of *What goes around comes around.* An old boxing adage, you think.

You do want to see Katie again. You do want to see your mother . . . You are not so certain about visiting the cemetery, in fact. He never forgave you, he was not ever going to forgive you, that was his prerogative.

But yes, you would like to drive along Howard Street, in daylight.

**At the** entrance to the Thruway you stop to call Tyrell Jones on your cell phone.

Clutch of panic, the phone might have lost its power. Or, worse—there is no such number.

Your relationship with Tyrell Jones is so mysterious to you, so forged in inexpressible yearning, silences and ellipses—in uncertain moments you wonder if it is real, and not a dream. You wonder if, away from you, Tyrell Jones feels the same way.

The need you have of him. The hunger.

As the damned little dog has of you. Might as well admit it.

Hearing the phone ring at the other end. Biting your lower lip in anguish, that the might not be answered . . .

He will see your caller I.D. It is the man's prerogative, to answer, or not answer.

Then, you hear Tyrell's voice. For an instant you are unable to speak, there is a tight band around your chest.

"Violet? Hey. H'llo."

"Hello . . ."

"Where are you? What has happened?"—Tyrell's voice is clear and assertive. It is always a surprise to you, to hear this adult voice over the phone, so different from your own, hesitant voice.

You tell Tyrell that your visit home has not gone so well as you'd hoped, and you are returning to Mohawk early. Quickly you speak, briskly enough, so that Tyrell doesn't ask *why.*

You have not told Tyrell much about your background. All that he knows of the Kerrigans has little to do with you. He has never asked you about your family. He has never asked you about your (notorious) brothers. He could have no idea that one of them had been released from prison, still less that this brother might be living with your mother, and that there was a likelihood of your encountering him.

Tyrell asks when you estimate you will be home and you tell him—you hope before midnight.

He will wait up for you of course. He is bringing take-out Chinese food home, he will make sure there is enough for you.

Close to the edge. Close to tears. You feel your throat ache, as if someone had kicked you there. *I love you. Forgive me. All of us—forgive us.*

Such a declaration would only embarrass Tyrell. No possible way he could reply to it.

Seeing how he looks at you sometimes, with what bemused affection, you wonder if Tyrell understands you as you have never dared to suppose another person might understand you. As if you stood before him naked, in the illusion of being fully clothed.

Tyrell has fashioned himself into a professor of American history, after all. He is much altered from the shy tongue-tied high school boy terrorized by the white-devil math teacher. He has brilliantly triumphed over that devil, and has moved on. Shrewd, crafty, if it is revenge Tyrell Jones requires, this is the perfect revenge: knowledge. Not emotion, not the waywardness of desire, or the ecstatic joy of violence, but rather knowledge, and the power of knowledge.

Now, you must move on. Your old, wounded life, the perverse pride in your scarred face, you must surrender.

You have lost the thread of what you've been saying. This hurried conversation in your car, by the Thruway entrance at dusk, as a succession of headlights glides over you like rippling water, is domestic, pragmatic. Yes, before midnight. If all goes well. And yes, Chinese food will be perfect. You are weak with gratitude. You are close to tears. Tyrell, protective by instinct, is quick to assure you that it's wonderful news you are returning home sooner than you'd planned—"Brindle has been pining for you."

# HARPER LUXE

## THE NEW LUXURY IN READING

We hope you enjoyed reading
our new, comfortable print size and found it
an experience you would like to repeat.

**Well – you're in luck!**

HarperLuxe offers the finest in fiction and
nonfiction books in this same larger print size and
paperback format. Light and easy to read, HarperLuxe
paperbacks are for book lovers who want to see
what they are reading without the strain.

For a full listing of titles and
new releases to come, please visit our website:

**www.HarperLuxe.com**